CAMMIE & ALEX'S
adventures in

SKATING HISTORY

CAMMIE & ALEX'S
adventures in

SKATING HISTORY

OLGA JAFFAE

TATE PUBLISHING & *Enterprises*

Published by Tate Publishing & Enterprises, LLC
127 E. Trade Center Terrace | Mustang, Oklahoma 73064 USA
1.888.361.9473 | www.tatepublishing.com

Tate Publishing is committed to excellence in the publishing industry. The company reflects the philosophy established by the founders, based on Psalm 68:11,
"The Lord gave the word and great was the company of those who published it."

Book design copyright © 2010 by Tate Publishing, LLC. All rights reserved.
Cover design by Brandon Wood
Interior design by Lynly D. Grider

Published in the United States of America

ISBN: 978-1-61739-278-8
1. Juvenile Fiction, Fantasy

10.09.20

DEDICATION

To my family: Mom, Dad, Ksyusha, and Kostya.
You guys are the best. God bless you!

TABLE OF CONTENTS

SHOW CAST

In her dream, Cammie saw the sun skate on the blue rink of the sky. The sun spun and jumped, and then it stretched its long arm and tickled Cammie on the nose. Cammie laughed, opened her eyes, then quickly shut them again. The sun, bright and hot, shone right in her face. Cammie bolted up and glanced at the digital clock by her bedside. 7:57 a.m. Why was she still in bed? Morning practice started at six. Cammie looked at the bed across from hers and sighed with relief. Sonia, her roommate, was still asleep, which meant Cammie wasn't in trouble. Unlike Cammie, Sonia had never, ever overslept. Then Cammie remembered that it was Saturday. How cool! No morning practice today.

Cammie leaned back on her pillow again, thinking how great it would be to have Saturday every day. Instead of two practices, they would only have one public session at the Silver Rink and ... oh, no!

Cammie sat up in bed. "It's today!"

She couldn't help raising her voice, and the covers on Sonia's bed slid off, exposing long, red locks and one half-open blue eye.

"What 're late?" Sonia mumbled.

"The show cast, remember?"

"Oh!" Suddenly looking amazingly alert, Sonia tossed her covers to the side and jumped on the sun-lit floor.

"Do you mind if I shower first?" Without waiting for Cammie's answer, Sonia sprinted to the bathroom.

Cammie closed her eyes and smiled excitedly. Yesterday afternoon, a notice had appeared on the bulletin board saying that all skaters were expected at the Silver Rink at ten o'clock Saturday morning for a very special meeting. Both the theme and the cast of the annual Skateland show would be announced—something everybody had been dying to find out. The show would take place at Main Square Rink; all residents of Skateland would be there to watch the presentation. And of course, Cammie's parents wouldn't miss the opportunity to see their daughter skating in the spotlight.

The auditions for the show had taken place last Saturday. For the whole week, skaters had been talking of nothing else. As challenging and exhausting as the audition had been, Cammie thought she had done okay—very well, actually. She had landed all of her jumps without mistakes. Well…Cammie frowned slightly. Perhaps, her double flip had been slightly underrotated, and she hadn't attempted her double lutz. But Cammie had hoped the judges wouldn't be too picky.

"I'm done. You can go ahead." Sonia ran out of the bathroom and opened the closet door.

Cammie walked into the bathroom and stepped in the shower. *Oh please, let me get a leading part in this show*, she prayed. She really, really wanted a decent part this time. Last year she had skated in a group number—one of six girls. But now she was a much more advanced skater; she had all of her double jumps…Well, almost all of them.

Cammie wrapped herself in a thick towel and ran to the closet to pick out an outfit. On Saturdays, the skaters didn't have to wear their rink signature colors. Cammie skated at the Green Rink, one of the eight official rinks of Skateland, so Monday through Friday she was expected to show up for practices in a green skating dress. Cammie actually looked good in green, but sometimes she got tired of wearing the same outfit. Today she would put on something nice. Cammie quickly got into black leggings and a pale blue, long-sleeved T-shirt with Cool Skater emblazoned in silver on the front. Instead of her usual green warm-up jacket, she pulled on a blue cashmere sweater.

Breakfast was served in the dorm dining room on the first floor—cereal and toast.

"I think it will be something wintery, like *The Snow Queen* or *The Nutcracker*," Liz, a petite Asian girl, said as she buttered her toast.

The Nutcracker *would be great*, Cammie thought. Two years ago, she had skated her first program to a piece of music from Tchaikovsky's famous ballet, and she had won the gold medal. The president of Skateland had been one of the judges then. So if they were really going to do *The Nutcracker* this year, chances were that Cammie would get the part of Clara.

"Well, I don't think so." Dana, a tall blonde, sipped her tea and gave Liz a snooty look. "I'm sure they will go for something…hmm…not so popular."

"*Four Seasons*, maybe?" Sonia said.

"Uh, perhaps."

"What do you think, Cammie?" Liz reached for the sugar bowl.

Cammie felt her cheeks get slightly warm. "I don't know. I wouldn't mind *The Nutcracker*. The music is nice."

"So who would dance the lead, then?" Dana asked, a butter knife in her hand.

"They would give it to Sonia, of course. She is the best skater." Liz shrugged her shoulders.

Cammie's heart sank. Liz was right; Sonia was really a much better skater than Cammie. She had been skating since she was two, while Cammie had taken her first lesson at the ripe old age of eight.

"Not necessarily. They may want some-one…better looking. Like me, for example." Dana studied her reflection in the spoon. Today she wore a black shimmering skating dress that looked great with her long blonde hair.

Good looking, big deal! Cammie thought. Skating was about technique, not looks. She would have made it clear to Dana right away if it hadn't been for Mrs. Page, their dorm supervisor.

"It's a quarter after nine, girls. Aren't you going to be late?"

"Ah, yes!" Cammie jumped up, gulped down her tea, and grabbed her toast. She would finish it on her way to the rink.

Cammie ran out of the dorm, zipping up her parka. Sonia already sat on the steps, taking off her skate guards. They were facing a long trip to the Silver Rink. Residents of Skateland never walked; they were expected to skate to their destinations. And while the Green Rink, where Cammie and Sonia usually trained, was only eight blocks away, the Silver Rink was much farther—in a huge octag-onal sport center.

"Come on, Cammie!" Sonia stepped on the icy sidewalk.

Cammie put her skate guards in her backpack and followed her friend. It was a beautiful morning. The tall trees on both sides of the road cast shadows on the snow; slight frost bit their cheeks and noses.

They crossed Axel Avenue and were heading toward Main Square, when someone called Cammie's name.

Cammie turned around. "Alex!"

Alex caught up with them, grinning. "Hi, Cammie! Hi, Sonia! All ready for the big news, huh?"

Cammie smiled happily. Alex was an old friend from her home rink. Tall and blond with bright, green eyes, Alex was very good looking. He was fourteen—two years older than Cammie. Together, Cammie and Alex had gone on wonderful adventures in the past. This year, Alex had finally moved to Skateland to train at the Yellow Rink. Though he had only been in Skateland two months, Alex already had the reputation of a very promising skater.

"I hope it will be a good show, not the kid's stuff we had back home," Alex said.

"Skateland shows are always interesting," Sonia said. "I'm really excited."

"Yeah, me too," Cammie said. *Especially if I get a solo part*, she thought. Oh, how great would it be to skate in the middle of Main Square Rink, everybody's eyes fixed firmly on her. Her parents would be so proud. And—

"The show will be televised," Sonia said, as though overhearing Cammie's thoughts.

Cammie closed her eyes and said a quick prayer. She had to get the lead; she absolutely had to.

The glass, octagonal building of the Sport Center appeared at the end of the street. Cammie, Alex, and Sonia picked up speed. They crossed the big, circular Main Square and approached the building. The glass walls of the Sport Center sparkled in the sunlight. Cammie shivered with anticipation and looked back at Main Square Rink, admiring its smooth, gray surface. For a moment she closed her eyes, picturing herself in the middle of the square wearing a gorgeous pink dress...no, perhaps this time she would skate in a purple outfit with lots of sequins and—

"Cammie, come on. What are you waiting for?" Alex and Sonia were already at the entrance.

"Uh, sorry!" Cammie hurried after her friends. She would think of her costume later, when she knew exactly what her part would be. But one thing she was sure of: she would look really, really good.

The spacious lobby was almost empty; most of the skaters were probably inside. At the entrance to the Silver Rink, they separated. Cammie and Sonia walked up the steps to the left, while Alex went right to join the other boys from the Yellow Rink.

The smooth, silver ice arena was empty; no one was skating. The whole skating population of

Skateland sat in the stands, and there was a lot of excitement in the air.

"A minute left," Sonia whispered.

Cammie looked up at the huge digital clock hanging directly across from where she sat. It said nine fifty-nine.

"Look! Wilhelmina is here already!" a voice behind Cammie said.

Cammie turned around and saw Jeff, a boy from her class and Sonia's best friend. Jeff was short but muscular, with dark, curly hair and big, brown eyes. Like Sonia, he was a very good skater. Even though he was of the same age as Cammie, Jeff had already started working on his triple jumps. Cammie sighed at the thought of how long it would take her to get to that level.

The clock clicked over to ten o'clock.

"Now!" a girl in the front row squeaked.

Cammie licked her lips and squeezed Sonia's hand. Sonia gave her a weak smile and turned away, her eyes fixed firmly on the entrance to the ice. Whether Sonia was nervous or not, she surely wasn't showing it.

Before the clock changed its reading again, a collective sigh swept across the rink. Cammie looked at the entrance, through which Wilhelmina, the president of Skateland, had just appeared in her wheelchair. A group of ten or twelve people—most of them coaches—followed. Wilhelmina was a short woman with a shrewd, narrow face; short, gray hair;

and bony legs. How the woman could skate on those skinny limbs had always been a mystery to Cammie. And yet Wilhelmina didn't merely skate around the rink; she performed brackets and rockers with blinding speed, and her spins … Would Cammie ever be able to spin as fast as the president? Nobody who ever saw Wilhelmina skate could ever suspect that the older woman suffered from any health problems at all. And yet the president of Skateland had a bad case of arthritis that kept her confined to a wheelchair, except for the times when she was on ice.

Cammie watched Wilhelmina glide gracefully across the rink on her right foot, her knee perfectly bent, the free leg extended gracefully, the toe pointed. When the older woman reached the middle, she turned around and addressed the excited skaters.

"Good morning and welcome to our annual Skateland show practice. First of all, I would like to thank all those who auditioned for a part in the show. You all did a wonderful job. I'm truly impressed with the high level of skating you demonstrated. And while not all of you will get solo parts, I kindly ask you not to get disappointed. Whatever small role you will have to skate, it is not a reflection of your lack of competence as a skater. I hope you understand that no show consists of leading parts only. There are quite a few group numbers, and of course, we will need a lot of skaters in the corps. What I want you to understand is that there are no major or minor parts in our show. No matter what your role is, you are still a skater, and we all expect you to do your best."

The rink was quiet as the students drank in every word of Wilhelmina's speech. Sonia sat next to Cammie, her back perfectly straight, her hands folded on her lap. On Sonia's other side, Jeff smoothed the fabric of his skating pants and nodded appreciatively. Cammie took a deep breath and slowly exhaled. Okay, whatever Wilhelmina was saying was great, but when would she finally announce the name of the show? And the cast, of course?

"The title of this year's show will be *The History of Figure Skating*," Wilhelmina said.

Everything became quiet, so quiet that Cammie could discern the sound of her heartbeat. Fearing that everybody at the rink would hear it too, she quickly pressed her hand against her chest.

"*The History of Figure Skating?*" Jeff muttered.

Yes, that's different, Cammie thought, still not knowing whether the news was good or bad. The History of Figure Skating was one of the subjects she was taking at her Skateland school, and unfortunately, it wasn't her favorite. Actually, she found all those historical facts pretty boring.

"We are going to show how figure skating developed into the beautiful sport we all enjoy," Wilhelmina said. "There will be special numbers featuring the evolution of jumps and spins. But we will also spend quality time teaching the audience about compulsory moves or figures. Of course, you all know from your skating history course that it was the figures that gave our sport its name. School figures were eliminated from official competitions in 1991, and personally, I didn't support that decision. Only figures can give the skater a true mastery of edges. Drawing patterns on ice requires precision and impeccable technique. In our show, we will bring back the lost beauty of edges and turns, of lines and symmetry. For this purpose, I expect all of you to master basic school figures. Of course, the so-called special figures like the beak or the anvil require years and years of practice. Those would be too challenging for you, so we will leave them to our more experienced skaters, like Mr. Walrus, Mr. Reed, as well as your humble servant."

Two gray-haired men from the group surrounding Wilhelmina raised their hands in a greeting. Meanwhile, Wilhelmina spread her arms, put her feet in a perfect T-position, and performed a series of small twists and turns. As soon as she was done, the tracings on the ice darkened, revealing a perfect cross.

"Cool!" Jeff breathed out.

"That was awesome!" Sonia said quietly.

Everybody around Cammie clapped enthusiastically. Cammie cast a furtive glance at her friends and shrugged. Honestly, she didn't understand what was so great about using blades as a … hmm … a pencil. Drawing figures on ice—big deal! And besides, when Wilhelmina was working on that cross she looked awfully unattractive. She kept looking down, and her skating leg was bent most of the time. No, Cammie definitely didn't care for figures. Jumps and spins—that was real skating.

"It is also important to know about the great skaters of the past," Wilhelmina said. "We will give the audience a chance to meet Axel Paulsen, Ulrich Salchow, and Sonja Henie. And of course, we will show the evolution of the four divisions of our sport: ladies' and men's singles, pairs, and dancing. The audience will see how single jumps evolved into triples, basic lifts into throw jumps, elementary dancing steps into beautiful programs. This part of the show is very demanding, so we have chosen our best skaters to demonstrate the most difficult elements."

So there were going to be jumps and spins after all! Cammie straightened up in her seat. Of course, Wilhelmina was going to let her do some of those demonstrations. Cammie was a good skater; she deserved a good part.

"Jessica McNeil and Peter Deveraux will do the pairs demonstration."

The audience cheered. Cammie brought her hands together too. She knew Jessica and Peter. The junior-level pairs skaters trained at the White Rink, and they were really good.

"Dancing demonstration will be performed by Sandra Newman and Kevin Sawyer."

More applause came. Okay, Sandra and Kevin would surely do a good job.

"In men's singles, the leading part goes to Steve Duncan."

A burst of applause erupted from the corner, where the boys from the Yellow Rink sat. Cammie looked in their direction and saw Alex give Steve Duncan a playful shove on the side. Steve, a tall and lean African-American boy, grinned widely.

"And in ladies' singles…"

Cammie squeezed tight in her seat and crossed her fingers. *Oh please, ple-ease let it be me. I did so well in my audition…well, perhaps the double flip wasn't perfect, but—*

"Sonia Harrison."

"What?" Cammie said out loud.

Nobody seemed to hear her; her words were drowned in an avalanche of cheers and applause.

"Yes, yes, yes!" Jeff patted Sonia on the back heartily.

Cammie twisted her face in a perfect grimace of dejection and moved away from Sonia. So her roommate had just got a lead in some stupid show; was that a good reason to go nuts about it? Come on! But the rest of the skaters apparently disagreed with Cammie. They clapped and shouted and whistled, and Wilhelmina was saying something— Cammie didn't exactly hear what it was. Oh yes, she was inviting the skaters who had gotten the leading parts to come down to the middle of the rink.

Yes, there they were: Jessica, Peter, Sandra, Kevin, Steve, and ugh, Sonia, looking her usual calm self in black leggings and a white sweater. Cammie's blue sweater would definitely look better against the silver ice.

Cammie had a burning sensation in her eyes. She felt so lonely and sad; she was sure she was going to cry. But she couldn't cry, no, not at the rink with so many people around. They would laugh her to scorn. Cammie bit her upper lip so hard that it began to sting and stared at the dark gray linoleum floor under her feet.

"It's not fair," Cammie whispered, barely keeping the tears from flowing down her cheeks.

"Now the rest of the parts and the cast for the show will be posted on the bulletin board in the lobby," Wilhelmina said.

Oh! Cammie raised her head, her tears drying off immediately. So there would be other parts too. Well, perhaps she would get something decent after all. And with renewed hope, Cammie joined the crowd of skaters who were already pouring out into the lobby.

DREARY PRACTICES

I t's not fair!" Cammie said as she stared at the red and brown circles of her quilt. She sat on the edge of her bed, still fully dressed. She hadn't even taken off her skates.

"Look, I'm really sorry. I wish you had gotten a lead." Sonia slid off from behind the table piled with her homework and approached Cammie.

Cammie felt Sonia's warm hand on her shoulder and jerked away angrily. "Look, you don't have to be sweet, all right? I'm a horrible skater, that's it."

Sonia shook her head. "It's not true. You're very graceful, and your jumps are getting good. Just keep working hard, and you'll get a better part next time."

Cammie looked away. *Next time.* It was easy for Sonia to say. How could she understand? Sonia was going to be the star of the show, while Cammie hadn't even got any of the solo parts, just a stupid group number. And of course, she would be in the corps doing figures. What would her parents say? At that point, Cammie couldn't contain herself any longer; she began to sob.

"Come on, Cammie; it's not the end of the world."

Cammie gritted her teeth, grabbed her parka, and ran out of the room. Her skate guards banged against the steps as she sprinted downstairs. She had absolutely no idea where she was going. She simply wanted to get out of the dorm, away from Sonia's sympathetic looks. It was easy for Sonia to feel sorry once she had the lead. Well, okay, Sonia was a better skater. So what? Was it Cammie's fault that her parents hadn't started her in figure skating when she was two?

Cammie turned the front door handle, but before she had a chance to open the door, a heavy hand landed on her shoulder. Startled, Cammie turned around and stared right into Mrs. Page's broad face.

"Well, well, well, and where do you think you're going?"

Cammie rolled her eyes. It wasn't that she was afraid of Mrs. Page. Their dorm supervisor was actually very nice. Someone who saw Mrs. Page for the first time might think that she was a harsh woman, but it wasn't true. Short and plump, with a low voice, Mrs. Page was the kindest person on earth. The homely, middle-aged woman genuinely loved the skaters who lived in her dorm. She was the one who summoned the girls to breakfast and dinner and also saw to it that everybody was up in the morning in time for their practices. Mrs. Page was also a terrific cook, and even though Skateland authorities required that all young skaters eat healthy, balanced food, Mrs. Page often tried to sneak in some forbidden stuff, like blueberry pancakes, chocolate chip cookies, or even a piece of cheesecake. Cammie had never seen Mrs. Page without a smile, yet now her face was grim.

"Do you know what time it is, Cammie?"

Cammie wrinkled her nose. "Uh, actually I don't. What time is it?"

Mrs. Page sighed gravely and pointed to the clock hanging on the wall across from the front door. "It's after eight, and there is no business for a young girl to be out of the dorm after dusk."

"Oh please, Mrs. Page. I need some privacy."

Mrs. Page put her hands on her hips. "Still grieving over not getting a solo, huh?"

"I really don't care about that stupid show," Cammie said defiantly.

Mrs. Page chuckled; the fine lines under her eyes deepened. "Really? Look, I have lived in Skateland long enough to know how you kids act when you don't get what you want. Let me tell you something: you are actually better off not being in the spotlight."

Cammie frowned. She couldn't understand. How could someone in her right mind feel happy about not being in the spotlight?

"You are much safer than those skaters who have solo parts."

Safer? Now Cammie had completely lost Mrs. Page's train of thought.

"Top skaters are easier prey for witches," Mrs. Page said solemnly.

Ah, so that was it—the witches! Cammie smiled for the first time since she had found out about the show cast. At least Mrs. Page believed in witches. That was refreshing, because most Skateland adults—and not only adults, kids too—didn't. It was useless to tell anybody that Cammie and Alex had confronted several witches twice themselves; that they had delivered Jeff and Sonia from the wicked women's clutches. Last year, Cammie and Alex had barely escaped the witches themselves after being locked in at the Black Rink, where skating outcasts hung out. Yes, all that was true, but Cammie still couldn't understand why having a solo in the show increased a skater's chance of being attacked by witches.

"Mrs. Page, do you seriously think the witches will show up during the performance? There will be security and—"

"Enough! I'm not supposed to discuss those things with you."

"But Mrs. Page, you started it."

"I only wanted to make you feel less miserable."

Cammie sighed in frustration. "No one is going to see me in that stupid number."

"Sure they will. They aren't blind."

"But I wanted to have a decent part."

"Every part in the show is good."

Cammie gave the dorm supervisor a dubious look. "You're talking just like Wilhelmina."

"And she's right, isn't she? Now it's time for bed."

"At eight-thirty?"

"Then get started on your homework. Now go upstairs, Cammie; you're not getting out. Forget about it."

With a grimace of defiance, Cammie turned around and walked up the steps back to her room.

The next three weeks were the worst in Cammie's life. Show practices turned out to be even more boring than Cammie had expected. Now the only time Cammie could work on her own skating was during early-morning practices; afternoon skating was devoted entirely to show rehearsals. Everybody was supposed to report to the Silver Rink promptly at three o'clock, and they stayed on the ice till six, practicing hard. That in itself wasn't too bad; Cammie was used to skating for hours and hours.

The problem was that Cammie saw absolutely no point in spending precious ice time working on edges. That kind of exercise was for beginners, for crying out loud!

After defeating the Witch of Injuries, who also went by the name of Winja, two years before, Cammie had never had any problems with her backward edges again. But practicing school figures? Who in her right mind could even suggest that? No one in the skating world did figures anymore. They had been banned from competitions because they were totally useless. And yet, Wilhelmina seemed to be oblivious to the rules. Every afternoon, she positioned the skaters across the shiny surface of the Silver Rink. Each of them was given a patch of ice for practicing figures.

Wilhelmina had explained to them that each figure had to be traced several times, and the new tracings were supposed to be positioned directly on top of the old ones. Overlapping was an absolute no-no. Cammie found the exercise irresistibly boring, difficult, and of course, useless. Drawing circles and paragraphs would never help her with her jumps.

"It's such a waste of time!" Cammie said to everybody who listened. "I wish I had spent all those hours working on my double lutz. I would have landed it already."

For some mysterious reason, none of the skaters seemed to share Cammie's revulsion for school figures. On Thursday, when they were having a late lunch before the afternoon practice, Cammie expressed her concerns for the fourth time. Liz merely shrugged.

"Big deal," she said as she took a bite of her tuna salad sandwich. "I know it's not easy, but imagine doing figures in front of all the guests. My mom will freak out when she sees me doing perfect eights."

"True." Dana sipped her iced tea. "My dad used to tease me, saying that I would never be as good as him because my brackets weren't perfect. Now guess who's going to laugh? And by the way, Mr. Reed has promised some special effects for figures."

"Wow!" Sonia leaned forward. "I can't wait."

Mr. Reed was Skateland's most famous skate sharpener, and he was known for his gift of inventing magical skating equipment.

"My parents always told me how disappointed they were that school figures were eliminated," Sonia said in her usual meek manner. "Mom called yesterday, and when I told her about the show, she was so excited. She told me my technique would improve by leaps and bounds once I starting practicing figures."

That was surely more than Cammie could handle. "Yeah, right. *You* don't have to practice school figures like everybody else.You are a star!"

Cammie's face became very hot as everybody in the dining room stared at her. Oh no, she shouldn't have said that. Now everybody would think that she was merely jealous of Sonia. It wasn't true; Cammie wasn't jealous at all. She simply hated doing stupid, useless things.

Sonia, however, didn't seem hurt at all; there was nothing but usual sweetness in her blue eyes. "But Cammie, Wilhelmina has me do patch sessions just like everybody else. School figures are mandatory for every skater who is involved in the show."

"They are?" Cammie felt genuinely surprised.

"Well, of course! See, you missed the last two practices, so you didn't hear Wilhelmina criticize my paragraphs. She actually assigned me an extra patch session."

Before Cammie could speak, Mrs. Page appeared from the kitchen, carrying a huge tray filled with something that looked like dry tree twigs.

"Special treats for show skaters. Chocolate-covered pretzels."

Now Cammie realized that the objects she had taken for twigs were indeed pretzels. What made them look unusual was the fact that they were shaped like skate guards. She reached for a pretzel, took a big bite, and squealed with delight.

"It's delicious! Can I have one more?" Liz reached for a brown skate guard, but Mrs. Page promptly took it away from her. "Sorry, hon, you can't have more than one. Coaches' order."

"Ugh!" Liz made a nasty face.

"I know it's hard. But your skating comes first."

Mrs. Page arranged the remaining pretzels on the tray in a neat pile and sighed. "I wish I could sell them to Sweet Blades. But they won't accept my baked goods; how about that?"

"And why not, Mrs. Page? They taste great." Liz cast a covetous look at the pretzel tray that now sat on the counter.

Mrs. Page folded her arms on her chest. "Yes, but it's the way the pretzels look that they have a problem with: 'All Sweet Blades goods must be molded in perfect, skating-related shapes.' That's what they say. Since when have skate guards not been considered skating-related shapes, huh?"

Cammie nodded sympathetically. Even though she couldn't but admit that Mrs. Page's pretzels really looked more like tree limbs than skate guards, she felt sorry for the woman. Who but Cammie understood what rejection felt like? She was a good skater yet couldn't get the part she wanted. Mrs. Page was a good cook, yet Sweet Blades didn't want her. Cammie put the last piece of pretzel into her mouth, savoring the rich chocolate flavor.

Cammie waited for Mrs. Page to look away, bunny-hopped to the counter, and grabbed another pretzel from the tray.

"Don't you dare!" With agility uncharacteristic of a nonathlete, Mrs. Page grabbed Cammie's hand.

"Didn't I tell you not to have more than one? Didn't I?"

Cammie pouted and walked out of the kitchen, ignoring Dana's smirks. A pretzel, big deal! She had another burning problem on her mind—how to get out of the afternoon practice session. So far, Cammie had managed to skip the last two afternoon practices. She had asked Sonia to tell Coach Ferguson she had a sore knee, and it worked.

This morning, however, Coach Ferguson had demanded an explanation. "How come you show up for morning practices but can't make it to show rehearsals?"

Cammie gave her coach an innocent look. "Well, I think I can only skate for a couple of hours before my knee gets sore."

Coach Ferguson's face hardened. "Oh, I see. Perhaps, it would be best to have a doctor look at your knee."

That wasn't what Cammie wanted. Any doctor would be able to tell right away there was nothing wrong with her knee. But still, Cammie absolutely dreaded the idea of wasting time doing figures. The last couple of days, after everybody had left for the afternoon practice, she had sneaked to the Icy Park and practiced her double lutz at one of its frozen ponds. She was definitely getting the hang of it. Cammie was sure a couple more practices would do it. If only Coach Ferguson were a little more understanding! Well, if Cammie wanted to skip another practice, she'd better find a better excuse than a sore knee. And she'd better do it soon.

In their room, Sonia was changing into black leggings and a matching sweatshirt.

"You'd better get ready fast; we need to leave in fifteen minutes," Sonia said.

"Hmm." Cammie twirled her ponytail around her fingers, thinking hard. She had to find a good enough excuse to miss the practice.

"What's wrong? Are you coming?"

Gosh, how Cammie hated those authoritative notes that sometimes appeared in Sonia's voice. The girl was her age, but she often acted as though she were Cammie's mother. Or even worse—her coach.

"Uh … no, I don't think so," Cammie said.

Sonia's blue eyes became cold like steel. "And why not?"

"Hey, don't look at me like that. I'm … I'm not feeling good, okay?" Cammie snapped. She still hadn't thought of what could be wrong with her, but she knew she would make something up in a moment.

"If this is your knee again, it's not going to work," Sonia said sternly. "Coach Ferguson said she would take you to a doctor if you didn't show up."

How come Sonia always knew everything?

"Well, it's not my knee," Cammie said. "It's … well, I'm just sick. Maybe I'm coming down with something."

Yes, that was good. She could send a word to Coach Ferguson that she had a slight cold. After all, she spent so much time skating back and forth in the cold. It had to work.

Sonia eyed her. "Are you *really* sick?"

"Of course I am." Cammie plopped on her bed and grimaced, pretending she was in pain.

"And what exactly is wrong with you?"

"Uh, I have a headache, and my throat is sore." To add credibility to her words, Cammie coughed a couple of times.

Sonia's face softened a little, but she still didn't look as though she quite believed Cammie.

"Then we'd better let Mrs. Page know. Perhaps she could give you some aspirin." Sonia whirled around and left the room.

Cammie quickly got into bed and pulled the covers up to her chin. Good. Now all she needed to do was convince Mrs. Page that she really wasn't up to practicing this afternoon and everything would be all right. She would tell the dorm supervisor she needed a nap, and then she would go to the Icy Park and work on her double lutz.

The door slammed. Cammie looked up. Mrs. Page had entered the room, a thermometer in her hand.

"Let me take your temperature, Cammie."

"Uh, you don't have to. I'll just take it easy and everything will be all right," Cammie said sweetly.

"Now I'm the one who will make this decision. Sonia, you may go to practice now," Mrs. Page said.

Sonia nodded, gave Cammie another long look, and walked out of the room.

"Open your mouth!" Mrs. Page commanded.

Reluctantly, she opened her mouth and felt the cold thermometer slide under her tongue.

"Lie still now, and I'll check on you in ten minutes." Mrs. Page tucked Cammie in and walked out of the room.

The minute the dorm supervisor was gone, Cammie took the thermometer out of her mouth. What was she going to do? Once Mrs. Page saw that Cammie had no fever, she wouldn't believe she was sick and might send her to practice after all. Actually, it would make things even worse for Cammie, for Coach Ferguson loathed skaters coming late. Cammie had to do something and fast.

Cammie looked around the room. What could she do to make her temperature rise? Would a quick workout help? No, it might take time, and Cammie only had a few minutes. Bingo!

She leaped out of bed, wrapped the thermometer in a towel, and pressed it against the radiator. One, two, three... She had no idea how long she had to hold the thermometer like that. She had heard of the trick from her father, who had sometimes resorted to it when he was afraid of his English tests. Nine, ten... that had to be enough. Cammie unwrapped the thermometer, slipped it back in her mouth, and got into bed right before the door opened. When Mrs. Page walked in, Cammie lay quietly under the covers. Her face felt hot, but it was probably all right: Mrs. Page would have no doubt that she had fever.

The dorm supervisor took the thermometer out of Cammie's mouth.

"Ugh!" She stared at Cammie's hot face then at the thermometer again. "Do you have a sore throat?"

Cammie nodded eagerly.

"Your temperature is almost a hundred and three. That's high. Perhaps I should take you to the doctor's office."

"No!" Cammie sat up and folded her hands pleadingly. "Please, Mrs. Page, it's not that bad. It's just a slight cold. It was so windy today, I couldn't get warm. I'll be all right."

Mrs. Page still looked worried. "Tell you what, I'll give you some aspirin and hot tea and then try to get some sleep. Maybe you'll feel better. But if not—"

"Oh I'll be fine, Mrs. Page. I promise."

"Okay. Now stay in bed. I'll be right back."

Mrs. Page left the room, closing the door quietly behind her. Cammie threw off the covers and did a quick somersault on the bed. How cool! Now she would just wait for the aspirin and hot tea, and then once Mrs. Page was sure that Cammie was asleep, she would sneak out to the Icy Park and work on her double lutz.

She put on her wool leggings and a thick white sweater. Skating outside meant beating cold wind, so she had to be dressed warmly. Cammie walked down the steps on her toes, stopping occasionally to make sure Mrs. Page didn't hear her. She lifted the latch on the door, trying to be as quiet as possible. So far so good. Before leaving the dorm, Cammie cast a furtive look at the kitchen door. Mrs. Page was nowhere in sight. Perhaps she had gone to her room to rest. It was just what Cammie needed. Cammie swung the door open and ran out into the cold. The Icy Park was really close; she would make it in no time. There would be enough time to work on her lutz, and she would be back in the dorm for dinner. Brilliant!

Cammie was already halfway down the street on her way to the park, when someone grabbed her by the hood of her parka from behind.

"Witch!" Cammie screamed. Yes, she knew there were wicked witches in the Icy Park, but she hadn't expected them to catch her so soon. Well, Cammie wasn't going to give up so easily. She whirled around and raised her leg, ready to kick the evil woman hard, and gasped in horror. It wasn't a wicked witch who had attacked her; it was Mrs. Page, glaring at her from under the hood of her heavy blue coat.

"What did you call me?" Mrs. Page asked coldly.

"Ah, ah, I said *twitch*. You know…er…you seized me, and I twitched." Cammie smiled coyly, but Mrs. Page's grim expression didn't change.

"So this is how you're resting."

"Mrs. Page, I—"

"Quiet! Follow me now."

Mortified, Cammie skated back to the dorm after Mrs. Page. She couldn't understand what had gone wrong. Why had Mrs. Page suddenly decided to check on her again?

Mrs. Page didn't say a word until they reached the dorm. Inside, the dorm supervisor escorted Cammie to the dining room. "Take your seat."

Prepared for the worst, Cammie sat on the edge of the chair across from the woman.

"I'm waiting for an explanation," Mrs. Page said.

Cammie stared at her trembling hands without saying a word.

"Obviously you don't want to talk to me. Well, perhaps you're right. I'm sure your coach will handle the situation better."

"No!" Cammie looked at the dorm supervisor with horror. Was she going to tell Coach Ferguson that Cammie had tried to weasel her way out of the afternoon practice?

"Mrs. Page, please, please, don't tell Coach Ferguson anything!"

"Why not? She's your coach, and you won't talk to me."

Cammie grimaced. "Look, I wasn't really planning on sneaking out. It's just...I hate those show practices, okay? It's such a waste of time. I mean, we spend the whole session drawing stupid figures on ice. And my double lutz is still nowhere. No wonder I didn't get a solo part. And I want to get better; I have to work hard, and instead I have to draw loops and paragraphs."

Tears flowed down Cammie's cheeks, but she didn't care anymore.

"Cammie..." Mrs. Page chuckled, which made Cammie look up in surprise.

"Oh Cammie, what a silly little girl you are! Don't you think Wilhelmina knows what she is doing? Why do you think has she come up with a history show? Why? Tell me."

Cammie tried to think, but she didn't have a good answer.

"Because she wants all of you kids to get better. That's why."

Cammie stared at the dorm supervisor incredulously.

"That's true. When I skated as a little girl, we spent most of our sessions working on school figures. And you know what? We had much better control of our edges, and there were fewer injuries than nowadays."

"Oh!" Cammie looked at Mrs. Page with interest. "Were you a skater too?"

"And what do you think? Skateland is the land of past, present, and future skaters. Everybody who lives here either was a skater or skates now. And to answer your question, yes, I skated competitively. Unfortunately, I lost my jumps when I started developing hips and breasts." Mrs. Page patted her massive thighs.

"So I understand what you're going through, Cammie. But I suggest that you trust Wilhelmina. She is a wise woman, and she only wants the best for you. And if this show makes you a better skater, why not try your best?"

Cammie contorted her forehead, thinking hard. Perhaps Mrs. Page was right, and if those stupid figures could improve her skating, she might as well practice them.

"Now be a good girl, Cammie. Of course, it's too late to go to the afternoon session today. You may take this afternoon off, but if you miss tomorrow's practice, then your coach will know everything. I'll take care of that. Is it a deal?"

Feeling relieved, Cammie nodded. So Mrs. Page wasn't going to talk to Coach Ferguson, after all. Good! And tomorrow Cammie would go to the afternoon practice. She had no choice—the show was only two weeks away. Two more weeks of torture, and then Cammie would forget about stupid figures for the rest of her life.

FIGURE CANDIES

Cammie looked at her patch and gritted her teeth in frustration. She had spent the last twenty minutes desperately trying to trace at least one outside eight on top of the other—all in vain. Now she almost wished she hadn't missed three practices. Somehow Cammie hadn't realized that while she had spent her afternoons in the Icy Park working on her double lutz, the other skaters had become more and more proficient in school figures. While at the last practice Cammie's figures had been only slightly worse than those drawn by the other show participants, now she was way behind everybody else.

Cammie couldn't help admitting that her brackets and paragraphs were the worst at the rink. Today Cammie's failure was even more obvious because Melvin Reed had appeared at the rink to demonstrate his special effects. First of all, the elderly man asked Wilhelmina's permission to get all the skaters off the ice. Then he circled the arena himself, stopping occasionally, muttering something, stomping his feet, and smoothing the ice with both hands. Cammie watched all those strange manipulations with awe bordering on suspicion. Her attitude toward Mr. Reed was complicated.

Last year Mr. Reed had invented self-spinning boots that allowed a skater to land multi-revolution jumps safely without ever falling. The most exciting thing about those boots was the fact that you could program them to do as many revolutions as you wanted. Last year, Cammie had tried the boots herself and landed several triples. Mr. Reed himself could do beautiful quintuples. Unfortunately, Skateland authorities didn't allow skaters to compete in those magical boots or even to use them for practices. But Cammie still remembered the wonderful feeling of flying and spinning in the air.

Mr. Reed lived in a wood cabin hidden in the thickets of the Icy Park and skated at an outdoor rink with beautiful purple ice. The Purple Rink was one of Skateland's official rinks, though nobody ever skated there except Mr. Reed himself. Cammie knew why: the purple ice had magic powers. Only honest, dedicated skaters could step on the purple ice. An evil person would suffer horrible pain.

Therefore, Mr. Reed's special effects could be either good or bad news for Cammie. Either way, she was a little nervous when the tall, gray-haired man took a small bottle out of his pocket, unscrewed the lid and sprinkled white powder on the ice. The ice absorbed the substance immediately.

Mr. Reed nodded and turned to Wilhelmina. "It's ready. Let the skaters do their figures now."

Feeling slightly uncertain, Cammie skated toward her patch. Standing in the T-position, she pushed off the ice with her left foot. When her first eight was completed, Cammie looked at the ice to check on her progress. "What's that?"

The ice was no longer silvery clean. Something black and dirty was drawn on the clear surface; something looking like a very crooked figure eight. And it was Cammie who had done it.

Shocked, Cammie looked around to see if anybody had witnessed her disgrace. Luckily, the rest of the skaters were too preoccupied with their own progress.

"Hey, I did an outside eight, and here it is on the ice!" Alex's excited voice came from the other end of the rink.

"That's my paragraph!" Jeff shouted.

Coach Ferguson appeared in the middle of the rink. "So what do you guys think of Mr. Reed's special effects? You can't get away with cheating anymore, right?"

The skaters laughed approvingly.

"And you can see your mistakes easily. Now does everybody understand what you need to work on now?"

"Sure!"

"It's great!"

All the kids looked excited, and Cammie was the only one who couldn't share everybody's joy.

"Now I can tell that all of you have improved tremendously." Coach Ferguson's voice sounded somewhere really close to Cammie.

Cammie made a feeble attempt at shielding her pathetic figure eight from the coach's inquisitive eyes. No luck. Coach Ferguson was staring right at Cammie's patch, her face harsh. *Oh please!* Cammie stiffened, too scared to move.

"Keep working," Coach Ferguson finally said and skated away.

Cammie stared at the coach's back, her mouth wide open. That was it? *Keep working.* Blinking hard to cast away angry tears, Cammie looked at the ice where the crooked figure eight screamed silent rebukes at her. Well, merely standing there wouldn't do her any good. With a deep sigh, Cammie pushed off the ice again; another eight and even worse than the first one. Today definitely wasn't her day.

Cammie glanced at the clock. Four more minutes and the torture would be over. No, she couldn't wait that long. Four minutes weren't going to make her figures any better.

Cammie turned her back on the crooked circles on her patch and skated away. She didn't care that Coach Ferguson would be upset with her. The coach might even take Cammie off the show cast. So what? Cammie didn't want to skate her stupid group number anyway. She put on her skate guards and clomped away.

In the aisle, Mr. Reed was talking to Wilhelmina.

"That was good, Mel. The kids are definitely getting better," Skateland president said.

A mischievous smile touched the man's lips. "Not bad, but still a bit dull. I'll think of something better for the show."

Wilhelmina grinned appreciatively. "I bet you will."

Yeah right, there was Mr. Reed planning something to humiliate Cammie even more. She galumphed to the locker room and yanked her parka off the hook. She didn't even bother to change into jeans and a thick sweater. She knew it was cold and windy outside, but she didn't care. Cammie put the parka over her yellow T-shirt and black leggings and stormed out of the Sport Center.

Outside, the wind grabbed her with its ice cold hands right away. Cammie shivered and skated in the direction of Main Square. Perhaps she could take a shortcut through the Icy Park. The park was usually out of bounds for skaters because that was the place where witches lived, but now Cammie couldn't care less. All she wanted was to get out of the cold.

"Cammie, wait!"

She looked back, bending under gusts of cold wind.

Alex was skating fast in her direction. "Hey, what's the rush? I thought I'd never catch up with you."

At the sight of her friend's smiling face, Cammie relaxed a little. Boy, it was great to have Alex train in Skateland with her. Alex always understood her. Somehow, Cammie had failed to become close with any of the girls in Skateland. Sonia was nice, but…well, too perfect for Cammie's taste. There were other girls in the dorm, but all of them were so competitive. All they ever talked about were the new jumps and spins they had mastered. And Cammie knew the girls always watched her closely to make sure she wasn't ahead of them in any way. If she was behind, they treated her as their best friend. But if she was ahead…well, they didn't like her that much anymore.

Alex was different, of course. He was two years older, a much more advanced skater, and it didn't bother Cammie in the slightest. On the contrary, Cammie was proud that Alex had shown interest in her. He often gave her skating tips; he complimented her on a good move; he critiqued her programs. But most importantly, Alex was always there for her.

Last year, Cammie had moved to Skateland all alone, and the girl whom Cammie had considered her best friend turned out to be a witch-in-training. Alex had been the one to battle the wicked witches. And if it hadn't been for him—

"Are you okay?" Alex asked.

Cammie hung her head. The question sounded simple enough, but to give her friend an honest answer, she would have to explain a lot.

"I have an idea! Let's go to Sweet Blades," Alex said. "I don't know about you, but I could use a snack after this practice. Those school figures are driving me nuts. Can you believe it? My ankles hurt so badly; I never feel so tired after a jumping session."

Cammie felt encouraged. "Exactly. And I don't even understand why we need those figures. No one does them anymore. We'll look like a bunch of idiots during the performance. Okay, I know figures are important and stuff, but I still hate them. Making them part of the show is a crazy idea. "

They walked into the brightly lit bakery. Delicious smells of vanilla, hot chocolate, and cinnamon hung in the air. It was very warm inside. Fortunately, the line to the counter wasn't very long. Cammie and Alex scanned the long menu printed on the wall. Sweet Blades was Skateland's most popular bakery and candy store that specialized in skating-related sweets. Skaters could try skating pastries made of white or dark chocolate; the store offered hard candy shaped like icicles and cookies that looked exactly like skating dresses. Today, however, Cammie wanted to order something new.

"What's Crossover Cocktail?" Cammie asked, rising on her toes.

The saleslady chuckled. "Oh, you'll love it. Though called cocktail, it's a non-alcoholic drink, of course. We don't allow any alcohol in Skateland, you know. Crossover Cocktail contains hot red grape and cranberry juices with lots of sugar, a little lemon, and honey. Nothing can warm you up better after a long, hard practice."

Cammie and Alex exchanged eager looks.

"That sounds good. But I still don't understand why it is called Crossover Cocktail. Does it help you to improve your crossovers?" Alex asked innocently.

The saleslady smiled brightly. "Oh, I wish it did. No, unfortunately, the only thing that can help you with your crossovers is practice. As for Crossover Cocktail, we chose this particular name because it's sort of a cross between a soft drink and real cocktail. It warms you up, but it won't make you tipsy."

"Okay, we'll take it," Alex said. "And we also want two cans of Special Figure Skating Candy."

"What's that?" Cammie asked Alex. She had never heard of this candy before.

"Wilhelmina suggested we all try it."

"It's our new promotion item," the saleslady said proudly as she pointed to a huge poster on the entrance door.

The poster showed a group of skaters wearing multicolored clothes and intertwined in an intricate dancing pattern. The sign over the picture read: "Special Figure Skating Candy. Preferable for show skaters, but also perfect for show spectators."

They carried their drinks and candy to a table next to the huge window that offered a perfect view of Main Square. The multicolored lights around the rink were already on, and from where they sat, Cammie could watch people skating in the middle. A little boy of about four stomped on the ice, apparently feeling uncomfortable in his new figure skates. His mother pulled the child tightly by the hands, trying to get him to glide.

"Not bad," Alex said as he sipped his Crossover Cocktail.

Cammie took her eyes off the toddler and sampled her drink. It had nice fruit flavor; but what was even more important, it seemed to have lit a fire in every limb of Cammie's body.

"Want to try these?" Alex opened one of the metal cans decorated with geometrical figures. The lid slid out of Alex's hand, and a bunch of multicolored candy spilled out of the can and scattered across the red-and-white checkered cloth.

"Oh no!" Alex scooped as much candy as he could and stuffed them back into the can.

"What is it?" Cammie picked up a bright blue candy twisted in an unusual shape. It looked like the beak of a bird.

"It's a beak, one of the special figures." Alex twisted a yellow candy between his fingers. "Hey, look, this is an anvil and...wait, okay, this is a grapevine."

Alex showed Cammie a green and purple candy.

Cammie stared at the strangely shaped object, unable to believe her eyes. "Special figures? Hang on...are these the figures from the show?"

"Sure. And look, here are the ones we can do. This is figure eight, and this is a bracket..."

"And you want me to *eat* them?" She turned around and saw that everybody's eyes were fixed on her. Embarrassed, Cammie lowered her eyes. A colorful display of special figures that looked like hard candy glittered on the table in front of her. With repulsion, Cammie took a pink candy shaped like an intricate cross and carefully put it in her mouth. The candy had a pleasant cherry flavor.

"Here, try this orange snowflake." Alex pushed another bright candy into Cammie's hand.

With a deep sigh, Cammie dropped the snowflake in her mouth, enjoying the taste of tangerine on her tongue.

"What's wrong? Don't you like it?" Alex asked, his mouth full.

Cammie gave him a sad look. "Sure I do. It's just I don't need another reminder of that stupid show."

"It's not stupid. I think showing the history of figure skating is a great idea."

Cammie made a nasty face. "It's bo-oring. And for your information, history is my least favorite subject."

Alex swirled the straw in his drink. "So are you ready for the test?"

"Test? What test?"

Alex looked genuinely surprised. "Don't you know? All the participants of the show are required to take a test on the history of figure skating. Wilhelmina mentioned it three days ago. I've already gone through half of the book. It's quite exciting, you know. Can you imagine: for many years, there were no toe picks, and still some skaters could do jumps and spins... What's wrong?"

Alex must have noticed Cammie's horrified facial expression.

"I didn't know about any test." She pushed her glass away. "Yes, that's it. First the figures, now some crazy test. I didn't even know we had to study history before the show."

"But how could you miss Wilhelmina's announcement?"

Cammie sighed. "I missed three practices."

"Whoa! What happened?"

Cammie grimaced and put another beak in her mouth. "Nothing. I just skipped them. I had to work on my double lutz, okay?"

Alex gave her a funny look, though she couldn't miss a mischievous glitter in his green eyes. "Cammie, you are really something. How did you manage that? Did you honestly believe you'd get away with that?"

"I told Mrs. Page I was sick. She believed me…until yesterday. Anyway…Gosh, how am I going to take that test if I know nothing about history?"

"But you're taking it at school."

Cammie rubbed her forehead. "I don't think I remember anything."

"You still have two weeks to study. The test is on Friday, two days before the show."

"All right," Cammie said reluctantly. She hated the idea of studying about skaters of old. Why did that matter anyway? Skating was about what *you* could do. Knowing that people had skated without toe picks once wasn't going to help her land her double lutz.

"Cammie!"

She shook her head.

Alex was looking at her with concern. "Don't think you're wasting your time. I believe Wilhelmina knows what she is doing. After all, she was a world champion and an Olympic silver medalist. She is a great coach too. She wouldn't want us to waste our skating time on something that wouldn't help us with our technique."

Cammie nodded slowly.

"Hey, remember how we both hated practicing basic moves before our first competition in Skateland? Edges, three turns…Remember?"

How could Cammie forget? She picked up the multicolored candies and let them run through her fingers, watching the hearts, flowers, and circles drop on the table. Maybe Alex was right.

Cammie put a green bracket in her mouth and smiled, trying to look cheerful. "Okay, I'll try to do my best."

"Good!" Alex said, looking relieved. "Believe me, you may end up liking figure skating history after all."

Cammie pouted. "No way. I'll study for the test, and I'll practice stupid figures because I have to, but I won't enjoy it."

After talking to Alex, Cammie never missed another show practice. She still hated drawing figures on ice, but she told herself that she wouldn't have to suffer long. *The History of Figure Skating* show would soon be over, and then Cammie wouldn't attempt another school figure for the rest of her life.

Melvin Reed never showed up at their practices again. There were rumors that he was working on more special effects, and Cammie wondered if his inventions would make her incompetence at school figures even more obvious. But as the days slipped by, and the skate sharpener hadn't shown up, Cammie slowly began to relax.

She dutifully drew eights, brackets, and paragraphs on the assigned patch, stopped, looked, sighed, and drew them again. Her figures still looked dreadful, but Cammie hoped that during the actual performance no one would pay attention to her asymmetrical shapes. There would be better numbers to watch. Not the French group number Cammie was supposed to skate, of course. There was too much flailing of arms and very little skating to Cammie's taste. Stupid swan-like positions, spread eagles on bent knees, as though Cammie couldn't do a real one! At the conclusion of the French number, the girls were supposed to do a three-revolution two-foot spin, which made Cammie feel like a toddler.

"But this is what they did back then," Liz said when Cammie shared her frustration with her.

How stupid! Why should skaters of the twenty-first century care about some old traditions?

Days dragged by slowly, like a beginning skater going around the rink. Cammie's parents booked tickets for the show. Judging from the sound of their voices over the phone, they were really excited to see their daughter skate in the big gala. If only Cammie had a real part! Her heart sank each time the first boring part of the show was over, and soloists moved to the center of the rink to perform their routines. As Cammie watched her friends doing jumps and spins, she couldn't help thinking that if only she were given a chance, she would do a much better job. Her worst moments came when Sonia appeared on ice, small and agile, skating so fast that whenever Cammie took her eyes off her roommate's tiny figure, it instantly disappeared from her field of vision. Sonia's job was to show the evolution of jumps and spins through history. She started with simple waltz jumps then moved up to singles, doubles, and finally, triples. Two-foot spins were followed by layback and change foot spins, and finally, Sonia would raise her leg high behind her and grab her blade in a perfect bielmann's position.

Inspired by Sonia's performance, Cammie started stretching hard, so she could do a bielmann spin too. Yet she still couldn't get her leg up high enough. And as for triples...well, it would probably be a long time before Cammie could even start working on those. Sonia was a much stronger skater.

"Why do you have to compare yourself with Sonia?" Alex asked Cammie after she shared her disappointment with him.

That was a weird thing to ask. "How else would I know whether I'm good or bad? Every competition is about comparing yourself with other skaters."

"But this is a show, not a competition. We aren't supposed to beat anybody. Just relax and have fun."

It was easy for Alex to say; his part was good enough.

They kept practicing, and all of a sudden the time started moving ahead faster and faster; days swept by in a blur like Sonia doing backward crossovers.

Before Cammie knew it, there were only two days left before the performance, and all the show participants gathered in the Sport Center computer room for their written Figure Skating History Test.

Cammie felt drowsy. Although she had promised Alex to study hard for the test, she hadn't managed to finish her skating history book. Whatever her friend might have said, Cammie still found the stories about skaters of old boring. The night before the test, she had tried to do some last-minute studying, but still she could barely remember the stuff she had read.

Mr. Stevens, their skating history teacher, positioned everybody in front of a computer. Cammie stared at the blank screen, hoping for the best.

```
Toe picks were first introduced by:
a. Ulrich Salchow
b. Axel Paulsen
c. Jackson Haines
d. Dick Button
```

Hmm, that was a tough one. Cammie scratched her head, desperately trying to remember the page from the history book where toe picks were mentioned. No, she didn't have a clue. *Okay, think logically!* she told herself. *Ulrich Salchow? He is known for his salchow jump. Could he have introduced toe picks too? Nope, that would have been too much for one person. Axel Paulsen?* Same thing: he was the first to land the axel jump—that was obvious. Cammie wished there had been a skater named *Toe Pick*; that would be a big help. Anyway, was it Jackson Haines or Dick Button? Cammie had never heard of Jackson Haines, which meant he couldn't have designed blades with toe picks. And as for Dick Button...That name really rang a bell; Cammie had definitely heard it somewhere. Feeling relieved, Cammie clicked on "d" and moved to the next question.

Pick the name of the three-time Olympic gold medalist:
a. Katarina Witt
b. Peggy Fleming
c. Sonja Henie
d. Michelle Kwan

Piece of cake! Of course, it was Michelle Kwan, the world's greatest skater. Cammie quickly clicked on "d."

Which of the following is the name of a school figure:
a. a flip
b. a loop
c. a twizzle
d. a bunny hop

Cammie wasn't quite sure, but the correct answer was probably a twizzle. It had to be. Of course, a loop was a jump, and so was a flip, and as for bunny hops...Cammie laughed as she remembered how she had once been scared of bunny hops. Now she liked them, but they were jumps; definitely not figures. Twizzles, of course, were multiple circles, and all figures involved circles. Okay, a twizzle had to be the right answer. Cammie clicked on "c" and moved to the next question.

```
Which of the following is not a
school figure:
    a. a beak
    b. an anvil
    c. spectacles
    d. a can opener
```

Cammie frowned. Okay, a beak and an anvil—those were school figures for sure, Cammie thought of the candy from Sweet Blades and mentally thanked Alex for taking her to the bakery. Now how about spectacles and a can opener? In Cammie's opinion, both sounded too weird for school figures. So out of those two, which one would be more difficult to do on ice? Cammie closed her eyes and pictured a can opener and spectacles sitting on a kitchen counter next to each other. Well, if she had a choice of which one to do on ice, she would definitely go for a can opener. One big circle and a knob inside—yes, that figure was doable! So the correct answer had to be spectacles. Feeling relieved, Cammie clicked on "c."

Cammie went through the next sixteen questions, feeling more and more confident. The test wasn't that difficult after all. She finished it just in time and followed the rest of the skaters out of the building, squinting at the bright sun. How awesome! They would have the rest of the day to themselves, and then tomorrow the dress rehearsal would finally take place. The show was scheduled for Sunday night, the day after tomorrow, and after that, Cammie would be free to work on real skating.

DRESS REHEARSAL

C ammie wrapped her warmup jacket tighter around her body and shuffled her feet. Jammed between the other show participants, she couldn't wait for the rehearsal to start. Moving around would definitely make her warmer. The temperature had dropped after sundown, and Cammie's hands and feet were beginning to complain. *It's time. Come on. Let's begin!* Cammie looked at the clock on top of the tower on Main Square again. No luck: its hands seemed to have frozen. The last time Cammie had checked, there had been two minutes left before the beginning of the rehearsal. Now it said one minute, but it couldn't be true. The show participants had been milling around Axel Avenue leading to Main Square for what seemed like long hours.

The long hand of the clock began to move, slowly, reluctantly and finally settled on five. Immediately the air was filled with huge golden snowflakes. They glittered in the light of lanterns, swirled over the ice, landed, flew up again. It was impossible to tell where the air ended and the ice started. It had to be another special effect from Melvin Reed. The audience erupted in a loud applause. Though it was only the dress rehearsal, not the actual show, many of Skateland residents had shown up. The roofs of the stores had been turned into stands, and from where Cammie stood she could see dozens of eager faces staring at the play of lights on the ice.

"Welcome to our annual Skateland show dress rehearsal."

Cammie rose on her toes to see who had spoken. Wilhelmina stood on the edge of the ice, a microphone in her hand. Tonight, Skateland president wore an ankle-length black dress embroidered with golden threads. The dress covered her bony legs and made her look younger.

"Music, please!" Wilhelmina said.

Slow music poured out from the speakers, and a dozen little girls dressed like snowflakes skated to the middle of the rink.

"Cammie!"

Cammie turned around.

Coach Ferguson stood next to her, looking stern. "You failed your skating history test."

"Oh!" Cammie didn't know what to say.

"You don't look surprised. Did you study hard for you test like you were supposed to?"

In spite of the cold air, Cammie felt hot. Unable to meet the coach's eyes, she looked away.

"I assume your silence means you didn't study."

Cammie sighed gravely and tugged at her new velvet dress. It was gorgeous—black, trimmed with silver. If only she could skate a solo in it!

"I could pull you off the show, of course," Coach Ferguson said.

Cammie looked up, startled. Oh no, even though she hated her part, not skating at all would be a disaster. She had already told her parents she would be in the show.

"Coach Ferguson, I—"

"Yes, that's what I should do," the coach said as though she didn't hear Cammie at all.

Cammie's heart skipped a beat. Yes, that was it, she wouldn't skate. Boy, what an embarrassment! Perhaps she could tell her parents she was sick or …

"Unfortunately, pulling you off would require too many changes. We would have to shift the figures pattern, and then you're in a group number … how unfortunate!" Coach Ferguson seemed to be thinking out loud.

Cammie waited anxiously.

"I'll tell you what," the coach finally said. "I'll let you do the rehearsal, but after it's over, you are going back to the dorm to study. You will be given another opportunity to take your test at one o'clock tomorrow. And if you fail it again, you won't skate in the show, and I will have a serious discussion with your parents. Is that understood?"

Cammie nodded miserably. Coach Ferguson really knew how to make her suffer. For crying out loud, tonight was supposed to be the time to relax and have fun. Cammie had been planning to go to Sweet Blades with Alex. Now she would have to return to the dorm and spend the rest of the night reading about skating history.

Coach Ferguson turned away from Cammie. "Attention, everybody! School figures are next, after the Dutch waltz!"

There was a wave of excitement as the skaters formed a long file, ready to skate to the middle of the rink.

"Go!" Coach Ferguson waved her hand.

Cammie glided forward alongside her friends. Each of them took a small patch. As Wilhelmina had explained earlier, school figures were normally performed without music. However, the president had decided to add some background music during the show so that the audience wouldn't get bored and distracted. This time, Cammie really tried her best. Inspired by the music and the people in the stands, she concentrated on executing each of her figures perfectly. She thought she was doing fine, yes, much better than at practices. Okay, the second tracing of her figure eight was completed; she could leave her patch now. Relieved, Cammie moved away.

Someone giggled next to Cammie, and the wind carried the sound to the other side of the rink.

Now Cammie felt as though she were swimming in a sea of laughter. "What?"

She looked around, trying to find the source of the chuckles; she glanced at her figure pattern.

"Uh-huh!" Dana said, staring at Cammie's patch.

"Oh no!" Cammie took a quick step back, slipped, and almost fell.

"Out, everybody!" Coach Ferguson motioned them off the ice.

Before skating away, Cammie looked at her tracings again. She couldn't suppress a groan. Instead of being positioned directly on top of the first figure, Cammie's second eight stood almost half a foot away. Perhaps, under different circumstances, the audience might have missed the obvious mistake. After all, who could see tracings on ice from the stands? However, Mr. Reed had made sure the skaters' mistakes wouldn't be missed.

Cammie could almost hear the skate sharpener's English-accented voice, "Just wait till the dress rehearsal, fellows, and you will see the big surprise I have prepared for you."

Apparently, Mr. Reed had kept his promise about special effects, and now his surprise had played a bad trick on Cammie. Somehow the skate sharpener had made the first figure appear bright red; the second was canary yellow. And while everybody else's figures had acquired a nice solid shade of orange, Cammie's patch had two individual tracings—red and yellow.

"You know, your figure is actually nice, like a zebra." Dana giggled.

Before Cammie could think of a decent answer, Coach Ferguson shooed them off the ice, so room could be given to Mr. Reed, Mr. Walrus, and to Wilhelmina herself. The older skaters were about to demonstrate special figures.

While the other girls crowded at the entrance to the rink expressing their admiration of the adult skaters' skills, with "wow's" and "oh's," Cammie lurked in the corner. Perhaps it would have been better if Coach Ferguson had pulled her off the show after all.

"Cammie, wake up! French group number, remember?"

"Keep your belly tucked in, Cammie. What's the matter with you?" Coach Ferguson slapped Cammie on the butt. It didn't hurt in the slightest, but Cammie felt humiliated. She gritted her teeth. If the coach thought Cammie couldn't do the stupid French number, she was going to see she didn't always know everything.

Cammie kept biting her lower lip during the whole performance, never allowing even a trace of smile to appear on her face. Other than that, she did okay. When the girls finally stepped off the ice, Cammie caught her coach's approving grin. Still, she didn't allow herself to get excited. At least she was done for tonight, except for the final parade of skaters, of course, but that would be easy.

Cammie's friends rushed to the stands to watch the rest of the show, but witnessing Sonia's triumph was the last thing on Cammie's mind. She zipped up her warmup jacket and skated away from the noise and excitement of Main Square to a side street. To justify the name—Straight Line Footwork Street— it was straight and narrow. Cammie plopped down on a small marble bench without even bothering to brush the snow off, put her hands in her pockets, and closed her eyes. From where she sat, she could still hear all the action, yet no one saw her. She felt tired; her muscles were sore.

Cammie must have drifted off to sleep, although she was sure she had been keeping track of the show's progress. She remembered loud march music—it had to be Jeff playing the part of a famous skater; Cammie couldn't remember the name. Then Cammie was aware of herself swinging to soft tango music—those had to be Sandra Newman and Kevin Sawyer demonstrating the evolution of ice dancing. When Cammie heard the famous Chaplin music, she pictured Alex doing a huge axel. Though only a single, the jump was supposed to be over twenty feet long; Cammie remembered Alex telling her about it.

The music stopped; everything was quiet. It meant the snow was over; that was good. Cammie opened her eyes and jumped off the bench. Her feet must have gone to sleep, for they wouldn't hold her. Cammie squeaked as she fell into the deep snow, face first.

"How silly!" She sat up and massaged her thighs and calves, feeling blood rush to her cold limbs. Brushing the snow off her clothes, Cammie skated back to Main Square.

Even before she reached the rink, Cammie knew something wasn't right. There was no usual excitement that normally signaled the end of a successful show practice. She could hear no laughter, no words of approval. Instead, when Cammie approached the square, she saw people in the stands stretching their necks as though looking for something. A tight group of skaters stood on the edge of the rink, holding hands.

"What's wrong?" Cammie asked a girl from the Blue Rink.

Before the girl could say a word, Mr. Nielsen, one of the Blue Rink coaches, stepped forward, looking very determined.

"Now don't panic, we'll find her." He tapped the girl Cammie had been talking to on the shoulder and hurried away.

"What's he talking about?"

The girl swallowed hard and shook her head. Flabbergasted, Cammie stared at her.

"All the skaters will return to their dorms promptly!" a deep voice said.

Cammie looked around and saw two uniformed policemen getting off a sled that bore the sign *Skateland Police* on its silver side.

"Coaches are requested to accompany the children to their places of safety. No panic!" a middle-age policeman with a mustache said.

No panic. It was the second time Cammie heard those words. But gosh, could someone explain to her what had happened?

"Back to the dorm now!" Coach Ferguson separated herself from the crowd and grabbed Cammie by the hand. "Do you need a special invitation, Cammie Wester?"

"No, please!" Cammie wriggled her hand free. "What's wrong? Why are the police here?"

Coach Ferguson's pale blue eyes narrowed. "Didn't you hear the announcement?"

"What announcement?"

Coach Ferguson gave her a very disapproving look, but Cammie didn't care. "Coach Ferguson, please!"

"A skater is missing."

"What?" Cammie couldn't even understand what the coach was talking about. Missing? How was that possible? Everybody was right there, skating or watching the show.

Coach Ferguson let out a very sad sigh. "It's Sonia."

"Sonia?" Cammie stepped back and pressed her hands against her mouth. It was impossible. Sonia couldn't have gone anywhere. She had a part to skate. And …

"Did she … did she skate her solo?" Cammie asked weakly.

The coach shook her head. "No. She disappeared right before her number."

"But it can't be true. Sonia is so disciplined, she just couldn't—"

"Well, she's gone."

"But then …" Now the truth was beginning to sink in. And before the coach could say another word, Cammie knew exactly what had happened.

"Coach Ferguson, I know what happened."

Coach Ferguson, who had already started gathering the scared girls around her, stopped abruptly. "What did you say?"

"It's the witches!" Cammie explained. She caught the coach's skeptical look and hastened to explain that Skateland witches had a plan of attacking the top skaters, that Sonia was on their list. Cammie and Alex had been accidentally locked at the Black Rink a year before, and they had overheard the witches' evil plot. Cammie even knew exactly which of the witches was supposed to attack Sonia.

"It's the Witch of Fear, Coach Ferguson. She lives in a big castle in the Icy Park. I'll tell the police about it, all right?"

The coach's cold eyes flashed furiously. "Now I don't want to hear that nonsense. There are no witches in Skateland, all right? Sonia probably got lost, and that's it."

"But she couldn't have just walked out of the show!" Cammie shouted.

"Keep your voice down, will you? Now she may have gotten abducted, but certainly not by witches. How ridiculous! The police will do their best to find her. Sonia will definitely be back soon, perhaps even tonight. Now I want you to go to the dorm now. And for goodness sake, don't spread those ridiculous rumors about witches. The skaters are scared enough already."

Cammie looked at the group of girls from her dorm standing nearby. They really appeared frightened. Cammie pressed her lips tight. Perhaps Coach Ferguson was right when she did her best not to cause panic, but why didn't she believe Cammie? For some stupid reason, most of the residents of Skateland didn't accept the fact that there were quite a few witches in the Icy Park. Cammie had met most of them personally, and because of their evil attacks, she had been close to the end of her skating career more than once. The witches had skated competitively, too, at some point, but for one reason or another, they had had to give up the sport.

Instead of retiring gracefully, they had become extremely jealous of good skaters who still had a chance at the worlds, the nationals, or even the Olympics. They had made it their purpose to put an end to the skating careers of good skaters. Cammie didn't understand why. Perhaps seeing other people suffer made the witches feel better about themselves. Anyway, Cammie found the witches extremely dangerous, and she didn't think that merely denying their existence was the right thing to do. The witches were very creative when it came to attacking skaters. The Witch of Injuries could cause a bad fall, resulting in an injury. The Witch of Fear, who often hung out at Skateland's official rinks, could somehow frighten a skater so badly that she would never attempt another jump in her life. The Witch of Pride would usually make a skater so haughty and self-confident that he would come to a false conclusion that practicing hard wasn't necessary at all. Inevitably, his skating would deteriorate. And it had happened so often! Two years ago, Cammie and Alex had come across four skaters who had gained so much weight after having an encounter with the Witch of Pride that they had stopped skating altogether.

Shaking her head angrily, Cammie joined the other girls on their way to the dorm.

"She probably eloped with a boyfriend," Liz said, widening her eyes.

"Don't be stupid!" Cammie snapped.

Liz clenched her fists. "Don't you dare insult me, Cammie Wester!"

"Stop spreading idiotic rumors about Sonia, then."

"*You* don't know where she is."

"Oh I do."

Cammie shouldn't have said that, for a split second later, the gang of girls was all over her.

"Where?"

"Come on, Cammie, tell us!"

"She doesn't know anything. Don't you see she's just showing off?" Dana was batting her long lashes, looking very self-confident.

Cammie felt very tempted to say that Sonia was most likely in the Witch of Fear's castle in the Icy Park, but she had promised Coach Ferguson not to spread rumors about the witches. She didn't want to get in more trouble by disobeying her coach. Surely failing her skating history test was enough.

"I told you, she doesn't have a clue." Dana turned away from Cammie.

Cammie kicked the ice hard.

"Do you think what I think?"

Cammie wheeled around. Alex stood beside her, his face red.

"It's the Witch of Fear," Alex said without the slightest doubt.

Cammie nodded. "I know. Remember the Black Rink?"

Alex grinned wryly. "How could I forget? So what are we going to do?"

"We?" Cammie stared at Alex, feeling slightly shocked. What could they do? The coaches had just told all the skaters to stay put.

"We've got to rescue her. We are the only ones who know where she is. The policemen don't have a clue, and they won't listen to me."

"Did you talk to the cops already?"

Alex nodded. "It was useless, though. They only laughed at me. So it's now or never. We have to sneak out before your coach locks you up in the dorm. I'm sure you won't be able to get out tonight."

Cammie looked around. They were already approaching her dorm; from where they were, she could see the brightly lit porch and the green letters "Juvenile Girls' Dorm." There was only a block left, and Axel Avenue was straight and narrow as a blade. There were a few snow-covered trees on both sides of the street. The trees weren't thick enough to give Cammie and Alex enough cover, but using them as a temporary hiding place was still worth a try.

Cammie glanced at Alex and caught his wink, which meant he understood. They had to get out of the crowd.

"Now!" Alex mouthed to Cammie and dashed to the side.

Cammie bent down as low as she could and rushed after him. *Bang!* She got on her toe and crashed hard on the irregular ice. She grimaced with pain but didn't squeal, unwilling to get the coach's attention. She crawled a couple feet toward Alex's outstretched hand.

"Cammie Wester! What on earth are you doing?"

Coach Ferguson. For a split second, Cammie still hoped that perhaps she would be able to crawl away fast and then skate along the twisting Cross Roll Street to the Icy Park. But it didn't take Cammie long to realize that she wouldn't be able to skate away from Coach Ferguson. The woman was older, faster, and a much better skater. Another second, and the coach's strong hand grabbed Cammie by the collar.

"Now didn't I tell you to follow the group? Don't you understand English?"

Cammie tried to say something, but the collar held by the coach's hand pressed her neck hard, and she only managed a feeble *meh-heh-heh*.

"And now of all times, when everybody is focused on finding Sonia. No, I'm not going to listen to any more gibberish. You are grounded. Do you hear me? No more walking around. You are only allowed to go to practice and to school, and then you'll go back to the dorm. And I'm warning you, Cammie: disobey me one more time, and I'll write to your parents."

Coach Ferguson let go of Cammie's collar and pushed her toward the dorm entrance, where the girls stood watching them. Cammie looked away not to meet Dana's smirk and swallowed angry tears.

"And you?" Now Coach Ferguson was yelling at Alex. "You have just been accepted to Skateland, and here you are setting a bad example for younger skaters."

"But Coach Ferguson, Cammie and I are only trying to help. We know exactly where Sonia is."

Cammie saw that Alex was doing his best to sound calm and reasonable.

Coach Ferguson folded her arms on her chest. "Oh really? And where, may I ask, is she?"

"In a castle in the Icy Park. We believe Sonia has been abducted by the Witch of Fear."

"Now enough. I won't hear any of this nonsense again." Normally a cold and reserved woman, Coach Ferguson looked like a furious dragon.

"But look, what if Sonia is really there?" Alex didn't look intimidated at all, and his calm demeanor seemed to be working. At least Coach Ferguson wasn't yelling anymore.

"If Sonia is really in the Icy Park, the police will find her. They are already searching all of Skateland."

"But we could help!"

"Young man, I don't think qualified investigators need any assistance from you or your little friend."

Cammie fidgeted at the look of scorn the coach had flashed her.

"Now, Alex Bernard, if you just go to your dorm … no, wait a minute! I will escort your personally. I don't trust you anymore." Coach Ferguson squeezed Alex's arm and led him away.

Cammie saw that Alex tried to look back, but the coach wheeled him around immediately. Apparently she didn't want him to send Cammie a cryptic message.

"Coach Ferguson, I still think … " Alex's voice sounded weaker and weaker, and finally Coach Ferguson and Alex turned around the corner, and Cammie couldn't hear them anymore.

With a deep sigh, Cammie followed the rest of her girls into the dorm building. Why hadn't the coach believed them? They had already helped Sonia once, and they could surely do it again.

"Now, sweeties, don't you worry. Everything will be all right," Mrs. Page crooned as the girls walked into the lobby. "I've made hot chocolate for you girls, and then there is a special treat."

"Chocolate-covered pretzels again?" Dana asked.

The dorm supervisor's lips spread in a shy smile. "Actually, I decided to try something new. Now how about … mitten cookies?"

Liz giggled. "Mitten cookies? What kind of dessert is that?"

"They taste good. I put in lots of butter and vanilla. And they are decorated with different patterns made from strawberry, cherry, and blueberry preserves."

The cookies tasted soft and rich. Unfortunately, Mrs. Page had failed to give her baked goods a decent shape again. Though called mitten cookies, the shapeless lumps of dough looked more like donkey's ears. Cammie didn't mind, although she couldn't help thinking that Mrs. Page's products would probably be rejected by Sweet Blades again.

It was cozy in the dining room. A fire roared in the fireplace, hot chocolate warmed Cammie up instantly, and she would have been happy if it weren't for Sonia's disappearance. The other girls had to feel the same, for there was little talk at the table.

"Where is she sleeping now?" Liz sighed as she looked at the window. It had started snowing again, and snowflakes swirled in the wind like little girls in their group number.

"Sonia will probably be back soon," Mrs. Page said reassuringly.

Cammie tried her best to believe the dorm supervisor's words. But as she went up to the room she shared with Sonia and got into bed, she felt almost sick. The room was well heated; Cammie's bed felt soft and comfortable and outside the wind howled and cast snow against the dorm walls. Lying in bed, the covers up to her chin, Cammie thought of poor Sonia, scared and lonely in the Witch of Fear's castle. Tears streamed down her cheeks onto the covers. Cammie wiped her eyes off with her fingers, thinking that she would give everything only to have Sonia back in their dorm room.

"Oh please, please, Sonia, come back," Cammie whispered. "Let everything be all right with you, and I will never feel jealous of you again." As Cammie thought of how stupid she had been, she felt hot and miserable. Really, why had she been so upset about Sonia getting the lead in the show?

Cammie sat up in bed and tossled her pillow. Even though nobody took Alex and her seriously, they were not giving up. Tomorrow the two of them would definitely think of something. And then they would go after Sonia, and they would rescue her. They had done it once, and they could do it again.

A Night Stroll Around the Icy Park

Cammie was determined to start looking for Sonia as early as Sunday morning. Unfortunately, sneaking out of the dorm proved to be impossible. When Cammie walked into the dining room to have breakfast, Mrs. Page showed up with an official-looking paper. As it turned out, the paper contained a long list of security measures that everybody was expected to follow.

"No skater is allowed to leave the dorm unless accompanied by an adult," Mrs. Page read. "It means I will be taking you to your practices, girls."

Cammie groaned.

"Do you have a question, Cammie?" Mrs. Page looked unusually strict.

"No, sorry." Cammie looked down. How on earth was she going to visit the Icy Park with Mrs. Page on her tail?

"After practices and school, the skaters will proceed straight to the dorm," Mrs. Page went on.

Cammie leaned back in her chair, feeling upset. Just school and practices, nothing else.

"Skateland annual show is postponed until further notice." Mrs. Page finished reading, folded the paper, and looked up at the frustrated skaters.

"Why did they have to cancel the show?" Dana grumbled as she toyed with her cereal.

"The show isn't canceled; it's only postponed. Once Sonia is back, the performance will take place," Liz said.

"Couldn't they find another skater to replace Sonia?" Dana dropped her spoon and stared dreamingly into space. "I mean … who knows for sure that Sonia was abducted? Perhaps she just sneaked out to take a vacation. So if she isn't serious about her part, there are plenty of other skaters. Like me, for example."

Only a couple of days ago, Cammie would have agreed with Dana. In fact, she would have been happy to replace Sonia in her leading part; she would have thought of it as her best chance. But since Sonia's abduction, something had changed inside Cammie. Now as she thought of how badly she had treated her roommate before the dress rehearsal, she had a strong sense of guilt. The reality was that Cammie had barely talked to Sonia. She had never compli-mented her, no matter how beautifully Sonia had skated. That was wrong, and Cammie was ashamed of herself. Of course, she couldn't change the past, but at least she could protect her friend from unfair attacks, especially from Dana's snide remarks. How could Dana assume that Sonia had walked out on them when she was now suffering in the castle of the Witch of Fear?

"Shut up, Dana, or I'll make sure you never skate another part in your life!" There, Cammie had said it.

Cammie expected Dana to really snap at her. Dana wasn't the kind of person who took insults with dignity. But miraculously, Dana did shut her mouth, allowing but an occasional dirty look at Cammie as she finished her cereal. Cammie did her best to ignore Dana.

"Okay, girls, now back to your rooms. You have homework to do." Mrs. Page began to clear the table.

Dana pushed herself away from the table. "What? It's Sunday, remember? Liz and I were plan-ning to go to Smiling Skater. I need new gloves."

Mrs. Page put the sugarbowl back on the table with a loud clang. "Didn't you hear what I just said, Dana? No one is leaving this dorm without me. And I have things to do this afternoon."

She picked up the stack of dishes and headed for the kitchen.

Dana glared at Mrs. Page's back. "It's sick."

Shaking their heads, muttering under their breath, Dana and Liz headed for their room. Cammie, however, stayed at the table, feeling miserable. So that was it; Mrs. Page had been dead serious. So there would be no more fooling around at outdoor rinks. No feasting on ice cream and candy at Sweet Blades. No shopping at beautiful stores at Main Square. Okay, those things weren't that important; they could wait. But looking for Sonia? That was an emergency.

Cammie waited for Mrs. Page to return to the dining room for another portion of dirty dishes.

"Mrs. Page, I need to go to the Icy Park today," Cammie said, adding as much determination to her voice as she could.

Mrs. Page literally jumped away from her, her face reddening. "Cammie…I don't even know what to say. The Icy Park? You aren't supposed to go there even without high security measures in action. But now? It's completely out of the question."

"But Mrs. Page, I—"

"Cammie, one more word, and I'll have to call your mother." Mrs. Page no longer looked like a sweet, kind woman; in fact, if Cammie didn't know the woman, she might think she was looking into the furious eyes of a witch.

"Back to your room. Now!"

With a deep sigh, Cammie rose from the table and slowly walked toward the steps, her head down.

"And if I see you trying to sneak out … "

"All right, all right." Cammie twisted her face in an ugly grimace and headed for her room. Well, if Mrs. Page thought Cammie Wester would give up that easily, the woman was in for a big surprise. The dorm supervisor might be able to keep Cammie locked in today, but not on weekdays. Cammie would find a way to visit the Icy Park. Of course, she wouldn't want to try it on her own. She needed Alex. And if Cammie wasn't mistaken, her best friend was spending the Sunday in the same way, locked in his dorm. Well, so they would have to put off their quest till some other time. Too bad, considering that Sonia would have to endure another day in the witch's castle, but there was nothing Cammie could do.

Unfortunately, Monday morning brought no relief. Getting away from Mrs. Page proved to be almost impossible. The dorm supervisor dutifully took the girls to their morning practice, watching them closely as they skated eight blocks to the Green Rink. When the session was over, Cammie wondered if it would be a good idea to bag school and head to the Icy Park instead. Yet she hated the idea of confronting the witches alone, so she decided it would be better to talk to Alex first. Though they trained at different rinks, they still attended the same school, and Cammie was sure Alex would do his best to find her during recess.

Even the trip to school turned out to be a supervised affair; Coach Ferguson skated along with the kids. From time to time, the coach slowed down, looked at the skaters' feet, and barked instructions concerning their stroking.

"Liz, you are bending forward too much."

"Jeff, where are your edges? Bend your knees more!"

"Cammie, could you please hurry up a little? We don't have all day."

Cammie rolled her eyes. Skating to school was supposed to be a relaxing experience, not another practice. At least the school wasn't that far from the rink. Finally, Coach Ferguson stopped in front of the school building.

"I'll meet you all here at 3:30."

Cammie looked up. "But we are done at two. Can't we go to the dorm first and rest?"

Coach Ferguson pressed her lips. "Unfortunately, your dorm supervisor can't accompany you to the dorm this afternoon. So I suggest that you stay at school and do your homework till it's time to go to practice."

"But—"

"Cammie, I won't hear any objections. See you all at 3:30." The coach nodded at the bewildered skaters and glided away. Even when she was skating leisurely, she still maintained a perfect posture.

Cammie stomped her foot angrily. That was so unfair. Now they weren't even allowed to have any free time. She wished Coach Ferguson herself would try skating and studying without even a little break.

The first bell rang. Reluctantly, Cammie slipped her skate guards over her blades and opened the heavy door. Her only hope was that Alex would find her, and together they would come up with some plan.

The school day dragged on and on, like a show practice. After the last class, the kids stayed in the classroom to do their homework. Cammie took out her math notebook and tried to work on her geometry problem. She couldn't concentrate. The only thing on her mind was Sonia. *Oh please, let me not miss Alex*, she prayed silently.

At twenty after three, Cammie was in the lobby craning her neck to spot Alex in the crowd of the kids milling around. And finally, Alex did show up, his eyes shining angrily.

"Oh, here you are. I've been looking for you everywhere." Alex grabbed Cammie by the hand and dragged her to the corner where no one could hear them.

"I need to talk to you too. Can you believe it? They won't let us go anywhere without an adult."

Alex made a nasty face. "You don't have to tell me about it. How silly! Anyway, do you know what I heard? The police have already searched Skateland twice and still haven't found Sonia."

Cammie's mouth dropped open. "But she is in the Icy Park! Gosh, I told Coach Ferguson about it. Why couldn't she let the police know?"

Alex snorted. "I bet she did. So what? Those cops are nothing but a bunch of idiots. I tried to talk to them yesterday; they wouldn't even listen to me."

"Only because they think kids don't know anything."

"Well, we'll show them what we can do," Alex said excitedly.

Dana approached them. "Cammie, it's time to go. Coach Ferguson is here."

"All right, all right. I'll be out in a moment." Cammie brushed the girl off.

Dana walked away but not without giving Alex a curious look.

"So what are we going to do?" Cammie whispered.

"Pay the Witch of Fear a visit, of course."

"But how? Mrs. Page is watching me like a hawk."

"Alex Bernard, we're all ready to go." Jessica McNeil winked at Alex from under the beak of her red cap. Jessica was a petite fifteen-year-old pairs skater who had already won the gold in the novice division of the Junior Nationals. Jessica was a good skater, but she was also a big flirt. Now she wouldn't tear her big gray eyes away from Alex.

Cammie turned away from the girl and lowered her voice even more. "We need to do it soon. We can't let Sonia spend another day with the witch."

Alex nodded. "Sure. Okay, I'll meet you outside your dorm at eleven o'clock tonight."

"But how on earth am I going to get out?"

"Alex!" Jessica sang again.

Alex turned to the pairs skater. "I'll be right out."

"Think of something!" he whispered to Cammie.

"Mrs. Page locks the building at ten. But if I sneak out, how will I be able to get back in? I don't have a key to the front door. So..." Cammie tried to think out loud, but her mind was blank.

"There has to be a way. So I'll see you at eleven. Bye." Alex quickly took off his skate guards and skated into the blustery afternoon with Jessica chirping by his side.

Cammie shook her head angrily. She still had no idea how she was going to get out of the dorm in the middle of the night, but she knew she would think of something. She had to. She slowly put on her gloves and left the building. The skaters from the Green Rink, led by Coach Ferguson, had already gathered in the middle of the schoolyard.

At half past ten Cammie sat on her bed, fully dressed, listening to the sounds in the hallway. Everything was quiet except for the slight buzz of the radiators. Ten o'clock was the official lights-out time, so the rest of the girls had to be in bed already. The rigorous Skateland schedule usually left the skaters so tired by the end of the day that they rarely had any desire to play or even to watch the big-screen plasma TV in the living room. All they had strength for was a quick study for the next day's classes. Of course, Sonia often stayed up late reading in bed or doing her homework. A perfectionist, she always tried to be the best at everything. Not only did Sonia have the best skating technique in Skateland, she also received straight A's at school. How she could pull it off, Cammie had no idea. Personally, Cammie could barely scrape together a B average.

Ten thirty-five. Cammie sighed. She was exhausted. If it were not for her promise to Alex, she would be in bed already. Squirming at the very thought of having to go outside in the bitter cold, Cammie put on her wool hat, making sure her ears were completely covered, and reached for her gloves. She'd better leave now; it might take her more than twenty minutes to sneak out of the building unnoticed.

The thick carpet of the hallway muffled the sound of Cammie's steps. As she reached the stairs, she grabbed the banister hard, trying to make as little noise as possible with her skate guards. One flight, another flight…she was in the lobby.

A door slammed on the second floor. Cammie froze for a second then quickly tiptoed across the lobby and dove under the round table on which

Skateland promotional flyers were displayed. Cammie remembered Mrs. Page spreading them around the table on Friday night in case some of the show spectators might want to look at them. Well, the show had been postponed, but the table proved handy. The navy blue velvet cloth stretched almost to the floor, hiding Cammie from view. Cammie hugged her knees and listened. She knew whoever was coming couldn't see her, yet her heart pounded so hard against her ribs that Cammie was afraid it would wake up everybody in the building.

The clock chimed a quarter to eleven, and in another second, there came a sound of shuffling footsteps down the stairs. Cammie lifted the edge of the table cloth and peeked out. Mrs. Page appeared in the lobby in a light blue robe and matching slippers, her hair disheveled. The woman headed toward the kitchen, and a minute later, Cammie heard a click of the microwave being opened, and a familiar smell of hot chocolate reached her nostrils. Cammie smiled. Mrs. Page tried her best to watch the skaters' diet, yet she wouldn't say no to a midnight treat.

Cammie had to wait another fifteen minutes for the dorm supervisor to walk by on her way upstairs. Finally, she heard the door to Mrs. Page's room close. The clock struck eleven. Alex had to be waiting already. Cammie crept from under the table and crossed the lobby in four leaps. It took her seconds to reach the window at the end of the long hallway on the first floor. She pushed the window up. Cold air burst inside. Cammie zipped up her parka and jumped out of the window onto the cold, hard snow. She carefully pulled the window down, leaving a small crack, so she could open it again once she returned. Cammie only hoped Mrs. Page wouldn't want another cup of hot chocolate till the morning.

Cammie brushed the snow off her clothes and skated onto the street. Alex already waited in front of the dorm, hopping impatiently in place.

"Good. I thought you weren't coming," Alex said, sounding positively relieved.

"Mrs. Page got in my way. But it's okay; she didn't see me."

They reached the Icy Park in silence. The trees were thick with several layers of snow and looked like huge bulky monsters. The ice on the winding path was rock hard, and Cammie was sure the scratching of their blades could be heard miles away. The park looked deserted, yet Cammie had a weird feeling that they were being watched. The Icy Park wasn't just an ordinary park. It had several enchanted rinks scattered around the thicket, and witches had chosen it for their dwelling place long ago.

"It's eerie, isn't it," Alex said as though overhearing Cammie's thoughts.

"I wonder when the witches are going to show up," Cammie said nervously. She peered hard into the grove, trying to detect some motion, but everything appeared serene.

"Can't wait to see them, huh?" Alex chuckled, but he, too, appeared tense.

"No, I just don't believe they will let Sonia walk away peacefully. They will try to fight us, but at least we'll see where the attack is coming from. Now it looks like there is a witch under every tree. But you know what? I still don't understand why the police didn't find Sonia in the Witch of Fear's castle."

"I bet they never bothered to search it properly. They probably knocked on the door, the witch came out, they asked her politely if Sonia was there, she said no, and they left. Just like that." Alex snapped his fingers.

Cammie giggled. "They were probably afraid the witch would make them do waltz eights, like she did to us."

"No way. The cops wear hockey skates, so they wouldn't have a chance."

They skated another couple of minutes, abusing Skateland cops further as they moved along. Cammie's fingers began to sting with cold. She took off her gloves and blew on her stiff hands.

"How much farther, do you think?"

Alex looked around. A huge bird that looked like a hawk landed on a branch directly above them, sending dry snow into their faces.

"The castle is supposed to be close to the Sport Center," Alex said as he swept the snow off his face. "Remember last time we were on Mr. Walrus's zamboni machine, and it took us very little time to get to the competition."

"True, but the zamboni machine is much faster than us."

"Hey, I remember this pond with a bridge across it. We need to turn right now." Alex skated ahead of Cammie.

Cammie put her gloves back on. "That's right. Now I remember too; the witch's castle is just around the corner."

They dashed forward past bushy fir trees.

"There it is!" Alex exclaimed.

A snowy white castle stood no more than a hundred feet away. The heavy clouds parted, and the silvery moonlight slid down the ornate walls. The intricately curved figures of dragons and serpents encircling the façade suddenly came to life; it seemed as though they were about to slither off the walls right onto the path where Cammie and Alex stood, mesmerized.

Cammie took a tentative step back.

"It's okay," Alex said quickly. "They won't attack you. They aren't even real; it's a play of light."

"I know," Cammie whispered. She couldn't take her eyes off the skull above the front door. It was definitely smiling at her—the long, sharp teeth glittering in the light of the moon.

"Cammie, they are only here to scare people away."

"I know," Cammie said again. She could also add that the Witch of Fear was doing a great job of intimidating anyone who dared approach her castle. Cammie wasn't really that scared of the monsters living in the castle; she had seen quite a few horror movies. The worst thing would be developing fear of ice, not being able to skate a decent program. That was exactly what had happened to Sonia two years ago.

"Where is the witch hiding Sonia, anyway?" Cammie asked, turning away from the shimmering skull.

"Let's look around, okay?" Alex suggested, and together they skated around the edge of the witch's property.

They did their best to avoid stepping on the witch's rink, although the ice was irresistibly beautiful. It was smooth like silk and pink in color. Yet when you came to a witch's rink, you could never be sure that she hadn't concealed several traps under the seemingly innocent surface. One of Skateland witches' favorite tricks was bewitching the ice, so whoever stepped on it could only perform certain elements. In most cases, those were moves-in-the-field, something most skaters hated. Besides, the witches' rinks were ready to pick on every little mistake that even judges might overlook. Edge shifts, scraping the ice with the toe pick—the victim who skated on the witches' ice couldn't get away with anything. Now that Cammie skated past the pink rink, she didn't feel like struggling with double threes or brackets. Therefore, she made sure her blades stayed firmly on the path.

"There is definitely nobody outside," Alex said when they came back to where they had started. He rose on his toes, trying to look through the dark windows of the first floor.

"What if they are asleep?" Cammie stared at the black windows, too, but all she could see was thick darkness.

"Perhaps we could ring the doorbell," Cammie said.

Alex grinned. "Yeah, and then we can say to the witch, 'Excuse me, are you hiding Sonia in you castle by any chance?' Do you really think she will tell you the truth?"

"Of course not, but we can watch her reaction. If she looks guilty, it means Sonia is with her."

"You're funny, Cammie. Of course, she won't look guilty. She's a witch."

"We may still try. But—"

Before Cammie could finish her sentence, a branch cracked on their right, and a deep voice shouted, "Freeze! Don't move!"

"The witch!" Cammie shrieked and darted forward.

"Stay where you are, Cammie Wester."

The voice definitely didn't belong to the Witch of Fear; in fact, it was a man's voice.

Cammie turned back, surprised. Silhouetted against the pink ice stood two dark figures. The taller man held Alex firmly by the hand. As Cammie looked closer, she recognized Skateland police uniforms—light gray pants and jackets with matching wide-brimmed hats. The front of the jackets was decorated with Skateland logo—a skater with her leg raised in the scratch spin position, holding a multicolored flower. Each of the petals represented one of Skateland's different rinks: green, pink, blue, yellow, white, silver, purple, and black.

"Well, well, well, here are the rebels," the shorter, younger man said. He stretched his hand in Cammie's direction.

Cammie balanced on her toes, her mind running through all the possible options. So the police had already seen them—that was bad. Now the two of them were in serious trouble. On the other hand, they still hadn't found Sonia. And because their disobedience was no longer a secret to the authorities, breaking more rules probably wouldn't change anything.

"You'd better give up, we got you," the younger cop leered.

"No, you didn't!" His face reddening, Alex jerked his hand away from the taller man's grip. The impact must have been strong, for the policeman almost fell over.

"Run, Cammie, run!" Alex leaped away from the cop and raced away from the castle into the bushes.

"Cammie Wester, don't you dare!"

Ignoring the young cop's warning, Cammie followed Alex, leaving the startled policemen behind.

Unfortunately, the cops got over their initial shock fast. In about two seconds, Cammie heard the scratching of their blades right behind her.

"Alex!" Cammie called.

"Hurry!" he shouted without looking back.

They skated along a winding path that led somewhere deep into the forest. The policemen were right over Cammie. In another moment, they would grab her.

"Alex!" she shouted again.

Alex turned his sweaty face in her direction. "Cammie, do a bunny hop. Quick!"

Cammie's mouth dropped open. "A bunny hop?"

Then she understood. If she took a long leap forward, she could skip a loop of the winding icy path. It would give her a huge advantage over the cops.

"Look!" Alex got on his left toe and jumped forward, skipping two loops.

"Yes!" Cammie picked up speed and rose on her left toe. It was truly a wonderful idea. The cops would never be able to do bunny hops—not with their hockey skates. They would have to take the winding path one loop at a time; that was great. A couple of bunny hops, and Cammie and Alex would be outside the cops' reach.

Cammie swung her right leg and landed smoothly on the hard ice. Someone caught her; it had to be Alex.

"Cool, huh? Let's do it again!" Cammie exclaimed.

"Not so fast, young lady."

What? The voice wasn't Alex's, and the strong fingers that pressed deep into her flesh surely didn't belong to her friend either. Cammie gasped as she stared into the unblinking yellowish eyes. Oh, no, it was the shorter of the cops, a young man not much older than Alex, probably eighteen or nineteen. The policeman had a long nose and very full lips that he curved all the time, so his expression kept changing from open triumph to deep loathing.

"How could you jump here ahead of me in your hockey skates?" Cammie asked. It really didn't make any sense.

The young man jerked his chin up. "Hockey skates? Are you crazy? I am a figure skater. My name is Bob Turner. Don't you know me?"

Cammie furrowed her forehead. Bob Turner? Hmm, it didn't ring a bell.

"Your name is surely not in the history book," Alex said angrily.

Bob Turner straightened up, looking scandalized. "I *should* be in the history book. I won the silver medal at the Junior Sectionals four years ago. You are supposed to know that, stupid brats."

"Sorry, I must have missed your name when I was studying for my test," Alex said sarcastically.

Bob Turner's face reddened. Cammie giggled but bit her lip when she saw that Alex, too, was being held firmly by the older cop.

"Why didn't you run away? You were ahead of me," she asked Alex softly.

"Not without you," Alex said simply.

Bob Turner guffawed. "How deeply touching!"

"That's enough, Lieutenant Turner," the older policeman said.

He turned to Cammie and Alex. "My name is Captain Greenfield. I'm sorry we had to resort to violence, but it wouldn't have happened if the two of you had obeyed the president's orders and not gone out wandering in the middle of the night."

"We had to go look for Sonia," Cammie said stubbornly.

Bob Turner rolled his eyes. "Oh, the noble spirit of the young!"

"Get your filthy hands off me!" Cammie tried to set herself free. The cop's long fingernails pierced her skin.

Lieutenant Turner's face became rigid. "What did you say? How dare you insult a man of authority. Captain Greenfield, I think we need to blade brake this little lawbreaker. And him too, of course." He nodded in the direction of Alex, who glared at the young cop with an expression of deepest contempt.

Captain Greenfield sighed deeply and shifted his eyes from Alex to Cammie. "I hate to be doing it to you, young people, but I'm afraid my colleague is right. The two of you have broken a lot of Skateland laws already. So we have to restrain you for your own protection. Blade brake them, Lieutenant."

"Yes, sir!" With a nasty grin, Lieutenant Turner reached into his pocket and produced two pairs of what looked like funny-looking skate guards. They were made of metal with rubber discs attached to the bottom.

"Your right foot please, miss!" The young cop crouched next to Cammie, grabbed her foot, and quickly attached the metal skate guard to her blade. *Click!* Cammie glanced at her skate and saw a small combination lock dangling from the bulky device. It meant that she wouldn't be able to take off the stupid thing herself. In the meantime, Lieutenant Turner trapped her other blade in a similar skate guard and stood up, grinning from ear to ear.

"Cool, huh?" Lieutenant Turner said as he attached the same guards to Alex's blades. "These are called blade brakes. Now you can't skate away from us, kiddies."

"Let us escort the two of you to the ice mobile, then," Captain Greenfield said.

"All right, let's move on." Lieutenant Turner rubbed his hands excitedly. "We'll take a nice ride."

"To jail?" Cammie asked faintly.

Lieutenant Turner's lips curved in a malicious smirk. "Perhaps."

Now Cammie was actually dizzy from fear. Oh, no, they were arrested; they were criminals. What would her parents say once they found out that their only daughter was in jail?

"No, no." Captain Greenfield patted Cammie's arm. "There is nothing to worry about, kids. We simply don't want you to roam around the Icy Park at night. It's not safe. Come on."

Supported by Lieutenant Turner's hand, Cammie moved forward. Immediately she discovered that the blade brakes attached to her skates made gliding absolutely impossible. The rubber discs had a firm grip on the ice, so she could still walk, though it was extremely uncomfortable.

"Could you please take these blade brakes off us?" Cammie asked Captain Greenfield, who seemed nicer and friendlier than Lieutenant Turner.

"Oh, no, no!" Lieutenant Turner said slyly. "You're under arrest."

"She's not talking to you!" Alex barked.

Cammie glanced at Captain Greenfield pleadingly. "They are so uncomfortable."

The captain looked Cammie in the face, and for a split second she saw something like genuine pity in his hazel eyes. Then the cop shook his head. "I'm afraid not. We don't want you to skate away again."

Cammie sighed and clomped further, wondering how far they would have to walk.

"Are you taking us to the dorm?" Alex asked with a note of hope in his voice.

Oh, that wouldn't be too bad, Cammie thought.

Captain Greenfield gave Alex a funny look. "Actually, we are heading to Mrs. Van Uffeln's house."

Alex stopped so abruptly that Cammie walked into him. The stupid blade brakes were definitely a big nuisance.

"Who?" Alex breathed out.

"See? They don't even know Skateland president's name," Lieutenant Turner said pompously.

"We are going to Wilhelmina's?" Terrified, Cammie gasped first at Captain Greenfield then at Lieutenant Turner.

The younger man bared his big healthy teeth. "Exactly. Not ready to face the consequences of your misdemeanor, right?"

"Oh, no!" Cammie clasped her hands shaking her head. "Oh, no, no!"

Things were even worse than they could have ever expected. Wilhelmina was the highest authority figure in Skateland. Being called to her place could only mean that the two of them were in serious trouble. The president of Skateland didn't normally handle cases of minor misbehavior; she only got involved when some serious crime had to be addressed. Last year, for example, Wilhelmina had personally dealt with Isabelle, Cammie's friend, who had been caught cheating at a competition.

Isabelle had been disqualified from all future competitions for a year. Unable to cope with the humiliation, Isabelle had stopped practicing altogether and decided to become a skating witch instead. The last time Cammie had seen Isabelle was at the Black Rink, where the girl she had always liked had joined the gang of other witches in their attacks against Cammie and Alex. But okay, Isabelle had really committed a very serious offense; she had been dishonest. Cammie and Alex, however, had really done nothing wrong; they had merely wanted to rescue Sonia.

Cammie glanced at Alex; her friend's face was pale. She cast a pleading look at Captain Greenfield then at Lieutenant Turner.

The four of them got in the ice mobile, a very fast vehicle that had skating blades instead of wheels. Captain Greenfield pressed a silver button shaped like a blade, bent down, and said softly, "Mrs. Van Uffeln's house."

The vehicle shot forward; everything around them swirled; ice cold wind rushed in their faces. Cammie bent her head as low as she could, but there was no protection from the bitter cold.

Wilhelmina's house looked like a gingerbread cottage from a Christmas card. Frost-covered trestles of ivy glided down the stone walls, the roof was laid with red tile, and a huge wreath decorated with skating figurines hung on the oak wood door.

"Here we are," Captain Greenfield said. He took off his glove and touched the silver bell that dangled from the middle of the wreath.

WILHELMINA'S HISTORY BOOK

The bell clanged softly; the sounds blended into the melody of "The Carol of the Bells." Low hissing followed, and finally, Wilhelmina's familiar, slightly husky voice came from the inside.

"Who is it, please?"

"Captain Greenfield and Lieutenant Turner here with Alex Bernard and Cammie Wester," Captain Greenfield said.

The door opened with a click, and Wilhelmina stared at the four of them from her usual wheelchair. Though it was way past midnight, the older woman was perfectly made up, as though she were going to a party. Her cropped gray hair looked perfectly done, and she was wearing a long navy blue dress complete with a silver broach shaped like a skater in a perfect spiral position.

"Come in, please," Wilhelmina said, and the four of them walked into the brightly lit foyer. The walls were panelled with dark wood and decorated with old-looking paintings in gilded frames.

"I appreciate you bringing Cammie and Alex to my place," Wilhelmina said to Captain Greenfield.

Lieutenant Turner stepped forward. "We caught them roaming around the white castle in the Icy Park, Mrs. President. They know the area is off limits. It means they deserve the most severe punishment. I would suggest expulsion or disqualification."

Cammie and Alex exchanged worried looks.

"Thank you, Bob. I think I can handle the rest of the procedure without your help," Wilhelmina said dryly.

"Wait! How about these blade brakes?" Alex called. He raised his leg, displaying his blade still trapped in a metal skate guard.

Captain Greenfield slapped himself on the forehead. "My apology. Unbrake them, Lieutenant."

Still pouting, Lieutenant Turner crouched next to Alex and removed the blade brakes from his skates. He did the same to Cammie's blades and stood up, looking at Wilhelmina expectantly.

"Have a good night, officers," the president said politely.

The cops walked out, Lieutenant Turner still skulking as he followed the captain. Wilhelmina turned the latch; there was a click of the lock, and the older woman smiled at Cammie and Alex. "You may take your skates and coats off and put them in the closet to the right of the front door. "

Cammie tried to read the president's facial expression to figure out what sort of punishment was awaiting them, but the woman looked completely calm and relaxed.

"Don't mind Bob Turner; he has a chip on his shoulder," Wilhelmina said as Cammie and Alex did a quick job at smoothing their hair and straightening their clothes.

"Bob showed a lot of promise when he was a junior skater, but he could never land his triple axel. So he retired from the sport and went to the Police Academy. Now he is a Skateland policeman."

Wilhelmina pushed her wheelchair around the corner, motioning for Cammie and Alex to follow her. They walked along a corridor lit by sconces shaped like pine cones. The wallpaper pattern resembled a tangle of frosted limbs. The thick green carpet cushioned their steps, and for a split second, Cammie had a funny sensation that they were back in the Icy Park.

"Yes, what young man wouldn't be excited about protecting skaters from villains and witches?" Wilhelmina said. Somehow the older woman managed to get a lot of speed in her wheelchair; Cammie actually found it hard to keep up.

"But Bob isn't happy, you see." Wilhelmina stopped, waiting for Cammie and Alex to come closer. "His dream is to become a skating judge, yet I won't give him a recommendation. He is too headstrong, too judgmental. Too obsessed with power. Well, at least Captain Greenfield is there to keep an eye on him. Anyway, welcome to my home!"

Cammie looked around. They had just entered a spacious room with brown leather furniture. Almost every inch of the walls was covered with oil paintings depicting various skating themes.

"This is *Children Skating* by Leopold Till." Wilhelmina pointed to a canvas, where a group of little boys played on a small pond. The setting sun cast a pinkish glow on the ice, and the children's faces were alive with joy.

"It's beautiful," Cammie said.

"Isn't it really? I like the simplicity of their moves and the genuine excitement their postures portray. How about this painting? It's called *Dr. Syntax Skating*, and it was done by Thomas Rowlandson, an English artist. What I find particularly interesting here is how Thomas Rowlandson captured some of the famous historical skating positions. Do you recognize any?"

Cammie stared at the figure of a guy in the foreground skating on one foot, his free leg behind. She would probably identify his posture as the attitude position, if his skating leg weren't bent, and if he didn't hold his right arm high over his head. There was also some kind of a sword in the man's right hand, probably to make his body line appear longer. Anyway, Cammie didn't like what she saw. In fact, if someone tried this position now at one of Skateland rinks, he would surely be laughed at.

"I think it's the flying Mercury position," Alex said.

What? How did *he* know that? Cammie stared at her friend, trying not to appear too shocked.

"That's right." Wilhelmina gave Alex a bright, encouraging smile. "It's really the flying Mercury position, one of the key postures that characterized the English style of the eighteenth century."

"And there is a man practicing figures in the background," Alex said. He looked positively more relaxed.

Oh, gosh, of course, the guy with a red shirt and a funny hat was drawing figures! Cammie wished she had spoken up. Now Wilhelmina would know she was a total dummy when it came to figure skating history.

"Good, Alex. I see you have been reading your history book. But we'll talk about history later. You are my dear guests, and I would like to offer you some tea. What would you prefer, Stop or Position?"

"Excuse me?" Cammie and Alex said in unison then looked at each other and exchanged shy smiles.

Cammie had absolutely no idea what Wilhelmina was talking about. The older woman was surely not a typical president. First, she had told the police to bring the two of them to her house, so naturally they expected a severe punishment, and now she was offering them tea. And another thing—how was tea related to stops and positions?

"I mean tea." Wilhelmina apparently saw that both of them were confused. "I have two kinds of tea at home—Tea Stop and Tea Position. They are my favorite."

"T-stop and T-position!" Cammie exclaimed.

"Of course!" Alex slapped himself on the forehead.

Now it all made sense. Wilhelmina had been talking about skating related tea. Most of the ice exercises were supposed to be started from the T-position when a skater kept his feet perpendicular to each other, like in the letter *T*. T-stop was basically the same, though of course, at the end, you were expected to slow down and come to a complete stop.

"Personally, I wouldn't say no to a cup of Tea Stop," Wilhelmina said. "It's very rich and strong, and it clears your mind. Although Tea Position is also delicious. What I really like about it is the delicate rose flavor. So what will it be?"

"Stop," Alex said eagerly.

Cammie smiled. "I would like a cup of Position please."

Wilhelmina shifted in her wheelchair. "Christel!"

The door at the end of the room opened, and in walked a petite woman wearing tight black jeans and a white sweater. She looked younger than Wilhelmina, though Cammie saw the resemblance between the two women right away. Christel had the same narrow face and gray eyes as Wilhelmina, but her hair was long and shiny black. Christel crossed the living room and stopped in the middle, facing Wilhelmina, her arms folded on her chest. Cammie couldn't help noticing that the woman moved like a ballerina—her feet turned out, her back perfectly straight. Perhaps Christel could be described as a beautiful lady, if it were not for the aloof, slightly sarcastic facial expression. Wilhelmina was much nicer and kinder, even though she could be pretty tough at times. Christel's gray eyes were firmly fixed on Wilhelmina. She totally ignored Cammie and Alex as though they weren't even there.

"I thought you were resting," Christel said coldly.

Wilhelmina beamed at her. "Could you please bring us two cups of Stop and a cup of Position? Oh, and those chocolate-covered pretzels, all right?"

Christel pressed her lips so tightly that they almost blended with her pale skin. "At one thirty in the morning?"

Wilhelmina chuckled. "Well, life is full of surprises. Who could know that my dear guests wouldn't arrive till after midnight?"

Heat rushed to Cammie's face, and she lowered her head, but deep inside, she felt excited. Wow, Wilhelmina had actually called Alex and her *dear guests*. She wished Dana and Liz could hear that.

"Cammie and Alex, I would like you to meet my daughter, Christel," Wilhelmina said good-naturedly. "Christel, these are Cammie and Alex, our students."

Cammie and Alex hastened to say hello, but Christel didn't even look in their direction.

"How many times do I have to tell you? Not getting enough rest is detrimental to your health, Mother. And yet each night it's either a history arti-cle or…a bunch of hard-headed brats."

Cammie frowned. Christel had never met Alex and her before, and yet she hated them already. That was so unfair!

Wilhelmina, however, seemed completely unperturbed by her daughter's rudeness. "Christel, we have a serious issue to discuss here. Now if you could please give us that tea? I'm thirsty, and Cammie and Alex have had a tough day."

"A serious issue, huh?" Angry creases sprouted on Christel's forehead. "I bet it's all about Sonia Harrison. I only hope you're not going after that poor girl yourself. Because if you do—"

"Oh, no, I'm afraid I can't." Wilhelmina smiled mischievously. "Although it's not a bad idea at all. Now please, don't make a scene. Actually, Cammie and Alex are the ones to help me with the rescue mission."

The rescue mission? Was Wilhelmina talking about Sonia? And she was going to ask Cammie and Alex to help? Cammie stared at Wilhelmina, her pulse racing.

Christel looked interested. "They are? Hmm, okay, so it's one Position and two Stops, right?"

She headed for the door.

"And the pretzels!" Wilhelmina called after her.

"She used to be a good pairs skater. Unfortunately, skating is the only thing she can do. She competed for a while; then she had to retire. We all have to do it sooner or later. Christel absolutely loathes coaching—she's not a people person, and she has no patience for mistakes. And she hates everything else. So now she takes care of me. I can use all the help I can get."

Wilhelmina cast a sad look at her deformed knees, and Cammie felt sorry for the older woman.

"Tea is coming." Christel wheeled in a tray with three steaming mugs of tea and a bowl of brown things that looked vaguely familiar.

Cammie craned her neck and recognized Mrs. Page's chocolate-covered pretzels.

"Help yourselves." Wilhelmina sipped her tea and smiled warmly at them.

Alex took a big swig of his tea. "I like it."

Cammie tried her Tea Position. It was really good—pleasantly hot and strong, with a somewhat unusual flavor of rose petals. A perfect drink for a skater.

"Try some of these." Wilhelmina pushed the bowl of pretzels closer to Cammie. "By the way, do you know who made them?"

"Mrs. Page?"

"That's right. She offered them to Sweet Blades, but unfortunately, they turn down everything short of perfection. So I bought some of them for my guests and myself. Why not? They taste great, and I have a very sweet tooth. Go ahead, have some. You too, Alex."

Wandering around the Icy Park had made Cammie not only tired but ravenously hungry. After the third pretzel she finally felt she couldn't swallow another bite and thanked Wilhelmina, who had offered her another cup of tea. As much as Cammie was enjoying herself sitting in a soft leather armchair, sipping tea with delicious pretzels, her mind was on other things. Okay, so far they had been treated as guests, even offered refreshments. But how about their punishment?

"Now let's get down to business," Wilhelmina said. "So why do you think I wanted to see the two of you tonight?"

Cammie flinched. Next to her, Alex let out a deep sigh.

"We're sorry, Mrs. Van Uffeln," Alex finally said.

"We understand we shouldn't have gone to the Icy Park at night. But—" Cammie hung her head, wondering what Wilhelmina was going to do.

The older woman tapped her nose with her index finger. "Sneaking out at night, hmm. Yes, you really deserve to be punished. So what am I going to do with you two?"

There was a very uncomfortable silence. Cammie flinched in her armchair that didn't feel particularly comfortable anymore. *Oh please, don't let her expel us*, she prayed silently. *Anything but that!*

"Ah, well, I'll think of something," Wilhelmina said lightly. "Now, however, we have a more important issue to discuss. Cammie and Alex, I need your help to find Sonia."

Well, that was a statement Cammie hadn't expected. She rose in her armchair and stared at Wilhelmina, unable to utter a single word. Alex looked equally stunned, with his mouth wide open. And yet in another second, the two of them began to talk.

"But that's exactly what we did in the Icy Park!"

"Sonia is in the white castle. We know for sure."

"It was the Witch of Fear who abducted her."

"The wicked witch already jinxed her once; she couldn't even skate."

"It was all the witches' plot; they are after certain skaters. We heard them speak about it."

Wilhelmina grimaced and raised her right hand, motioning them to be quiet. "Now could the two of you stop talking for a moment, please?"

Cammie, who was about to say that she was on the witches' list too, shut her mouth eyeing the older woman impatiently. Wilhelmina was now looking at Alex and her with unmistakable warmness, and the corners of her lips twittered slightly as though the woman was trying to suppress a smile.

"I see I was right about the two of you. You know a lot about what is going on in Skateland, and as Mr. Reed informed me, you've had a valuable experience battling the witches. And you seem to deeply care about your friend, which, of course, is commendable."

Cammie felt her lips spread in a happy smile. Alex winked at her; he looked equally delighted.

"Unfortunately, you've got it all wrong. Sonia is not with the Witch of Fear," Wilhelmina said.

"What?"

"Of course, she is!" Cammie said, probably a little louder than necessary.

"No, she isn't." Wilhelmina shook her head slowly. "The police told you the truth. They really did a thorough search of Skateland and couldn't find any trace of Sonia. If you had taken Captain Greenfield's words seriously, you wouldn't have had to sneak out of your dorms in the middle of the night. You put yourselves in danger for nothing."

"But…" Alex seemed to have forgotten what he wanted to say.

Wilhelmina slapped her hand against the table. "Unfortunately, I don't have all the facts straight myself. All I know is that Sonia has really been abducted by the witches. They are holding her captive, though not in Skateland."

"Not in Skateland?" Cammie simply couldn't imagine the witches operating in the real world, where people did other things rather than skated all the time.

"But where?" Alex asked huskily.

Instead of answering them, Wilhelmina turned her wheelchair around and picked a thick book from a lectern.

"Sonia is here." Wilhelmina smoothed the cover and lowered the book on her knee. Cammie leaned back in her armchair, feeling completely confused. She wasn't even sure she had heard the president right. How could a skater be hidden inside a book?

Next to Cammie, Alex let out a small cough. "Mrs. Van Uffeln, hmm, I think we didn't quite understand you."

"It's not an ordinary book," Wilhelmina said. "Take a look at it."

Cammie accepted the thick volume from the lady's wrinkled hands. It was the oldest book Cammie had ever seen. Its pages were thin and yellowish and creased in some spots. The cover was made of grayish blue leather, and the title *Figure*

Skating through Time was embossed in silver. The name of the author was underneath, printed in much smaller letters, and Cammie wasn't surprised to read *Wilhelmina Van Uffeln.*

"You wrote it!" Cammie exclaimed, feeling excited. She had never met an author before.

Wilhelmina chuckled. "Well, if it says so on the cover."

"Cool!" Alex moved closer to Cammie, and together they began to turn the pages.

Wilhelmina's book was nothing like the battered copies of *Figure Skating History* they both had in their dorms. When Cammie touched the frayed pages, she had a weird sensation that they were alive. There were dozens and dozens of illustrations picturing skaters in various positions. Even though the book was definitely old, the colors on the skaters' clothes hadn't faded a bit, and their faces were full of emotion. Cammie wouldn't be surprised if the famous champions suddenly walked off the pages of the book into the night to perform their routines at Main Square Rink.

"See, these are the Protopopovs, famous Russian pairs skaters. They won the Olympics twice," Wilhelmina said. "And look: this is Peggy Fleming, one of the most graceful skaters of all times. You know her, of course. Here is Janet Lynn. I used to call her sunshine skater. I've never seen anyone bring so much joy to her performance. Now the dancers—look at this couple. Janet Torvill and Christopher Dean—total perfection."

On and on went Wilhelmina, turning the pages of the book, telling them about the famous skaters of old. Fire roared in the grate, the room smelled of fresh tea, and soon Cammie forgot that Sonia was missing, that they had been delivered to Wilhelmina's house by the police ice mobile, that she had failed her history test. She wished she could sit in the comfortable armchair, listening to the president's stories forever.

"Oh, my goodness, it's almost two in the morning." Wilhelmina closed the book with a snap. "I shouldn't have gotten carried away. But skating history is my true passion, you see. Anyway, back to Sonia. I know you find it hard to believe, but the witches took her to the past, to one of the periods in the figure skating history."

"But—" His forehead furrowed, Alex leaned forward.

Wilhelmina waved her hand at him before he could say anything else. "This book has magic powers. You see, when I wrote it, I poured so much of my soul and passion into the text that it literally became alive. Do you believe it's possible?"

Cammie thought of what the older woman had said. Well, of course, there was nothing extraordinary about making things happen once you truly believed in them. How many times, for example, had she succeeded in landing difficult jumps only because she wanted it to happen so badly!

"I studied all the facts about the famous skaters; I looked through hundreds of articles; I read dozens of books," Wilhelmina said. "Eventually, I felt that I knew each of the champions personally. They became my sisters, my brothers, my best friends. As I sat writing about their successes and failures, it was as though I were skating next to them at the same rinks. I repeated their moves, and the experience really helped me with my special figures. The champions of old became my coaches; they turned me into a much better skater. Sometimes, I even talked to my beloved stars. They answered me; it was the most exciting experience. And then one day something happened."

Wilhelmina closed her eyes for a moment. Cammie exhaled quietly.

"You know Mr. Reed, of course."

Cammie nodded. "The skate sharpener."

Wilhelmina looked at her with her bright gray eyes. "He's not only a skate sharpener. Mr. Reed is an extremely talented engineer whose knowledge and skill go far beyond boot fitting and sharpening. Mr. Reed is an inventor, a designer! And on top of all this, he has magic powers."

Fire swirled in the grate casting shadows at Wilhelmina's face.

"You're familiar with Mr. Reed's work, I presume," Wilhelmina said.

"Sure," Cammie whispered, remembering his self-spinning boots.

"It was several years ago that I thought of a Skating Museum," Wilhelmina said. "I figured it would be good for young skaters to familiarize themselves with the history of our sport. I pictured the museum as a large area with many halls, each of them representing a certain historical period. I imagined a rink in each hall and waxed figures of skaters dressed in skating outfits of that period. So I talked to Mr. Reed about my project, and he was very enthusiastic about it. He started working, and very soon the museum was ready. It turned out to be even better than I had anticipated. Mr. Reed actually designed a mechanism that could cause the wax figures to perform skating routines that were popular in a certain skating period. I was very pleased with what Mr. Reed had done. Very pleased, indeed. Until..."

Wilhelmina let out a deep sigh and folded her hands on her lap. Cammie waited for the older woman to go on, but the president seemed to be deep in thought.

"Now I almost wish we had never built that museum in the first place."

Alex's green eyes became round. "But why?"

Wilhelmina's face stiffened. "Because the witches managed to sneak inside, that's why."

Alex shrugged. "So what?"

Personally, Cammie didn't understand what the problem was either. If the witches wanted to have fun watching wax figures skate, what was so dangerous about it?

"You don't seem to understand what skating witches are like," Wilhelmina said. "Yes, I know, the two of you managed to defeat them twice, but let me warn you: don't think of those women as a bunch of comical figures. They are extremely evil; they are eaten up with pride, jealousy, and revenge. Their bad inclinations feed off their emotional energy, giving them enormous evil powers. They are capable of magic themselves; only unlike Mr. Reed or me, they use it for destruction, not blessing. And what is most unfortunate, the witches aren't merely nasty; they are also incredibly smart. So they are the ones who found out something I had apparently missed."

Wilhelmina rubbed her forehead. "Now I think, perhaps, if I hadn't dreamed of that Skating Museum... if Mr. Reed hadn't built it... well, no, they would have still thought of something to hurt other skaters. Witches can't survive without attacking innocent people; it's their nature. Anyway, I used to keep my book in the lobby of the Skating Museum on a special lectern. I thought that was the appropriate place for it. I should have remembered: you need a magical connection for a miraculous thing to happen. And then one day, the witches somehow discovered that if they brought the book to a hall with waxed figures, opened it on the page that described the same period, placed the book on the ice, and stepped onto it, they could be magically transformed into that moment of time."

"Wow!" Cammie couldn't contain herself.

"Just like a time machine!" Alex blurted out.

Wilhelmina nodded. "Exactly. Though it's not quite the same. Using my book, you can only travel through the history of figure skating; it won't take you anywhere else, which brings me to Sonia again. I believe that when the witches abducted her from the show practice on Saturday night, they brought her to the Skating Museum and carried her to the past."

"To the past!" Cammie echoed. That was unbelievable. So Sonia was somewhere back in time, probably skating on some frozen pond doing figures. They had to bring her back, and the sooner the better!

"Where exactly is she?" Alex asked softly.

Wilhelmina shook her head. "That I don't know."

The president looked grave. "If only I hadn't left the book in the museum. What was I thinking? Now it's here, of course. And I want you to have it."

"You're giving it to us?" Alex exclaimed.

Wilhelmina stroked the leather cover. "Well, someone has to go after Sonia. Of course, originally, I thought of doing it myself. Sonia's parents called me after her disappearance. I promised them I would do my best to find their daughter. And I know skating history better than anyone else, of course. But unfortunately, my body isn't as strong as it used to be."

Wilhelmina looked at her arthritic fingers with apparent disgust. "Of course, I can still spin and do figures, but skating through time may be too much of a challenge. The two of you, however—"

"So...so you want Cammie and me to look for Sonia in the skating history book?" Alex blurted out.

Wilhelmina gave him a nod of approval. "Yes, this is exactly what I want you to do. So? Do you think you can handle it?"

"Of course!" Cammie clapped her hands.

"We'll search the whole book. We'll find her!" Alex jumped off his armchair.

Wilhelmina tilted her head. "Don't forget, though, it can be dangerous."

"We're not scared."

"We faced those witches before."

"We'll do it."

"You can count on us."

"Okay, okay." Wilhelmina raised both hands. "It's great that the two of you are so brave, but I don't want you to become overconfident. Your assignment isn't easy, and, I repeat, is quite dangerous. Don't take your mission lightly. Before you go, I need to let you know that there are several rules about travelling through time that aren't supposed to be broken under any circumstances. Are you listening? I want your complete attention now."

Cammie straightened herself and fixed her eyes on Wilhelmina's calm face.

"First of all, I want you to remember: history can't be changed. Ever. Do you understand that?"

Alex creased his forehead. "Not really."

"All right, let me explain. What we now think of as figure skating didn't appear overnight. The very first skates people used were made from leg bones of large animals. Actually, a skate is called *schenkel* in Dutch, which means leg bone. Then wood skates appeared, and finally people began to manufacture metal blades. Of course, those primitive skates had no toe picks. Figure skating elements also took centuries to develop. The very first skaters focused on geometrical figures and edges, and it took a lot of time for our sport to evolve into modern freestyle.

"Now," Wilhelmina went on as she studied Cammie and Alex's blank facial expressions, "what do you think will happen if you show up, let us say, in the eighteenth century wearing your custom-made boots and blades with toe picks and, even worse, start doing double jumps and camel spins?"

Cammie looked at Alex and saw him shrug.

"People will be astonished," Wilhelmina said. "Naturally, they will want what you have."

Cammie smiled. "Well, why not? We could teach them how to jump and—"

"No way!" Wilhelmina cried out. "See, this is the reason I'd rather travel to the past myself. I can't count on kids, no, no."

Skateland president put her elbows on the table and rested her chin on her hands, looking displeased.

"Uh, I didn't mean that," Cammie muttered. "Of course, if we aren't supposed to—"

"That's right, you aren't supposed to!" Wilhelmina said sharply. "Gosh, girl, I thought you would be smarter than that at your age. Teaching eighteenth century people how to do doubles! It would be similar to teaching a beginner how to do an axel. What would happen? Ah? Cammie, I'm talking to you."

Cammie thought for a moment. "The beginner skater could get injured."

"That's right. You need to be prepared for the moves you're learning. Eighteenth century skaters weren't ready for the twenty-first-century style. The evolution of skating is a natural progression; it takes time. People need an opportunity to invent their own skates, to come up with their own styles. Don't take this chance away from them. If you intervene with the natural course of history, disastrous things will happen, which brings me to my next point. Once you are in the past, you must never, and let me say it again, *never* show off. Never demonstrate what you can do! When you see people practice elementary moves, you may be tempted to try your axels or double flips. You'd better forget about it right now, or you aren't going anywhere."

Now Wilhelmina sounded really harsh, and for a split second, Cammie wished she were someplace else. Why did the older woman think Alex and Cammie were such dummies? Of course they wouldn't want to brag about their skating skills to eighteenth century people.

"Also, you can't leave any of your possessions behind, and you aren't supposed to bring anything from the past to our time," Wilhelmina said. "Don't attract too much attention to yourselves. Blend in with the crowd. Before you go to a certain period, make sure you change into appropriate skating clothes. You will find them in the Skating Museum. Each hall has a closet full of the appropriate skating attire."

Alex raised his hand. "What about our skates? They are custom made, and they have toe picks. Are we supposed to wear old skates, too?"

Wilhelmina thought for a moment. "Well, as great as it may sound, no, you'd better not. See, you feel comfortable in your skates, and security should be your top priority. You may have to flee the area fast. In this case, antique skates may impede your progress. So let's hope people won't study your blades closely. I would recommend that you use covers for your boots, though. You will find boot covers in the closet, alongside skating clothes."

Wilhelmina twisted the silver chain that supported her eyeglasses. "At least I'm glad you had an opportunity to practice school figures for the show. Those will be safe to do any time in skating history."

Cammie felt slightly uneasy as she thought of her poor performance during the dress rehearsal. She only hoped that perhaps, in the past, not everybody could do school figures perfectly well either.

"The Skating Museum is temporarily closed to the public now. So you can use it. Here is the key." Out of her pocket, Wilhelmina produced a huge keychain and took off a big silvery key. "You're older, Alex, so I want you to keep it. And the book too."

Alex put the key in his pocket and gently put the book on his knee. The thick volume looked very heavy.

"Don't worry. Once you try to put it in your pocket, it will shrink to the size of a wallet," Wilhelmina said brightly.

Looking skeptical, Alex brought the huge volume close to his jeans pocket. The moment the book came in contact with the fabric, it immediately became smaller. Alex stuffed it in his pocket easily and smiled.

"But how did it happen?" Cammie whispered.

Wilhelmina spread her arms. "There are so many things in life I can't explain. So you can start tomorrow morning. Just put the book on the ice in the hall. Then open it to the period you want to visit and step on the book. Let us say, if you are planning a trip to 19th century England, go to the English Hall. And once you are there, you'll need to open the book to page 242—see 'Skating in 19th Century

England.' You will move to the past instantly, and the history book will go with you."

"But do you have any idea where exactly Sonia may be?" Alex asked softly.

Wilhelmina shook her head sadly. "I wish I did. But no, you may actually have to visit several places before you find her. Try Holland—my intuition is telling me that it might be a good choice. And definitely visit England, though you never know. Use your mind, as well as your skating skills. I'm sure you'll do fine. Now you may need several days to locate Sonia. Therefore, you will be exempt from your classes and practices. I will talk to your teachers and coaches, so they won't worry about you. I will tell them you are on a special mission. Of course, I won't divulge all the details. And I urge you not to share what you are about to do with your friends and relatives. Let it be our secret, all right?"

Cammie and Alex nodded at the same time.

"Oh yes, before I forget. When you need to return to Skateland, open the book on the 'Introduction' page and step on it. All right? And remember: even though I can't go to the past with you, you can always come back to me if you need help or advice."

Wilhelmina reached for her cell phone. "I'll call Captain Greenfield and ask him to take you to your dorms. It's too late for you to skate back. I'll also let your dorm supervisors know that you're on your way."

Skateland president squeezed Alex's arm and hugged Cammie. "Stay in touch. And please, *please*, be careful!"

THE FROZEN SHIP

When Captain Greenfield brought Cammie to the dorm, it was three in the morning. Mrs. Page opened the door for them looking puffy-eyed and disheveled, yet she didn't say a word. Feeling exhausted, Cammie clambered up the steps to her room and fell asleep before her head touched the pillow.

When she woke up the next morning, the sun shone brightly through her window, and the dorm was quiet. No wonder; all of the skaters were at their morning practice. Cammie glanced at the clock; it showed a quarter after ten. Oh no, actually, the practice was over, and everybody was at school.

But it was okay. Wilhelmina had actually suggested that Cammie and Alex sleep in, for they had a difficult and important mission ahead of them. For that, they had to be perfectly rested.

Cammie took a quick shower and put on several layers of clothing, making sure she was warm enough. Today they were going to visit Holland, and it would probably be freezing cold there.

In the kitchen, Mrs. Page stood near the stove, stirring something in a huge pan. "Oh, you're up. Good. Let me fix you a quick lunch. How about split pea soup and a tuna salad sandwich?"

"Thank you, it would be great," Cammie said cautiously. She was surprised that Mrs. Page was making no comments about her not being at school. Then she remembered that Wilhelmina had called her the night before.

The dorm supervisor must have noticed Cammie's uncertain look. "But of course, I know you are doing an important work for Wilhelmina. Here's your soup, and you'd better finish it. Who knows when you're going to eat next?"

Cammie stirred her soup and ate a bite of her sandwich. "Everything tastes great, thank you, Mrs. Page."

"You're welcome. Oh, it breaks my heart to even think what poor Sonia is eating now. Just do what you can, Cammie, and bring her back soon, okay?"

So she was right: Mrs. Page knew everything.

"You don't have to give me any details. Just be careful. And remember, Alex and you are in my prayers," the dorm supervisor said.

The grandfather clock struck eleven. Cammie finished her tea in two big gulps and stood up. "Thank you very much, Mrs. Page. I've got to go now."

She rushed out of the living room onto the porch without even zipping up her parka. She didn't want to keep Alex waiting.

"Wrap your scarf around your neck; it's cold outside!" Mrs. Page called.

"Thank you, I will." Cammie shut the door behind her and ran down the steps.

As she kneeled on the lower step to take off her skate guards, Alex grabbed her by the hand. "Ready to go?"

"Sure!" Cammie straightened up and gave her friend a big smile.

"Did you talk to anybody about you-know-what?" Alex asked as they headed in the direction of the Skating Museum.

"Of course, not. Mrs. Page knows, though. Wilhelmina must have explained everything to her."

"Yeah, Mr. Gordon wished me good luck too. But I didn't see any of the guys, so—"

"We probably won't have time to talk to any of the skaters anyway," Cammie said as she pulled on her wool hat tighter to cover her ears.

"True. We have so many countries to visit, I doubt we'll have any time to chat with anybody."

They were already approaching the Skating Museum that was only a block away from Wilhelmina's home. Cammie had never been in this part of Skateland before. When the huge, perfectly round building emerged from around the corner, for a split second, Cammie had a weird feeling that she had suddenly gone forward in time. The Skating Museum definitely had a futuristic look about it—smooth with white stucco walls and a glass dome on the roof. Cammie looked around. Cold wind was swirling snow powder across the icy path. For some reason, Cammie felt a little uneasy.

"Let's make sure no one sees us." She lowered her voice, although the area was deserted. The museum was the last building on the block; it bordered the western side of the Icy Park and that bothered Cammie.

"Where's that key?" Alex grumbled as he patted his sides. "Ah, yes, here it is."

He inserted the intricately carved key into the lock, and the warm, slightly stale air of the museum rushed outside.

"It's great that Mel Reed keeps it heated," Cammie said as she unzipped her parka.

"Yep!" Alex locked the door behind him. "Okay, here we are, and there was nobody behind us."

"Good." Cammie looked around. They stood in a spacious lobby. It was completely devoid of furniture, except for the long counter than ran around the walls, an oval table in the middle, which was probably for the receptionist, a leather couch next to it, and an empty lectern that stood about four feet from the table.

"That's where Wilhelmina kept the book before," Cammie said. She ran her finger along the glassy surface of the lectern. It was dusty, for her finger left a long trail.

"Wait a minute! How did the witches manage to use the book? It means they have a key to the museum." Alex looked around as though expecting to see the witches lurking somewhere close.

Cammie brushed him off. "Of course they don't. They probably did it during museum hours. See, if the book just sat here, they probably took it without anyone noticing."

"Hmm. You're probably right. Okay, where is that Dutch Hall?"

Alex got the answer to his question right away. As they approached a huge directory that hung on the right wall, they discovered that Dutch Hall was on level two of the museum. A spiral staircase led up to the higher levels. Cammie and Alex ran up the steps and opened the door that bore the sign "Dutch Hall."

"Oh wow!" Alex said.

Cammie, too, felt extremely excited. They stood in a round hall, two-thirds of which was occupied by a rink with real ice. There were about a dozen skaters on the ice frozen in different positions. Of course, those were wax figures, not people, but they looked so real that Cammie felt like saying hi and introducing herself.

"Look at their skates!" Alex bent down in front of one of the skaters and examined the blades that were perfectly smooth in the front and were attached to the boots with a worn-out belt.

"And the clothes! Boy, I could never wear such a long dress for skating. I would trip." Cammie tugged at the hem of a green skating skirt that belonged to the smiling figure of a girl about her age.

Alex smirked. "Well, today you'll have to."

Cammie rose from her knees. "What do you mean?"

"Wilhelmina told us to change into these clothes, remember?"

Cammie groaned. "Oh, no! Are you sure we'll have to do that?"

"Well, of course! We have to blend in with the crowd. Come on, let's find something we can wear."

They rummaged through the huge closet that took all the space along the ice-free part of the hall. Cammie changed into a dark green skirt and a yellow jacket; then pulled on a pair of thick wool socks and covered her head with a tight-fitting cap. She took a quick glance at herself in the mirror that hung on the closet door. Hmm, not bad. She looked like a character from some historical movie. And the good part about those skating clothes was the fact that they were thick. Perhaps it wouldn't be particularly easy to skate in them, but at least they would protect her from the cold.

"The boots, Cammie!" Alex said.

"Ah, yes." Cammie quickly covered her boots with pieces of cloth that made them look as though the blades were fastened to old-fashioned boots with the help of leather straps.

"So how do I look?" Cammie did a quick pirouette on the ice and smiled at Alex. "Oh, my gosh, what a sight you are!"

Alex had already changed into a pair of loose pants that barely reached his ankles and was now adjusting his wool hat.

"What really matters is that we look just like those kids from the display."

"That's true." Cammie looked at the wax figures again. From what she could judge, the kids weren't doing any fancy moves; they were just skating around chasing each other.

"But don't forget that the Dutch started using their edges pretty early," Alex said. "So if you want to try the Dutch roll once we are there, you'll be safe."

Cammie twisted her face in concentration. "The Dutch what?"

"The Dutch roll. Alternating forward outside edges around the rink. We had to practice them before the show, remember?"

"Ah, of course." Outside edges—that was easy. It was the fancy name that Cammie couldn't identify.

"Okay, let me see." Alex sat down on the floor, turning the pages of the history book. "'Skating in Holland,' all right. Hmm, there are two long chapters about Holland. So where should we go?"

"To the very beginning, of course." Cammie was getting too hot in her warm clothes, and she was eager to go outside.

"You're right. We'd better make sure we search every period. If Sonia isn't there, then we'll go later in history. Now come here."

Alex gently put down the open history book. The minute the volume touched the ice, it began to grow until it became about six feet long. Now both Cammie and Alex could easily step onto it.

"Ready?" Alex took Cammie by the hand.

She nodded.

"Holland!" Alex shouted.

The book became even bigger; then Cammie heard the sound of wind whistling in her ears. Next thing she felt was an invisible force sucking her inside the book; she was falling down, farther and farther. The objects in the room around her began to spin; she closed her eyes…

They stood in the middle of a frozen canal with hard, scratched-up ice. The sky hung low over them, laden with gray, angry clouds. Cammie took a tentative step forward; her blade caught something.

She looked down and saw that the ice was bumpy, with ruts and holes. Tall black trees with bare limbs lined the sides of the canal. Something dark and huge loomed about a hundred yards ahead of them. First, Cammie thought it was a house, but as her eyes got used to the gloomy gray light, she saw that the big structure was, in fact, a ship. Yes, it was a real sailboat with five sails and an orange, white, and blue flag hanging loosely on a tall mast.

"Cool!" Alex breathed out next to Cammie. He rushed forward, apparently to take a better look at the ship.

"Be careful!" Cammie called after him, but Alex wouldn't listen.

Before Cammie could take a few faltering strokes on the rough ice, Alex had already approached the ship and was now gazing at it with admiration.

"Can you believe it?" Alex jerked his head so high that his wool ski hat slid down all the way to his neck. Alex pulled it back impatiently.

"So what?" Cammie skated closer and ran her hand along the side of the ship. The peeling wood felt rough. "What's so exciting about an old boat?"

"An old boat?" Alex looked at her with obvious disdain. "What do you girls understand? It's an authentic Dutch war ship. Wow! Just wait till I tell the guys at the rink."

Cammie raised her head too and studied the ship, trying to understand what had impressed Alex so much. Well, of course, the big boat had straight flowing lines, and the decks must have looked strong and polished one day, and the sails had probably been clean and smooth, with wind blowing into them. The tricolor flag must have waved proudly as the ship sailed across the ocean. But now everything was different. Cammie touched the splintery wood again and sighed at the sight of the faded flag and the dingy sails that hung loosely from the masts as though in surrender. Poor ship!

"But why is it here, in the middle of the canal?" Cammie asked. That didn't make sense to her. War ships were supposed to be cruising deep waters, fighting enemies.

"It probably didn't leave the canal in time before winter struck," Alex said. "Now the water is frozen, of course, so the ship can't leave. I wonder where the people are."

"They probably left." To Cammie, it seemed like a logical explanation. Who would want to spend winter locked inside a wood structure that probably didn't even have central heating?

"What century are we in anyway?" Cammie asked.

"Wait, let me see." Alex took the *Skating through Time* book out of his pocket and turned several pages. "Can you believe it? We are in the year of 1572."

"Are you serious?" Cammie clapped her hands with excitement and looked around eagerly. "I can't wait to get back to Skateland and tell everyone at school about it. Mr. Stevens will be dying to hear every word of it. I bet he won't even have me retake that history test. Let's look around, okay?"

Alex closed the book and put it back into his pocket. "We're here to rescue Sonia, not to look at the sights. Besides, we don't know any Dutch."

"Well, there's nobody here anyway." Cammie rose on her toes and scanned the area. The canal stretched far ahead; she couldn't see where it ended. The gray light made it hard to see the details, though Cammie could vaguely discern the outlines of several small houses on both sides of the canal. A windmill stood on the right side, the tallest structure in the area.

"What time is it here?" Cammie asked. She couldn't figure out whether it was early morning or late afternoon.

Alex looked at his watch. "One thirty, just like in Skateland. Wilhelmina told me that no matter what period of time we visit, the time of the day will always stay the same."

"Well, that helps." Cammie cupped her hands and shouted as loudly as she could, "Sonia!"

"Are you nuts?" Alex grabbed her arm.

"But why? If she is here, she'll hear us."

"Yeah, right. What do you mean *here*? Do you expect Sonia to hang out next to the abandoned ship waiting for us to come?"

"She might be."

"Cammie," Alex said. "Sonia doesn't expect us to come and look for her. And the witches wouldn't just let her wander around on her own. We need to search the place, maybe talk to some folks. But we must be careful."

"But how are we supposed to talk to people if we don't speak Dutch?" Cammie asked impatiently. The gloomy atmosphere of the Dutch afternoon was beginning to get to her. Perhaps Alex was right and making noise wasn't the best idea, but there was no one to ask about Sonia. At least if they made noise, someone might show up and give them a clue. And surely they wouldn't attract much attention. In their new clothes, they looked very Dutch. Alex couldn't be always right, and Cammie was determined to take the matter into her hands.

Drawing as much oxygen into her lungs as she could, Cammie called again, "Can anybody hear me? Sonia!"

"Cammie, stop that shouting now!"

Before Alex could say another word, a strange noise came from the right. First, Cammie took it for a strong gust of wind, but then she saw a dark cloud approach them. The weird thing about it was the fact that instead of floating across the sky, the cloud rolled over the canal at high speed. Startled, Cammie looked at Alex. He, too, stood glued to his spot, his eyes wide open. A thought flashed through Cammie's mind that it would be better for them to hide somewhere, but she couldn't move.

"Those are people!" Alex exclaimed.

What she had believed was a cloud was actually a horde of men wearing dark pants, matching coats, and wide-brimmed hats. Judging by the look of the men, they were warriors. Each of them was armed with a sword and a shield, and Cammie thought that they probably belonged on the frozen ship. The unusual thing about the combatants was the fact that they all wore skates. Those weren't shiny figure skates like Cammie and Alex's but rough metal blades attached to the boots with the help of ropes. And yet as Cammie understood, it was the primitive-looking skates that allowed the warriors to move on the chipped ice of the canal with almost blinding speed.

The men skidded to a stop next to Cammie and Alex and stared at them. Apparently, they didn't expect to see anybody next to their ship.

After a moment's hesitation, a tall blond man with a beard spoke up. "*Goedemiddag. Wat bent u hier doen?*"

Cammie and Alex exchanged puzzled glances.

"Uh, I'm sorry, we don't speak Dutch," Alex said apologetically. There were red patches all over his face.

The men studied Cammie and Alex's confused faces then exchanged quick words in Dutch. Finally, a stocky guy in a cocked hat with a plume stepped forward. He wore brown velvet breeches that barely reached his knees and a cloak fastened at the throat with a shiny clasp. There was also a ruff about his neck, but in spite of the fancy outfit, he looked like a man who had spent a lot of time outside in the ghastly wind. Though he was definitely tired, his eyes had a bright vivid look.

"Are you from England, lads?" For a split second, a pair of light brown eyes skimmed Cammie's blades.

"No, we are from Amer—"

Alex kicked her hard on the shin. Cammie gave him an angry look. What was the matter with him?

"Uh, yes, sir, we are visiting from England," Alex said quickly.

"Welcome to Amsterdam," the man said. "I don't want to sound unfriendly, but I'm afraid the two of you must leave the canal as soon as possible. The Spanish will be here any minute."

"Sir, we are looking for a friend. It's a girl her age." Alex pointed to Cammie. "Her name is Sonia Harrison, and she has red hair. And oh yes, she's from England too."

The man with a cocked hat translated Alex's words into Dutch. The rest of the warriors shrugged and shook their heads.

"There are no more English lasses here," the man said.

"Who are you?" Alex asked.

"We are *watergeuzen*, which means sea beggars in your language. The Spanish have taken control of our land. We are fighting them in the name of our lord, William the Silent."

"*In naam van onze lord, William Stil,*" echoed the warriors.

"But you lads must be careful," the man went on. "Our scouts have just told us that the Duke of Alva and his army will be here soon. Of course, we'll defeat him because we have *schaatsen*."

Cammie was confused. "You have what?"

"These." The man pointed to Alex's skates. "Fortunately, the two of you have *schaatsen*, too. But—"

Before the warrior could finish his sentence, a shout came from the left so loud that Cammie grimaced and put her hands over her ears.

"*¡Vamos a triumfar! ¡Viva España y el Duke de Alva!*"

Cammie wheeled around and saw another group of armed soldiers move in their direction, though not even remotely as fast as the Dutch. All of the men had deeply tanned faces, and dark hair was spilling out of their metal helmets with plumages. The Spanish were greater in number than the Dutch, but in Cammie's opinion, the Dutch looked much more intimidating. Unlike the Dutch warriors, the Spanish soldiers didn't wear skates.

"Get out of here, lads! Quickly!" the man in the cocked hat said to Cammie and Alex.

Then he turned to his warriors and waved his hand at them. "In the name of William the Silent!"

"*In naam van William Stil!*" The Dutch warriors skated right at the fast-approaching Spanish troops.

The Spanish had apparently not expected the speed that the Dutch could achieve on their blades. For a moment, the Spaniards looked stunned; then the tall man who was leading the procession gave his soldiers a quick order in Spanish. Immediately, the air filled with a terrible blasting sound. Fire erupted about thirty feet from where Cammie and Alex stood, and a hard explosion shook the ground.

Cammie shrieked and darted to the right.

"Down!" The Dutch warrior grabbed Cammie and Alex's hands at the same time and pulled them down on the hard, uneven ice.

"You must leave this place, do you hear me?" he barked at them. "But don't get up; crawl over there."

He pushed them under a tree. Unfortunately, its bare limbs provided very little protection.

The Dutch leader turned to his soldiers. "*Brand!*"

Cammie had no idea what the man was saying, but his quick order was followed by another explosion, this time closer to the Spanish army.

"What's that?" Cammie whispered. She could barely move her lips.

"A cannon ball," Alex said huskily.

"But why?" Cammie asked dully.

Alex didn't say anything. The Dutch were advancing fast; apparently the skates were really giving them a huge advantage. From where Cammie lay, she could see the straight line of the Spanish soldiers shake as the people tripped and fell. Some of the warriors crawled under the trees.

"*Krijg hen!*" the Dutch leader shouted, and several Dutch soldiers jumped at the desperately resisting Spaniards, fighting them to the ground.

Cammie rose on her elbows, unable to tear her eyes away from the scene that was unfolding in front of her. For a split second, she had a weird feeling that she was at a movie theater, and she almost reached for popcorn...A cold feeling in her knees brought her back to reality. She had been sitting on the cold ice too long, and obviously the Dutch folk skirt wasn't thick enough to give her the protection she needed.

"*¡Hola, muchacha!*" a deep voice snarled next to Cammie.

The next thing she felt was a strong arm grab her wrist. She pulled it back, but the attacker was stronger. As Cammie glanced at the Spanish soldier, she saw that he was an olive-skinned man with a black beard. His dark narrow eyes glowered menacingly under a pair of thick eyebrows.

"Let me go!" Cammie gritted her teeth and kicked the evil man hard in the stomach with her blade.

The soldier groaned and fell on his back, his hands clutching his midriff.

Cammie sighed with relief, but the next moment, the man was on his feet again.

"*¡Te voy a matar!*"

The soldier was next to Cammie; he was about to grab her again.

"Cammie! Over here!"

She felt Alex's strong arm pull her backward. She took a step in her friend's direction, still unable to take her eyes off her attacker.

"*¡Déjela! Es mía,*" the soldier growled. He was still advancing on Cammie.

"Cammie, step on the book. Quickly!" Alex shouted.

Cammie looked back. The history book sat on the gray ice, Alex standing next to it. The page fluttered in the wind, and Cammie read the word "Introduction" at the top.

"Cammie, come on!" Alex stepped on the book.

The soldier tried to leap upon Cammie but fell short lying prostrate on his stomach. He grabbed one of Cammie's ankles. Cammie fell down on the edge of the page. Alex clutched her hands pulling with all his might, but the soldier clung to her firmly.

"Cammie, kick him off! We can't take him with us!" Alex yelled.

The man's grip was strong. Cammie raised her free leg again, aiming at the soldier's hands. He flinched, apparently remembering the first contact with Cammie's steel blade. The soldier loosened his hands only for a split second, but it was enough.

Cammie lurched forward unto the book, completely free of the Spaniard.

"Skateland!" Alex shouted.

The canal and the black trees blurred around Cammie as though she were doing a very fast scratch spin. The wind carried them farther and farther away. Feeling slightly nauseated, Cammie closed her eyes, and when she opened them again, they were back in the Skating Museum.

WAX FIGURES

What was that? A war?" Cammie jumped onto the linoleum floor and brushed the dust off her long skirt.

"It was the battle between Duke Alva of Spain and Dutch Sea Beggars," Alex said excitedly. He took off his wool hat and ruffled his hair. "Did you see those cannon balls? Wow, it was just like a movie—no, way better! The Dutch rocked. Did you see their skates? That's how they won that battle; they had way more speed. Of course, the Spanish took over again later. It's a shame."

Cammie pulled off her tight cap. "How do you know all that stuff?"

Alex shrugged. "From our history course. Where else? Do you know that after that battle Duke Alva ordered seven thousand pairs of skates for his own troops?"

Cammie stared at Alex blankly. How come she didn't remember anything of what he was saying? Although something about the war between the Dutch and the Spanish rang a bell, but where had she read about it?

"Don't look at me like that. It was on our skating history test."

"Ah!" Cammie slapped herself on the forehead. Of course! She saw herself sitting behind a computer monitor, and the question about the battle flashed in her mind:

```
In 1572, Dutch Sea Beggars defeated
the Spanish army because they had:
  a. cannon balls
  b. skates
  c. better food
  d. courage
```

"I chose cannon balls," Cammie said feebly. "I thought that was the right answer for sure. I mean, people used cannon balls to blast one another, right? But now I think the Spanish army had them too. So the correct answer would be—"

"Skates, of course!" Alex exclaimed. "Come on, Cammie, that's the whole point. The Dutch won with the help of skates."

"For crying out loud!" Cammie plopped on a chair against the wall. "No wonder I failed the test. I probably got every question wrong."

Alex grinned. "Well, now after we rescue Sonia, you won't even have to study for that test. You'll know skating history better than Mr. Stevens himself."

Cammie rolled her eyes. "Is that what you think? Anyway, where are we going next? Personally, I'm not looking forward to another battle. And you know what? I don't think the witches could hide Sonia in the middle of a battlefield. The witches may think they're scary, but they are actually cowards. I bet the mere sight of a cannon ball would scare them out of their wits!"

Alex gave her a thumbs up. "Now you're thinking like a guy. Well, I have good news for you: there are no more fighting scenes in this book. I read it from cover to cover last night."

Cammie looked at him doubtfully. "When did you sleep?"

"I didn't," Alex said lightly. "So what? Knowing what we are facing is far more important. Anyway, what would be the most likely place for Sonia to be?"

"You know what? We probably went too far back," Cammie said. "Maybe the witches hid Sonia in a more recent time period, like ten years ago."

Alex thought for a moment. "I don't think so."

"But why not?"

"Think. Ten years ago, skating was pretty much the same as now. So what would happen if Sonia appeared at some rink at the end of the twentieth century? People would start asking questions; she would tell them she was from Skateland; and with all the modern technology, her parents could be easily contacted. And would it change Sonia's skating career? I doubt it. No, the witches are smarter than that."

"Okay, how about fifty years ago?" Cammie asked.

Alex shook his head. "Same thing. Fifty years ago, people already had television, and figure skating was very popular."

"Then I don't know," Cammie said angrily.

"Hmm." Alex looked pensive. "You know what? Let's stick to the original plan. We decided to start from the beginning, so let's move on." He turned a couple of pages. "See? There is more information about skating in Holland."

"But we've just come back from Holland."

"So what? We'll go three centuries forward. Look—there is a picture of skaters, and many of them are kids. The witches could easily hide Sonia among those children skating on the canals. There was no television, no radio in those days, so who could find her?"

"But are you sure there were no more cannon balls?" Cammie asked nervously.

Alex laughed. "I'm positive."

"Okay. At least, we'll be able to wear the same clothes," Cammie said. "Are we going now?"

"Uh, no, it's almost seven o'clock, and I'm starving. I hope Mr. Richter has left me something from dinner. We'll go to Holland tomorrow morning. How about that?"

Cammie nodded. "Sure. I hope Mrs. Page hasn't forgotten about me. Let's skate to our dorms, then."

At six o'clock in the morning, Cammie ran down the steps of her dorm building, zipping up her parka. Alex already stood leaning against a tree, looking glum.

"You're late!" Alex snapped the moment Cammie reached him.

"Oops, sorry! For some reason, I was more tired last night than after two practices."

"Yes, me too." Alex looked positively upset. "But that's not the point. Do you know who cornered me this morning?"

Cammie looked up at him.

"It was Jeff. Boy, I shouldn't have gone down for breakfast. But I was hungry, and I didn't want to wait for everybody to leave, so I walked straight in, and there he was waiting for me."

Cammie felt confused. "But what did he want?"

"Well, he knows that we are going after Sonia."

Cammie's heart sank. "But Wilhelmina told us to keep it a secret."

"Do you think I blabbed it to him?" Alex snapped.

"No, of course, not. How did he find out?"

Alex jumped over a frozen limb in the middle of the path. "Actually, it was easy to figure out. The two of us aren't at practices, we're cutting school, and then our dorm supervisors tell everybody who's interested that we're on Wilhelmina's special mission. What would you think?"

Cammie slowed down. "You're right. Boy, I didn't think about it."

"Anyway, Jeff sounded pretty upset. He said he was coming with us and wouldn't take no for an answer."

Cammie stomped her foot against the rough ice. "No way!"

"Well, that's what I told him. But he was adamant. He started shouting at me that Sonia was his best friend, so he had to help her. But I knew we couldn't take him with us."

Cammie winced. "So what did you do?"

"Well, I said he could go. But I told him it would be awfully cold wherever we went, so he had to put more warm clothes on. So he went to his room, and I slipped out of the dorm. The rest of the guys were still finishing their breakfast, and they gave me funny looks, but I pretended I didn't notice and walked away. So there I was in front of your dorm at a quarter of six, and you were late."

"Oh, no! Alex, I'm really sorry."

Alex waved his hand in a thick black glove. "It's all right; just be there in time tomorrow."

"But what're you going to tell Jeff tonight?"

"I'll think of something later," Alex said nonchalantly.

Before entering the Skating Museum, they looked around to make sure no one was following them. The street looked deserted; even the window shades in the houses were down. Satisfied, Cammie slammed the heavy door shut behind her and followed Alex to the Dutch Hall on the second floor.

They took the same clothes out of the closet. Alex spread the pants and the jacket on the floor, while Cammie walked inside the closet to change.

"Are you ready?" Alex called.

"Yes, pretty much." Cammie smoothed out her long skirt and walked out of the closet, tying the strings of her cap under her chin.

A loud scraping sound came from downstairs as though someone had turned a key in the lock.

"Hey, did you hear that?" Alex froze in his spot, his hat in his hand.

"Now budge, you stupid Winja. We don't have all day!" a cold voice barked from the lobby.

"My knees hurt. You don't know what it's like," a high-pitched voice whined.

"Well, to each her own. My job is to scare, and as for you, Winja…hmm, I think you don't have a bone to spare." An evil cackle followed.

"What's that?" Cammie whispered.

Alex's eyes were wide with horror. "The witches! They are here."

"What are we going to do?"

They looked frantically around for a place to hide.

"In here!" Alex pulled Cammie by the hand and together they ran inside the closet and crouched behind layers of old clothes hanging on the racks. The air smelled strongly of moth balls.

"Now where's the book? It was here last time."

This time, Cammie recognized the voice. It belonged to the Witch of Pride, the one who had brought Cammie to Skateland last year and had almost destroyed her career later.

"What do you mean the book is missing?" The voice was deep and low, almost manly.

"That's the Witch of Destruction," Cammie said feebly.

Alex put his finger against his lips.

This time, the witches started screaming all at once, sounding positively panicky.

"It wasn't me!"

"I haven't crossed the threshold of this place ever since we all left last time."

"I wasn't here either!"

"Neither was I!"

"Why should I? I thought we were finished with the girl."

"Hey, that's right. Listen, Fear, are you sure we need to go back?" the Witch of Pride exclaimed.

"Quiet, everybody!" the Witch of Destruction roared. "We know the girl is in a safe place, but it never hurts to double check."

"Destruction is right. We planned on paying Sonia a nice visit, and I hate it when someone interferes with my plans," the Witch of Fear hissed.

"You know what? We probably misplaced the book," a dreamy voice drawled.

Cammie wondered who the strange voice belonged to; she didn't remember meeting that witch.

The Witch of Pride guffawed loudly. "I bet it was you, Confusion. I won't be surprised to find the book in your washing machine."

"Ha-ha-ha, the washing machine! That was a good one, Pride." Winja giggled sycophantly.

"Quiet, everybody!" the Witch of Destruction barked. "Confusion is right. We probably did misplace the book. Now what are you all waiting for? Search the place!"

Cammie and Alex stared at each other horrorstruck. What? The witches were going to rummage through the museum. It meant they would find Cammie and Alex in no time.

"Two witches per hall. Now!" The Witch of Destruction's voice was so loud that Cammie had to cover her ears.

There was a scuffle of footsteps on the first floor. Apparently, the witches were entering the first hall that displayed skates made from animal bones. Next thing Cammie heard was the telltale stomping sound of skate guards against metal steps; it meant that the witches were climbing up the stairs. They would walk into the Dutch Hall any minute and then—

"Cammie, over here!" Alex jumped out of the closet.

"What are you doing?"

The door opened with a crack.

"Now budge, Winja, we haven't got all day!" the Witch of Fear grumbled.

"I can't grab the railing; I have my crutches to carry." Winja sniveled.

"It's your problem, useless scum!"

"Cammie, come on!" Alex already stood on the ice next to the wax figure of a boy about his age.

Still uncertain about what her friend was about to do, Cammie stepped on the ice too.

"Now take this spot and freeze!" Alex pointed to the rosy-cheeked figure of a Dutch girl slightly taller than Cammie.

"Oh!" Now Cammie understood. They were going to pose as wax figures. With their Dutch clothes, they would probably be able to fit into the skating scene. As scared as Cammie was, she had to admit that Alex had indeed come up with a brilliant plan.

"Don't breathe when the witches are here!" Alex whispered.

Before Cammie had a chance to ask him how she could possibly not breathe for more than ten seconds, the door swung open, and in walked the Witch of Fear wearing loose white clothes. Her long gray hair hung limply down her spine, and she looked livid.

"Do you know how long it will take us to search this place?" The Witch of Fear glanced at the rink. Then she approached the closet and started throwing the clothes out of it onto the floor.

"Ugh!" Winja hobbled inside, panting, her limbs heavily bandaged. She threw the crutches on the floor and sat down next to them. Her face bore an expression of boredom.

"You'd better help me here, Winja!" the Witch of Fear said angrily.

"Ah! You're doing a great job. I just need to catch my breath." Winja waved her bandaged hand at the Witch of Fear and stared at the rink absent-mindedly.

Cammie had no choice but to hold her breath and stand perfectly still with her arms to the sides, one foot slightly behind the other. The worst thing about not moving was the fact that her mouth was slightly open. She had started saying something to Alex and then the witches came in, so she hadn't had a chance to close it. Now Winija sat directly across from her, and Cammie was desperately trying not to blink.

Next to her, Alex obviously had a hard time staying immobile. His posture looked about as uncomfortable as Cammie's. Alex's fists were clenched, his left knee was bent, and his torso was slightly leaning forward. His face was twisted in a weird smile—Cammie was sure that Alex had put on that facial expression at the exact moment when the witches walked into the Dutch Hall. Alex had probably been trying to blend in with the crowd of Dutch skaters, all of whom were smiling cheerfully. Looking at Alex's funny posture, Cammie fought a strong desire to chuckle. To suppress the urge, she sank her fingernails deep into her palms.

The Witch of Fear turned away from the closet, her face red. "There's nothing here. Hey, Winja, how about looking into the pockets of those figures?" The Witch of Fear nodded in Cammie and Alex's direction.

Cammie gasped, and the only reason the Witch of Fear didn't notice it was because she was urging Winja to get up.

"Nay, those aren't even real clothes; that's all wax," Winja said lazily.

Cammie slowly exhaled. The wax figures' clothes *were* real, but she only prayed the Witch of Fear wouldn't want to search their pockets herself.

"Besides," Winja said, "who would put the skating book into the wax figures' pockets?"

"True." The Witch of Fear sighed and wiped beads of perspiration from her forehead. "I think we're done here. Let's go upstairs."

The door closed behind them with a thud, and only then did Cammie allow herself to relax her muscles. Next to her, Alex flexed his fingers and hopped on the spot.

"That was close!" Cammie shook her head.

"Okay, time to go." Alex spread the skating history book on the ice. As the thick volume began to grow, Alex let out a loud chuckle. "Stupid witches couldn't even imagine that the book was in my pocket."

Cammie laughed too, feeling elated. "At least they will never be able to go back to the past."

They stepped on the page describing skating in nineteenth-century Holland. Cammie closed her eyes and let the swirling wind take her back to the past.

SANNE AND SVEN

The ice on the canal was sparkling clean; it glittered in the afternoon sun. The air was still chilly; wisps of steam came out of Cammie's and Alex's mouths, and there was a pricking sensation in Cammie's fingers. In spite of the frosty weather, Cammie still found nineteenth century Holland warmer and more pleasant than the grayish landscape they had seen three hundred years before.

"Alex, look!" Cammie pointed to a woman skating past them, a bundle of clothes tied to her back with a thick wool shawl. The bundle stirred and let out a faint whine. The lady stopped, loosened the shawl, and the bundle turned out to be a baby. The woman said something softly to the red-cheeked infant, inserted a pacifier into his mouth, readjusted the shawl, and skated away.

A busy-looking man in a long black coat floated by, his skates making deep curves on the ice.

Another man appeared, pushing what looked like Wilhelmina's wheelchair with blades instead of wheels. The occupant of the chair, a small woman dressed in a sleek gray fur jacket, sailed by without looking at Cammie or Alex.

"It's Skateland!" Cammie exclaimed, smiling broadly. "Don't you see? It's exactly the same as back home!"

"Wow, you're right!" Alex looked around and whistled. "Everybody is wearing skates."

It was true. Even though the area wasn't particularly crowded, probably due to the early afternoon hour, the few people Cammie and Alex had seen so far wore skates. Of course, they were not figure skates like Cammie's or Alex's. The blades were attached to people's boots with leather straps, and the front of the blades was long and rounded, curving over the front of the boots. There were still no toe picks.

Cammie shook her head in amazement. "How can they skate like that?"

"Don't underestimate them. Dutch skaters were famous for their beautiful edges even back then. Look!" Alex nodded in the direction of a young man who looked like a college student. He had a stack of books in his hand, and he was gliding forward in long strides on deep outside edges.

"The Dutch roll," Alex said. "This is exactly what Wilhelmina taught us to do for the show, remember?"

Cammie nodded absentmindedly. "Yeah, I think I do. But Wilhelmina, wow! Do you think she really modeled Skateland after Holland?"

"Perhaps. She's Dutch, after all. And she did encourage us to visit Holland."

"You know what? I bet Sonia is somewhere here. Her Dutch roll must be terrific."

Alex shrugged. "Actually, Sandra and Kevin can do a better job. They are dancers, and the Dutch waltz is the first dance they teach you."

Cammie was getting impatient. "If it's true, why didn't the witches abduct Sandra and Kevin?"

"They may still try." Alex looked worried. "Sandra and Kevin are on the witches' list too, remember?"

Cammie stared at Alex, her mouth open. "You're right!"

How come she had never thought that the witches' attacks might not stop after Sonia's disappearance? The evil women were likely to go after other skaters too. Even though they no longer had the skating book, they could surely think of other ways of attack. Skating witches wouldn't be satisfied until they destroyed the career of every promising skater in the world!

"I think we need to talk to someone," Alex said. "If Sonia is really here, they would know."

"But we don't speak Dutch."

Alex shrugged. "I'm sure most people here know English. It's an international language, after all."

"You're right." Cammie remembered that her father had once been to Germany on a business trip, and he had told Cammie and her mother that almost everybody could speak English.

"We Americans need to become more serious about foreign languages," Cammie's father had said. "Everybody in Europe speaks three or four languages, and we only know English."

Now that Cammie thought of her father's words, she wished she had spent more time practicing her Spanish at her Skateland school. Although how would that help her? It was Dutch they needed now.

"I think we would be better off talking to kids," Alex said. "I wonder where they are, though. I've only seen adults on the canal so far."

Alex got the answer to his question two minutes later when the two of them skidded to a stop in front of a two-story light yellow building. There was a metal plaque on the door with the words *School* engraved in bold letters.

"See?" Alex said excitedly. "The Dutch language is so much like English."

"The lessons probably aren't over yet." Cammie rose on her toes, trying to see something through the school windows, but they were too dark against the bright afternoon light.

"It looks like we are the only ones cutting classes," Alex said.

And practices too, Cammie thought. She wondered if all the travelling through time would affect her skating. She hadn't practiced any of her elements for two days already. That was completely unacceptable.

Cammie looked around. The canal across from the school building was empty; no one could see her. Satisfied, Cammie lowered herself into backward crossovers, made a circle, picked up speed and flew up in the air in a tight double loop. She wobbled a little on the landing, but overall the jump was good.

"Hey, what're you doing?" Alex grabbed her by the hand, his face red.

Cammie shrugged. "We're waiting for school to be over. Why waste time?"

"Don't you remember what Wilhelmina said? What would the Dutch think once they saw double jumps?"

"But there's nobody here." Cammie looked at the peaceful silhouette of the village stretching far in both directions. The small wood houses with gabled roofs seemed to be asleep. The window shutters were closed; the polished front doors appeared locked. Tall, weeping willows stood along the sides of the canal, their bare limbs almost touching the ice. A windmill towered behind the houses, its wanes spinning slowly, lazily. Apparently it wasn't windy enough. And most importantly, no one watched Cammie and Alex.

"Someone may be looking through the window; you never know," Alex said.

Before Cammie could say another word, a loud sound of the bell came out of the school building. In another moment, the heavy door burst open, and out came children of all ages ranging from six to probably seventeen or eighteen. Cammie saw that the boys wore wide pants with short, tight jackets and small felt hats or caps. The girls had long skirts and jackets, pretty much like Cammie's. Laughing excitedly, the children opened their schoolbags and produced skates with dangling leather straps. Cammie watched the kids as they quickly attached the blades to their boots and rushed onto the ice. Another minute, and the canal was filled with brightly clad figures whizzing past Cammie and Alex, chasing one another.

"Skateland again!" Cammie said. "It's just like back home when our classes are over. Except that they don't have to rush to practices afterwards."

Alex grinned. "It looks like they are practicing already."

Alex wasn't exaggerating. Of course, the Dutch children could hardly be called figure skaters, and their skates weren't up to modern standards, but overall they were skating really, really well. The children's edges were long and secure, and they developed tremendous speed on their primitive blades. Some kids even attempted one- and two-foot spins. Both Cammie and Alex gasped at a short boy who did an unmistakable back flip.

A tall pretty girl whooshed past Cammie with a cheerful smile. The girl shouted something in Dutch. Cammie smiled weakly and shrugged.

The girl came back and looked at Cammie and Alex with her bright blue eyes. It was then that Cammie saw how pretty the girl was, with delicate features and golden curls spilling out from under her bonnet.

The girl spoke again, and again Cammie shrugged then spread her arms, showing that she couldn't understand a thing.

"Uh, we're sorry, but we can't speak Dutch," Alex blurted out next to Cammie.

Cammie glanced at her friend and saw that his cheeks were bright red, and that he was watching the beautiful girl with a mixture of admiration and embarrassment.

The girl seemed to think for a moment; then her face lit up with a flash of recognition. "You two are from England, yes?"

Remembering their experience in the sixteenth-century Holland, Cammie was ready to say yes. How shocked was she, however, when Alex mumbled, "No, actually we are from the United States of America."

Cammie stared at Alex in confusion. Hadn't they agreed to tell people they were from England?

"Is that right?" The girl's eyes looked even bigger now, like two ponds with blue ice.

"Did you arrive in Holland by ship?"

By ship? How stupid. No one covered such long distances by ship anymore. At least, there had to be some credibility to their story if Alex had decided to tell everybody they were from America.

"No, actually we flew by pl—"

Bang! Alex kicked her hard, and this time, Cammie was really upset. What? He couldn't even keep their story straight?

"Of course, we came by ship, and it was lots of fun," Alex said.

The girl looked very impressed. Apparently she had never met anyone who lived so far from Holland.

"What's your name?" the girl asked Alex.

"Alex."

The girl turned to Cammie. Reluctantly, Cammie introduced herself.

"I'm Moniek," the girl said. "So what is your business in Holland?"

Moniek spoke with a strong Dutch accent, but at least she knew English.

"We're looking for a friend," Alex said. "Her name is Sonia Harrison. She's twelve, small, with red hair. She's a very good skater. Have you seen her?"

Cammie looked at Moniek, her hopes rising.

The girl shook her head, the corners of her mouth twitching. "Everybody is a good skater here. We Dutch are the best in the world."

Now wa-ai-t a minute! Cammie actually didn't remember any Dutch skaters winning medals at worlds or Olympics, except Wilhelmina. In fact, the only Dutch skater she knew was their president, but she had been a U.S. citizen for quite a while, so it didn't really count.

Cammie was about to explain it to Moniek, when the girl spoke up again. "But I think your friend is here."

"She is?" Cammie and Alex shouted in unison.

"Well, my classmate, Renate, has her cousins, a boy and a girl visiting from … hmm … it must be America. Or is it England? But I can ask her. Can you wait?"

"Sure!" Cammie and Alex said.

Moniek skated away, Alex's admiring eyes following her.

"Ye-es!" Cammie did a quick split jump then bent her left knee and went into a very low sit spin followed by a scratch spin. "We have found Sonia! We have found Sonia!"

"Cammie, will you stop showing off *now*?"

Alex's voice sounded harsh, and as Cammie came out of her spin, she saw that his face was contorted with anger. It wasn't the Alex she knew.

"Stop bossing me around, okay?" Cammie said angrily. What was the matter with him?

"I told you—we don't want to be noticed."

"Nobody cares. They are all skating and not looking at us."

"Oh yeah? How about them?"

Cammie looked in the direction Alex was pointing. Her friend was right; a group of girls dressed in brightly colored skirts and jackets were now eyeing them with apparent curiosity. Moniek was also part of the group.

"Hmm." For a moment, Cammie thought of agreeing that she was indeed wrong, but then she remembered another thing.

"Why did you hit me again? Tell me!" She kicked the ice with her blade.

Alex's green eyes rounded. "What're you talking about?"

"When I said we came by plane."

The surprise on Alex's face was immediately replaced by sarcasm. "There were no planes in the nineteenth century. Any first grader knows that."

"So why did you tell them we were from America, not from England?"

"Because in the nineteenth century, everybody knew about America already. Of course, in the sixteenth century…"

Cammie felt really hurt. Why did Alex always have to treat her as though she were a hopeless dummy?

"I'm sure the Dutch have met quite a few English people already, or they may have visited Great Britain themselves." Alex was talking calmly as though he didn't notice Cammie's sulky face expression. "They may find something unusual about the way we talk or skate—anything. At least, we can tell them it's our American way."

"Okay." Cammie sighed. Perhaps Alex was right, after all.

"Here you go!" Moniek was back, accompanied by a shorter girl. The girl was not as pretty as Moniek, but her gray eyes looked soft and kind.

"This is Renate Molenaar, and she is the one who has cousins visiting from America." Moniek said.

Renate blushed. "Not America, England."

Moniek waved her hand. "Whatever."

"It's okay, I haven't been to either of those countries," Renate said. "And you know I just met Sanne and Sven myself."

Cammie's heart raced in her chest. "What did you say?"

Renate looked slightly surprised. "Sanne and Sven. Those are my cousins' names. They never visited us before. You see, their mother—"

Cammie wasn't listening anymore. Wow, *Sanne* sounded just like *Sonia*! It had to be her roommate;

there was no doubt about it. Cammie glanced at Alex, who looked as excited as she felt, and saw him nod. So it looked like they had really found Sonia. Now the question was, how were they getting to Renate's house?

Renate had probably guessed what they were thinking. "Where are the two of you staying?"

Cammie and Alex exchanged looks again. Actually, they hadn't thought of spending the night in Holland, but now that they had probably found Sonia, why not?

"You two can stay with us," Renate said. "I'm sure my parents won't mind, especially now that we have my cousins visiting. And perhaps Sanne is the friend you're looking for."

"Cool!"

Cammie felt ecstatic. They were about to see Sonia. Besides, the air was getting colder, and Cammie longed for a warm shelter and hot dinner.

"Come on!" Renate said. "My house isn't that far from school."

Sanne was not Sonia. Only the name sounded similar; other than that, the girls had absolutely nothing in common. First of all, Sanne was much younger, only ten years old. Although Sanne lived in England (not America) and spoke perfect English, she looked like a typical Dutch girl, with very fair hair and light blue eyes. Sanne's brother Sven was eight, but the two of them could be twins. Both kids were quiet and shy. Renate, too, was timid, but very nice. Cammie liked her more than Moniek, who never stopped batting her long eyelashes at Alex.

Even though it was fun to be able to talk to someone who understood English, Cammie and Alex had absolutely no business spending the night in Renate's home. Except that it was cold and dark, and they were hungry. Of course, getting back to Skateland by the skating history book would only take seconds, but ... Cammie pictured a long run to her dorm across Skaletand. Hopefully, Mrs. Page would have something nice and hot for Cammie to eat. But what if they came too late? Mrs. Page might be in bed already. Of course, the dorm supervisor would let Cammie in, but would she have a hot dinner ready for her? And here, in Renate's house in Holland, fire roared cheerfully in the fireplace, and Mrs. Molenaar had a sumptuous dinner of beef stew with potatoes ready for them. Herring and pickles were also served, and for dessert, they had delicious gingerbread cookies.

Moniek had stayed for dinner too. For some reason, now that they were in Renate's house, the pretty girl no longer flirted with Alex. Instead, she sat next to Cammie, asking her all kinds of questions about her skating. Moniek's interest made Cammie uncomfortable, for she wasn't sure what aspect of figure skating was already known to the nineteenth-century Hollanders. On the other hand, Cammie didn't want to appear impolite, so she spoke about school figures. Renate's parents were listening to her too. As Cammie spoke about loops and brackets, Mrs. Molenaar nodded her head, knitting a long white scarf at the same time.

"We need them for our cold weather, dear. I make wool clothes for the whole family," the lady said to Cammie with a kind smile.

Mr. Molenaar kept quiet most of the time, smoking a thick brown pipe. He puffed and puffed the whole evening until Cammie got worried that either the man would suffocate or the house would be set on fire. Back home, she had never seen anyone smoke so much. But luckily, nothing happened, and finally, Mrs. Molenaar covered her mouth with her hand to stifle a yawn and announced that it was time to go to bed.

Although it was still early—just a little past nine,—Cammie felt really tired. It had been a long, hard day, and tomorrow they would have to travel again. They said good night to Moniek, who took a long time putting on her coat and attaching her blades to her boots in the lobby.

As Cammie lay in bed that had been previously warmed by a hot water bottle, she thought of England. Sanne and Sven were English. Perhaps that was the place where the witches had hidden Sonia. She would have to talk to Alex, and perhaps, they could visit England tomorrow. At least it was good that the witches could no longer travel through time, because they didn't have the history book. It meant they couldn't hurt Sonia any further.

Cammie lay in bed thinking about Sonia, but then the witches somehow found a way to sneak into Renate's house, and now the Witch of Pride was kneeling over the chair on which Alex's carefully folded clothes sat, and she was looking for something. Cammie was about to jump out of bed and grab the history book before the witch could steal it, but the Witch of Fear bent over her and stared at Cammie with her bloodshot eyes. Cammie tried to scream, but she couldn't open her mouth; she wanted to kick the witch, but her legs wouldn't move, so she closed her eyes and floated in complete darkness...

"Cammie, wake up, we've got to go!"

She opened her eyes. Alex stood by her bed, fully dressed. Renate, too, was by his side, a bashful smile on her lips.

"Mother says breakfast is ready," Renate said softly and walked out of the room.

Then Cammie remembered her nightmare. "Alex, the book. It's been stolen!"

Alex frowned. "What're you talking about?"

He put his hand into his pocket and extracted the history book. "Here it is."

"Oh, great!" Cammie sighed with relief and leaned against the pillows. It had been nothing but a dream; they would get back home after all. And they would also be able to go to England to find Sonia.

"Come on, get dressed!" Alex left the room.

Cammie quickly got into her Dutch clothes. She pulled a pair of cotton socks over her tights. The socks made her feet a little too snug in her skating boots, but she had to wear them when she knew she would spend the whole day outside.

Cammie walked into the dining room. Unlike the bedroom, it had no carpets on the floor, and the cold tiles felt hard against Cammie's feet.

"I still don't like you walking on the floor without shoes on." Mrs. Molenaar said, shaking her head. She had made the same comment last night when she saw Cammie leave her skates in the lobby.

"But I couldn't walk on the floor with my skates on," Cammie explained for the second time already. Of course, if she wore her skate guards, that would be possible, but oh, she would feel extremely uncomfortable.

"And I don't see why somebody would want her blades attached to the boots," Mrs. Molenaar said as she ladled porridge into Cammie's plate. "It seems so unpractical."

The problem was that as hard as Cammie and Alex had tried, everybody in Renate's family had noticed that their skates were different from what the Hollanders wore. Perhaps if they hadn't spent the night…

Sanne giggled as she toyed with her oatmeal. "I want skates like Cammie's, auntie!"

Uh-huh, Cammie thought.

Mrs. Molenaar shook her head. "I don't think your father would like blades that come together with boots. It's strange. Besides, they don't even sell them in Holland or England."

"I'll go to America when I grow up!" Sven, who had been silent all the time, suddenly announced. "And then I'll buy such skates for both me and you, Sanne."

Cammie wondered how disappointed the grown-up Sven would be once he came to America and couldn't find modern skates. She glanced at Alex, caught his worried look, and quickly lowered her head.

"Thank you very much, but we have to go," Alex said as he finished his second cup of fresh English tea.

Cammie stood up, too. "Thank you all for your hospitality."

"But where are the two of you going now?" Mrs. Molenaar looked worried.

"Uh, our parents are meeting us in Amsterdam," Alex lied.

"Ah!" Mrs. Molenaar nodded. "So you lads are skating to Amsterdam?"

"Yes, ma'am."

"Take some gingerbread with you, then." Ignoring Cammie and Alex's protests, the kind lady stuffed their pockets with slices of gingerbread. "You'll get hungry even before you reach the city.

And don't argue with me—Amsterdam is six miles away."

Cammie thanked Mrs. Molenaar again and stopped by Mr. Molenaar to say good-bye. He nodded, his brown pipe still in his hand.

Alex was already in the lobby lacing his skates. Cammie sat on a low wood stool and reached into the corner with her hand. Her fingers felt nothing but emptiness. She knelt on the floor and patted the tile surface. Again, she found nothing.

Still unable to believe what had happened, Cammie turned to Alex. "Have you seen my skates?"

Alex raised his head, a soaker in his hand. "What?"

"My skates aren't here."

"What're you talking about?" Alex crouched and ran his hand along the empty floor in the corner. He frowned, looked around the lobby—

"No, I left them right here." Cammie patted the spot where she had put her skates the night before.

"Someone may have moved them accidentally." Alex knelt on the floor, peering into every corner. He straightened up and looked Cammie in the eye, his face troubled. Cammie's skates were gone.

STOLEN SKATES

I'm sorry Cammie. What a shame it happened in our house. I don't even know what to say." Mrs. Molenaar stood in the middle of the lobby, her arms dangling limply by her sides.

"Are you sure you didn't leave them in the bedroom?" Mr. Molenaar boomed.

"Why don't you take a look, Renate?" the girl's mother suggested.

"It's no use, Mother, I've already looked everywhere." Renate shook her head sympathetically.

"It never hurts to double check, does it?" Mr. Molenaar lit his pipe, shaking his head.

Renate shrugged. "I guess." She hurried out of the lobby.

"What a shame! Those skates are really expensive, but I can't imagine…" Mrs. Molenaar's face was red, and her light brown hair hung loosely along her cheeks.

"The skates aren't in the bedroom." Renate was back in the lobby, breathing hard. "But you know what? I know who took Cammie's skates. It was Moniek."

"Moniek?" Cammie exclaimed. Why, sure! Boy, how stupid she was. Moniek was the one who had shown the greatest interest in Cammie's boots and blades last night. Perhaps without the pretty girl's detailed questions about the design of modern skates, Renate's family might not have noticed that Cammie's and Alex's skates were any different from traditional Dutch blades. Yet Moniek had never stopped asking Cammie questions about her skating.

"But why would Moniek want Cammie's skates?" Mrs. Molenaar thought out loud. "Her parents are rich. Surely, they can afford to buy her anything she wants."

Renate shook her head. "Not skates like Cammie's, Mother. You can only get them in America."

"But stealing...I don't know. It's a sin!" Mrs. Molenaar spread her arms helplessly.

"When Moniek wants something, she has to get it right away," Renate said angrily.

"What am I going to do?" Cammie whispered. She felt her eyes fill up with tears.

Alex clenched his fists. "Isn't it obvious? We'll go after Moniek and get your skates back. Where does she live?"

Mrs. Molenaar shook her head. "You'd better be careful, young man. Moniek's father is a lawyer, one of the best in Amsterdam, by the way."

"A fairly decent man, actually," Mr. Molenaar said, swirling his pipe in his mouth.

"True, Mr. Termeulen is pretty honest, but when it comes to his little princess…" Mrs. Molenaar sighed gravely.

"The real problem is that you have no proof," Mr. Molenaar said. "Did any of you see Moniek take Cammie's skates?"

Alex and Cammie looked at each other dubiously and shook their heads.

"But there was no one else in the house!" Renate exclaimed.

"How about all of us?" her father asked firmly.

"Us? But—"

"Renate, we know that we didn't take Cammie's skates," her mother said. "But we can't prove it to Mr. Termeulen. And when he asks Moniek whether she stole them, she will probably say no. So it will be her word against your word. And because Mr. Termeulen practically worships his daughter—"

"But it's not fair!" Cammie's lips quivered.

Alex put his hand on her shoulder. "We'll think of something."

"Look, Renate, why don't you talk to Moniek at school," Mrs. Molenaar said. "And don't be rude. Simply ask her if she borrowed Cammie's skates to take a look at them."

"Take a look of them? Without permission?" Alex said with indignation. "How is Cammie supposed to skate now?"

Mrs. Molenaar slapped her forehead. "Of course! You poor dear, you need skates. Tell you what; I have a pair of old skates here in the closet. I used them myself years ago before my feet grew too big. But I think they are in fairly good condition."

Before Cammie could say no, Mrs. Molenaar rushed out of the lobby. She returned carrying a very rusty pair of blades. Cammie gasped in horror.

Mrs. Molenaar must have noticed her terrified look. "Nothing to worry about, dear. Of course, they need a little bit of polishing and sharpening, but it will only take a minute."

"How far does the skate sharpener live?" Cammie asked dully. She thought longingly of Mr. Reed's sharpening shop in Skateland. Somehow, she doubted that there were real sharpening experts in the nineteenth-century Holland.

Mrs. Molenaar looked at Cammie with surprise. "Skate sharpener, dear? What are you talking about? Mr. Molenaar will take care of your skates in no time."

"Sure." Mr. Molenaar said tersely. He picked up the blades and left the room.

Cammie shook her head in frustration.

Alex bent down to her. "Look, it's better than nothing. And it's kind of fun, what do you think? Who would ever have a chance to skate in antique blades?"

Alex winked at her. Cammie tried to hold back tears. As much as she appreciated her friend's desire to cheer her up, all she wanted to do was cry.

Ten minutes later, Mr. Molenaar was back. He handed Cammie the skates, and as she examined them, she saw that they really looked better. The blades were sharp and appeared almost new. Of course, there were no toe picks, and that was what scared Cammie the most.

"Oh, and you need a pair of boots too," Mrs. Molenaar said.

It was funny, but Cammie actually liked the boots Mrs. Molenaar had brought her. They were made of fine leather and looked almost modern. The size was right, and the boots felt really comfortable.

Cammie laced her boots, and Mrs. Molenaar helped her to attach the blades, strapping them around Cammie's heels and insteps.

"Now you look just like a Dutch girl," Mrs. Molenaar said sweetly.

Well, perhaps that was true, but Cammie still wasn't sure whether she would be able to skate without toe picks.

The morning was bright but breezy, the vanes of the windmills flapping in the wind. As they left the house and headed for the school building, Cammie tagged behind Alex and Renate. Mrs. Molenaar's blades appeared to be dull; they simply refused to hold an edge. Cammie's legs wobbled. The closest feeling to skating in antique blades was the sensation of stepping on the ice with her skate guards on. That had happened to Cammie once or twice, and she had never forgotten the experience.

"Cammie, are you all right?" Alex had stopped and was now studying Cammie's clumsy moves.

"I'm fine, but the skates ... " Cammie skidded to a stop, panting. "Just wait till I see Moniek again."

"That bad, huh?" Alex looked at her blades sympathetically.

"You'll get used to them," Renate said.

"I guess. Okay, let's go." Cammie moved forward, Renate and Alex skating by her side.

By the time they approached the school, Cammie's skating had got significantly better. She glided past the multicolored houses in big smooth strokes, wind whistling in her ears. They were almost at the entrance—no more than a hundred feet away. Determined to squeeze the truth out of Moniek, and the sooner the better, Cammie rushed forward, ahead of Alex and Renate. She bent her left knee, went into a three turn ... her left foot twisted; she had no control of her blades ... bang! She fell forward on her right knee. Oh, no, how could she forget? The antique blades had no toe picks.

"Ouch!" Cammie rubbed her knee.

"What's wrong?" Alex helped her to get on her feet.

"There are no toe picks, all right?"

"Of course, there aren't. What did you do a three turn for?"

Cammie shrugged. How could she explain that for a split second, she had forgotten that she wasn't wearing her skates?

"Moniek!" Renate called.

Cammie whirled around, still clutching her knee. The pretty girl was approaching the school building, wearing a sleek light blue jacket trimmed with white fur. At the sight of Cammie and Alex, Moniek's eyes twitched. She turned her face away, and her hands clad in blue embroidered mittens clasped nervously. But the pretty girl's shock didn't last long; within a couple of seconds, she was her usual cheery self.

"Hello, how do you do?" Moniek asked Cammie.

"I've been better," Cammie snapped.

"Oh!" The pale blue eyes widened; apparently Moniek was faking surprise.

Before Moniek could say another word, Alex stepped forward. "Did you see Cammie's skates, Moniek?"

The pretty girl's eyes slid down Cammie's legs to her blades. "Oh, of course, I saw them. They are great. I'll ask my father to buy me skates like hers."

"He won't have to bother," Alex said sarcastically.

"What?" Moniek wrinkled her nose, but before she could keep acting surprised, Alex grabbed her wrist hard.

"Oh please!" Moniek's bright lips parted, she looked around nervously. Then her eyes darted toward Renate as though begging for help.

Renate, however, remained silent, staring at Moniek with quiet disdain.

"I…I didn't take her skates," Moniek bleated.

"Yes, you did," Renate said calmly. "You were the only guest in the house. And my family doesn't have them."

"Now what are you waiting for?" Alex's tall, strong frame towered over Moniek, looking menacing. "You heard us. Cammie needs her skates back. Now!"

But Moniek seemed to have recovered from her initial shock of being singled out as the primary suspect. She licked her lips, straightened up, and looked at the three of them with the expression of complete innocence.

"I don't understand what you're talking about. She has her skates." Moniek nodded in the direction of Cammie's feet.

Cammie glanced at her antique blades. "Those aren't mine, and you know it. I want my boots and blades now!"

"I don't have your skates!" Moniek said sweetly. There was a slight twinkle in her eyes that reminded Cammie of the way the Witch of Pride had spoken when she had told Alex and her that they would never be able to skate again.

"Now look—"

Before Cammie could say another word, the school bell rang. The children around them hastened to take off their skates.

"I need to go," Moniek chirped. "I have math as my first lesson, and I can't be late."

She walked away from the three of them, her curls bouncing on her shoulders. As Moniek reached the porch, she knelt down and unstrapped her blades.

"You're a thief!" Alex yelled.

Moniek pulled the polished door and looked back at Cammie and Alex. "Have a nice trip home!" With a cheerful wave, Moniek disappeared inside the building.

Renate sighed. "See? That's what my mother said would happen."

"But she is a thief!" Cammie felt tears pouring down her cheeks. "What am I going to do?"

"You can keep my mother's skates," Renate said.

"But I can't!" Cammie couldn't contain herself any more. She pressed her fists against her eyes and began to sob.

"Cammie, I…" Renate shifted her feet. "I'm sorry, but I have to go to class now."

"Go!" Alex nudged her to the front door. "We'll think of something."

Renate's eyes were full of concern as she stared at the sobbing Cammie. "I'm really sorry."

"It's not your fault. Now go!" Alex waved at Renate, who still looked reluctant to leave. He led the girl toward the school building. Cammie saw Alex say something to Renate and the girl nod.

The heavy school door closed with a bang. Cammie bawled louder.

"Cammie, stop it! Everything will be all right."

Cammie shook her head. What was she going to do without her skates? They were still new. She had only gotten them three months ago and had barely broken them in. Those were custom-made Riedell boots, and Cammie really liked them. After she had endured three weeks of blisters trying to practice in her new skates, the boots finally felt comfortable. Now what was she going to do? Her old skates sat in her father's garage; the boots didn't fit anymore. Cammie's feet had grown a size during the last year.

"Cammie, look!"

"Oh, no!" Cammie pictured herself showing up for her lesson with Coach Ferguson wearing toe-pick free blades attached to old-fashioned boots with the help of leather straps. Everybody in Skateland would laugh her to scorn; she might as well quit skating.

"Cammie, be quiet! Of course, all you girls are like that. The moment something goes wrong you bawl like babies."

"That's not fair!" Cammie snapped. "If she had taken your skates—"

"So how is crying going to help? Let's think what we can do."

Cammie dried her face with her sleeves and took a couple of deep breaths.

"Problem is, we can't do much here." Alex seemed to be thinking out loud. "Moniek will keep denying everything, and I don't think she'll invite us to her house, so—"

"So what? I'll be stuck with these for the rest of my life?" Cammie raised her foot, demonstrating the long blade, curved and smooth in the front.

Alex rolled his eyes. "Of course, not. But you can buy another pair in Skateland."

Cammie gritted her teeth. "Do you think my parents will pay for another pair of custom boots and blades only three months after I got those?"

Alex's face darkened. "Yeah, they probably won't be too happy to do it. But look, I'll think of something. Why don't we head home now and then—"

"Without my skates?" Cammie cried out.

"Just give me time, okay?" Without waiting for Cammie's answer, Alex spread the history book on the ground and stepped on it.

Cammie had no choice but to follow her friend.

TOE PICK TRAP

"Don't worry, I have a plan," Alex said when the two of them approached Moniek's school building the next day.

"What is it?" Cammie sighed as she looked at her old-fashioned skates.

Alex pointed to the quiet school building. "The best thing is to watch Moniek. If she has your skates, she will start showing them off sooner or later."

"You're brilliant!" Now Cammie wondered how she hadn't thought of it herself. If they saw Moniek wearing Cammie's skates, the pretty girl wouldn't be able to deny that she had indeed taken them. Although...

"But what do we do then? I mean, after we have seen her wear my skates?" Cammie asked. "What if she says that her father brought them from America or something?"

Alex frowned. "True. Even if we tell her you can't buy skates like yours in America now, how can we prove it? Tell you what; we can't talk to Moniek. Not yet. We'll just watch her."

"And then?" Cammie felt disappointed.

The bell rang. In another minute, kids would come out of the building.

"In here!" Alex grabbed Cammie's hand and pulled her to the place where the big canal split into a fork. They crouched behind a big boat frozen into the ice. Now they were completely hidden from the eyes of anyone who would leave the school.

"We'll just wait, okay?" Alex rubbed his hands excitedly.

"But what if Moniek won't try her new skates today?" Cammie felt she couldn't wait another day. She needed her skates now.

Alex smirked. "Do you seriously think that Moniek would miss an opportunity to show off?"

"But won't she be afraid to wear them with us still in the area?"

Alex brushed the snow off the tile pavement and sat down. Cammie knew he was trying to make sure none of the kids leaving school could see him. "I took care of that. I spread the rumor that we were leaving for the U.S. today."

Cammie felt her mouth open wide. "When did you do that? I didn't hear a thing."

"Right before Renate walked into the building. You were crying your heart out and wouldn't have heard a bomb explode if someone had set it off."

Cammie pouted. "How would you react if your skates were stolen?"

"Relax. I'm only making a point. Anyway, when you were moaning and howling—"

"Alex!"

"I made a big deal of saying goodbye to Renate," Alex said, ignoring Cammie's annoyance. "I hugged her and told her how we appreciated her and her parents' hospitality, and how we might be able to meet again one day."

Alex chuckled. "I bet half of the school heard that."

Cammie's hands were getting cold even in her thick wool mittens. She rubbed them hard. "That was cool. But—"

Alex raised his index finger. "Look!"

The canal was already filled with happy kids. They laughed, they chased one another, they swirled, they spun. But then, about ten minutes later, Cammie noticed something different in the children's skating style. No longer were they doing tricks on ice. Instead, a wide circle had formed, and the skaters were apparently staring at someone in the middle.

Cammie craned her neck, trying to see what had attracted the children's attention. But she couldn't see anything. The crowd pressed tight against what looked like a lonely figure of a skater. But when the chain of *ah-ing* and *wow-ing* girls broke for a second, Cammie saw who was showing off in the middle of the circle. It was undoubtedly Moniek wearing Cammie's skates. The pretty girl had taken off her light blue jacket and was now skating in a shiny white sweater, apparently to go with Cammie's white boots. As Moniek skated back and forth, her golden locks danced around her face. The other children clapped and cheered.

"Nasty thief!" Cammie muttered. She had a strong desire to make a snowball and throw it right at Moniek. Oh, how she wished the Dutch snow wasn't so dry and powdery!

"Just wait!" Alex whispered. "Remember, he laughs best who—"

Cammie understood the wisdom behind Alex's sentence even before he finished it. The next thing Moniek did was get on her toe pick. She crashed hard on the ice. "*Aye!*"

Cammie stood up excitedly. Alex pulled her back down.

Meanwhile, a gang of boys rushed to Moniek's side, helping her to her feet. The girl pushed them away, her pretty face now red with humiliation. She shouted something in Dutch that Cammie couldn't understand. Judging from the pretty girl's gestures and the boys' reaction, Moniek was assuring everybody that it had been nothing but a small blunder, and she would be all right in just a moment.

Cammie snickered. Moniek was so self-confident, and yet she didn't know that learning to skate properly in figure skates took time. Toe picks were figure skaters' friends, but they could be a menace for beginners.

Moniek's admirers skated away from her, clearing the space in the middle of the canal. Apparently, they expected their princess to demonstrate another cool move on innovative American skates.

Moniek rewarded the crowd with a bit of a white-tooth smile, spread her arms, and raised her left leg behind her.

"Oh, no, she's going to do a spiral!" Cammie exclaimed.

"Hush!"

Cammie brushed Alex away. Nobody would be able to hear her; everybody's eyes were on Moniek. Actually, the girl was pretty flexible; Cammie had to hand it to her, although—

There was a collective gasp as Moniek leaned forward too far; she was now on her toe pick; Cammie knew what was coming…

Splat! A moment later, Moniek lay sprawled on the ice, screaming at the top of her lungs, "*Hulp! Hulp!*"

The kids huddled against Moniek talking excitedly. Two girls rushed into the school building and returned with a stout woman wearing a stiff white bonnet. The nurse bent over Moniek, and the crowd tightened around the girl lying on the ice. Cammie and Alex could no longer see what was going on.

A girl pushed through the crowd, a pair of Dutch blades in her hand. A couple of minutes later, the crowd spread, and Moniek appeared, supported by the nurse.

"She has different skates on!" Alex exclaimed.

Now Cammie, too, could see that Moniek's blades were strapped to her shiny leather boots.

Cammie pressed her fingernails hard into her palm. "Where are my skates? What did she do with them?"

Moniek skated away slowly, the nurse still by her side. It looked as though the pretty girl was favoring her right leg.

"She looks all right. At least she hasn't broken anything," Alex said.

"Well, hopefully she has learned her lesson," Cammie snapped. She was still scanning the canal. Perhaps someone else was using her skates now. But no, the rest of the kids were wearing their antique Dutch skates.

"Don't move!" Alex said warningly.

Cammie hugged herself, battling a strong desire to rush forward. "What about my skates?"

"Be patient, just another minute."

The crowd had finally dispersed. Most of the kids were following Moniek, who seemed to have completely recovered. Now the pretty girl didn't even look upset as she smiled at the gang of boys around her. Several girls joined them too, bombarding Moniek with questions. From what Cammie and Alex could hear, the girl sounded cheerful enough. Even her old habit of tossing her curls from her shoulders to the front had returned.

"Alex!" Cammie couldn't wait another minute.

"Come on!" Alex shot forward toward the spot where Moniek had tripped. Cammie followed, her knees weak. What if they never found her skates? Not only wouldn't she able to skate her program, Wilhelmina probably wouldn't even allow Cammie to train in Skateland. Cammie's skating career would be over. *Oh no, no, please!*

"Here they are!" Alex picked up a white boot from a small patch of snow in front of the school building. "She just threw them away, see?"

"Wow!" Cammie grabbed the boot and pressed it hard to her chest.

"Go ahead, put them on."

Cammie unlaced Mrs. Molenaar's boots. "I wonder why none of the kids wanted my skates."

Alex kicked a small piece of ice. "Isn't it obvious? They don't want to get hurt."

Cammie quickly changed into her boots. She stood up and glided along the canal, enjoying the wonderful feeling of security the toe picks gave her.

"Hey, what are we going to do with these?"

Cammie turned around. Alex stood in front of the school building, twirling Mrs. Molenaar's blades between his fingers. The leather boots sat on the snow by his side.

"Oh, I completely forgot." Cammie skated back.

"You know what? I'll write Renate a note. I'll tell her we found your skates, and I'll thank her for everything again." Alex took a pencil and a piece of scrap paper out of his pocket and quickly scribbled a short note. He put the boots and blades on the porch of the school building and slipped the note into one of the boots.

"Alex, but why were you so sure Moniek would throw my skates away?" Cammie asked as the two of them skated along the canal away from the school. They wanted to make sure they wouldn't be seen before going back to Skateland.

Alex shrugged. "It was pretty obvious. You have to know how to skate on figure skates. And Moniek isn't really a tough cookie. A couple of falls, and she has given up. Actually, all of you girls are like that. "

Cammie went into a T-stop and glared at him. "What? I don't give up."

"And who was flooding the place with tears not too long ago?"

Cammie dismissed him with a wave of her hand. "It doesn't count. If you lost your skates … but you know what?"

She looked at the vanes of the windmill that were now going fast. "It's just what Wilhelmina said, huh? These people aren't ready for figure skates."

Alex's green eyes widened. "That's right!"

Still thinking about Skateland President's wisdom, they stepped on the history book and flew back to the twenty-first century.

"So when are we going to England?" Cammie asked.

They had just changed back into their clothes, and Cammie didn't feel like putting on another weird outfit.

Alex thought for a moment. "I think it's a little late to go to another country today. Let's wait till tomorrow."

Cammie sighed with relief. As they closed the heavy door of the Skating Museum behind them, Cammie already anticipated Mrs. Page's scrumptous meal. Then she could catch up on her homework, or maybe even watch television in the dorm.

As it was still early in the afternoon, most of Skateland's residents were still at work. The streets were empty, except for a couple of women gliding fast in the direction of their homes with grocery bags in their hands. A short, plump grandfather skated by holding a red-cheeked boy no older than two in a harness. The toddler could barely stroke; he mostly walked on his toe picks, yet he looked happy.

Alex looked at his watch. "We'd better hurry. Classes are over, so the kids will be going to their afternoon practice now."

"I know." Cammie sped up. "I don't want to answer Dana and Liz's questions. They are so nosey."

"Well, in my case, it's Jeff I don't want to talk to. I still haven't thought of a good reason why he can't join us on our trips."

Cammie shrugged. "Just tell him we're supposed to go alone. Wilhelmina's orders."

"Well, I did, but he—"

Something leaped in front of them, blocking their way. "Here you are!"

Startled, Cammie stopped abruptly to avoid a nasty collision and almost fell backwards. She waved her arms violently to steady herself.

"Jeff!" Cammie heard Alex yell. "What are you doing here?"

"Looking for you!" Jeff was breathing hard. His normally cheerful face now looked grim.

"Are you okay?" Cammie asked.

"I'll ask the questions from now on." Jeff turned to Alex, shaking his finger at him. "I waited for you this morning. You promised to take me along with you, so I stood in front of the dorm for forty minutes, and you never showed up. So I went to practice, because what choice did I have? And I was late, of course, and the coach yelled at me, and—"

A muscle on Alex's cheek twitched. "Hmm, look—"

"You lied to me!" Jeff's brown eyes looked almost black with anger.

"It's not that I had a choice. I didn't want to bump you!" Alex said, sounding apologetic.

"But you did!"

Alex was speaking in a calm voice, apparently expecting Jeff to relax too. "Jeff…how do I explain it? It's a very dangerous mission, and Wilhelmina doesn't want many people involved—"

"Sonia is my best friend!" Jeff shouted.

"I understand, but—"

"And you can't stop me. Nobody can, okay? I'm coming with you tomorrow. And I don't care if you say no. I won't leave your side; I'll—"

"All right, all right!" Alex raised his arms as though in surrender.

Jeff's lower lip trembled; Cammie could see that the boy was having hard time controlling his emotions. She understood what Jeff was going through. He and Sonia had been friends since they were little kids. Both of them had lived in Skateland for many years, separated from their parents. Two years ago, both of them had been viciously attacked by witches who had kept them from skating for a long time.

In fact, it was Cammie and Alex who had broken the witches' curses over Jeff and Sonia. Jeff and Sonia were of the same age as Cammie—twelve years old, in the seventh grade—but they were much better skaters. Both of them could land a couple of triple jumps already, something Cammie could only dream of. Jeff and Sonia worked hard like no one else, and they actually seemed to enjoy Skateland's rigorous training. At least Cammie had never heard Sonia complain about anything; her roommate endured sufferings with calm patience. And Jeff had a great sense of humor. When something went wrong, he would merely laugh the problem away. Cammie liked him for that.

So now as she looked at Jeff's contorted face, she understood that the boy simply couldn't go on with his daily activities while Sonia was tortured by the witches. Looking for Sonia was Jeff's duty as a friend; Cammie could see it very clearly. And if she had to explain it to Alex, she would.

"Alex!" Cammie called.

Alex ignored her, his eyes fixed firmly on Jeff's shaking chin. "Listen, buddy, I understand. If something happened to Cammie, I would feel the same way."

What? Had he really said that? Cammie turned her face away so none of the boys could see her flushing cheeks. Deep on the inside, she had a really nice warm feeling.

"You can come tomorrow," Alex said.

Jeff still didn't look convinced. "How can I be sure you won't leave without me again?"

"I promise," Alex said simply.

Cammie stepped forward. "We both promise, okay?"

Jeff stared at both of them, apparently wondering if they could be trusted. There was a long silence. Cammie stared at the house across the street. A big marmalade cat sat on the windowsill, peering at the three of them with his yellow eyes. Apparently the cat didn't consider them trustworthy. With a quick sigh, Cammie looked away.

"I have to go to practice." Jeff bent down and tucked a loose lace into his boot.

"Don't let the coach work you too hard; you'll need strength tomorrow," Alex said.

Jeff grinned, his brown eyes looking like two big truffles. "Speak for yourself."

The three of them crossed Loop Corner. Now Cammie and Alex would have to turn left on Axel Avenue and head to their dorms.

"So where have you been so far?" Jeff slowed down.

"Only to Holland," Alex said.

"Wow!" Jeff looked impressed.

"Well, Sonia isn't there. So it's England tomorrow."

"England?" Jeff slapped himself on the knees. "What year?"

"I'm not sure." Alex took the history book out of his pocket and started turning the pages.

"I know. Let's make it 1864!" Jeff said excitedly.

"And why do you think Sonia is there?" Alex asked.

Jeff looked a little sheepish. "Well, I can't be sure, of course, but she might be. See, that was the year when Jackson Haines visited England. Everybody watched his performance; there were a lot of people at the rink, so if the witches wanted to hide Sonia in the crowd, it would be a perfect place."

Cammie creased her forehead. "Who is Jackson Haines?"

Alex and Jeff glanced at each other then at Cammie. Cammie hated that look. The boys acted as though Cammie were an ignorant little kid. Cammie found it extremely nasty, because person-ally she couldn't see how knowing who Jackson Haines was could help her skating.

"Jackson Haines was a famous American skater," Jeff said. "While everybody in England did figures, he danced on ice. It was unusual in those days. I really wish I could meet him."

Cammie gave him a questioning look. "So? There were other good skaters. Why do you want to meet Jackson Haines?"

Jeff's cheeks reddened. "Hmm, I play Jackson Haines in the show."

So it was that stupid show again. Cammie sighed and looked away.

Cammie and Alex should have turned left long ago; instead they were skating next to Jeff toward Main Square. A tall, skinny woman was moving in their direction, leaning heavily on crutches. Her wrists were bandaged too. There was something familiar about that woman, only Cammie couldn't remember—

Alex jumped backwards. "Winja!"

Jeff stopped abruptly and collided with the woman.

"You stupid brat. Watch where you're skating!" the Witch of Injuries squeaked. She swung one of her crutches and hit Jeff hard on the leg below the knee.

"Ouch!" Jeff bent over, clutching his leg.

"Are you okay?" Cammie rushed to Jeff's side.

"Get out of here, stupid Winja!" Alex darted forward and snatched both crutches out of the witch's hands.

Winja collapsed on the ice.

"Here you go!" Alex dropped the crutches on top of the whining witch.

"And don't come close to us again!" Alex shouted.

"You jerk!" With surprising agility, Winja picked up the crutches, jumped to her feet, and scampered away without looking back.

"Bye, bye!" Alex gave the witch an exaggerated wave and leaned over Jeff. "Hey, what's up?"

Jeff looked pale but otherwise okay. "I'm fine."

"Are you sure?" Cammie sat on the ice next to Jeff. "Does your leg hurt?"

"I don't think so." Jeff touched the knee gently then ran his fingers down to the ankle. "It's a little sore, but nothing is broken. There may be a small bruise on the calf, but it's nothing. I can still go to practice."

"Perhaps you'd better take it easy today." Cammie knew how deceptive injuries could be. A skater might think he was all right until the next morning when he couldn't get out of bed.

"No, I feel great, really." Jeff stood up, did several tentative strokes, moved into a fast sit spin, then tried a waltz jump. "Nothing hurts, thanks."

"Good!" Cammie sighed with relief.

"You'd better be careful, Jeff." Alex said seriously. He was looking in the direction of the corner behind which Winja had disappeared. "Winja has you marked. We heard it last year when we were at the Black Rink. Remember, Cammie?"

Cammie nodded.

"Oh, I'll be fine. Next time I see her, I'll just kick her hard." Jeff giggled and brushed the snow off his pants. "I've got to go. So when do we meet tomorrow?"

Alex thought for a moment. "Seven in the morning in front of the Skating Museum, okay?"

Jeff nodded. "I'll be there."

English Skating Style

W hat's wrong with that guy?" Alex asked angrily. He sat on a high-back chair in the English section of the Skating Museum, leafing through the history book. Alex was already dressed in the common style of nineteenth-century English skaters—a medium-length black coat and dark pants. He had also replaced his wool hat with a felt cap.

Cammie thought Alex looked very distinguished in his new outfit. The English clothes made her friend appear older and more mature. Cammie looked at her own clothes and admitted regretfully that they were much less suited for skating than

Alex's dapper attire. Cammie wore a long skirt that covered her legs down to the ankles. *No wonder those skaters of old never tried doubles,* Cammie thought angrily. She had also put her long hair up in a chignon and secured it with bobby pins. The bobby pins kept sliding out, and Cammie had to keep tucking them back in as though she had nothing better to do.

This time, Cammie and Alex didn't have to cover their boots with patterned cloth imitating leather straps. In fact, Alex had made no alterations to his skates at all. He had explained to Cammie that in the nineteenth-century, some people already wore blades attached to their boots. Of course, toe picks were still non-existent, but they hoped no one would notice. But Cammie still had to cover her boots with black boot covers, because in the nineteenth century, women's boots were black, just like men's.

So Cammie and Alex were all set and ready to go, and the only thing that was missing was Jeff. He still hadn't come, and Alex was upset.

"I wish I hadn't promised to take him along with us," Alex said angrily.

He glanced at the clock hanging on the wall. The big hand came to life and jumped to thirty-one.

Alex closed the book with a snap. "We don't have all day!"

"Maybe his coach didn't let him miss practices. Let's just go without him, okay?" Cammie was tired of waiting too.

Alex sighed, looking uncertain. "But I promised him. You saw how upset he was yesterday. I don't want to be called a liar again."

"What if he's sick? Hey, do you think his leg is still bothering him? Winja hit it pretty hard."

Alex shook his head. "It didn't look bad to me. Besides, Jeff said he was fine."

"I don't know, then." Cammie jumped off her chair and began to pace the English Hall. She couldn't sit still anymore. Cammie approached one of the wax figures and gave it a critical look. The young man appeared to be drawing a beak, his right leg bent deeply, his left toe touching the right ankle. She grimaced as she remembered that in nineteenth-century England skaters did nothing but figures. Probably their trip to England would be very much like a show practice, with Coach Ferguson drilling them in school figures.

"A quarter of eight, that's it!" Alex stood up. "We'll just have to explain to Jeff that we couldn't wait all day. Who knows how much time we'll need in England?"

"Okay." Cammie walked away from the figure of a woman tracing perfectly round circles.

Alex spread the history book on the ice and opened it to the chapter entitled "Skating in England, 19th Century." They stepped on the page, the English Hall vanished, and they were pulled forward.

Cammie closed her eyes, and when she opened them again, they stood on a snow-covered lawn surrounded by dark trees. About a hundred feet ahead lay a huge frozen pond. The ice was dark gray and looked smooth, and about a dozen of skaters zoomed back and forth. Cammie immediately noticed that most of the skaters were adults, although she did see some boys in their late teens and two girls closer to her age.

The people's skating levels were very different. The children seemed to be unable to do anything more challenging than merely gliding around the perimeter of the rink. But even basic stroking appeared different from what Cammie was used to. The skaters pushed off their inside edges, keeping their feet in a turned-out position. Cammie thought it was ugly and, judging from Alex's facial expression, he felt the same way. Adult men, who looked very polished in their long coats, did three turns, rockers, and brackets one after another. They seemed to be trying their best to make the ice tracings just right.

Cammie also saw that as the skaters moved around the rink, their legs were perfectly straight, and their arms hung loosely alongside their bodies. Any Skateland coach would yell at a skater who did that, and yet Cammie had to admit that the figures that appeared from the English skaters' blades were the best she had ever seen. Even Coach Ferguson, who was a stickler for perfection, couldn't come close to the nineteenth-century English skaters. Of course, Wilhelmina was probably that good too.

Cammie approached the pond and stared at a tall, skinny boy, a couple of years older than Alex, who drew three smaller circles in a row, all on one foot. The end result was something looking like an exotic flower. Cammie had never seen anything like that.

"It's a shamrock, miss," the boy said. He had obviously noticed Cammie's admiring look.

"I want to try it," Alex said from behind Cammie. "May I?"

Cammie watched the English boy nod.

Alex stepped on the ice and tried to repeat the English boy's moves. Apparently, the shamrock figure was more challenging than it looked. Though Alex managed to draw three circles on the ice, they were lopsided and different in size.

"Hmm, you need to work more on it," the English boy said, now looking a little smug. He stretched his hand to Alex. "I am Thomas. What's your name?"

Alex introduced himself. Thomas turned to Cammie, and she gave him her name too.

"You fellows must be Americans?" Thomas asked with interest. His English accent made him appear snobbish, though the boy was quite friendly.

"That's right." Alex bent down and tightened his laces.

"Welcome to London Skating Club or merely Skating Club, which is the common way of referring to it," Thomas said.

"Oh, so you have a club here?" Alex sounded very interested.

"Right you are. Do you skate too, Cammie?"

"Of course," Cammie said.

"I invite the two of you to join me and my colleagues for this skating session," Thomas said.

"Thank you, we appreciate it," Alex said. "But actually we're looking for someone here, a friend."

"Can I be of assistance?" Thomas asked.

"It's a girl; she's from America too, and her name is Sonia Harrison," Alex said.

Thomas tightened his face in concentration. It was then that Cammie noticed that the boy was quite good looking with slightly wavy, light brown hair and deep, gray eyes.

"And why are you sure your friend Sonia is here? What is she doing in Great Britain? Is she meeting relatives?"

"No!" Cammie and Alex said in unison.

It was always difficult to explain to strangers why Sonia was expected to be in this or that historical period. How could Cammie and Alex tell Thomas, a sophisticated young man from nineteenth-century England, that Sonia had been abducted by skating witches?

"Someone…hmm…some bad people took Sonia away to England…or maybe, not even to England, to some other place…" Alex stammered. Cammie could see he was struggling to find the right words.

Thomas furrowed his dark eyebrows, looking positively confused. "So you are not even sure your friend is in England. But supposing she is, why do you think she is at the rink?"

"Because she is a skater," Alex said.

"A very good skater," Cammie hastened to add. "The best in Skateland…hmm, our club."

"Oh, I see." Thomas lowered his head for a moment, appearing deep in thought. "Of course, a rink is the first place a skater would rush to, no matter what country of the world she is in. I would surely do the same thing. So what's Sonia's surname?"

"Harrison," Alex said.

Thomas thought for a moment then shook his head. "No, I don't find the name familiar. You say she is a good skater. What figures is she able to perform particularly well?"

"Figures?" Cammie repeated dully.

"Well, she can probably do some, but that's not her strength," Alex said.

"Sonia is one of our best jumpers, and her spins are pretty good too," Cammie exclaimed, surprised at herself. She couldn't believe she had just called Sonia a good skater without feeling jealous.

Thomas, however, looked positively annoyed. "Spins and jumps? But this is fancy skating, fellows. Not English style."

"Fancy skating? What do you mean?" Cammie had never heard the term before.

"This is what we call dancing on ice," Thomas said. "It's completely inappropriate. Figure skating isn't ballet; it's a serious sport. The beauty of figure skating lies in the symmetry and precision of figures that one can trace on the ice."

Cammie and Alex's facial expressions must have spoken more eloquently than any words.

"What? Do you disagree?"

Cammie didn't say anything. Alex shrugged.

"Okay, do you see this chap?"

Cammie turned in the direction Thomas was pointing. An older man skated on his left blade, drawing a perfect letter *Q* on the ice. He completed the figure, switched feet, and repeated his moves. The two letters looked absolutely identical.

"Wow!" Alex exclaimed.

"He has been here since the club first opened in 1830," Thomas said. "His *Q* figure is the best in the club. It took him four winters to master it."

Cammie thought she had heard Thomas wrong. "Four months?"

"No, four winters. For figures, you need perfect edges. See, I finally got my outside edges right. That was pretty quick; it took me only two seasons. Let me show you!"

Thomas skated away from them. He took the T-position and moved forward on his right outside edge, nice and deep. So what?

Cammie glanced at Alex and saw that he was trying hard not to laugh. Outside edges, that was kids' stuff! Okay, Thomas did a good job with figures; Cammie had to hand it to the young man. But two years to learn outside edges? Cammie would die from boredom!

"So what do you think?" Thomas was back, beaming with unmistakable satisfaction.

Trying to be polite, Cammie forced a pleasant smile. "Yes, your edges are good."

Alex, however, remained silent. Instead he gave Thomas a very meaningful look and skated to the middle of the rink. He stroked hard around the perimeter of the pond, causing other skaters to duck, though he evaded the club members who were busy doing figures. Alex got on his right forward outside edge, making it deep and long. He did a change of edge, a Mohawk. Now he was on his right backward outside edge. He stepped forward … Cammie gasped, fearing that her friend might go for an axel. Of course, she realized how strong the temptation was. She too was eager to show the snobbish club members what real skaters could do. Yet at the last minute, Alex must have remembered Wilhelmina's warning, for he slowed down, did a three turn, and skated back to the edge of the rink, where Cammie and Thomas were waiting for him.

"Jolly good!" Thomas said.

Actually, Cammie expected the young man to scream or jump with excitement. Alex was a much better skater. Well, perhaps, the British skaters were more reserved by nature.

Now it was Cammie's turn. She demonstrated flawless outside and inside edges on both feet, did alternating three turns, and finished her routine with a fast scratch spin. She skated back, expecting a better reception than Alex had got.

To her utter disappointment, Thomas didn't look pleased.

"That last thing you did was fancy skating." The young man's lips, already narrow, looked like a fine thread now.

"But it's beautiful!" Cammie exclaimed.

"It's sloppy. Totally asymmetrical. Of course, you are allowed an occasional pirouette on ice, but an excessive use of ballet moves is completely inappropriate. Besides, pirouettes look much better when performed on both feet."

"Two-foot spins? But they are for tots!" Cammie shouted indignantly.

Thomas raised his eyebrows. "I beg your pardon? What was the last word you used? I'm not familiar with American slang."

"Tots are toddlers, kids under five years old," Alex explained. "What Cammie meant is that two-foot spins are only done by beginner skaters."

Thomas looked at the ice. "Hmm, I see your point. A pirouette isn't a particularly difficult move. You can probably learn it in one year. But you have to be older and a much more advanced skater to master figures."

"But figures aren't even that hard; they are just boring!" Cammie snapped.

Now it was Thomas' turn to be amused. "Not hard? Do you really think so? All right, how about trying a heart?"

Without waiting for Cammie's answer, Thomas jumped back on the ice and did what looked like a simple three turn connected with a triangle. The figure that appeared on the ice really looked like a heart. Cammie noticed that Thomas had held the inside edge until the shape was completed. So that was the heart figure. Cammie remembered seeing a heart among the candies from the Sweet Blades store ... well, whatever Thomas might have said, the figure didn't look particularly difficult to her.

"Piece of cake!" Alex declared. He went into an outside three turn—that was really nothing. He held the inside edge long enough, and ... well, perhaps, technically everything was fine, but the shape that had emerged from Alex's blade looked more like an ear than a heart.

Alex stopped and examined the results of his unfortunate attempt. "Hmm."

"Actually, it's not bad for the first time." Thomas gave Alex a reassuring smile.

"What do you mean *not bad*?" Alex grumbled. "It's not even close to yours. I drew an ear, not a heart."

"So it means you're playing it by ear." Thomas giggled.

He must have noticed Alex's angry look. "Don't worry, you'll get it. I've been working on mine for three seasons."

"Well, I've been skating for four years, and not just in winter, in summer too." Cammie said angrily.

Thomas's gray eyes widened. "In summer too? But where do you find ice then? Does it get that cold in America?"

"Hmm, sometimes." Cammie felt she was on a shaky ground. She turned her face away from Thomas and caught Alex's warning look. He was right; she'd better not say anything else.

"You are lucky, then," Thomas said with a tone of jealously in his voice. "Would you like to try a heart now, Cammie?"

Cammie knew she wasn't strong at drawing shapes on ice. Besides, the heart wasn't even on the list of the mandatory figures for the show. But she had to prove that four years of skating meant something. Besides, what could be so difficult about doing a three turn followed by a long inside edge?

She glided forward, trying to look confident. The three-turn part was fine, but when she tried to hold her inside edge, it kept pushing her in a wrong direction. She stopped and studied her tracings.

The shape on the ice looked more like a lip than a heart.

"Now you're giving me a lip service," Thomas spoke up from the edge of the rink.

That guy really had very unique sense of humor.

Cammie clenched her teeth. She would get that stupid heart whatever it took her. She glided forward again, determined to do a better job this time. She still couldn't draw a discernable heart.

Alex puffed next to her, apparently trying his best too. His hearts were definitely better than Cammie's—not missing show practices must have paid off—but they didn't even come close to Thomas's perfect figures.

"I can't do it." Cammie finally gave up.

Alex stopped next to her, wiping perspiration from his forehead. "Yeah, it's more difficult than I thought."

"Well, I can also do a Q figure, and do you know what you will get when you do two in a row?" Thomas looked at them excitedly.

Cammie and Alex shook their heads at the same time.

"Spectacles!"

"Spectacles? Wait!" Cammie rubbed her forehead. She had heard the word somewhere before. Of course! It was in one of the questions on the history test. She had had to choose the object that was *not* a school figure. Gosh, and she had selected spectacles. Oh, no!

"So spectacles is a school figure?" Cammie asked sadly.

"Sure. Let me show you." Thomas moved forward eagerly.

Cammie looked at Alex. "Can you believe it? I thought *can opener* was a school figure. "

Alex stifled a giggle. "You'd better not tell him that; he'll laugh you to scorn."

Thomas was skating back, looking at the two of them expectantly. No doubt he was waiting for a compliment.

"Well, you are very good, of course, but freestyle…I mean fancy skating is still better," Cammie said firmly.

Thomas shrugged. "I guess it's a matter of taste. Fancy skating probably appeals to American people more. Actually, your champion is going to skate at our rink tonight."

"Who are you talking about? What champion?" Alex asked.

"Jackson Haines. You ought to know him. He's the champion of America; this is what is written on the advertisement."

"Oh yes!" Cammie exclaimed. So that was the guy Jeff wanted to see so badly.

"No, we never saw him perform," Alex said to Thomas.

"The tickets are very expensive, but I'm sure I can get you free passes from the club. Would you like to see the show?"

Cammie looked at Alex, not knowing what to answer. On the one hand, they had to look for Sonia. On the other hand, seeing Jackson Haines would be exciting. Cammie pictured herself telling Jeff how they had met his idol in person. Well, it would serve Jeff right. He should have come to the museum this morning. Boy, he would be so jealous!

"Of course, we'll be happy to see Jackson Haines's performance," Alex said.

"Good decision. Please wait for me here. I'll be right back. Oh, and I'll ask around if someone has seen your friend Sonia." Thomas stepped off the ice and walked on the pressed snow in the direction of a brick house that housed the quarters of the Skating Club.

"Are you really so excited about watching Jackson Haines's show?" Cammie asked Alex.

Alex was watching Thomas. "Uh, why not? He's a historical figure, after all. Jeff likes him."

"But how about you? What male skater would you like to meet?"

Alex thought for a moment. "I don't know. Evan Lysacek, probably. I like his quad toe loop."

"Me, I would like to meet Johnny Weir," Cammie said dreamily. "He is so graceful."

"Are you fellows still talking about fancy skating?" Thomas had already returned, two tickets in his hand.

"So they gave us tickets?" Alex asked.

"Sure. You are our guests. Unfortunately, no one has seen Sonia Harrison. I'm afraid your friend isn't here."

Cammie caught Alex's disappointed look. So Sonia wasn't in England either. They would have to travel to another historical period. Well, Wilhelmina had warned them they might have to try several places.

"Let's just enjoy the show, okay?" Alex whispered.

Cammie shrugged. "Sure."

For nothing better to do, Cammie and Alex spent the time before Jackson Haines's performance practicing figures for the show. Amazingly, toward the end of the session, Cammie's figure eight looked much better. There was hardly more than an inch separating the tracings of the first and the second figure.

I wish Coach Ferguson could see me now, Cammie thought as she repeated her figure over and over again.

And then the skaters were asked to leave the ice, and a group of people armed with brooms and mops walked to the center of the rink. Cammie watched them in total amazement. She had completely forgotten that there were no Zamboni machines in nineteenth-century England. The workers swept and swept the ice as though it was a living room floor, not a pond. Somehow, Cammie doubted that they would make the ice smooth enough with their primitive-looking tools. But to her great surprise, the workers did a very good job. When they walked off the pond, the rink sparkled clean, as though no one had ever skated on its gray ice.

Thomas led Cammie and Alex to their seats in the fourth row, very close to the edge of the rink.

"We'll have the greatest frolic of our lives," Thomas said, and Cammie believed him.

Jackson Haines's Show

Jackson Haines's show was nothing like *Stars on Ice*. The performance was going to be held not in a nice hall, but outside, at the pond rink. As evening approached, the cold wind had picked up, and Cammie was beginning to feel chilly. She sat on a long bench between Alex and Thomas, and the rest of the seats in their row were occupied by other Skating Club members. With its high straight back and hard wood seat, the bench was quite uncomfortable.

A group of musicians dressed in wool tailcoats and dark breeches positioned themselves on the edge of the rink. Cammie recognized a clarinet and a violin, but there were other instruments she had never seen. She asked Thomas what they were.

"That's a French horn, and the chap on your right is going to play the trombone. Isn't it queer, though? Who would fancy skating to music?"

"And why not?" Alex asked.

Thomas looked at him as though Alex were a child who didn't understand elementary things. "Music is distracting."

"But look—"

Before Alex could say something in defense of freestyle skating, the musicians began to play a cheerful piece.

A gaunt man wearing a top hat skated to the middle of the rink. "Ladies and gentlemen, let's extend a warm welcome to Jackson Haines, the American champion!"

Automatically, Cammie and Alex brought their hands together to greet the famous skater. To their great surprise, the audience remained stiff and quiet. Cammie saw Alex's cheeks turn pink as he quickly put his hands down. Feeling ill at ease, Cammie stuffed her hands into her pockets.

The orchestra struck up a drum roll, and Jackson Haines skated to the middle of the rink. Though short, he appeared very muscular. The American champion wore a bright red jacket trimmed with gold. A high hat with a plumage sat tight on his head; Cammie thought he looked like royalty. Jackson Haines's boots were high, almost reaching his knees, and they were trimmed with fur. But what was most encouraging, his blades were attached to the boots. Cammie leaned against the hard back with satisfaction. Finally, there was a real skater.

Next to her, Thomas fidgeted nervously. "Look at his attire. And the boots! The blades are glued to the soles."

"Not glued but fastened with screws," Alex said.

Cammie could see that her friend was trying hard not to smile.

"It's actually very comfortable," Cammie said, thinking that perhaps they could sell Thomas on real skates. Surely Wilhelmina wouldn't mind. Jackson Haines's blades were attached to his boots, and that was acceptable.

"I wonder where he leaves his street shoes before stepping onto the ice," Thomas asked. "Isn't he afraid they might be stolen?"

Cammie shrugged. "He probably leaves them in the locker room."

Alex kicked her.

Cammie felt herself blush. "I mean—"

Before Cammie could finish her sentence, the orchestra started playing a dazzling waltz. Jackson Haines's eyes lit up; he spread his arms gracefully and went forward on a deep outside edge. There was something electrifying in the way he carried himself. Jackson Haines wasn't merely going through the motions; Cammie could see that he was truly enjoying himself. The music became faster; Jackson

Haines's blades rushed forward too, in perfect harmony with the tune.

When the famous skater leaped forward, for a split second, he looked as though he were about to fly off the ice. He glided, he jumped, he pirouetted—all in one smooth motion. His moves were graceful and perfectly polished. As Jackson Haines circled the rink in deep backward crossovers, he looked as poised as a ballet dancer. His edges were impeccably clean, and his arms seemed to have a language of their own. They flew like birds; they swerved and flowed; they shot up in triumph then pleaded for mercy.

"Wow!" Cammie blurted out.

Jackson Haines hurried to the middle of the rink and whirled around in a fast scratch spin. Before Cammie could take it all in, the skater performed an equally gorgeous spin in the opposite direction.

"Amazing!" Alex muttered.

Cammie knew what he meant. Few skaters could spin equally well in both directions.

Meanwhile, Jackson Haines went into a series of high leaps. Cammie recognized a ballet jump and a mazurka jump. Of course, she could do those too, but hers were not as high as Jackson Haines's. She sighed, feeling slightly jealous.

When the first number was over, Jackson Haines skated to the side of the rink and pulled off his red coat. Cammie watched him change into a blue jacket and fasten a matching belt around his waist.

"I like his outfits," Cammie whispered to Alex.

He nodded without taking his eyes off the skating champion.

This time, the music sounded like a march. Jackson Haines bent his left leg deeply and went into a very low sit spin. His free leg was perfectly parallel to the ice.

"Hmm, now I understand why Wilhelmina drilled Jeff so much on that sit spin," Alex said.

Cammie nodded, knowing that Alex was thinking about his own sit spin. Cammie had to hand it to Jackson Haines; he was a better spinner than Alex. The amazing thing was that whatever Jackson Haines did, he made it look easy, as though there was no effort to it. And yet Cammie understood how much practice it had taken the famous skater to get to that level. She shook her head in admiration, thinking that if Jackson Haines could join them on their trip to the twenty-first century, he would definitely get an invitation to *Stars on Ice*, or perhaps to *Disney on Ice*.

Next to Cammie, Alex was clapping hard. It meant the dance was over, and Cammie hadn't even noticed it. Cammie joined Alex happily as Jackson Haines stepped off the ice again and reappeared two minutes letter dressed like ... a bear!

"Disgusting!" a woman in a gray tweed jacket hissed.

"That's right. He's making a goose of himself," Thomas said indignantly.

Cammie giggled. "Not a goose; a bear!"

Thomas tightened his lips and looked away.

"What do you understand, anyway, figure freak," Alex said very softly, but Cammie could still hear him. She suppressed a chuckle.

Down at the rink, Jackson Haines was performing a fast joyful dance. Even the bulky furry outfit of a bear didn't take away from the skater's perfect posture.

Cammie could barely stay in her seat, watching the skater's every move. She wanted to skate like him; she pictured herself doing the same number, sharing a story with the audience, becoming one with music. She wanted to forget about the fear of not landing a difficult jump. What did it matter anyway? The important thing was to let go, so everyone could enjoy the beauty of her sport.

Jackson Haines did a series of very quick turns then threw himself in the air, landed on his right blade, and went into a back spin.

"A toe pick would help a lot," Alex said.

"What? His skates don't have toe picks?" Cammie was shocked. Jackson Haines could do jumps... well, those were only half-revolution jumps, but they still looked graceful.

"A quadrille on ice. Doesn't it look preposterous?" the woman in a tweed jacket said to the man next to her.

"Right you are, dear, and all those cheap tricks..."

Cammie made a nasty face and turned slightly away, so she could see only Jackson Haines.

Perhaps Jackson Haines's technique wasn't up to modern freestyle skating standards—he didn't land any multi-revolution jumps—yet his energy was contagious. At some point, Cammie stopped paying attention to what the skater was doing. The technique didn't matter.

Jackson Haines stood in the middle of the ice, taking his bows. Cammie hadn't even noticed that an hour had passed. The famous skater was breathing hard, yet he never stopped smiling.

"Yes!" Alex applauded so fervently that a man with a newspaper frowned and moved slightly away. Alex ignored him.

Unable to contain herself, Cammie rose from her seat and waved at the American champion. Jackson Haines seemed to have noticed her, for he smiled and waved back.

"U.S.A.!" Cammie cheered.

She felt half a dozen eyes stare at her with apparent disapproval. All around her, people were moving away, their lips tightened, their eyes narrowed. Even Thomas looked fidgety.

"I'm afraid I'm going to take my leave now. It was nice meeting you," Thomas said stiffly. He started walking away from them.

"Bye!" Cammie and Alex shouted.

Thomas turned around, his gray eyes cold and sad. "Farewell, then."

He joined a group of teenagers, all of whom stared at Cammie and Alex as though they were some exotic animals.

"Never mind them. What do they know? Come on, let's talk to Jackson Haines!" Alex said excitedly.

"Oh, absolutely. Maybe, we can even get his autograph."

They pressed through the crowd against the flow of people exiting from the park. As Cammie looked back, she saw dark outlines of carriages outside. The horses clicked their hooves against the cobblestone pavement. Cammie felt sullen looks on her; then someone hissed at Alex after he stepped on somebody's foot and apologized. Well, clearly the Londoners hadn't liked Jackson Haines's performance. How unfair! The American champion was so much better than the snobbish figure-lovers Cammie and Alex had seen, yet he had received such a cold reception.

Jackson Haines stood next to the entrance to the rink.

"Hello, Mr. Haines," Alex said timidly.

The skater's brown eyes slid down Alex's face, and rested on his skates.

"Mr. Haines, we just wanted to let you know how much we enjoyed your performance," Alex said passionately.

"Oh, yes, that was pretty cool!" Cammie exclaimed.

"Oh, thank you. You may call me Jackson," the skater said.

His eyes brightened. "Are the two of you Americans?"

They nodded.

"Oh, it's wonderful. And thank you for your support. This crowd was so ... so cold." Jackson Haines did an exaggerated shudder, making Cammie and Alex giggle.

"Although back home, they don't like my skating that much either," Jackson Haines said. "I'm heading for Vienna now. Hopefully the Austrians will be more open to my style. After all, the Viennese appreciate music so much more. You must have heard of Johannes Strauss."

"Of course!" Cammie had once skated a program to a waltz by Strauss, and she had enjoyed the music.

"Oh, you'll be a real hit in Vienna!" Alex said confidently.

Jackson Haines laughed heartily. "I appreciate your vote of confidence, young man, what's your name? Alex? Okay, Alex, thank you for your support, but you never know—"

"I'm telling you, they will be falling off their seats. You will become a skating celebrity," Alex said.

Cammie pinched Alex. What did he think he was doing? Of course, they both knew that Jackson

Haines would be a success in Vienna, but how could they explain that to the skater?

Jackson Haines was smiling broadly. "You two are the best. Hey, I like your skates."

His eyes shifted from Alex's blades to Cammie's then to Alex's again. "Do you mind if I take a look?"

Alex hesitated for a moment. He cast a quick glance at Cammie. She shrugged. Of course, it would be better for Jackson Haines not to see their modern blades. On the other hand, saying no would be a very rude thing to do, and Jackson Haines had already been unfairly spurned by the British public.

Alex must have been thinking along the same line, for he quickly took his left skate off. "Here!"

Jackson Haines accepted the boot gently, carefully, as though it were a porcelain cup. "Your blade is attached to the boot, I see. Good. Just like mine. And the blades are nice and sharp—you must be taking good care of them... good steel, yes. You can probably get good, deep edges, right?"

Alex nodded. "I hope my edges are good. So are Cammie's. Her name is Cammie, by the way.

"Oh hi, Cammie. Nice to meet you," Jackson Haines said absentmindedly.

He ran his index finger along the bottom of the blade. "It's not as rounded as mine, more flat—it should help with balance. Goodness gracious! What on earth are these?"

The skater's fingers rested on the toe pick. "What are these claws for? How ridiculous! Why would you want the claws? Don't you trip over them?"

Alex's facial expression changed from delightful to patronizing. "Of course, not. I—"

"Are yours the same?" Jackson Haines interrupted. He was staring at Cammie's skates.

"Do you mind lifting your foot, Cammie?"

With a very strong feeling that they weren't doing the right thing, Cammie raised her foot obediently.

"Fascinating, really fascinating! But what's the point? I'd surely trip," Jackson Haines muttered.

Feeling they had nothing to lose, Cammie began to speak very fast. "Toe picks help you to get a better grip of ice on jumps and spins."

"Is that so?" Jackson Haines asked sharply.

"Naturally!" Cammie demonstrated the basic entry to a scratch spin. "See, right before you get on the backward inside edge, you stay on the toe pick for just a split second. It makes the change of edges much easier."

"Hmm," Jackson Haines said.

"Toe picks help with jumps too," Alex said. "You're supposed to land on your toe pick before gliding backwards on your outside edge. That's the only way you can control your landing on multi-revo—oops, big jumps."

Cammie saw Alex's cheeks turn very red.

"How interesting! To tell you the truth, I've never thought of this. Although I did feel something was missing in my skates. I wish I could jump higher, but it's a little dangerous. So—"

"Jackson, if you want to leave tonight, we'd better get going. The musicians are all packed and ready to move," a deep voice said from the darkness.

A split second later, a tall bulky man in a black leather coat appeared from behind Jackson Haines.

"Sure!" The American skater was now studying the screws of Alex's blade.

"Or, if you'd rather spend another night in England, I'm game." The man in the leather coat rubbed his hands. "We could go to that Irish pub and—"

"Oh, not another night in this cold place! I want to leave tonight." With obvious reluctance, Jackson Haines handed the skate back to Alex. "Thank you, my friends. I'll definitely think of improving my skates now that I've talked to you. I wish we could chat longer, but duty calls."

The famous skater turned around to leave, but Cammie shouted, "Wait!"

Jackson Haines looked back, but Cammie paused. There were a lot of things she wanted to tell the American champion. That one day, his style would be accepted by everybody. That he would be known as the father of freestyle. That in the future, all skaters would use music for their routines. That one day, joy and excitement would be considered an advantage, not sloppiness. That judges would reward artistry and audiences would give skaters standing ovations for their big jumps and fast spins. Costumes would become very important in figure skating, and skaters who would be able to tell a story on ice would be considered the best performers.

Yes, there were many things Cammie could tell Jackson Haines, but she knew she had to be quiet, because the time had not come yet. And because history couldn't be changed. Instead, she looked Jackson Haines in the eyes and said timidly, "Could we please have your autograph?"

Jackson Haines looked both excited and surprised. "Sure. Do you have a piece of paper?"

Cammie rummaged in the pockets of her sweater that she wore underneath her English-style jacket and produced a flyer with "Green Rink Practice Schedule" written on top. Making sure Jackson Haines couldn't see the inscription, Cammie asked the American skater to sign the other side.

For a moment, Jackson Haines stared at the ballpoint pen. Apparently, he wanted to ask where Cammie had gotten it. Cammie realized she had made another blunder, but—

"Jackson!" the American skater's companion called again.

"Coming!" Jackson Haines shouted back.

He took the flyer from Cammie's hand and quickly wrote, "From Jackson Haines with love. Skate well!"

"Thank you so much!" Cammie and Alex yelled in unison.

Jackson Haines raised his hand, bidding them goodbye. "Enjoy your nice skates. Yes, and I'll definitely be working on improving mine. Definitely. "

"Have a good time in Vienna!" Alex waved at Jackson Haines.

The American champion waved back, and a moment later, darkness swallowed him.

"Well, it's time for us to go too," Alex said and took the history book out of his pocket.

"Alex, what if Wilhelmina finds out that we showed our skates to Jackson Haines?" Cammie asked after they changed into their streets clothes.

Alex looked a little worried. "You think it changed figure skating history?"

"I don't know. Perhaps. No one had skates with toe picks back then."

"Well, actually, it was Jackson Haines who first used toe picks."

Cammie's heart leaped in her chest. "He did? No, wait! Remember how surprised he was when he was looking at our blades? He surely knew nothing about toe picks."

"But it says so in the history book. Look." Alex opened the book and read, "Toe picks were first introduced by the American skater Jackson Haines in the 1870s. See? Oh wait, gosh!"

"What's wrong?" Cammie came up to Alex and stared at the history book too.

"In the 1870s," Alex said slowly. "And we were in England in 1864."

"Oh!" Cammie contorted her face in concentration.

"Which means Jackson Haines really knew nothing about toe picks then."

"But we told him," Cammie said slowly. "And—"

"And it means that we did change figure skating history," Alex said angrily.

"Oh, no!" Cammie plopped herself on the floor and hit the hard surface with her fist. "Wilhelmina's going to kill us."

"Do we have to tell her?" Alex closed the book and put it back into his pocket.

"I guess. What if everything isn't lost yet? What if she can do something? She has powers."

Alex let out a deep sigh and shook his head. "Man, I tried so hard not to say something I wasn't supposed to."

"Yes, me too."

"Well, you did start talking about indoor rinks and locker rooms and—"

"Come on, Thomas didn't notice anything!"

Alex stood up. "I hope he didn't. Let's go."

As they closed the heavy museum door behind them, Cammie remembered another thing. "Hey, what're we going to tell Jeff?"

"We don't have to tell him anything!" Alex said angrily. "He was the one who didn't show up."

"But what if he's sick?"

Alex chewed his lip pensively. "You can come to our dorm with me if you want. We can talk to Jeff together. It's only seven-thirty now; that's not too late."

"Okay." Cammie hurried after Alex. The more she thought about Jeff, the more worried she was. He had been so adamant about joining them. She only hoped nothing terrible had happened to him.

The boys' dorm was about four blocks away from where Cammie lived. Unlike the girls' dorm building that had an old classical look, the boys' five-story dorm had a distinctly modern appearance. Alex pulled the front door, and together they walked into the spacious lobby, where three walls were made of glass. There were two elevators along the fourth wall and a skating calendar hung on the panel between them. The picture on the calendar showed Jeremy Abbot.

"He landed a good quad at the Grand Prix Final this year," Alex said. "And I hope I'll be able to do quads too one day."

"Sure you will."

Alex pressed the elevator button.

"May I help you?"

Cammie looked back at the security desk near the entrance. When they walked into the building, there was no one there. Now, however, the chair next to the table was occupied by a man who looked like a boxer. He wore tight black jeans and a tight T-shirt that did nothing to conceal his bulging muscles.

The T-shirt was decorated with a Skateland logo of a spinning skater holding a flower representing rinks of different colors. The letters underneath the logo said, "Skateland Security."

"Oh hi, Rick!" Alex said sounding slightly surprised. "Are you on duty tonight? Where's Mr. Simpson?"

"Taking the night off. The authorities voted for tougher security," Rick said in an important voice.

Alex looked confused. "But why now?"

"Should have done it long ago, right after the girl had been abducted. Would have been safer for all of you kids. And now another kid got attacked, so we have strict orders not to let any strangers in. Now she doesn't live in this dorm, does she?" Rick nodded in Cammie's direction.

Alex raised his hand. "Whoa, wait a minute! Did you say someone was attacked?"

"Yup. Yesterday evening, actually. But I didn't find out till this morning, so—"

"But...hey, who was attacked?"

"Jeffrey Patterson," Rick said.

"Jeff!" Alex yelled.

"Do you want to visit Jeff? I'm sure it won't hurt him. It's suspicious-looking hoodlums that I'm instructed not to let in. Believe me, I can tell a witch from a distance, and this girl isn't one of them."

Cammie suddenly felt there wasn't enough air in the lobby. She grabbed the side of Rick's table. "Witches?"

"Well, sure. Who do you think attacked Jeff? Only a witch could do that."

"What exactly happened?" Alex asked quickly.

Rick shrugged. "All I know is that some witch approached him, and he got hurt. You'd better ask him all the details. What a shame, though! Jeff is an excellent skater, and he has one of the leading parts in the show. Now who knows if the performance will even take place! Okay, he's in room 401, if you don't know. What's your name, young lady? Cammie Wester? Okay, I have it written down. Go on, then."

Whispering a quick "thank you," Cammie followed Alex to the elevator. She still couldn't recover from the shock. So Jeff was injured. But what had really happened? Yesterday he had told them his leg didn't hurt. Unless... Cammie stopped abruptly. Of course, if it was really one of Winja's attacks, Jeff could be plagued with recurring injuries again. Just like two years ago when Cammie and Alex had first met Jeff at Winja's rink. Jeff had told them back then that injuries never left him. He would fall and break his left wrist; then, after he had barely recovered, he would break his right ankle. And then the same would happen on the other side.

Jeff had battled injuries for a year; the doctors had merely shaken their heads, unable to explain what had been happening to the poor boy. One doctor had suspected that Jeff didn't have enough calcium in his body and warned him that he might have to give up skating for good. However, after a battery of tests, it had been decided that Jeff's calcium level was perfectly normal. Still, Jeff couldn't skate, and then Cammie and Alex had come across Winja's rink and rescued Jeff by performing a series of perfect edges. And now Jeff was hurting again.

"It's Winja again; I have no doubt about it," Alex said angrily as he pressed the fourth floor button.

"Stupid witch!" Cammie shook her fist in the air as though Winja could see her.

They walked along a long corridor covered with a thick navy blue carpet with white stars. There were doors on both sides, and most of them were decorated with pictures of famous skaters in the middle of their jumps and spins. Some doors had warnings and instructions. Apparently the owners took them very seriously.

Cammie slowed down and read: "Knock and Get Knocked Out of Your Skates," "Best Skateland Men," "Sucky Spinners, Keep Out!" "Don't Jump in if you are Not a Jumper," "Come and Try to Beat Me in the Short Program."

"These signs don't look particularly welcoming," Cammie said.

Alex chuckled. "Ignore them. It's our style."

The sign on Jeff's door said, "Double Axel Dudes Only."

"Boy, I'm not even allowed. I can't do the double axel yet." Cammie took a tentative step back.

"Oh, take it easy; it's just a joke. I know most of these guys, and believe me, half of them can only land double axels in their sleep."

Cammie looked at him sideways. "Half of them?"

"Hmm, okay, maybe, one third, or…a quarter. Who cares?" Alex knocked on Jeff's door and without waiting for an answer, kicked the wood surface with his skate guard. The door opened, and Alex stepped aside to let Cammie in first.

The small rectangular room was almost dark, except for a lonely lamp on the nightstand next to the bed to the right of the floor-length window. The venetian blinds were drawn. The bed on the left was empty, although Cammie saw hand weights sticking out from under it. Next to the bed stood a hockey stick. A boy lay on the right bed on top of the covers holding a book. His left leg was propped on a stack of pillows. There was no doubt Jeff had heard Cammie and Alex walk in, but he behaved as though he were still alone in the room. His eyes were staring stubbornly at the open book that, as Cammie had just noticed, he held upside down.

"Jeff!" Cammie called softly.

Jeff's shoulders twitched a little, but he still didn't raise his head. He continued ignoring his guests until Cammie approached the bed and snatched the book out of his hands. She glanced at the book cover and saw that it was *The Great Eight* by Scott Hamilton.

"Hi!" Alex said, perhaps a little too loudly.

Jeff raised his red and swollen eyes at them, blinked, and turned away quickly.

"Who plays hockey here?" Cammie pointed to the hockey stick.

Jeff folded his arms. "My roommate. His name is George. He's a good skater, but he won't say no to a game of hockey. Is that why you're here? To ask about George?"

"Could you just relax?" Alex asked.

Jeff turned away from them and stared at the beige wall as though it were a wide-screen TV showing men's Olympic free skate program.

"We aren't your enemies, you know," Alex said.

Jeff stopped studying the wall, his brown eyes now shooting fiery darts at Alex. "And what do you expect me to say? Okay, I'm injured again. So good-bye skating, and I won't be able to look for Sonia with you either. Now go ahead, laugh!"

Jeff's upper lip shook; he turned his head away angrily.

"Is it really that bad?" Cammie asked carefully. Merely admitting that you were injured wasn't enough. Skating injuries could be different. Most of them healed sooner or later, but some could destroy a skater's career. Cammie's worst fear was that Jeff was injured beyond repair.

"Well, it's a sprain. Not a bad one, at least, that's what the doctors say. I should be fine in a couple of weeks," Jeff said irritably.

"A couple of weeks? But that's great!" Cammie cried out. She felt tremendous relief.

"So what are you so upset for? Cheer up!" Alex patted Jeff on the shoulder.

Jeff jerked away from him.

"Look, buddy, what's your problem? Two weeks will be over before you have time to think about it. Just do what the doctors say, and you'll be fine. Actually, taking a break from skating isn't that bad. Sometimes this pressure really gets to me. I almost wish I could have some minor problem, so I could just take it easy."

Alex winked at Cammie, and she responded with a smile of understanding. She, too, felt that way sometimes. Especially on cold winter mornings when even the air froze in her lungs, making her fight for breath.

"You still don't get it, do you?" Jeff bolted up in his bed. The stack of cushions shook and fell. The abrupt move must have irritated Jeff's leg, for he grimaced

"I'll get them!" Ignoring Jeff's obvious annoyance, Cammie quickly readjusted the pillows.

"Jeff, you'll be up and healthy before the opening night of the show," Alex said.

"It's not the show I'm worried about."

Jeff leaned back, breathing hard. He closed his eyes for a moment. "Sorry, I didn't come this morning."

"Oh, we understand," Cammie said quickly.

"It happened during practice yesterday," Jeff said gloomily.

"But you said your leg didn't hurt after Winja hit it with her crutch," Alex said.

Jeff smiled wryly. "That's what I thought. I came to the rink and started skating, but something didn't feel right. I don't know. For some reason, I felt weak all over. I decided to keep pressing on, but then my leg sort of seized up, and then it buckled under me. Before I realized what happened, there I was sitting on the ice, and my ankle hurt like crazy. Why? I hadn't even tried any difficult moves."

Jeff exhaled slowly and rubbed his forehead. "I still thought I could skate the problem away, but I couldn't put weight on that leg."

Jeff blinked, and Cammie saw a tear roll down his cheek.

"So Coach Ferguson called the Medical Center, and they came and took me away," Jeff said miserably. "Now I'm not supposed to put any weight on that leg for a week, and I'm off ice for two weeks."

"It's not that long," Cammie said again.

Jeff hit his healthy leg with his fist. "Why do those injuries always have to happen to me? Does it mean I'm weak? Does it?"

"Don't be dense, man. It's a witch's attack, and you know that," Alex said.

"I wanted to go after Sonia with you, don't you understand?" Jeff took a deep breath. "Okay, tell me about your trip. Did you find her?"

"No, she wasn't there." Alex sounded apologetic.

"So what's next? Where are you going tomorrow?"

"We're not sure yet," Alex said. "I'm going to look through the history book again tonight, and we'll think about it tomorrow. Don't worry, we'll find her. Now look, we have something for you. It's sort of a surprise."

Alex gave Cammie a meaningful look, and Cammie nodded excitedly. She shook her small backpack off her shoulders and took out her Green Rink practice schedule with Jackson Haines's autograph on the back.

"Here!" Cammie handed the flyer to Jeff.

He turned it around and stared at the words written in slanted, old-fashioned handwriting,

"From Jackson Haines with love. Skate well," Jeff read slowly.

He raised his head, his eyes shining. "Is this … really from Jackson Haines himself?"

"Of course!" Cammie said.

"I can't believe it." Jeff reread the words, touching the letters with his finger.

Alex grinned. "Can you imagine? Jackson Haines was really shocked to see Cammie's ball-point pen with the Skateland logo. It's great that his companion took Jackson away right before he had a chance to ask us what it was."

"Tell me about him!" Jeff demanded.

Cammie and Alex spent the next half hour describing Jackson Haines's terrific performance. Jeff interrupted them bombarding them with questions, asking for details. By the end of their visit, Jeff looked positively better.

"I wish I had been there with you!" Jeff said for about the fifth time.

"Maybe you will one day," Alex said as the two of them got ready to leave. "You take care of yourself, all right? And we'll keep you informed."

"Thanks!"

WORLD'S GREATEST SKATER

"Tell you what," Alex said as the two of them met in front of Cammie's dorm at seven o'clock in the morning, "how about having a snack at Sweet Blades before we head to the past?"

"Uh, sure. Where exactly are we going?" Cammie asked.

"Well, I think it would be a good idea to go to Davos."

"Davos? Where's Davos?" Cammie had never heard the name before.

"Davos is in Switzerland."

"Switzerland? And what year will it be?"

"Well, I've been thinking a lot. It seems to me the year 1910 will be the best. See, there was a figure skating world championship that year in Davos, and it was really a big deal. By the way, Ulrich Salchow competed there. Can you imagine?" Alex smiled dreamily. "It would be really exciting to meet him. He landed his first salchow jump just a year before, at another world's."

"Wouldn't it be better to go there, then?"

"I thought about it." Alex slowed down a little for Cammie to catch up. "But you see, back in 1909, nobody knew that Ulrich Salchow was going to land that jump. A year later, however, there was a lot of excitement about it, and the crowd was larger. By that time, more skaters had tried to land a salchow. So it would have been logical for the witches to take Sonia to Davos. I don't believe they hid her somewhere where she would stand out. They would want her to blend in with the crowd, so the more people the better."

Cammie thought for a moment. Something didn't make sense. "But a single salchow isn't a big deal for Sonia. She can do a triple. So she'll definitely stand out. Maybe we need to go to a later period in history when skaters already did triples?"

"I told you," Alex said patiently, "at the time when triples became popular, people already had television. If the witches had sent Sonia to that period, every channel would have shown her big jumps. And people would have asked her where she was from and stuff. It would have changed skating history. It's not what the witches want to do; they are only trying to hurt Sonia."

"Okay, what will happen if people see Sonia do a triple salchow in 1910?"

Alex slowed down. Apparently, he was thinking of the same possibility. "Probably nothing. Sonia couldn't compete in Davos anyway."

"She might try."

Alex took his gloves off, blew on his frozen fingers, and pulled the history book out of his pocket. "See, it says here that only men competed in Davos. The ladies' event took place a week later in Berlin."

"Wow. Not even in the same country. Why did they do that?"

Alex shrugged. "How should I know? The point is, there is a good chance Sonia is in Davos."

"Okay." Visiting Switzerland might be an interesting experience.

"But we don't want to get there too early," Alex said. "It's still dark, and official practices won't start till probably nine o'clock. So we have time for hot chocolate or something."

"I'll have a skate pastry. A white one," Cammie said excitedly. Skate pastries were her favorite treats. Nothing could be more delicious than a rich, cocoa-filled cream boot topped with white chocolate. Add to it the sweet-and-sour flavor of the hard candy shaped like a blade and the fruity touch of the lace—you could choose any color you liked. Skate pastries were incredible.

"I want Three-Turn Ice Cream," Alex said enthusiastically.

"You're nuts. It's freezing."

Alex grinned at her puzzled expression. "I'll have a skating cocktail too. It will warm me up perfectly."

When they approached Sweet Blades, it was still pretty dark, though the first purplish pink streaks had already appeared in the horizon. The reflections of the brightly lit display windows of the stores and cafes circling Main Square shimmered on the ice.

At this early hour of the morning, the bakery was almost empty except for an older man in hockey skates. He sipped his coffee, perusing the latest issue of the newspaper *Skateland Daily News*. Cammie and Alex sat down at their favorite table facing the square. Cammie took off her gloves and shoved them into the pockets of her parka.

The smiling saleslady brought them their snacks. Cammie wrapped her fingers around her cup filled with steaming skating cocktail and stared at Alex's ice cream. It was a bright swirl of three colors—pink, yellow, and white.

"Is this why they call it Three-Turn Ice Cream? Because of the colors?" Cammie asked.

"Yes, but it also has these." Alex dug his spoon into the bright substance, and Cammie saw that the ice cream was sprinkled with chocolate chips in the shape of threes.

Cammie laughed. Of course! Everything in Skateland was skating related.

The door opened, bringing in a draft of cold air. A woman walked in with long blond hair spilling down her shoulders like a shawl. She wore a long fox coat, and big gold hoops glittered in her ears.

She must be a judge, Cammie thought. Because judges spent most of their time at cold rinks, they always wore very warm clothes. But this lady's outfit wasn't merely warm; it was gorgeous. Though tall and bulky, the lady carried herself like a skater. Keeping her shoulders perfectly straight, the woman approached the counter and exchanged quick words with the saleslady. The saleslady nodded. The classy-looking lady turned around, and Cammie saw with great surprise that she wore sunglasses.

"But it's still dark," Alex muttered.

The woman looked around the bakery; her eyes glided past the man with the newspaper and finally rested on Cammie and Alex. Looking determined, she walked right to their table and put her hand on one of the empty chairs. "Do you mind if I join you, young people?"

Though the lady had said *young people*, it was obvious that she was talking to Alex. She pierced him with her sunglass-covered eyes, a coy smile playing on her lips.

Immediately, Alex turned red. "Uh, sure." He gave Cammie an uncertain look and pushed his unfinished ice cream away. Then as though remembering something, Alex jumped to his feet and pushed one of the empty chairs closer to the woman, inviting her to sit down.

"Oh, thank you very much! You're so gallant!" the woman sang. Her voice was low and throaty; it reminded Cammie of someone she had heard before. But who could it be? Oh, yes! Auntie! That was what Cammie's friend, Isabelle, had called the Witch of Pride, even though the witch wasn't really Isabelle's aunt. It was funny, though, that Cammie had thought of the Witch of Pride. She looked at the lady again. The lady had removed her long coat and now sat in black jeans and a white cashmere sweater. A gold pendant in the shape of the letter *p* sat on her massive chest.

I wonder what P *stands for?* Cammie thought.

"So how are you doing this morning?" Again, the woman was talking to Alex as though Cammie wasn't even there.

It made Cammie feel uncomfortable. She stared at her skating cocktail.

"Uh, we're fine, thank you." Alex was apparently trying to figure out why the woman was addressing only him.

Who is she? Cammie thought. *Could it be the Witch of Pride? No, the Witch of Pride has dark hair. It has to be someone else, probably, a judge. Oops, she'll definitely ask us why we are not at practice. But we can't tell her the truth.*

"What's taking them so long?" The woman looked at the counter. The saleslady was gone, probably working on the woman's order. The woman tapped her fingers on the table as though playing an invisible piano and turned to Alex again.

"Enjoying your practices, Alex?"

What? Had she really said *Alex*? Cammie stared at the lady in unbelief.

"D-do you know me?" Alex stammered.

The woman smiled widely. Cammie noticed that her teeth were very white, especially against bright raspberry lipstick.

"Honey, is there anyone in the skating world who doesn't know you?"

"Wh-what?" Alex looked totally shocked.

"Your skating is exceptional; not of this world." The woman smacked her lips as though she wanted to take a bite out of Alex.

So the lady had seen Alex skate. That explained everything. She was definitely one of the judges.

"Nice, graceful lines, perfectly centered spins—you've got the whole package, Alex."

"Here you go!" The saleslady put a cup of coffee and a crystal glass of pungent-smelling substance on the table.

"Finally!" Without giving the saleslady another look, the woman brought the glass to her lips. "To the best skater!"

Alex's normally pale cheeks were now of bright raspberry color—a perfect match for the woman's lipstick. "Are you a judge?"

"Sort of." The woman put the now-empty glass back on the table and pushed her coffee closer. "As I said, you have the whole package, though of course, your true strength is in the jumps. Your triples are very powerful and springy, and the landings are nice and soft—yummy!"

The woman sipped her coffee. "Ever tried any quads?"

"Uh, no." Apparently, Alex didn't know what to do with his hands. First, he folded them on his chest; then he rested them on the table next to his already melted ice cream. He probably thought it wasn't appropriate enough, for now he grabbed both edges of the chair.

"I can only do two triples so far—the triple salchow and the triple toe-loop. I'm still struggling with my triple loop." Alex lowered his voice, looking embarrassed. Funny how Cammie had never thought that her friend suffered from any lack of self-confidence. Two triples, that was great! The rest would come when Alex was ready.

"Oh, don't worry about it. The triple loop isn't that hard!" The woman had finished her coffee and was now swirling the empty cup in her hand as though it were a skater going for a jump. "All you need to do is hold the edge as long as you can and bend your knee really deep right before your takeoff. And swing those arms as hard as you can; it will give you more height. Oh yes, and of course, pull everything in faster. Try it next time, okay?"

"Thanks!" Alex's face lit up. "Of course, I wish I would land it sooner, so I can move to my triple flip."

"Oh, you will. Nothing can be too difficult for a skater of your caliber."

Alex's green eyes were shining. He turned to Cammie then to the woman again. "Cammie is a good jumper too."

The woman didn't even bother to look at Cammie. "Actually, it's you whom I noticed, Alex."

Cammie pouted. That surely wasn't fair; she *was* a good jumper.

"On the other hand, good jumpers come and go, but the true beauty of skating lies in the ability to present yourself," the woman said. "You have that star quality in you, Alex. This is the only thing that matters. Remember, you are a star. Keep it in mind when you skate, and your triples will come in no time. In fact, you don't even have to think about triple jumps at this point. Keep your eyes on the quads."

Cammie didn't think she had ever seen her friend look so happy. Apparently, Alex had a hard time staying in his seat. He straightened up, a glazed look in his eyes. "Do you…do you really think I have potential? I mean…to become an Olympic champion one day?"

The woman rested her chin on her folded hands. There was a huge diamond ring on her right middle finger. "Your potential is unlimited, Alex. You just need to believe it; you will be an Olympic champion, and it will happen sooner than you think."

"The competition is going to be tough, though," Alex said. His face darkened a little. "It may take years for me to land all the big jumps."

"Do I hear doubt? Is this Alex Bernard speaking? Alex Bernard, the greatest skater of this generation?" The woman raised her index finger.

"The greatest skater..." Alex shook his head slowly.

Cammie could tell that he was savoring every word.

"Hey, I have something that will help you with your confidence." Out of her bright raspberry color pocketbook, the woman extracted a small crystal bottle. The label on the bottle said "P.E.P."

The woman pushed the bottle into Alex's hand. "Here...drink this."

Something stirred up inside Cammie. For some reason, she had a strong desire to snatch the bottle out of Alex's hand.

The woman turned slowly and looked at Cammie through her dark lenses. For a split second, it seemed to Cammie that the lady's eyes glistened like a cat's. Though it was warm in the bakery, Cammie suddenly felt cold. Perhaps someone had just walked in and opened the door. She looked around. No, the door was closed; there was no one else in the café except Alex and the strange woman. Even the man with the newspaper was gone.

Alex was studying the label. "P.E.P. What is it? An energy drink?"

The woman laughed. "Of course, not. No, it's something better than that. Try it. You'll like it, I promise."

Alex, don't! Cammie wanted to say, but the woman's lenses were fixed right on her, and the words stuck in Cammie's throat.

Alex brought the bottle to his lips and emptied it in three swigs. "Whoa, it tastes great!"

"And it will make you feel even better," the woman said coyly.

She turned to the counter. "Betsy! Another coffee and Napoleon cognac for me. Yes, and bring the best skater of our generation another Three-Turn Ice Cream. I'm afraid his is all melted. My treat!"

The woman took a stack of bills out of her pocketbook.

"Oh, you don't have to." Alex's face was scarlet.

"I want to." The woman stood up and messed up Alex's hair.

Cammie flinched. Something surely wasn't right.

Betsy, the saleslady, approached the table with coffee and Alex's ice cream. "Enjoy!"

"Oh, we will." The woman winked at Alex, and Cammie saw her friend return the wink.

Now Alex looked positively more relaxed. He pushed his chair slightly away from the table, crossed his legs, and took a big spoonful of his ice cream. The woman emptied her glass of cognac and took a sip of her coffee. When she was done, she rested the cup on the table and started singing, first softly, then louder and louder. Although Alex's name wasn't in the song, it was abundantly clear that the woman was singing about him.

> *Of all elite skaters*
> *You're truly the best.*
> *The greatest of the greatest,*
> *The top of the blessed.*
> *No one can come close,*
> *They cry with defeat.*
> *They shower you with roses,*
> *They bow at your feet.*
> *You're fast like a rocket.*
> *My son, this is true.*
> *The worlds are in your pocket,*
> *The Olympics are too.*

Alex put his elbow on the table and rested his head on his fist. His green eyes squinted; he looked like a cat that had just finished a delicious fish dinner. To her utter shock, Cammie heard him actually sing along with the lady, only he was changing the words, so they would fit him.

> *No one can come close,*
> *They cry with defeat.*

They shower me with roses,
They bow at my feet.

"Alex, we've got to go," Cammie said firmly.

Alex didn't seem to hear her. Now he and the woman were singing in perfect unison. The woman was tapping her hand on the table, and Alex was swinging his arms like a conductor directing a choir.

I'm fast like a rocket.
Oh, yes, this is true.
The worlds are in my pocket,
The Olympics are too.

"Alex, let's go!" Cammie said louder. She didn't like what was happening to Alex. She had never seen him showing off that much.

Alex's eyes shifted to her face. "Umm, later. So what were you saying?" he turned to the woman again.

"Well, one thing I know for sure; you have a bright future ahead of you, Alex." The woman went into a detailed description of how great it would be for Alex to skate with *Champions on Ice* then with *Stars on Ice* then—

"Alex!" Cammie called again.

Her friend didn't even move.

"But Alex!" Cammie didn't know what to do; she was about to cry. The woman was so mean; first, she had deliberately ignored Cammie, and now Alex was unable to stop listening to the compliments.

Finally, however, the woman looked at her tiny gold watch decorated with diamonds. "Oops! I've got to leave now. Duty calls. Well, it's been nice talking to you, champion!"

She bent down and planted a loud kiss on Alex's cheek. To Cammie's utter disgust, Alex chuckled, grabbed the woman's manicured hand, and kissed it.

The woman's skate guards thumped against the floor as she walked toward the exit swaying her hips. The door shut. *Finally!*

"Well?" Cammie glanced at Alex.

He was gazing through the window. Cammie followed his look. The tall figure wrapped in red fur was quickly gliding away. Alex sighed.

"Alex, let's go. We've got to find Sonia, remember?"

He rubbed his forehead, still looking as though he had just woken up. "Uh, sure. Come on."

"Wait! What's this?" Cammie crouched and picked up a small raspberry-colored day planner from the floor next to the chair where the woman had just sat.

"It must be the judge's!" Alex snatched the note-book out of her hand. "Wait!"

He ran out of the bakery. Cammie followed him. As she sat down on a step to take off her skate guards, Alex came back, breathing hard. "She's gone. I didn't catch her."

"Well, maybe we'll see her again one day."

"Yeah!" Alex smiled brightly, apparently anticipating another meeting with his new fan. "Here, you keep this."

Cammie wrinkled her forehead. "Me?"

"I have no room for it. The skating book is in my pocket, remember?"

"Ah, okay. Hey, maybe the notebook has the judge's name and address. Then we can mail it to her."

Cammie opened the planner randomly and read the schedule for December 3 out loud.

10:00—hair dresser
2:00—cosmetologist
5:00—shopping for a new skating dress
7:00—meeting at BR.

"BR?" Alex asked. "What's BR?"

"I don't know. Hey, it also says "Sonja Henie, page 178." What's that about?"

"Beats me." Alex shrugged. "Sonja Henie was a famous skater, a three-time Olympic gold medalist... What?"

He had obviously seen Cammie gasp.

"Oh no, oh no. Here's another answer I got wrong on the test. The three-time Olympic gold medalist. I chose Michelle Kwan... I mean, she's the best skater."

"Well, she is, but it was Sonja Henie who won three Olympic gold medals."

"Too bad. No wonder I failed that test." Cammie closed the day planner with a snap and put it in her pocket. "Let's go."

They skated in the direction of the Skating Museum. A gust of wind swept the snow off the lawn and threw it into Cammie's face and ruffled Alex's hair. Alex took his wool hat out of his pocket and pulled it on.

"*Of all elite skaters I'm truly the best—*" Alex sang.

Cammie slowed down a little. "Isn't it enough for today?"

He looked at her askance. "What? Feeling jealous, huh? Because *you* are not a top skater?"

She stopped abruptly. "What're you talking about? Wait!"

Alex was speeding way ahead of her. It was only now that Cammie noticed his exaggerated flourish—the perfectly pointed toes, the excessive flailing of his arms. Alex skated as though a big crowd were watching him.

"Alex, what's the matter with you?"

He finally skidded to a stop and looked down on her. Tall and slender, Alex had always towered over Cammie, who was petite, but now he appeared even taller. And more mature too. Well, she wasn't going to be intimidated by him.

"You don't have to run, you know?"

He stretched and stifled a yawn. "O-okay, I see you have trouble catching up with me. You aren't fast enough."

"Alex, that's not—"

He turned away from her and glided forward, now too slowly. Cammie threw her arms in the air in desperation. Something was very, very wrong, and she thought she knew who had brought this sudden change upon her friend. It was the judge, of course. And what if she wasn't a judge? Cammie braked hard, startled by a sudden thought. What if it was a witch? Okay, if it wasn't the Witch of Pride, perhaps it was someone else.

"Alex, wait! I think it was a witch."

Alex went into a T-stop and glanced at her with apparent annoyance. "Now what are you talking about?"

"I don't think the woman at Sweet Blades was a judge. She was a witch, and she did something wrong to you. We can't go to the past like this. We—"

"What?" Alex glared at her, his eyes flashing. "She was a judge, that's it, and you're jealous. It's because she didn't call *you* a great skater."

"But Alex, it's ridiculous. You aren't great, I mean, not yet." At the sight of Alex's contorted face, she quickly corrected herself, but it was too late.

"You know what? One more word from you, and I won't take you to the past with me. Who needs you after all? I can find Sonia myself." He whizzed around and skated forward, picking up speed with every stroke.

Disgruntled, Cammie rushed after him. As much as she hated Alex at this moment, she couldn't leave him alone. He wasn't himself; the woman from Sweet Blades had done something evil to him, and Alex didn't even realize that he was talking sheer nonsense. The Olympics were in his pocket, yeah right! It took skaters years and years of practice, of failures and successes to even make the Olympic team. Who was Alex at this point? A promising young skater—nothing else. Surely, one day…but it was too early to call Alex *the top of the blessed*. And the woman who had done it couldn't mean anything good.

They didn't share another word until they reached the Skating Museum and walked into the hall that specifically displayed the history of world championships. Unlike the other exhibits, the World Championship Hall did not have wax figures skating on ice. Instead, the round-shaped rink was built like a clock with many hands pointing in different directions. At the end of each hand there was a circle that contained the name of the country where that year's championship had taken place and the names of the winners in each category. Cammie studied the latest events: 2009—Los Angeles, U.S.A, 2008—Goteborg, Sweden, 2007—Tokyo, Japan, 2006—Calgary, Canada.

"Okay, come here!" Alex positioned the history book on the circle that said 1910—Davos, Switzerland, Men's World Figure Skating Championship.

Cammie bent down and read:

Ulrich Salchow, Sweden—1
Werner Rittberger, Germany—2
Andor Szende, Hungary—3

"Hey, Salchow won!" Cammie exclaimed.

"Like I don't know. Come on, step on the book!"

BERNARD JUMP

Cammie squinted and shielded her eyes from the light. The sun stood bright and warm in the cloudless sky. If Cammie didn't know that it was December in Switzerland— just like back home—she might think of a beautiful spring day. They stood on a brick path, and snow-capped mountains stretched as far as she could see. Women wearing long dresses and cloaks strolled by, leaning on the arms of men dressed in striped suits and felt hats. Two tall men carrying skis walked by, chatting animatedly in French.

"They are skiers!" Cammie watched the guys as they went up a path leading up into the mountains. As she looked at the slope closer to the top, she could discern tiny figures skiing down.

"Skiing looks so scary; I don't think I could do it." Cammie sighed.

"I'm willing to try it," Alex said nonchalantly. "Want to join me? Right now?"

"Don't be silly; we've got to find Sonia."

A muscle in Alex's jaw twitched. "Fine, but afterwards."

He moved forward then stopped short. "We can't skate here!"

Cammie looked down. Alex was right; there was no ice on the brick path. She bent down to put on her skate guards. Funny how living in Skateland had taught them to take skating for granted. They walked along the path, enjoying the warm air. Cammie unzipped her parka. Alex pulled off his hat and was whistling something. As Cammie listened in, she recognized the infamous "Of All Elite Skaters."

"Do you have to whistle that stupid song?" Cammie asked.

Alex gave her a haughty look. "If I were you, I'd show more respect to a world-class skater."

Cammie gritted her teeth. She needed to think of something smart to say to that idiot, something that would put him in his place—

"O-okay, and here is the rink!" Alex exclaimed. He was way ahead of Cammie, of course.

Cammie rushed forward. A huge outdoor rink surrounded by a low iron fence stretched in front of them. Although the air was unusually warm for a December day, there were no puddles on the ice. The blue sky and the mountains surrounding the rink gave the whole place a festive appearance.

"Look!" Alex pointed to the rink.

About a dozen skaters practiced on the ice. Some were doing compulsory figures; Cammie recognized different variations of figure eight. Most of the competitors were men, but there were two ladies as well, both wearing ankle-long dresses just like Cammie's. For the umpteenth time, Cammie wondered why no one had thought of a better skating outfit for women. A short, wiry man swirled in a fast sit spin. Cammie also saw some scratch spins and waltz jumps.

"And this is the world championship?" Alex asked from behind her. There was more than disappointment in the way he had said it. For some reason, his voice had an unfamiliar nasal twang; in fact, Cammie thought that her friend sounded pretty nasty.

"The year is 1910," Cammie said coldly, without looking at Alex.

A slender man with very short hair did a series of deep edges around the rink and flew up in the air in a single salchow. The jump looked a little swingy to Cammie's taste, but it was still a single jump. Better than a waltz jump, when a skater did only half of a revolution. And of course, a single salchow was far superior to those boring school figures!

"Ulrich Salchow, spitze! Hast du seinen Sprung gesehen? Er wird immer besser!" a voice said on Cammie's right.

Cammie looked around. The voice belonged to a woman wearing a long gray skirt and a jacket of the same color. She had taken off her hat decorated with roses around the rim and was now swirling it in her hands.

The woman must have noticed Cammie's questioning look. "He's adorable, isn't he?"

She nodded in the direction of the man who had just done a salchow jump. "This is Ulrich Salchow. Can you believe it?"

"Wow!" Now Cammie stared at the famous skater in admiration.

Alex grunted behind her.

"You fancy him, Elsa," another woman said.

Cammie saw that the other lady wore heavier clothes. Her long flowered coat was trimmed with white fur around the hem and the collar.

"I fancy his jumps, not him," Elsa said, sounding defiant.

"Yes, but—"

Before the other woman could say another word, Alex interrupted her.

"You call *this* jumping?" He nodded in Ulrich Salchow's direction.

"Alex!" Cammie was absolutely terrified. Criticizing another skater—and not just anybody, the famous Ulrich Salchow—in the presence of two adults was bad enough. It was absolutely uncharacteristic of Alex, who had always been modest and polite. What was even worse, however, was the fact that Alex was putting down someone from the past. That meant attracting unnecessary attention to them.

"If this is a world championship, I could beat each of these skaters faster than you can say *salchow*!" Alex declared.

Oh, no! Cammie gasped and pressed her hands to her lips.

The women exchanged uncertain glances. The woman in the flowered coat lowered her head and whispered something to her friend in German.

"I could beat this guy too." Alex pointed to Ulrich Salchow, who had just ridden out of another of his famous jumps.

"Can you really?" the woman in a wide hat asked. There was a mischievous sparkle in her gray eyes.

"Of course!" Alex said importantly.

"You are American, aren't you?" the woman in the flowered coat asked.

"Yes, and much better than all of them," Alex said.

"Alex, look, we've got to—" Cammie tried to say something, but Alex didn't even look at her.

"Are you competing too, then?" the woman in the flowered coat asked. "I didn't know there was an American skater entering the competition. Let me see. Salchow and Thoren are Swedes, of course. Then Rittberger, he is German, and Szende is Hungarian. Have they added another competitor? Why aren't I aware of that?"

Elsa giggled. "*Ach so?* It only means you don't know everything, Anna."

Anna wrapped her coat tighter around her body, although it was warm. "I've got to talk to Holtz. He should have told me. Anyway, I shall be watching you, young man. And if you are even half as good as you say…hmm. Are you saying you can do the salchow jump too?"

"A single salchow? Ha-ha-ha!" Alex jerked his head back. "It's a pre-preliminary level jump."

"Alex, what's the matter with you?" Now Cammie was really scared. Alex was ruining everything. It was as though he had never heard Wilhelmina warn them about the possible consequences of showing off their modern-day skating skills. And Alex wasn't stupid; on the contrary, he had always been the one to notice that Cammie had been doing something wrong. And now he was making one silly mistake after another. It was as though he was deliberately trying to mess up their whole mission.

"I could land a single salchow when I was a little kid," Alex exclaimed.

The women were staring of him with a mixture of amazement and unbelief.

"Just wait and see what else I can do," Alex took a step toward the ice.

"Alex, stop it, please! Are you completely out of your mind?" Cammie was starting to panic. Angry tears had formed in the corners of her eyes. Something was seriously wrong with Alex. Maybe the evil judge had given him some contagious disease? Or poisoned him? With a growing sense of foreboding, Cammie remembered the weird P.E.P. drink. Who knew what was in it? Oh why, why hadn't she stopped Alex from even travelling to the past? Now he was going to ruin everything.

"Alex, we are here to find Sonia, remember?" Cammie pulled Alex hard by the sleeve.

He jerked his arm away angrily. "Now you don't tell me what to do! Did you hear the judge? I'm the best in the world, so I can do what I want. "

Anna, who still stood close to them, must have heard Alex's bragging. "A judge told you that? Was it Holtz? Or Gunther? No, wait, it must have been Faith, the British judge."

"I don't know the judge's name," Alex said pompously.

"So what are we waiting for? Let's see what the boy can do. Go ahead!" Elsa nudged Alex in the direction of the ice.

"Alex, don't! Please!" Cammie begged.

Alex took off his skate guards and glared at her. "I'm just letting you know that I haven't forgotten anything."

He turned to the woman with the hat. "Excuse me, miss … hmm, would it be okay for me to call you Elsa?"

Elsa laughed heartily. "But of course."

"Okay, Elsa, you see, we are looking for a friend. She's an American skater too. Her name is Sonia Harrison."

Elsa thought for a moment and shook her head slowly.

Anna's dark eyes squinted in concentration. "I don't think I met a Sonia. She's American you say? I pretty much know everybody here. Of course, the women's championship is in Berlin … but maybe your friend Sonia is here to watch the men compete. Or she may be practicing for her own competition. They don't mind other skaters joining practice sessions. See those two ladies? Is one of them your friend?"

"No," Cammie said sadly. "But maybe she'll come here to practice. You'll recognize her immediately. She's a very good skater, the best in Skate— hmm, at our rink."

"She's not. I'm the best!" Alex said with disgust.

Cammie did her best to ignore his stupid comment. "So are you absolutely sure Sonia isn't here?"

"How can you tell with all these people milling around?" Elsa pointed to the bleachers.

Cammie looked around the rink. Even though the competition hadn't started yet, a large crowd had already gathered to watch the official practice.

"You may want to look around. Who knows, maybe your friend Sonia is here after all," Elsa said encouragingly.

Cammie smiled. "Thank you. I—"

"Wow, he's amazing!" Elsa jumped, her hand pointing in the direction of the ice.

Cammie spun around, expecting to see Ulrich Salchow land another jump. Her jaw dropped. It wasn't the reigning world champion who had caused such an excited *wow* from Elsa. Nor was it the second place finisher, Werner Rittberger. Elsa was screaming and pointing to no one else but Alex, who was circling the rink in fast backward crossovers.

"Oh no no!" Cammie pressed her hands against her cheeks as she watched her friend glide backward on his right outside edge then step forward into a three turn with a deep knee bend. He was probably going to do his own salchow, bigger than the one Ulrich Salchow had just landed.

"Who is he trying to impress, idiot?" Cammie muttered.

Alex vaulted in the air, spun once, twice...on no! He had just done a triple salchow. At an official practice in 1910. How could he? The idiot was completely insane!

"Ah-ah-ah!" A collective groan came from the rows of spectators.

I've got to do something, Cammie thought. *I've got to pull him off the ice before he does more triples. Maybe not everything is lost yet. Maybe if we leave quickly, people will think it wasn't really a triple jump. Maybe they will take it for a trick ... something magicians do in a circus?* Cammie remembered seeing a magician who had sawed a woman in two—of course, he hadn't really done it; it had only been an illusion.

Cammie started pushing her way through the crowd to get to the entrance to the ice. But there were so many people around.

"Excuse me, excuse me!" Cammie hopped on her toes, desperately trying to find an opening. It didn't work; the crowd was too dense.

"Alex!" Cammie shouted, but her voice was drowned out in the collective shouts of dozens of fans.

"Das ist doch fantastisch!"

"Das kann ich nicht glauben!"

Now Alex was gliding backwards, his left leg raised. Oh no, he must have landed another triple jump. And then something worse happened. A man holding what looked like a very antique camera separated himself from the crowd. He moved to the other side of the iron fence, crouched, and pointed his camera in Alex's direction.

"We've got to stop him!" Cammie cast a hopeless look at Anna, who was scribbling fast in her crocodile leather notebook.

Elsa was dancing on the spot, waving her hat at Alex.

"Did you see that?" Elsa asked Cammie. "He can spin in the air. I've never seen anything like that in my life."

I bet you haven't, Cammie thought. She made another hopeless attempt at getting to Alex, but the entrance to the ice was now blocked by three uniformed men. They were apparently trying to hold back the swarm of reporters who were doing their best to catch Alex's attention. Cameras clicked and flashed; the reporters stomped their feet angrily and shouted at the security guards in different languages.

Cammie turned to Anna, who was still scribbling something. "Anna, I've got to get to Alex. Please, help me!"

Whistling excitedly, Anna closed her notebook. "Why?"

Cammie bit her lip. "It's an emergency."

Anna cocked her head. "You know what? I'm sure the media will keep your friend busy for a while. Personally, I would like to talk to him also."

"Anna is on the board of the rink," Elsa explained.

"The board of the rink?" Cammie gasped. That was even worse. She still hoped the audience, even the reporters, might think of Alex's triple salchow as a cheated jump or a trick. But once the officials got involved ... there was no way skating history could be left intact.

"So how long did it take you to learn spins in the air?" an excited voice asked in a very accented Enlgish.

Cammie turned to look, and sure enough, Alex stood at the edge of the rink looking extremely smug, his cheeks flashing. A short man in a beige suit gawked at him as though Alex were an Olympic champion. Cammie also noticed Ulrich Salchow, who stood about twenty feet away, looking flabbergasted.

"Oh about two months," Alex said nonchalantly.

"Liar!" Cammie hissed. "It took you more than a year, I remember."

"This jump is actually easy for me." Alex gave the reporters a charming smile.

"A jump? Pardon me. I would call it a spin." The reporter drew three circles in the air with his pencil.

"Oh, it was definitely a jump," a tall reporter wearing a white sport coat said. "His feet left the ice, didn't they?"

"That's right, but he actually rotated around his axis. Like this." The man in the beige suit raised his hand and showed how Alex had spun in the air.

"So what was it—a jump or a spin, anyway?" Anna sucked the end of her pencil and looked at Cammie, apparently interested in her opinion.

Feeling she had nothing to lose, Cammie sighed heavily. "It was a jump all right."

"Incredible. Amazing. The young man is making history here!" Elsa's eyes sparkled.

"*Changing* history," Cammie said through clenched teeth.

Elsa's eyes widened. "What?"

"Excuse me!" Looking extremely determined, Anna began to push through the thick crowd. To Cammie's great surprise, the same people who had just blocked her way spread apart to let Anna come through. Realizing it was her only chance, Cammie grabbed the hem of Anna's flowered coat and dove into the crowd after the young woman. Anna didn't seem to notice; apparently her mind was on Alex's stellar performance.

"It was a jump, not a spin, people," Anna said. Her strong voice had a commanding presence, and Cammie saw the reporters nod.

"And as soon as it is a jump, we need to give it a name," Anna said. "As you know, there is axel jump, and salchow jump ... what shall we call this incredible athletic endeavor?"

"What did you say your name was, young man?" the reporter in the beige suit asked Alex.

"Alex," Cammie's friend said. Undoubtedly he was enjoying all the attention.

"Oh please!" Cammie jumped up and down, trying to get Alex to see her. She waved her arms frantically, but even if Alex did notice her, he kept pretending she wasn't there.

"That's a nice name. How about alex jump?" the reporter in the white suit suggested. Anna brushed him off with a casual wave of her hand. "That's not going to work. Alex sounds too much like axel. Axel jump, alex jump—people will get confused. What's your last name, Alex?"

Alex pushed his chest forward. "Bernard."

"That's it! Bernard jump, Bernard jump!" the reporters echoed all through the crowd. More clicking and flashing of cameras followed.

Cammie thought she was about to faint. Trying to stay on her feet, she grabbed Anna's arms. "Please! It's not a new jump."

She must have spoken loudly, for all the noise around her died as though someone had turned off the volume.

"What are you talking about, Fräulein?" the man in the white suit asked her, not even trying to hide his annoyance.

"It was a triple salchow he did. A salchow jump, do you understand?"

"Of course it wasn't a salchow. We all saw Alex do three revolutions in the air. You saw it too. Didn't you?" The reporter was talking to Ulrich Salchow.

"Well … that's what it 1-looked like to me," the famous skater stammered. He kept staring at Alex with a mixture of bewilderment and awe.

"But no, you don't understand! It was just a salchow, nothing different."

She turned to Ulrich Salchow. He was a skater, he had to understand. "This jump is your invention, nobody else's. But when you do it, you can spin in the air once or twice or three times or … more. Alex just did a triple salchow. What's the big deal? It's still the same jump."

A collective sigh rolled across the crowd. "No big deal?"

"Did you hear her?"

"The young lady is surely smug."

"How about you, Fräulein? Can you do what Alex just showed us?" The reporter in the beige suit now stood next to Cammie, eyeing her with obvious contempt.

Cammie's heart sank. Of course she couldn't do a triple jump. Even her double flip and double lutz weren't consistent yet. But it was unfair to treat her as a bad skater. If only Wilhelmina hadn't asked Alex and her not to parade their skating skills during their trips to the past, she could do a beautiful double salchow. Easily. Cammie pictured the same crowd cheering *her* with the same enthusiasm Alex was now receiving. Oh, how Cammie wished she could show them her double salchow! Surely a double wasn't a triple, but it was more than anybody, including Ulrich Salchow, could do. And yet Cammie knew she had to keep her impulse under control. It was enough that Alex had gone bonkers.

"Well, it looks like the young lady can't do a Bernard jump," the reporter in the beige suit announced. The crowd laughed again. To her total dismay, Cammie saw Alex join the audience in ridiculing her. Tears welled up in her eyes, and Cammie had to blink twice so no one would notice.

"Of course, Alex needs to land a Bernard jump in a competition, so it may be counted as a new jump," the reporter in the white suit said.

As much as Cammie hated the man, she was now grateful to him for taking everybody's attention off her.

"Oh, he will," Anna said and smiled at Alex.

Alex winked at her.

During the short time when the audience's attention wasn't on her, Cammie somehow managed to pull herself together. Ignoring the reporters' nasty looks, she elbowed her way through the crowd to the edge of the rink where Alex still stood leering at her.

"Get off the ice now!" Cammie hissed.

Alex didn't move a muscle. "And what if I don't?"

"Then … then I'll tell everybody at home what a cheat and a liar you are!"

Her last words must have worked. Blood rushed to Alex's face, and for a moment Cammie thought he was going to hit her. Fine, she wasn't about to back off. And if she had to fight the jerk, she would. She didn't care that Alex was stronger than her; she wouldn't let him get away with cheating. Cammie stared Alex right in the eyes. She saw that he hated her, but still, she didn't flinch.

Finally Alex let out a sigh of deep annoyance and addressed the reporters. "I'm sorry, folks, but I need to talk to my friend."

The crowd shouted in protest.

Alex beamed at them. "It won't be long."

The reporters glared at Cammie. She knew everyone at the rink loathed her for taking their new idol away from the public eye, but she couldn't care less.

"Don't keep him too long!" Elsa crooned.

The crowd guffawed; someone shouted something in German. It had to be funny, for the audience positively roared with delight.

Her eyes firmly fixed on the road leading away from the rink, Cammie squeezed Alex's hand and pulled him through the mob. They didn't exchange a single word until they made it to the end of the path and turned the corner.

"Let go of me!" Alex snarled, trying to free his hand.

"In a minute," Cammie said curtly.

They stopped in front of a small wood building with a steeple. The spot where they stood was in the deep shadow cast from the building, and the air appeared significantly cooler. Cammie unclasped her fingers and pushed Alex away from her as hard as she could. He almost fell backwards.

"What...what's wrong with you!" Alex yelled, rubbing his hand.

"What's wrong with *me*? How about you? How could you show off in front of that crowd after what Wilhelmina told us? Bernard jump, for crying out loud!"

The tips of Alex's ears reddened, but other than that, he looked quite composed. "Don't give me that, okay? I can become a world champion tomorrow."

"This competition took place 109 years ago."

"So? A champion is always a champion. Everybody knows Ulrich Salchow. No one cares that he lived a hundred years ago and that he could only do single jumps. Don't you see? I can beat him easily with my triples, and then—"

"Ulrich Salchow was the one who landed that jump first! No one could do it in his time. That's what skating was like a hundred years ago." Cammie pointed in the direction of the rink. "And Ulrich Salchow didn't have all those coaches walking him through every stage of the jump. It was a huge achievement for him, and he was a great skater. And you … you—"

Alex hung his head. Cammie could tell that he was thinking hard. "But nobody would know how I learned those jumps. And I could have a gold medal from a world championship. I mean a medal is always a medal. I would still be recognized as a world champion. Isn't it enough?"

"If this is enough for you, then you're a loser!" Cammie felt herself shaking with fury.

Alex clenched his fists.

"If you consider beating skaters who can only do singles a great achievement, I can only feel sorry for you!" Cammie shouted.

"Oh all right, you made your point!" Alex kicked the curb hard with his toe and looked away.

They were quiet for a while. All Cammie could hear was the distant rumble of the voices coming from the rink.

Finally Alex looked up at her, and she saw that his eyes were red. "Fine. What are we doing now, then?"

"Let's go home," Cammie said calmly.

"But we haven't looked for Sonia yet."

"She's not here," Cammie said firmly. "That's what Anna told me. Besides, if she were here, everybody would have already noticed her skating. And of course, you have attracted so much attention that if Sonia were here, she would have definitely come up and talked to you."

Alex straightened up, looking defiant again. "See? Mission accomplished. And it was because of me. I wouldn't forget that if I were you."

He took the history book out of his pocket, and they stepped on the introductory page without saying a word.

P.E.P. AND P.O.P.

Well, I'll see you," Alex said as soon as the museum door closed behind them. Cammie saw that he was still angry. Still, she hadn't expected him to leave so soon. She had thought they would spend more time together and talk about what had happened. They were a team, after all; they had a mission to accomplish, so how could Alex simply take off after they had had such a fight?

"Alex, wait!"

He turned around and looked at her with a weird facial expression. Then he stuffed his hands into his pockets and skated away as though she hadn't even spoken. Just like that.

Cammie stood glued to her spot until Alex disappeared around the corner. She sighed. Something was really wrong with her friend. Doing triples in front of an early twentieth century crowd wasn't something the smart, rational Alex would ever think of. Hadn't he realized that his behavior could change figure skating history? Cammie's heart skipped a beat. Changing history… and what if Alex had succeeded, after all? What if those Suisse reporters had really given him credit for landing a Bernard jump?

Cammie had to talk to Wilhelmina, and the sooner the better. Visiting another period in skating history with Alex calling himself the best skater in the world would be a very dangerous thing to do. Alex needed help, and Wilhelmina was the only person who would know what had to be done.

This time, Skateland President opened the door herself. She looked classy in a long gray dress that covered her arthritic legs. At the sight of Cammie, Wilhelmina's eyes widened.

"Oh, that's who it is. Come in. Is Alex with you?"

Cammie shook her head. "No, it's just me."

Wilhelmina cocked her head. "Is anything wrong?"

"Yes," Cammie said curtly. A lot of things had gone wrong; she didn't even know where to begin.

"Did you have lunch?" Wilhelmina asked as Cammie unzipped her parka.

That was one question Cammie hadn't expected. With everything going on, food was the last thing on her mind.

"Uh, thank you, Mrs. Van Uffeln, I'm not hungry."

"Well, *I* am. So why don't we have lunch together, and then you can tell me what's going on? I'm alone today," the older woman said. "Christel is spending the whole weekend with a friend. And I got so busy working on a book that I completely lost track of time. Can you believe it? It's a quarter after one."

Earlier today, Cammie had eaten the whole skating pastry at Sweet Blades. It had filled her up. But that was hours ago, and considering that Cammie had just come back from 1910 Switzerland, she could easily say that she hadn't eaten for almost a hundred years. Perhaps that explained why she was so ravenously hungry.

"Take off your skates, then," Wilhelmina said. "I want you to be comfortable. We'll have a nice lunch, and then we'll talk."

"Thank you," Cammie muttered and sank into a soft leather footrest in the lobby. As she unlaced her boots, she thought that living in Skateland had made her so used to wearing skates that without them she felt something was missing. And yet sometimes it felt nice to give her feet some rest.

Wilhelmina handed Cammie a pair of light green fluffy slippers shaped like frogs.

"Are these yours?" Cammie couldn't suppress a grin as she pictured the bulky eyes and big ears of a frog on Skateland president's feet.

Wilhelmina cackled. "You'll be surprised to hear that, but yes, these are mine. Of course, this isn't something I'd normally buy for myself. A former student of mine gave them to me. They really warm up your feet, but to tell you the truth, I never wear them. I tried them on once and then put them in the closet. Not my style. But you'll like them, I'm sure."

Cammie put on the froggy slippers. They hugged her tired feet like two soft cushions.

"Do you mind if we eat in the kitchen?" Wilhelmina asked. "It's too much trouble to carry the food to the dining room."

"Uh, sure. We always eat in the kitchen at home."

Wilhelmina's kitchen was large, just as every other room in her house. It was also very modern. It had a built-in microwave, a double-door stainless-steel refrigerator, a big dishwasher, and lots of other gadgets.

"Do you like French onion soup? It's my favorite." Wilhelmina opened the refrigerator.

"Uh, sure. Can I help you?" Cammie offered as she watched the older woman transport a soup pan from the refrigerator to her knee.

"That will be good. Put it on the stove, please, and I'll grate some cheese."

Cammie was surprised to see that Wilhelmina could navigate around the kitchen in her wheelchair relatively fast. Within a few minutes, she had cheese and garlic bread ready. Wilhelmina told Cammie to pour some iced tea into high glasses adorned with silver icicles, and then the two of them took their seats at the octagonal wood table in the middle of the kitchen.

The onion soup tasted so good that for a moment, Cammie forgot about her disastrous experience in Switzerland. Wilhelmina pushed the plate with garlic bread closer to her. Cammie took another slice gladly. She felt warm and comfortable.

"Thank you so much, Mrs. Van Uffeln. It's delicious," Cammie said.

"You are welcome. Now as I make tea, why don't you tell me what happened? I can tell you are upset."

Cammie sighed gravely and told Wilhelmina the whole story. She didn't miss the fact that Alex had landed several triple salchows in front of Ulrich Salchow himself and that a big crowd of spectators had also been in attendance. What was even worse—the reporters had taken Alex's picture and written down his name. But the worst thing was that they had called the triple salchow Bernard jump.

When Cammie said Bernard jump, her face felt so hot that her eyes began to water. She stopped mid sentence and looked down into her tea cup, frustrated. What would Wilhelmina do now? Would she rebuke Cammie for not having stopped Alex? But Cammie had tried hard, really hard.

"I really tried to stop him, Mrs. Van Uffeln, but he wouldn't listen to me," Cammie said despondently.

"Hmm. I see. So you say he didn't land the jump in a competition. Is that right?" Surprisingly, Wilhelmina didn't sound particularly upset.

Cammie exhaled slowly. "No. I wouldn't let him."

"So what made him leave the rink? You say he wouldn't listen to you."

Now even Cammie's nose was on fire. "I...I told him that if beating old-time skaters with single jumps was a challenge enough for him, then he was a loser."

Wilhelmina chuckled. "Fair enough. So what did he say to that?"

"Nothing really. But he agreed to come home."

"Okay. Now Cammie, I want you to remember when exactly Alex started acting differently. I don't remember him being overly focused on glory before. Is that right?"

"It was after he talked to a judge at Sweet Blades this morning."

The cup picturing two little girls skating on a pond froze in Wilhelmina's hand. "A judge? What judge?"

Cammie put her chocolate-covered pretzel back on her plate. "We never met that woman before. She was tall and blonde. She wore a fox coat."

"Hmm." Wilhelmina raised her eyes as though the answer to her question were written on the ceiling. "Did the lady actually tell you she was a judge?"

Cammie thought for a moment. "Uh, not really. We just assumed she was a judge because she knew so much about skating. And she can't be a coach, because we have met every coach in Skateland. Unless she was visiting, of course."

Wilhelmina looked pensive. "Hmm, it's a possibility."

"No, wait!" Wilhelmina exclaimed before Cammie could even think of what the older woman had just said. "What exactly did the lady tell Alex and you?"

"She spoke mostly to Alex. In fact, she didn't pay any attention to me at all." Cammie frowned as she remembered. "She said he had great potential, that he would be an Olympic champion one day…no, it was worse. She actually said that he was the greatest skater in the world *now*. And she sang that stupid song to him, like…"

Cammie creased her forehead, trying to remember the lyrics. "*They shower you with roses; they bow at your feet*. And also *the worlds are in your pocket, and the Olympics are too*."

Wilhelmina's spoon fell on the table with a loud clank. "What?"

Cammie nodded. "It's true. Then she told Alex he was ready for quads, which is strange because

Alex is still having problems with his triple loop, so—"

Bang! Cammie jumped off her chair, startled. Wilhelmina had hit her fist on the table. Her gray eyes were now almost black, shooting angry darts at Cammie.

"Did the woman touch Alex in any way?" The older woman looked as though she were trying hard to control her temper.

Cammie stirred in her chair, feeling scared. "No. But she gave him a drink."

"What drink? Did she buy him something from Sweet Blades?" Wilhelmina asked sharply.

"No, no, she had brought it with her. It was in a small bottle, bright red, and it's called P.E.P."

Wilhelmina slammed her fist against the table again. Her cup jumped in the air; the remainder of her Tea Position spilled on the dark green placemat. The woman ignored the stain.

"It was the Witch of Pride!" Wilhelmina exclaimed.

Cammie, who had rushed to the sink for a sponge, stopped abruptly. "The Witch of Pride? No, it wasn't her."

"Oh yes it was." Wilhelmina gritted her teeth and muttered something in a foreign language.

"Sorry!" Wilhelmina smiled vaguely as she saw Cammie gawking at her. "I'm really upset, that's what. Sometimes when I get overly emotional, I tend to lapse into Dutch. Do you know what P.E.P. is?"

Cammie shrugged. "First, we thought it was short for Pepsi, but the woman said no. So we believed it was some kind of energy drink."

"No! P.E.P. stands for Pride Enhancing Potion. It's the potion the Witch of Pride uses on skaters whom she wants to bewitch. See, in most cases, a witch will resort to physical contact to jinx a person. Winja hit Jeff with her crutch, and he got injured. And as for pride..." Wilhelmina's eyes flashed. "Just an ounce or two of P.E.P. combined with flattery turns a skater into a hopeless braggart."

"That's right: *a braggart*. That's how Alex acted all the time. He never stopped bragging about his skating." Cammie was stunned. So the Witch of Pride had gotten Alex. How terrible! First Jeff got attacked, now Alex. Although... "Mrs. Van Uffeln, but the Witch of Pride has dark hair. The woman who talked to us was a blonde."

Wilhelmina nodded. "I would expect that. See, pride comes in all forms and shapes. The Witch of Pride actually enjoys changing her appearance. Personally, I remember her with short red curls. Now you say her hair is blonde."

Cammie nodded. "It's straight and long too."

"Yes, very typical. How about her eyes?"

Cammie looked up. "Oh, she wore sunglasses. I was surprised that she needed them. It was early in the morning, not bright enough."

"See, she didn't want to be recognized. But you must be alert all the time, Cammie. What a shame Alex fell for her flattery! Of course, he's a young boy, and so many compliments can be hard to ward off, even for a more experienced skater." Wilhelmina rubbed her temples, looking sad.

"But Mrs. Van Uffeln, you are the president of Skateland. Can't you just kick all the witches out of here?"

Wilhelmina stared at Cammie as though seeing her for the first time. A small smile touched her lips. "Oh, Cammie, what a sweet little girl you are! I thank you for the vote of confidence, but do you honestly think skating witches can be merely sent away?"

Cammie didn't understand why not.

"There is good and evil in figure skating, just like anywhere else in the world. Figure skating is the world of athleticism, elegance, beauty, and music. Unfortunately, not everyone does it for sheer love of the sport. Some crave glory and fame; others do it for money. And if they don't succeed, they become bitter. They can't come to grips with the fact that they are not number one. What is worse, they will never agree that they failed because they aren't talented enough or don't have a good enough work ethic. They will start blaming everyone else around them: their parents for not being supportive enough, or their coach for not teaching them right, the other skaters, who are more talented, who placed higher. And if they don't stop, if they don't move on, they will become skating witches. Do you understand, Cammie?"

Cammie was thinking hard. "Well, sure, but still, why can't those witches be banned from Skateland forever? You are the president, so you could—"

"Even if I could, new witches would come to take their place. Don't you see? Figure skating is a competitive sport. Where there are winners, there are also losers, and not everybody can handle the pain of being unable to make it to the top."

Cammie was drawing circles on the tablecloth with her finger. Why did skating have to be evil? Why couldn't somebody do something about it?

"It's okay if you don't understand it now. One day you will. The important thing is to be able to recognize the witches' attacks and to be able to protect yourself. Now let's get to the more pressing matter, which is Alex. The young man needs help. Did you ask him to come to my place with you, by any chance?"

Cammie smiled wryly. "He wouldn't talk to me."

"I see. Now if you will excuse me for a moment."

Out of the pocket of her dress, Wilhelmina produced a tiny gold cell phone and punched in three numbers. "Captain Greenfield? Yes, this is President Van Uffeln. Yes, I need a favor. Could you please bring Alex Bernard to my house? He is in the Junior Boys' Dorm. Oh, yes, it's very urgent. Thank you."

"Do you mind heating up more water?" Wilhelmina said to Cammie. "I'm sure our friend will want tea too."

Cammie stood up obediently and put the kettle back on the burner. As she turned on the stove, she wondered if Alex really would be in the mood for tea. And he would surely be upset with her for squealing on him. He probably wouldn't even want to be her friend anymore.

"Mrs. Van Uffeln, do you mind if I leave now? Perhaps you will want to talk to Alex alone."

"Oh, no, this is something that concerns both of you. You are a team. Aha, here they are."

The doorbell had just come to life, playing something that sounded like a waltz. Wilhelmina wheeled herself out of the kitchen into the lobby. Cammie looked around frantically, hoping she would find a place to hide. The last thing she wanted now was to come face-to-face with Alex. Perhaps Wilhelmina would invite him to the living room.

"Thank you, Bob. I won't keep you any longer." Wilhelmina said.

"No problem, Mrs. Van Uffeln." Cammie recognized the voice of the young policeman who had caught Alex and her wandering around the Witch of Fear's property.

The door slammed in the lobby, and a couple of seconds later Wilhelmina reappeared in the kitchen, closely accompanied by Alex. At the sight of Cammie lurking in the corner, Alex stopped short, and then a grimace of haughtiness replaced his slightly sheepish expression.

"I see Cammie has already complained about me," Alex said smugly.

"Well, personally, I haven't heard any complaints," Wilhelmina said lightly as she pointed Alex to the chair across from Cammie's. "The truth is, however, that we have a situation that needs to be addressed. So why don't we all sit down and talk about it?"

Cammie unglued herself from the wall and took her seat. Alex, however, remained standing, his green eyes narrowed with anger.

"Sit!" Wilhelmina suddenly barked.

Alex jolted forward as though in pain but sat down slowly. He looked calm on the surface, but Cammie knew he was burning with rage.

"Now Alex, I want you to look me in the eye. Yes, go ahead!" Wilhelmina said sternly.

With obvious reluctance, Alex raised his head and stared at the older woman. There were red patches on his cheeks.

"Listen to me, young man, whatever happened in Switzerland wasn't entirely your fault. The truth is, you were attacked by the Witch of Pride."

Just a second before, Alex looked as though he were going to fight tooth and nail to thwart any possible accusation. Now, however, he appeared puzzled. "W-what? I don't understand."

"Wait a minute." Wilhelmina wheeled herself to one of the kitchen cabinets and scanned the shelves.

Cammie looked at Alex, trying to read his facial expression. Alex acted as though she weren't there.

"Here, drink this." Wilhelmina held a small bottle made from dark glass. The lable read P.O.P.

Alex snorted derisively. "Another Skateland signature drink, huh? First P.E.P. now P.O.P."

"I'm waiting." Wilhelmina had already unscrewed the bottle. The dark liquid swirled and bubbled.

"I don't want it," Alex said stubbornly.

"Yes, you do." Wilhelmina's eyes peered Alex straight in the face.

He folded his arms on his chest and crossed his legs. "What is it?"

"Something that will reverse the effects of the drink the Witch of Pride gave you at Sweet Blades."

Alex's eyes narrowed. "What if I don't drink it?"

"Then you're no longer a resident of Skateland. You may go back to your dorm and pack right now."

Alex stared at the pale green tiles of the floor, his lips pressed tight. Apparently he was weighing his options.

"And don't think you will be able to compete anymore. Any doping test will show the presence of P.E.P. in your blood."

Alex still wouldn't move. The dark bottle danced in Wilhelmina's hands; Cammie was afraid that the potion would spill over.

Finally, Alex let out a deep sigh. "All right."

He stretched his hand and accepted the dark bottle. He brought it to his nose and sniffed the dark solution. "Ugh! It stinks."

"Go ahead," Wilhelmina said calmly.

For a split second, Alex looked as though he were going to throw the drink against the wall. Finally he grimaced and emptied the bottle in one big gulp. "Ugh, ugh, I need water, please!"

Seeing Wilhelmina nod, Cammie filled up Alex's cup with water and handed it to him. He took a big swig.

"Wow!" Alex exhaled and wiped his forehead. "What was it all about?"

Wilhelmina cast a sideway glance at Cammie. "Tell him what happened."

Cammie cleared her throat. "Alex, the woman at Sweet Blades, the one we took for a judge, was the Witch of Pride."

Alex looked as though he saw Cammie for the first time in his life. "I don't understand."

"She told you how great you were because she was trying to bewitch you," Cammie said.

Alex's green eyes narrowed. "No way. She meant it."

"Oh-hoh!" Wilhelmina snickered. "So you really think you're great, huh?"

Alex clasped his hands tight.

"That drink she gave you, remember?" Cammie stammered.

Alex glared at her, but didn't say anything.

"It was … poison."

"Potion," Wilhelmina corrected. "For your information, Alex, P.E.P. stands for Pride Enhancing Potion."

Blood drained from Alex's cheeks. "Did she … did she poison me?"

"In a way." Wilhelmina's wheelchair squeaked against the tiles as she moved closer to Alex. "She bewitched you. Don't you worry, though. Older and wiser skaters fell into the same trap more than once. The Witch of Pride is very powerful. What she can really do well is detect the smallest sign of weakness in a person, the tiniest inclination to put himself above the rest. Apparently, she sensed it in you. She didn't attack Cammie, after all."

Wilhelmina's gray eyes slid down Cammie's face. It was only then that Cammie realized that the last statement was meant to be a compliment. She felt herself blush.

"Don't get too comfortable, though, young lady," Wilhelmina boomed. "Pride has destroyed many skaters, so you'd better be careful."

Cammie lowered her head.

"But that P.E.P. drink was delicious. It's the P.O.P. that tasted terrible." Alex's face was the color of ripe cherry.

Wilhelmina looked amused. "No surprises here. Anyone who has tasted pride will agree that it's the best feeling in the world. Euphoria mingled with joy, what can be more pleasant? As for P.O.P, it stands for Pride Obliterating Potion. The person who drinks it has to deal with the bad consequences of pride. I believe facing the truth of what you really are is hardly an enjoyable experience."

Alex looked down.

"Now let's remember what happened," Wilhelmina went on. "The Witch of Pride started telling you how great you supposedly were, right?"

Alex mumbled something inintelligible.

"When she saw that you were open to flattery and therefore already proud of yourself, she topped it with P.E.P," Wilhelmina said. "So you went to Switzerland and did things you would never have dreamed of otherwise. Am I right?"

Alex lowered his head. "Well … yeah. I did land a couple of triple salchows. And they … hmm … they … er … "

"I know about Bernard jump," Wilhelmina said calmly.

"You … " Alex bent over and buried his face in his hands.

"Yes, it's a serious offense, young man. What you did is more than just showing off; it's lying and cheating. You know you weren't the first skater to land a triple salchow. Many skaters of your generation can land triple salchows, so it's hardly an outstanding achievement. You're not a skating genius, Alex. Actually, you could be disqualified for that."

"No!" Cammie and Alex shouted at the same time. Cammie saw tears forming in the corners of Alex's eyes.

"Oh please, Mrs. Van Uffeln, don't do it to him! He didn't mean it; he just didn't understand." Cammie knew she didn't sound convincing enough. But how could she explain to Wilhelmina that Alex was an honest, hardworking skater, and that he would never, ever cheat. The boy who had shown off in front of the Suisse crowd wasn't Alex. Cammie clasped her hands tight, but still she couldn't keep them from shaking.

Wilhelmina's grave look lingered on Alex's miserable frame. "I don't think I heard a word of apology from you, young man."

"I'm … I'm so sorry!" Alex whispered. He looked away. His shoulders twitched; Cammie knew he was crying. She rose in her chair, ready to defend her friend. Wilhelmina couldn't disqualify Alex, no way!

Wilhelmina stopped Cammie with a wave of her hand before Cammie could even begin her defense speech.

"I want the history book, please," the old woman said calmly.

His fingers trembling, Alex took the book out of his pocket and handed it to the president. Wilhelmina put it gently on her lap and waited till the book grew to its normal size. Then she opened it and began to read silently.

Alex sat in the same position, with his face turned away. In the grave silence, Cammie could hear her heart pounding heavily against her ribs.

"So you didn't land a triple salchow in competition, did you?"

At the sound of Wilhelmina's voice, Alex turned around, his eyes red. "No, I didn't. She … Cammie made me leave."

"Well, it's good. Because it means that the skating history hasn't changed after all."

"Are you sure?" Cammie asked softly.

"Positive. See, it's all in here." Wilhelmina stroked the pages of the history book as though it were a living creature. "As you know, this book has magical powers. So if Alex had changed history, an account of it would have appeared in the book. However, I don't see any mention of the Bernard jump."

Cammie could swear the old woman was smiling, and yet when Wilhelmina looked at Alex, her face looked firm.

"Now before we discuss your punishment, young man, I need to know what other blunders the two of you made."

Wilhelmina's eyes moved from Alex's red face to Cammie, and Cammie felt she was going to shrink under the weight of that heavy look. She flinched.

"Is there anything else you want to tell me?" Wilhelmina asked.

"Yes!"Cammie and Alex said in unison then glanced at each other and quickly looked away.

"What is it?" Wilhelmina's voice sounded unnaturally calm.

Her voice shaking, Cammie told Wilhelmina about how Jackson Haines had gotten excited about their toe picks.

"And he said he would think about adding them to his skates," Cammie concluded miserably. She was afraid to look at Wilhelmina, but when she did, she saw that the old woman was actually smiling.

"So what year was it?" Wilhelmina asked.

"1864," Cammie said, surprised at the president's calm demeanor.

Wilhelmina's smile broadened. "Read this."

She turned several pages going backward then handed the book to Cammie.

"Toe picks were first used by Jackson Haines in the 1870s," Cammie read.

She looked at Wilhelmina, puzzled. "So it means…it means that we were the ones who gave him the idea of toe picks."

The old woman raised her eyes to the ceiling. "Perhaps. Who knows? But does it really matter? Inspiration is a tricky thing. No one knows when and under what circumstances it will strike us. The important thing is that in the 1860s, the world was ready for toe picks, so they appeared. Jackson Haines made them at the right time."

"But—"

"That's enough," Wilhelmina said. "Let's get practical. Do you know what the best cure for pride is, young man?"

Alex, who had been looking away all the time, shifted his moist eyes to the president's face.

"Work. Hard work," Wilhelmina snapped. "No more trips to the past for a while. You are going back to the rink, and you are going to train as hard as you can. And you are not doing the fancy stuff you like. No jumps and spins, only moves in the field—that's what you need. So let me see ... a week will do it. Do you understand me? Go back to the rink starting tomorrow and no freestyle, just the basics."

"And what about me?" Cammie asked gingerly. She didn't think she would be allowed to travel to the past alone, nor did she really want to.

Wilhelmina's eyes lingered on her. "What makes you think that you are immune to pride? Same thing for you; two moves-in-the-field practices daily for a week. And then we will see." Wilhelmina leaned back in her wheelchair and rubbed her hands, looking satisfied. "And now, how about some tea?"

A Page in the History Book

ammie didn't see Alex the whole week. They practiced moves in the field at their respective rinks. Every day, Cammie went through her juvenile moves, not even daring to do any jumps and spins. Wilhelmina must have talked to Coach Ferguson, because the coach never asked Cammie where she had been or why she hadn't been showing up at the rink lately. Every morning and afternoon, Coach Ferguson greeted Cammie, and when time came for Cammie's private lessons, the coach made her practice her double threes.

Coach Ferguson looked all business; nothing had changed in her attitude to Cammie. Even though Cammie found her new practice routine irresistibly boring, she never complained, remembering how strict Wilhelmina had been with Alex. The last thing Cammie wanted was to become the new target of Skateland president's fury. Even now, as Cammie repeated her patterns over and over again, she had a weird feeling that Wilhelmina skated right next to her, watching her every move, registering every little mistake. Cammie was sure that if she dared to disobey Wilhelmina and went into a jump or a spin, the older woman would somehow materialize out of thin air, shaking her crooked finger at her.

On Saturday night, Cammie left the Green Rink arena after a lonely afternoon practice feeling completely drained.

"You look tired, Cammie," Mrs. Page said when Cammie entered the dorm.

Cammie could barely move her fingers as she pulled her wool hat off.

"Let me make you some hot chocolate."

Cammie forced a smile. "Hot chocolate sounds great."

"Come to the kitchen with me, then. But first let's take this parka off." Mrs. Page tried to unzip Cammie's parka.

Cammie shook her head. "Oh please, don't. I'm too cold."

Mrs. Page looked at her sadly. "You poor thing! Okay, I'll let you eat first."

The first bites of hot, cheesy lasagna melted the ice inside Cammie's chest and sent fire to her limbs. And when she took a sip of hot chocolate, she felt good and strong. "Thank you, Mrs. Page."

"Oh, you're very welcome, sweetheart. Now wait a minute." Mrs. Page looked around surreptitiously and winked at her. From one of the cabinets, she took out a tray of cookies. The cookies looked like inkblots.

"What do you think of these?" Mrs. Page asked, looking very delighted.

Cammie bent down and inspected the funny-looking shapes. Now she could discern blades attached to the lower parts of the lumpy cookies. "Umm, these are ... skating dresses and skates."

Mrs. Page's exciement was immediately replaced with disappointment. "Come on! These are skating bears butter cookies."

"Oops, sorry!" Cammie wished she hadn't said anything. Now as she looked at the lumps closer, she could actually discern four paws and a tail. And there definitely were horns on the bears' heads. Bears were supposed to have ears, not horns.

Cammie gave Mrs. Page a guilty look. "I'm just tired, Mrs. Page."

"Oh of course you are! Stupid me. I completely forgot about your special mission. How is it coming anyway?" Mrs. Page lowered her voice almost to a whisper.

Cammie looked down. "Fine."

"Okay, you finish your chocolate now and go to bed. And try some of these cookies while no one is looking. They are really good." Mrs. Page patted Cammie on the shoulder and left her alone.

Cammie ate two cookies—they were really delicious—took the last sip of her hot chocolate and stood up. It was quiet in the dorm. Most skaters were spending the Saturday night with their families or at the movies. Cammie was all alone.

She went to her room, sat down on her bed, and unlaced her boots. She might as well go to bed early. Next week would probably be hard. Besides, Wilhelmina had told Cammie and Alex to come to her house on Sunday. Even though Sunday was everybody's day off, Wilhelmina probably thought they could waste no more time. Sonia had been in the past too long.

Cammie stood up and walked up to Sonia's neatly made bed. All of Sonia's school books and notebooks sat on the nightstand in impeccable order. Something looking like a card stuck out from underneath the math book. Automatically, Cammie pulled out the card. It had a picture of a very beautiful woman skating on a frozen pond. The caption underneath said, "Sonja Henie, a famous Norwegian skater, three-time Olympic gold medalist." Wincing at the thought that she was snooping,

Cammie nevertheless opened the card that turned out to be from Sonia's parents.

Dear Sonia,

Congratulations on your gold medal at the regionals. We are really proud of you. We believe that one day you will win the Olympic gold, like Sonja Henie. No wonder we named you after this famous skater. Way to go, champion!

Love, Mom and Dad

Sonja Henie, hmm. So Sonia had been named after her. Well, naturally, after all, Sonia's parents had been figure skaters too, and now they coached in Colorado. Of course they wanted their only daughter to skate, so they had named her after Sonja Henie. But where had Cammie heard that name before? *It was on that skating test, silly,* Cammie thought. *One of the questions you got wrong.* But no, she had seen the name somewhere else. And it was after the skating history test, not too long ago. Cammie stood up and started pacing the room. She had seen Sonja Henie's name written down somewhere, and it had only been a week ago … of course!

Cammie picked up her backpack from the floor and rummaged through the side pockets. It had to be somewhere there; she remembered stuffing it into a pocket … yes! In her hand, Cammie held the raspberry day planner that belonged to the Witch of Pride, the one that had fallen out of her pocketbook.

Cammie had told Alex that she would give the planner back to the woman when she saw her again. At that time, Cammie had thought the woman was a judge. And after Wilhelmina had explained to them that it was a witch, Cammie had forgotten about the planner altogether.

Cammie opened the notebook and went through the long list of the witch's activities. Most of them weren't interesting at all, like routine trips to the beauty parlor or meetings at the B.R. Hang on, B.R. probably meant Black Rink. Of course! Now where was Sonja Henie's name? Cammie remembered seeing it somewhere. Yes, there it was! Cammie stared at the note that said, "Sonja Henie, p.178." Okay, now she knew who Sonja Henie was, but how about "p. 178"? The witch had probably meant the page in a book. What book?

Cammie's heart skipped a beat. Why of course! The Witch of Pride had to mean the skating history book. Could it mean that they had taken Sonia to the time of Sonja Henie? Perhaps. But Cammie had to check out the page in the skating history book. What a shame Cammie didn't have the book with her! And what was even worse, Alex didn't have it either, not anymore. After rebuking Alex for his Bernard jump, Wilhelmina had taken the history book away from him and had never given it back. But Alex had read the book several times. Perhaps he remembered where Sonja Henie's story was?

Cammie thought for a moment. No, as smart as Alex was, it was most unlikely that he had memorized every page in the thick history book. Wilhelmina probably knew all the pages by heart, and she had the book now. Should Cammie call her? Cammie looked at her watch. It was only eight-thirty, and Skateland President was probably still awake, but... Cammie shook her head. She would ask Wilhelmina tomorrow. What if Cammie was right, and the witch had really written down the page that pinpointed the period of time to which the evil women had taken Sonia? Cammie smiled happily. It looked as though Cammie and Alex would be able to find their friend very, very soon.

"Mrs. Van Uffeln, could you please look what is written on page 178 of the history book?" Cammie asked Wilhelmina as the older woman led her into the living room the next morning.

Alex already sat in the armchair, looking distant. By the expression on his face, Cammie couldn't tell whether a week of moves in the field had really worked a big change in her friend. Yet she didn't want to think about it now.

Apparently, Wilhelmina hadn't expected Cammie's question. "Why do you ask?"

Cammie smiled feebly. "I'm not sure yet. I think I found a clue, but I need to check it out."

"Well, I guess your curiosity is easy to satisfy." With a shrug, Wilhelmina wheeled herself to the fireplace, where the history book sat on the shelf between a porcelain statuette of a skater in the spiral position and a vase filled with live, white roses.

Wilhelmina moved the book to her knees and put on a pair of silver-rimmed glasses that hung around her neck on a chain. Carefully, slowly, the older woman began to turn the pages. Her hands clasped on her lap, Cammie watched Wilhelmina's every move. Alex, however, acted indifferent, though Cammie couldn't miss a flicker of curiosity in his green eyes.

Wilhelmina finally found the right page. Her eyes scanned it, lingering on the bold print at the top. The president's eyes narrowed then her lips became perfectly round as though she was going to say "oh."

Finally, the older woman put the book aside and looked at Cammie sharply. "Let me tell you, young lady, that I'm quite impressed. The page you referred me to has the title that reads: 'Sonja Henie's last World Championship. Paris, France, 1936.'"

"Yes!" Cammie jumped off her armchair so fast that it hit the table, almost knocking over a vase of white carnations.

Cammie didn't have time to apologize. "That's where Sonia is!"

Wilhelmina smoothed over the yellowing page of the book. "And what makes you so sure? Of course, it's a possibility that the witches took Sonia to that particular moment in the past. Hmm. Sonja

Henie, Sonia Harrison—same first names. I wonder if it's a coincidence or—"

"Sonia was named after Sonja Henie. Sonja Henie is her role model!" Cammie cried out.

Alex was watching her, his mouth slightly open.

"Besides," Cammie put the raspberry day planner on the table and opened it to the page where Sonja Henie's name was written next to "p. 178." "This is what fell out of the pocketbook that belongs to the Witch of Pride."

Wilhelmina picked up the day planner. She scanned the witch's daily activities, her eyes lingering on Sonja Henie's name.

"Good detective work, Cammie!"

Cammie felt her cheeks turn warm, and she couldn't conceal a happy smile.

Wilhelmina twisted the witch's notebook in her hands and put it on the table next to the history book. Her face brightened. "Brilliant! What an uncanny attempt to change skating history and destroy Sonja Henie's reputation at the same time. 1936 Worlds, of all competitions!"

Cammie stared at Wilhelmina. She didn't understand what was so special about that particular year.

Wilhelmina must have noticed a question in Cammie's eyes. "The 1936 World Championship was Sonja's last competition. It was the zenith of her career, the celebration of her achievements as a figure skater. Apparently, the witches brought Sonia Harrison to that period of time, so she could teach the famous skater a lesson, show her that she wasn't the best. On the other hand..."

Wilhelmina ran her hand through her cropped gray hair, looking pensive. "I don't think the witches will let our friend win the worlds. Remember, they want to destroy her too. I wonder what they have plotted."

Skateland president leaned back in her wheelchair, apparently thinking hard. Cammie shifted her feet and glanced at Alex, who was looking in another direction. Cammie didn't understand why it was important to know every detail of the witches' plan. They knew where Sonia was, so all they had to do now was go to 1936 France, find their friend, and take her back home. As simple as that.

Wilhelmina took off her glasses, letting them dangle from the chain on her neck. "Well, I guess we'll never know the answer until we see Sonia. So it looks like the two of you are going to Paris."

Cammie winked at Alex and saw the corners of his lips twitch a little as though he was concealing a smile.

"One thing I want to tell you, my friends, watch out!" Wilhelmina said. "The witches apparently realize that you are close to finding Sonia. Their attacks are likely to intensify. Please, and I repeat it, ple-ea-se be extra careful. "

Wilhelmina shot a quick look at Alex, who averted his eyes. "Stay together. No matter what you do, try not to be alone. Of course, now that the witches don't have the history book, they can't follow you to the past. But neither of you can be safe even in Skateland. Look what happened to Jeff and Alex."

"Use your eyes," Wilhelmina went on. "Keep your conversations with other people to a minimum. Naturally, you can ask questions about Sonia's whereabouts, but don't go into many details if they wonder who you are. Tell people you are visiting from America, but don't divulge the exact place where you live. And…this I have told you many times, but apparently it still hasn't sunk in…no showing off! Demonstrating your excellent skating skills can wait till the show or your next competition. Is that understood?"

Cammie nodded quickly. Alex hung his head.

"You know what? I have an idea. Don't wear skates this time. Put on your street shoes," Wilhelmina said.

What? Cammie saw Alex raise his head. Apparently he hadn't expected that sort of suggestion either.

"But without skates…how?" Cammie stuttered.

"Very easily." Wilhelmina folded her arms on her chest. "What, you can't walk anymore? I probably went overboard with this continuous skating experience in Skateland."

"No, no, of course we can walk, but…what if we have to get on ice? Rental skates probably won't be good." Alex asked softly.

"No!" Wilhelmina said firmly. "You'll have no business to be on ice. If you see Sonia, just yank her out and bring her home."

Cammie saw there was no point in arguing any further. "Okay."

"If you have no more questions, get started," Wilhelmina said. She moved away from the fireplace.

Cammie took it as a sign that they were dismissed and jumped from her armchair. Alex rose too.

"See you soon! Yes and please, keep an eye on each other."

Sonja Henie

The 1936 World Championship appeared to be a much larger event than what Cammie and Alex had seen in Switzerland. They had arrived at the arena ten minutes before the official practice. The competition hadn't even started yet, but the grandstands were almost filled. Posters of Sonja Henie hung everywhere. The famous skater beamed at them from the lampposts and gave them winning looks from the signs in people's hands.

A huge picture of the famous skater hung right near the entrance to the rink. Sonja was shown with her arms spread gracefully, her leg frozen in the attitude position. Therefore, Cammie wasn't surprised that after they took their seats in the stands, Sonja Henie was the first skater they noticed. She was really hard to miss. Dressed in a pink knee-length skirt and a matching beret, Sonja Henie whizzed around the rink on very deep edges, blowing kisses to the audience. She did several high waltz jumps, evoking cheers and bravos from the crowd. Cammie was actually impressed at the sight of well-executed jumps, though she noticed very quickly that the famous skater did nothing more challenging than a single loop.

"Sonia must be here somewhere." Alex was scanning the crowd in the bleachers.

Cammie pointed to the ice. "There is Sonja Henie. Didn't you recognize her?"

Alex rolled his eyes. "I mean *our* Sonia. Why should I care about Sonja Henie?"

"Ah!" Cammie rose on her toes and began to study the spectators too. There were women in long fur coats and men wearing wool coats and hats. There was a cheering crowd of children wearing bright scarves and mittens. Cammie's eyes scanned them, and she sighed with disappointment, realizing that Sonia wasn't among the children. Cammie frowned at the sight of reporters flashing their cameras. The nosy journalists she had seen in Switzerland would stop at nothing to find another sensation. If Cammie and Alex made a mistake, those reporters would be the first to notice. Again and again, Cammie promised herself that she would be extra careful. She looked at the policemen in berets and older men with canes. Yet as hard as she looked, she didn't see Sonia's bright red hair anywhere in the crowd.

"She isn't here," Cammie said with a sigh.

"But she has to be." Alex stretched his neck, studying the skaters who whooshed across the ice. "Actually, I expected Sonia to compete here."

"Oh, she would definitely win," Cammie said.

On the ice, Sonja Henie rose on her toes, spread her arms like wings, and tiptoed forward. The crowd roared. Sonja went into a fast scratch spin and her blond curls swirled around her face, apparently clouding her vision. Sonja shook her head impatiently and curtsied. More clicking and flashing followed. The people in the stands jumped to their feet and gave the skating star a standing ovation.

"*Elle est ravisssante, vraiment la meilleure!*" A woman squealed somewhere behind Cammie.

Several reporters armed with pencils and note-pads rushed to the edge of the rink. A tall man wearing a long black coat was the first to reach the skating star. "Sonja, could I have a quick word, please?" "Sonja, how about an interview for *Paris Soir*?" a young curly-haired man interrupted.

The reporters clapped their hands, cheered, whistled, extinguished cigarettes, beckoned Sonja Henie to come closer.

The beautiful skater didn't seem to mind the attention at all. She flashed another toothy smile at the crowd, shook her curls, and approached the gang of journalists. Her hot pink lips were curved in a coy grin.

"Thank you, my friends!" Sonja Henie said in a very accented English and bent down to put on her skate guards.

"What does it feel like to skate at your last worlds?" one of the reporters shouted at her right in the ear.

"Oh, you know, it's—"

Alex tugged Cammie on the sleeve, and she didn't have a chance to hear Sonja's answer.

"You know what? I bet we could talk to her. If our Sonia is here, she can't have missed her," Alex said excitedly.

"Definitely," Cammie said, feeling hope coming back.

They began to push their way through the crowd to the spot where Sonja Henie stood, chatting fast in her broken English, showering the jostling crowd with enchanting smiles. The reporters scribbled frantically, drinking in Sonja's every word.

"She's kind of busy," Cammie said undecidedly. "Do you think we should wait?"

"No, let's do it now. Our mission is much more important than whatever they are trying to find out."

They made another attempt at coming closer, but the crowd thickened around them, making it impossible to get within twenty feet of Sonja Henie.

"Excuse me!" Cammie was trying to squeeze between two tall figures ahead of her.

A man in a gray felt hat, who looked like another reporter, gave her a funny look. "Young lady, autographs can wait. Miss Henie is in the middle of an interview."

"We don't want an autograph," Cammie said.

"We only want to ask her one little question," Alex said importantly.

"Whatever it is, it can wait." The reporter turned away from them with obvious indifference.

"Come on!" Alex said angrily as he tried to elbow his way through the noisy crowd of reporters.

Cammie bent down and dove between the reporter in the gray hat and a squatty photographer who was jumping back and forth, looking for the best shot. Alex jumped after her.

"I told you to wait!" the reporter hissed angrily and stepped in front of Alex, blocking the view of Sonja Henie.

Alex's face turned red. "Who do you think you are? I can knock you down easily; I'm in much better shape."

"Alex, don't!" Cammie pulled her friend by the hand, leading him away from the stampeding reporters. "Remember what Wilhelmina told us?"

She saw Alex relax a little, though his eyes were still narrowed in anger.

"So how long do you think we're going to wait? If each of these losers wants to talk to her, it will be a while!" Alex clenched his fists.

Cammie sighed as she watched Sonja give the reporters an eager nod then burst into a rippling laughter.

"We'll wait as long as we have to, and we'll talk to her anyway," Cammie said firmly.

"Are you sure you want to do it, mademoiselle? Sonja Henie isn't exactly a nice person."

Cammie looked back to see who had spoken to her and found herself staring into a pair of dark, sad eyes. They belonged to a gray-haired man wearing a crumpled gray suit. Next to him a woman stood, dressed in an elegant coat and matching hat. She looked slightly annoyed.

"I beg your pardon?" Cammie asked.

"You see, that little girl who is visiting with us has been trying to talk to Sonja Henie, too," the woman said grudgingly. "Only Miss Henie wouldn't spare the child a minute of her precious time."

"Well, Nadine, our guest wasn't exactly courteous with Miss Henie either," the man said. "She kept insisting she was a better skater. I'll be honest with you; no star would like the idea of being outshined."

"The girl is good, though. Perhaps even better than her." The woman nodded in the direction of Sonja Henie. "Shame she can't compete."

"Excuse me, but who are you talking about?" Alex asked politely. He looked puzzled.

Cammie, too, found the conversation strange. The couple was telling them of some girl who said she was better than Sonja Henie herself?

The man observed both of them wearily. "There is a girl staying with us, though we don't know who she is."

Cammie had a weird sensation in the area of her stomach. She looked at Alex and met his unblinking stare. *Could it be her?* his eyes asked.

Why not? Cammie thought. A girl who can be as good as Sonja Henie … well, Sonia was actually better than the famous skater.

"And what's your guest's name? Is it Sonia, too, by any chance?" Cammie asked.

The man winced as if in pain. "No, no, it's not Sonia. She's been telling us her name is Hilde Holovsky. But it can't be true, can it?"

Oh, so it wasn't Sonia, after all. Cammie sighed with disappointment.

"I mean, there is no way our guest could be Hilde Holovsky, right?" The man gave Cammie a very meaningful look, as though he was stating something obvious, something she was supposed to know.

"And why not?" Cammie asked absentmindedly.

"Because Hilde Holovsky died of appendicitis three years ago. Everybody knows that," the man said.

Cammie stared at the man.

"It's sad, because Hilde Holovsky was a really brilliant skater," the woman said. "She won silver at the worlds when she was only thirteen. Can you believe it? Back then, everybody said she might be able to dethrone Sonja Henie one day. I wish she had."

The woman scowled at the radiant Sonja Henie who was tapping her toe on the ice and nodding.

"Anyway, our little guest—we call her Hilde, because she will only go by that name—she is an excellent skater too. And we thought of entering her in the competition, but they won't let her." The man spread his chubby arms.

Alex frowned. "And why not?"

"Because she doesn't know her real name or the country she's from. She insists she is Hilde Holovsky and won't listen to any objections. So the authorities here at the competition say that she is either a liar or she is crazy," the man said dismissively.

"We know she's not a liar." The woman took off her left glove then pulled it back on angrily. "She's such a sweet little thing. We absolutely love her. But unfortunately, she's a little out of her mind. We considered taking her to a psychiatrist—perhaps she might remember who she is, but you know those doctors...they might lock her up and what good would that do? At least now she can skate. And this is about the only thing she likes."

"Yes, she skates all the time on a pond behind our house," the man said. "I wonder what she will do in spring, when the ice melts."

Cammie's heart pounded hard in her chest. At this point, she was almost sure...but she had to check one more thing.

"That girl...Hilde, can she be American?"

The man's features tightened, as though he was trying to remember. "You know what? She could be. Actually, I thought she might be English."

"No, she sounds more like an American to me," the woman said. "Why do you ask? Do you know her?"

"Is her hair red?" Alex asked fast.

The woman looked at him with surprise. "Why, yes. I don't like that color, but it looks good on her. So you do know her."

"And how old is she?" Cammie was ready to shout yes! But she knew she had to behave.

The man shrugged. "She says she is fifteen, but I would place her at around eleven. She is kind of small."

"She is twelve," Cammie said.

"So you do know her." The woman wasn't asking a question now.

"Yes, we do know her. She is twelve years old, and her name is Sonia Harrison," Alex said.

Cammie watched the man and the woman gasp. She turned to Alex and caught his happy smile. She felt as though a heavy burden had been lifted from her. They had found Sonia!

"Are you sure it's her?" Alex whispered excitedly as they got in the back seat of a black Peugeot.

"I'm positive," Cammie mouthed.

"So the girl is American, right?" the man asked as he turned on the ignition.

Cammie and Alex already knew that the couple's names were Monsieur and Madame Parmentier. During their trip from the rink to the couple's home, Cammie and Alex had told their friends about Sonia. Not everything, of course—only the things that could be shared. Naturally, they had left out the part about skating witches; they had merely said that Sonia had been kidnapped.

"She's a very talented American skater," Alex said. "We train together."

"Actually, she's my roommate," Cammie said. Her heart was beating fast; she could barely contain her excitement. Could it be true that they had finally found Sonia?

The car swerved to the right and stopped behind a long row of huge funny-looking vehicles. On her left, Cammie could see the hazy silhouette of the Eiffel Tower in the horizon.

"We live outside Paris in Chateaux de Champs," Madame Parmentier said.

"It's much nicer there, more quiet," Monsieur Parmentier added. "And she can skate there, our little Sonia. Hmm, so that's her name. How interesting!"

"Her parents named her after Sonja Henie. They wanted her to become a skating champion," Cammie said.

"Well, maybe, she will," Madame Parmentier said happily. "Now that we know who she is, we may try to enter her again. Oh, how I wish for that haughty Norwegian to be beaten and by no one else than our little guest."

Cammie caught Alex's worried look. She understood what it meant. There was no way they could allow Sonia to enter the worlds. Of course, with her triple jumps, Sonia could give the reigning world and Olympic champion a run for her medal, but... history couldn't be changed; it had to run its course. And it meant that Sonja Henie was bound to win her last gold medal.

The car rolled on a country road past a beautiful park with perfectly manicured lawns and a gorgeous mansion with a slanted roof and high windows.

"This is the castle of Chateaux de Champs. Our place is named after it. The gardens look very picturesque when the sun is shining," Monsieur Parmentier said.

"Our home isn't far from here," Madame Parmentier added.

They made a few more turns past dark wet trees, and finally the Peugeot slowed down in front of an old house.

Monsieur Parmentier turned off the engine. "Welcome to our home!"

Cammie looked around. "Where is Sonia?"

Madame Parmentier chuckled nervously. "Oh, she can only be at the pond. I told you before; skating is about all she does. It's hard to get her to bed or make her eat. This way now. The pond is in the back of the house."

The ice on the pond was surprisingly smooth, as though it had just been resurfaced. The ice was light gray in color, but the shadows of the high trees surrounding the pond made the surface of the rink almost black. Snow lay white and pristine around the pond, and the whole place was ghostly quiet, except for the scratching of the blades against the ice. A small girl moved forward on alternating forward outside edges in the middle of the pond. She did a three turn, swung her leg around, and whirled in a very fast scratch spin, not unlike Sonja Henie's. As the girl brought her arms together, her blue felt hat slid down to her neck. Long strands of red hair fell on her face.

"Sonia!" Cammie whispered.

"Sonia!" Alex called, waving his hands.

The girl kept skating as though she hadn't heard him.

Monsieur Parmentier put his hand on Alex's shoulder. "She is so focused when she skates, you need to practically shout to get her attention."

"But is it really your friend?" Madame Parmentier asked eagerly.

"Oh yes, that's her." Unable to wait another minute, Cammie dashed forward, her feet plunging deep in the snow. It was right before she jumped onto the ice that she remembered she wasn't wearing her skates.

"Sonia!"

Sonia, who had just gone from an outside to inside spread eagle, slowed down and skated to the edge of the rink. Cammie saw that there was a slightly distant look in her friend's eyes.

"Hello," Sonia said uncertainly.

"Sonia, it's me, Cammie!"

"Cammie? It's a pleasure to meet you," Sonia said politely. Even her voice sounded strange, unfamiliar.

Cammie's heart sunk to the pit of her stomach. What was going on?

"Sonia, it's us. We have come for you." Alex, who had just joined Cammie on the edge of the ice, stretched his hand toward Sonia.

"Why do you call me Sonia? My name is Hilde. Hilde Holovsky," Sonia said sharply.

Cammie stepped back and gasped at her roommate. Something was definitely wrong. The real Sonia would never ignore them like that. And she would definitely know her own name.

Cammie pinched herself hard to make sure she wasn't asleep. But no, she was wide awake, and Alex stood next to her and there was Sonia. She wore an unfamiliar black jacket, and the hem of a blue velvet dress showed from under it. Cammie didn't recognize the blue felt hat that perched on the girl's head either. But other than that, the girl who stood in front of her looked exactly like Sonia Harrison— petite with very pale skin and a spray of freckles on the bridge of her nose. And the girl's eyes were round and blue, like Sonia's eyes. The only missing thing was the expression of friendliness everybody knew Sonia Harrison for. Now all joy and excitement seemed to have drained from Sonia's eyes; they were empty.

"I'm sorry, but I don't know you," Sonia said after an uncomfortable pause. "I have to practice. I have a very important competition in a couple of days."

She nodded at them and skated away. Flabbergasted, Cammie watched the black-and-blue silhouette rush to the middle of the rink. Sonia lifted her left leg in a spiral position, and as she glided in their direction, Cammie noticed an expression of complete joy on her roommate's face.

"What's going on here? She won't even talk to us," Alex whispered.

Cammie didn't say anything; she was as shocked as Alex.

Monsieur Parmentier coughed behind them. "Now as you see, the poor girl isn't in her right mind. She didn't even recognize the two of you."

"But are you sure she is the friend you're looking for?" Madame Parmentier asked. Her lips were pressed tight; the woman looked as though she didn't quite believe them.

"We're sure!" Alex exclaimed, though Cammie could detect notes of uncertainty in his voice.

"But how can she go home with us if she doesn't even remember us?" Cammie asked sadly.

Madame Parmentier's lips curved in an expression of annoyance. She brought her hands to her mouth like a loudspeaker and shouted, "Sonia! Would you like to come here, please?"

Sonia, who was now doing a sit spin, ignored her completely.

Madame Parmentier slapped herself on the forehead. "Oh but of course! Hilde!"

Sonia skated to the edge of the rink immediately. "Yes, Madame Parmentier."

"It's a bit late for practice, dear. Anyway, these young people want to talk to you."

Sonia fixed her eyes on Cammie and Alex. "Are you reporters? Do you want to interview me?"

Cammie felt her mouth open wide, but the only thing she managed to say was a weak *meh-meh*.

"Er," said Alex, apparently too shocked to speak either.

"For I'm about to beat Sonja Henie at the worlds, you know. I just need to get my double salchow consistent, and then she won't stand a chance." Sonia was speaking very fast.

"What?" Cammie still couldn't believe what she had heard. Either it wasn't Sonia, or Sonia was putting them on, or her roommate was really crazy. Beating Sonja Henie, the famous skater, who had skated sixty years before Sonia Harrison was even born! And a double salchow, how about that? Sonia Harrison, who could land four triple jumps...unbelievable!

"I've been having problems entering the competition," Sonia said. "But I will make it, and I will definitely win."

Feeling dizzy, Cammie leaned against the trunk of the nearest tree. No, it didn't look like a prank; her roommate was definitely, hopelessly crazy.

"Now Sonia, stop it! We've been looking for you everywhere. We know who did it to you," Alex said meaningfully.

"Yeah, the witches!" The moment Cammie said it she realized it was another blunder. What would the Parmentiers think of her now? They would probably be sure all the three of them were crazy.

Luckily, the couple didn't seem to have noticed Cammie's slip. Monsieur Parmentier nodded sadly as his gaze travelled from Sonia to Alex's angry face. Madame Parmentier was chewing her lip.

"Everybody back home is worried about you." Alex stretched his hand, inviting Sonia to join them.

Sonia didn't make a move; she simply stared at Alex. His hand hung in the air.

"Sonia, let's go. You'll feel better once you're back in Skateland." Alex's voice was pleading.

Sonia's blank eyes slid from Cammie to Alex then she turned to Madame Parmentier. "Who are these people? What do they want?"

"They are Americans, dear. The United States of America, that's where you're from, remember? They are here to take you home with them," Monsieur Parmentier said kindly.

Sonia shook her head slowly. "My home is in Austria. I'm a two-time Austrian figure skating champion. But I can't go home now. I've got to compete at the worlds."

Monsieur Parmentier stepped back. He looked helpless. "You see? She keeps insisting she's Hilde Holovsky."

"That's right, it's me!" For the first time today, Sonia smiled.

The spark of joy on her roommate's face made Cammie even more scared. Panic rose within her. "Alex, what are we going to do?"

Madame Parmentier threw her arms around Sonia. "Why don't we go home and change now, Hilde? It's almost time for dinner."

"And the interview?" Sonia was obviously disappointed.

"There will be time tomorrow. Come on." The two of them staggered away.

"Where … where are you taking her? She's got to go home with us!" Alex yelled.

Madame Parmentier ignored him, her hand clenched tightly around Sonia's waist. Right before they entered the house, Sonia turned around and blew a kiss at them. Sonja Henie's kiss. Cammie felt a wave of nausea.

"She even acts like a skating star," Alex exclaimed.

The door slammed.

"But Sonia needs to come home!" Cammie looked up at Monsieur Parmentier, begging him to understand.

He averted his look. "Look, you can't force her to come with you."

"And why not? She needs to go home. Everybody is worried about her. Her parents are looking for her too," Alex boomed.

"It's true, but … so far we have no proof that the girl who is staying with us is indeed Sonia Harrison."

"And who else could she be? Hilde Holovsky is dead; you know that," Alex snapped.

Monsieur Parmentier spread his arms. "This I don't know."

"But we both know her. We train together. She's my roommate, I swear!" Cammie cried out.

Monsieur Parmentier looked her in the eye, and she saw that the man was really sorry.

"With all due respect, it's her word against yours," the man said. "Even if you're telling the truth, and the girl's name is Sonia, and she is American, something bad happened to her. You say she was kidnapped, right?"

Both Cammie and Alex nodded.

"See? Before we let her leave, we need to be sure she'll be safe with you. And from what I have just seen, the girl doesn't even recognize you."

Cammie and Alex exchanged nervous glances.

"So what are we supposed to do now?" Alex asked angrily.

Monsieur Parmentier shrugged. "Bring me some proof. If I see that you are really Sonia's friends and you can help her, I'll let her go. Now, do you need a ride back to the rink?"

The man's last sentence was a sign of dismissal, a signal for them to leave. Apparently they were not invited to dinner. Feeling hurt, Cammie cast the last look at the door through which Sonia had just walked.

"No, we'll be fine. Thank you," Alex said coldly. "Come on, Cammie."

And without saying another word, he took Cammie by the hand and led her away from the Parmentiers' house.

WILHELMINA'S ADVICE

S o we are going back to Skateland, aren't we?" Cammie asked as she watched Alex set the history book on the ground. They were a block away from the Parmentiers' house, so they could be sure the couple didn't see them anymore.

"Of course. We need Wilhelmina's advice. Perhaps she can come with us and take Sonia home."

"But Wilhelmina's too sick. Remember, she said it was too hard for her to travel through time."

"Well, it would just be one trip. It wouldn't kill her."

"Or perhaps Sonia's parents can come with us," Cammie said.

"Good thinking." Alex motioned for Cammie to step on the introductory page next to him. They joined hands, and the French forest vanished from their sight.

In the lobby of the Skating Museum, they took their skates from under the receptionist's counter and quickly started lacing them up.

"Well, at least we know where she is. I'm sure Wilhelmina will think of something," Alex said encouragingly.

"Yes, it's good that we found Sonia, but wow, isn't she crazy? She couldn't even recognize us."

"Right, and all that nonsense about beating Sonja Henie ... "

"Well, she could beat her easily. Though of course, the real Sonia would know it wouldn't be right to even try. Hey, wait a minute!" Cammie jumped off the chair wearing one skate.

"What?"

"Remember she mentioned a problem with her double salchow? I can't believe it. Sonia's triple salchow is very consistent. She can do a triple flip and a triple loop too; it's only the triple lutz she still can't land."

"So?" Alex's hands that were lacing his boots froze midway. "Ah, I see. Yeah, that's weird. How can someone lose all the jumps in a week. Well, it may happen if you grow too fast, but—"

"That's it! If you have a growth spurt or if you are injured, but Sonia hasn't grown an inch; she's exactly the way she was. And she isn't injured. Which means—"

"It's the witches!" Alex slammed his skate guard against the floor, his eyes flashing.

"Of course! Remember how Sonia could barely skate last time when the Witch of Fear attacked her? Sonia was scared."

"Do you think it's the Witch of Fear again? Sonia didn't look scared this time," Alex asked.

"No," Cammie admitted.

"She was proud, though," Alex said slowly. "Oh, yes, it's got to be the Witch of Pride this time. Oh, how I hate that woman!"

Alex finished lacing his boots with record speed and jumped off his chair. "Let's find her. Just wait till I see that witch again. I'll rip her apart."

"But how will it help Sonia?" Cammie asked soberly.

"I'll think about that later. Let me deal with the witch first. Okay, she almost destroyed me. I almost got disqualified. And if I let that go, it doesn't mean that the stupid witch can torture my friend. You stay here!"

Alex pulled on his gloves and headed for the exit.

"Alex!" Cammie rushed after him, one boot still unlaced. "Remember what Wilhelmina told us? We need to be extra careful."

"I will be careful."

"Alex, please! Let's talk to Wilhelmina, okay? She will tell us exactly what to do. Do you want to mess it up again?"

Alex stopped, his fists still clenched. He was breathing hard. "Ah, okay. But after Sonia's home, I'll—"

"Fine, but let's make sure Sonia is safe first." Cammie sighed with relief. Wilhelmina would think of something. She was smart, and she had powers that were greater than the witches' abilities.

They locked the front door behind them and skated along the icy path in the direction of Wilhelmina's house. After not skating for the whole day, Cammie's legs felt a little stiff. She tried to push off the ice harder to stay close to Alex. He flew forward with breathtaking speed as though all the hours off ice hadn't affected him at all.

"Just wait, you stupid, evil—" Alex muttered.

"Alex, don't think about her now!"

Alex went into a hockey stop and turned his angry face to Cammie. "Listen, you don't know what it feels like to be attacked by the Witch of Pride. She makes you feel so good; you really believe you're the best in the world, that you can beat any skater. Even Evan Lysacek is no match for you. But it's nothing but a lie, and you don't know it and then you think you don't really need to practice hard. So you get worse and then ... don't you understand she almost ruined my skating career?"

"Alex, I understand—"

"No, you don't. I hate her!" Alex shouted.

A big crow sitting on a branch of an evergreen tree fixed its black eyes on Alex. Cammie could swear there was disapproval in the way the bird took off, showering him with snow.

"You will never understand it unless you go through it yourself." Alex brushed the snow off his parka, turned away from Cammie, and skated on. The hard ice scratched loudly under his blades.

Cammie followed shortly behind.

The door to Wilhelmina's house opened at the first notes of "Winter Wonderland," and Christel's sour face stared at them. "Not you two again."

Cammie blurted a quick hello.

"Who's that, Christel?" Wilhelmina asked from inside the house.

"Your two closest friends," Christel shouted with obvious sarcasm. She still clutched the door-frame, apparently unwilling to let Cammie and Alex in.

There was a squeak of wheels, Christel's "ouch," and then the door opened wide.

"I can tell from your facial expressions that you have big news for me." Wilhelmina smiled at them from her wheelchair.

"Uh, kind of," Alex said uncertainly.

"We found Sonia," Cammie said, knowing that her voice didn't sound particularly happy.

Wilhelmina raised her eyebrows. "But?"

"She won't come with us. She's bewitched," Alex said.

Wilhelmina's gray eyes became huge like two frozen ponds. She grabbed her glasses, put them on, and took them off again. "Please come inside."

"Well, everything makes sense," Wilhelmina said after she heard a detailed story of Cammie and Alex's encounter with Sonia.

"It's the Witch of Pride's work, isn't it?" Alex asked excitedly. "Please, Mrs. Van Uffeln, let me deal with her myself."

The president's eyes studied his bright pink face. "I guess you don't understand that it's not about revenge. I asked you to bring the girl back, that's all. Once you do that, your mission will be over."

Cammie could tell that Alex didn't like the fact that he wouldn't be directly involved in punishing the Witch of Pride for bewitching Sonia. Alex's green eyes glared angrily at Skateland president.

There was an uncomfortable silence, and then Wilhelmina stomped her foot against the wheelchair. It must have hurt, for the older woman winced.

"How can you even think of venting your anger when your friend is in the past, not even knowing who she is?" Wilhelmina bellowed.

Alex raised his head and looked at Wilhelmina with defiance. Apparently he was trying to tell the older woman that he disagreed with her judgment.

He cared about Sonia; he knew rescuing her was their top priority. But he had already been attacked badly, he had succumbed to the Witch of Pride, and he had failed. So now it hurt. Wilhelmina's eyes rested on his forehead then slid down and met Alex's glare. It looked like a battle, and Cammie knew Alex expected to win. He blinked, clasped the armrests, stiffened up ... the older woman sat in her wheelchair, calm and relaxed. Cammie could see that Wilhelmina was even smiling. And finally, it was Alex who looked away.

"That's better. Now back to business," Wilhelmina said. "One thing you are right about is that the Witch of Pride had her share in manipulating Sonia's mind. Yes, this time, the witches attacked Sonia's mind."

Cammie saw Alex raise his head.

"That's right; the problem is in Sonia's mind now. Yet I believe it took more than one witch to bring the poor girl to the state she is in now. I strongly believe the Witch of Confusion got involved. Are you telling me she isn't sure about her identity?"

"Yes, she calls herself Hilde. Hilde ... " Cammie creased her forehead, trying to think of the last name.

"Hilde Holovsky," Alex said softly.

"Ah, Hilde Holovsky." Wilhelmina closed her eyes for a second, appearing deep in thought. "Yes, that was really a brilliant plan. Evil but genius. To use the name of a deceased skater, a young girl ... "

Wilhelmina shook her head, looking morose. "Do you know who Hilde Holovsky was?"

"No," Cammie said apologetically. She had never wished more she had spent quality time studying skating history.

Alex shook his head too. That surprised Cammie. She knew that her friend enjoyed memorizing different historical facts. It could only mean that Hilde Holovsky's name wasn't in their school book.

"Hilde Holovsky was an extremely precocious Austrian skater who became European bronze medalist and then world's silver medalist at the age of thirteen," Wilhelmina said. "It happened in 1931. Everybody had high hopes for Hilde, believing she might be able to challenge the invincible Sonja Henie one day. Unfortunately, Hilde died in 1933, at the age of fifteen."

"Oh yes, the Parmentiers did say that Sonia had been using the name of a deceased skater," Cammie exclaimed.

"And that was the reason she couldn't compete at the worlds, because everybody knew she couldn't be Hilde Holovsky," Alex said.

Wilhelmina nodded. "Exactly. So do you see the brilliance behind that devilish scheme? The witches took Sonia to 1936 France and gave her the name of a dead person. Now in the sight of everybody, Sonia is either a liar or a mentally sick person. Either way, she can't compete at the worlds. She is a good skater, and she knows it. Yet she can't get recognition for what she can do. On the other hand, people talk; they spread rumors about someone out there who can outskate Sonja Henie. That can be bad for Sonja Henie's reputation too. By the way, what did Sonia's skills look like to you?"

"Her skating is weird," Cammie said quickly. "I mean she's good, but she skates like Sonja Henie a lot. Her style is almost the same. But her toughest jump is the single axel, and she is still working on her double salchow."

Cammie saw Wilhelmina's eyebrows shoot up and started speaking even faster. "But I know Sonia can do four triple jumps up to the flip. But back in France, I only saw her do singles."

Wilhelmina clapped her hands, looking tremendously excited. "You know what? It's the proof I needed. Now it all makes sense. Sonia believes she's Hilde Holovsky, so she can only do the elements the real Hilde was capable of."

Alex stared at Wilhelmina, openmouthed. "But how can it be? If she could do triples before, what happened to them?"

"She couldn't just forget them, could she?" Cammie asked.

"As you see, she could. Our mind is much more powerful than our bodies," Wilhelmina said. "If Sonia believes the double salchow is her limit, she won't be able to do anything more challenging than that. Do you understand what I'm talking about, children? This is the reason why you always need to believe in yourselves. If you are sure you are capable of doing a certain element, it's only a matter of time and work before you nail it. But take faith and confidence away from a skater, and she is helpless."

Wilhelmina stared at the dancing flames in the grate, appearing pensive. Cammie rubbed her forehead, trying to digest what she had just heard. Poor Sonia! Just because she believed she was someone else, she could no longer skate up to her level. But it was awful; the scariest thing that could happen to anybody. Cammie imagined no longer being able to do the jumps she had been working on for months and years, and shuddered.

Cammie opened and closed her mouth several times. She had so many questions to ask Wilhelmina, but the older woman kept looking at the fire, mumbling something to herself. The grandfather clock ticked minutes away.

Finally, Wilhelmina raised her head and looked straight at Cammie then shifted her gaze to Alex. "Yes, that's the only way. And I need both of you to help again."

Alex frowned. "But Sonia won't recognize us, and the Parmentiers don't believe we are her friends. They want proof."

"Yes, we were thinking maybe Sonia's parents could go after her instead?" Cammie asked warily.

Wilhelmina jerked her head impatiently. "What good would that do? Sonia wouldn't recognize her parents either. Do you know the only way she can remember who she is? She needs to start doing difficult moves again; the ones Sonia Harrison could do. "

"What?" Cammie whispered. What Wilhelmina was saying didn't make any sense.

"Yes, once Sonia is able to land her triples, her recovered muscle memory will send a message to her brain. That's how her true identity will come back," Wilhelmina said.

Cammie and Alex stared at each other in amazement. Triples? But Sonia couldn't do them. She wouldn't even try.

"And this is where you guys come in," Skateland president said. "You will teach Sonia how to do the difficult jumps she has lost."

At that point, Cammie thought she had misunderstood Wilhelmina. She looked at Alex, hoping that he would know what exactly the older woman meant. Yet her friend looked equally dumbstruck.

"But...but Mrs. Van Uffeln, we aren't coaches," Alex protested.

Wilhelmina cocked her head. "So? Now is a perfect time to start acting as coaches."

"But...but I can't do any triples myself!" Cammie exclaimed.

"Er...I can only do a triple salchow and a triple toe-loop," Alex said uncertainly.

"Don't worry about that," Wilhelmina said reassuringly. "Most coaches who work with elite skaters can't land triple-triple combinations or quads anymore. So what? They can still teach others and do an excellent job. Let me tell you something; it's caring about others and wanting your student to succeed that makes you a good coach. Being able to explain how an element should be done also helps."

Cammie was frantically searching through her mind. She had to say something, so Wilhelmina would understand that Alex and she couldn't act as coaches. No way! What was the older woman thinking? They were students themselves, for crying out loud!

Alex, who apparently found Wilhelmina's idea ludicrous as well, started saying that perhaps Sonia wouldn't be willing to learn anything from them. Cammie and Sonia were of the same age, and Alex was only two years older. Sonia wouldn't even respect them!

Wilhelmina smiled brightly. "Oh, that's where you are wrong. Skaters are respected for their skills, not for their age. Besides, you are forgetting one thing. The Witch of Pride played a big part in bewitching Sonia. It means that at this point, your friend is very arrogant. She believes that she is the best skater in the world. So once she sees someone who is better than her, she'll respond to the challenge. Believe me; she would be willing to work extra hard to move up to your level."

"But teaching someone to do triples... I don't know." Alex looked worried. "Why can't a real coach do it?"

"There's another thing you're forgetting," Wilhelmina said. "You won't have to teach Sonia new things. She did those triple jumps in the past, didn't she? It means that her body remembers how to do them. The problem is in her mind. But once she lands the jumps, her memory will come back. You will see."

COACH CAMMIE AND COACH ALEX

"I still hope Wilhelmina will let a real coach teach Sonia," Alex said.

Cammie shook her head. "No way. She's already made her decision; it's got to be us."

They sat on a couch in the empty lobby of the Skating Museum. Alex held a notebook in his hand, where he had written down the list of jumps Sonia had to learn.

"Her double salchow is still inconsistent, so we'll start with it," Alex said and circled "double salchow" on the list.

"I hope it will take her less than a year to learn all those jumps." Cammie folded her arms and shook her head morosely.

The list really looked impressive. In addition to the double toe loop, loop, flip, and lutz, it included all the triple jumps. Any skater would agree that mastering all of them could take years.

"Sonia could do most of them before," Cammie thought out loud. "Except for the triple lutz."

"We've got to believe her muscle memory is still there. That's what Wilhelmina said, remember?" Alex said. "Look at it this way: have you ever been injured?"

Cammie nodded. "Yes, during my first year of taking lessons. I sprained my ankle, and I had to stay away from ice for three weeks."

"Well, what happened? Could you skate when you came back?"

Cammie rested her face on her folded hands. "Well, back then I could only do half jumps. And I remember being a little unsteady at the beginning, but I think I pretty much had all the jumps back by the end of the first practice."

Alex turned his excited face to her. "See? And Sonia didn't even get injured. Everything is fine with her body, so it won't be a problem for her to land those triples."

"Her mind isn't right, though." Cammie shivered as she remembered the distant look in Sonia's eyes.

"So what? When you land a jump consistently, you don't have to tell your body what to do next. You don't have to remind your knees to bend and your arms to pull in. You just … do it!" Alex jumped off the couch and peformed a beautiful double axel on the floor.

"Well?" he asked as he faced Cammie, his arms spread, imitating the landing position.

"Bravo!" Cammie clapped her hands with exaggerated flare. "Now, how about the famous Bernard jump … hey, I was only kidding!"

Alex advanced on her, looking furious. "I'll get you for that, Cammie Wester. Just wait!"

"Uh-huh! I think I'd better run for it." Cammie flew off the couch and sprinted to the middle of the lobby, Alex following her closely. She was three steps up the spiral staircase when his strong hands squeezed her arm and pulled her down. Cammie tried not to let go of the banister, but Alex's fingers were like steel. Cammie whirled around, aimed her foot at his shin, kicked, and missed.

"Gotcha!" Alex shouted but slipped, and both of them fell on the floor in a heap. Cammie was laughing so hard that her ribs hurt. Alex however looked mad.

"If I ever hear about that Bernard junk again—"

Cammie giggled. "Bernard junk? That was a good one."

The corners of Alex's mouth twitched; apparently he was trying his best to appear menacing, but finally he chuckled too. "You wait, Cammie!"

"Come on, Alex, do you seriously think I'll go around Skateland blabbing about that jump? It was the witch's fault, not yours. It could happen to anyone."

"Yeah!" Alex stared at the stand with brochures depicting the halls of the Skating Museum. For a moment, he appeared deep in thought. Then he cast a quick glance at the clock and jumped up off the floor. "What are we waiting for? We'd better start working on Sonia's jumps as soon as possible."

They approached the pond in Chateaux de Champs shortly after lunch. As they had expected, Sonia was already there, gliding smoothly around the rink on deep edges. She did a high waltz jump then raised her hands and ran forward on her toes, blowing a kiss to an imaginary audience.

"And here's Sonja Henie's signature move," Cammie said, shaking her head.

"I don't think it would have the same effect on our audience," Alex said.

"Sure. It's too showy. Besides, it's one thing if a skating star greets the audience like this, but who on earth is Sonia Harrison?"

"Nothing but a braggart," Alex said eagerly.

"Well, it's not her fault. Come on." Cammie took off her skate guards and jumped onto the ice. She began her warmup, moving around the rink in long fast strokes. As Cammie glided past Sonia, she gave her roommate a furtive glance. Sonia ignored her completely; apparently, the girl was too absorbed in her routine—no, not her routine, her showing off.

Cammie's heart sank. The showy, overly confident skater who was gliding next to her was so unlike the Sonia Harrison she knew that Cammie almost had to pinch herself to make sure she wasn't dreaming. Sonia Harrison was a modest, hard-working skater, perhaps a little shy but sweet. Ever since Cammie moved to Skateland, Sonia had always been there to help her and encourage her. Sonia had given Cammie advice on her skating; she had explained math problems to her. *Sonia, talk to me!* Cammie wanted to cry. She tried to meet Sonia's eyes, but the girl seemed to be looking through her.

Frustrated, Cammie turned to Alex, who had just joined them on the ice. "Listen, she behaves as though I'm not even here."

"Sonia!" Alex called.

Sonia's face hardened. She glared at Alex for a moment then looked away.

"How about that?" Alex grumbled.

"Sonia!" Cammie called again.

When the girl didn't even look at her, Cammie suddenly remembered. "Alex, I know. She doesn't go by Sonia anymore. Hmm, Hilde, hi!"

Sonia swirled around and pulled her blue hat down to cover her ears more. Her eyes slid down Cammie's figure then went up and studied her face. Cammie fought the desire to turn away. The cold empty look of her roommate's eyes was unnerving.

"I don't think it's the best time for an interview," Sonia said haughtily. "I'm in the middle of my practice now. You see, I have to work hard to beat Sonja Henie."

Before Cammie could think of an answer, Sonia skated away on the scratched ice without giving her another look.

"She's even weirder than I thought," Alex said angrily.

Cammie looked at Alex helplessly, expecting him to think of something, to come up with a plan. Alex shrugged, his face morose. Cammie glanced at the bare trees around the pond. The dark, tangled branches almost touched the gray rutted ice, and the whole place appeared cold and unfriendly. Cammie wished Wilhelmina were there. She had allowed them to come and see her if they needed advice. Well, now they had no clue what to do with Sonia, and Wilhelmina was in Skateland, separated from them not only by miles but by years.

The wind rustled through the crooked trees. A bird chirped somewhere in the thicket, and then everything went quiet again. All Cammie could hear was the scratching of Sonia's blades. Even Alex had stopped skating. He stood at the edge of the rink, gazing at Sonia as though she were a ghost.

Then Cammie had an idea. She wasn't sure it was going to work, but it was still worth trying. She got deep on her knees and started circling the rink as fast as she could. She went into forward crossovers, did a Mohawk to backward crossovers, stepped on her left outside edge. Now the timing was important; she couldn't take off too soon, yet staying on the edge too long could result in a loss of speed and then the jump wouldn't happen either.

Now! a small voice whispered in Cammie's ear.

She bent her knee, picked with her right toe, and swung her arms hard. She was in the air spinning fast. One, two...she landed securely, her free leg extended behind her. It was a perfect double lutz.

"Yes!" Cammie pumped her fist in the air.

"Good job!" Alex's voice came from a distance, but Cammie was too excited to stop. She had to try another double lutz to make sure it wasn't a fluke; she could really do it.

She landed another and another then moved to her double flip then her double loop.

"Wow, Cammie!" Alex stood by her side, clapping loudly.

Cammie blinked, looking into Alex's excited face. She felt as though she had just woken up.

"It was fantastic!" Alex exclaimed.

"Uh, was it?" Cammie shook her head, feeling elated. She still couldn't believe she had landed all those difficult jumps without a single mistake, without as much as brushing the ice with her free foot. She had been perfect.

"Wait a minute, what's your name?"

That was a nasty question considering that Cammie and Sonia had been sharing a dorm room for a year.

Cammie turned around and found herself staring into Sonia's cold eyes. "Cammie Wester," she said matter-of-factly.

A frown appeared on Sonia's smooth forehead. "Never heard of you. You're a good skater, you know? You might give old Sonja Henie a run for her title. Are you competing at the worlds?"

Cammie couldn't suppress a smile. "No."

"Why not?" Sonia's eyes became very wide; she looked genuinely surprised.

"Because I'm not ready yet."

"Not ready? Of course you are! You're better than Sonja Henie and even...better than me." At the end of the sentence, Sonia lowered her voice, looking worried.

"That's right; you're not the best," Cammie said calmly. "But you can be."

There was a glint in Sonia's eyes as though the girl were beginning to wake up. "What do you mean?"

"Do you want to learn those double jumps?"

"Me?" Sonia seemed to have shed all aloofness, staring at Cammie excitedly. "Could you teach me? Really?"

Cammie nodded importantly. "Sure. Do you want to start now?"

"Yes! Oh, wait! I'm not sure how much I can pay you. I have to talk to the Parmentiers. Maybe they can cough up a dollar or two an hour, and then, when I win the world title, I'll be able to pay them back."

"A dollar or two an hour?" Alex's voice came from behind. He sounded shocked.

Cammie knew why. For a dollar, you could probably get a one-minute lesson in Skateland, but nothing more than that.

"It's 1936, remember?" Cammie whispered to Alex.

She turned back to Sonia. "We'll not talk about money right now. If you're ready, let's start with your double salchow."

"Sure." Sonia quickly adjusted her hat, looking elated. "I enter it from backward crossovers, right?"

Without waiting for Cammie's answer, Sonia did four backward crossovers, executed a quick three turn, held her backward inside edge, and pulled in her arms.

Sonia landed her jump all right, but there wasn't enough height, so she had to put her free foot down.

"It's almost there," Cammie said, trying not to show her disappointment. She remembered too well Sonia Harrison's huge, flowing salchow. In fact, just a year ago, Cammie had taken tips from her.

Sonia skated up to Cammie panting, an angry glitter in her eyes. "The jump was two footed. That won't work."

"How about trying a single first?" Cammie suggested.

Sonia's eyes glared menacingly. "No way. Single jumps are for Sonja Henie."

Cammie sighed. She knew the whole coaching business was going to be tough, but she wasn't prepared to work with a stubborn student. Sonia Harrison would never have thought of challenging a coach's advice. But Cammie felt she'd better not be too hard on Sonia.

"All right, let me show you what you do wrong. For a clean landing, you need to go up in the air sooner and pull in your arms tighter. Look!" Cammie did her own double salchow, which she thought looked all right.

"Pick up more speed and bend your left knee more!" Alex's voice came from behind.

Surprised that Alex had thought of teaching her too, Cammie took her eyes off Sonia to watch Alex entering a double salchow. Boy, he was so tall! Cammie had always thought that being petite helped her skating. But Alex was almost a foot taller, and surely he got a lot of power from his height. Alex landed securely on his backward edge, holding it for what seemed like eternity. Cammie sighed. Alex's salchow was huge, his landing was light, and his ride out was smooth. Oh, how she wished she could jump like that!

"Look girls, you both complete your second revolution when you are almost down," Alex said. "Get more height but spin tighter, or you'll never move up to triples."

"Triples?" came Sonia's bewildered voice. "Are you talking about—"

"Just do what I say," Alex said. He sounded stern, like a real coach. "Do it again!" Alex was now speaking to Sonia.

Cammie stepped aside, watching her roommate closely. This time, Sonia copied Alex perfectly. Her double salchow was almost as good as his. Cammie clicked her tongue. Sonia surely had a lot of talent.

"Not bad," Alex said reassuringly. "This time, try not to drop your right shoulder. Do it again."

Cammie shook her head, mesmerized by what Alex was doing. Not only did he sound like a coach, he looked as though he had been working with students for years. No wonder he seemed to have gained Sonia's trust immediately. The girl's aloofness was gone. What Cammie saw on the ice was an eager, dedicated student.

Now Alex was explaining something, drawing circles in the air with both hands. Sonia listened to him, her mouth slightly open. As she nodded, signaling that she understood, the blue pom-pom on her knit wool hat bounced gingerly.

Feeling that she was no longer needed, Cammie stepped aside. After watching Sonia and Alex for about half an hour, she felt her feet getting cold. She took a couple of laps around the rink to warm up then tried another double salchow. Not bad. Alex's recommendations surely worked for her too.

"Cammie, how about showing us a double toe loop?" Alex called.

Cammie skidded to a stop. Alex smiled at her. Sonia stood by his side, her usually pale cheeks flushing, her eyes glittering.

"Can you do a double toe loop?" Sonia asked Cammie impatiently. "I need to learn it too, then."

"Sure." Now fully convinced that their plan was going to work, Cammie did a double-toe loop.

"Your turn now," Alex said to Sonia.

Her eyes widened. "Just like that? I've never tried it before."

"Sure you have," Alex said simply. He winked at Cammie then squeezed Sonia's shoulder. "You saw Cammie do it, didn't you?"

"Of course, I did, but—"

"No buts. Don't think about it. Let your body do the work."

Looking slightly uncertain, Sonia skated away. She went into forward crossovers, picking up speed.

"Are you sure she's ready for a double toe loop?" Cammie asked softly.

"Muscle memory, remember?" Alex was watching Sonia closely. He threw his fist in the air. "Yes!"

Sonia's double toe loop looked a little unsteady, but it was definitely a fully rotated double jump.

"Now watch me do it," Alex said.

Toward the end of the practice, Sonia could do all of her double jumps up to the flip. The only double jump she was still having trouble with was the double lutz. Unless Sonia switched to the backward inside edge at the last moment, the jump came out underrotated, and she had to put her free foot down to avoid a nasty fall.

"It's still…not right," Sonia breathed out. She was short of breath; her face was clammy with perspiration. Loose strands of red hair were glued to her cheeks.

Alex looked at his watch. "I think we'd better call it a day."

"No!" Sonia shouted. "Not until I get my double lutz."

Wow, that was some determination! Cammie looked at the girl with a mixture of awe and joy. Her own legs shook, and she would give anything in the world just to get out of her skates. Sonia, on the other hand, was so focused on her goal that she apparently was oblivious to the fatigue. On the other hand, that kind of behavior was so much more like Sonia Harrison's that Cammie felt positively elated. Fine, if burning herself out was what it took to deliver Sonia from pride and confusion, Cammie was ready to stay at the rink overnight.

Alex, however, shook his head. "We have been on the ice for eight hours. It's time to take a break. Anyway, I think it's too much for one day."

"But Alex, we still have triple jumps to work on," Cammie whispered, surprised that Alex was actually going to give up.

Alex frowned. "Not today. We don't want her injured, do we?"

"Sure, but—"

"Hilde dear, what's this supposed to mean?"

Cammie wheeled around to see Madame Parmentier standing on the edge of the rink, looking scandalized.

"I had lunch ready for you, but you didn't even touch it. Don't tell me you have been skating the whole day!"

"Madame Parmentier, I have learned all of the double jumps today," Sonia said, her lips spread in a huge smile. "Only my double lutz still needs work, but I can fix it. Let me show you."

"No!" Cammie and Alex said at the same time.

Madame Parmentier looked at them with visible annoyance. "So the two of you are here again. I don't think Hilde needs to be pushed that hard. Come on, Hilde dear, you need to eat something. I'm sure your friends need to be back home too."

"They aren't my friends. They're my coaches," Sonia said proudly.

From where she stood, Cammie could see Madame Parmentier roll her eyes. "Whatever you say, dear. Anyway, I want you to say goodbye to your … hmm … coaches now."

Sonia beamed at Alex. "Goodbye, Coach Alex. You are coming tomorrow, aren't you?"

She suddenly sounded scared, as though fearing that Cammie and Alex would let her down.

"Coach Cammie, can we please have another lesson tomorrow?"

Coach Cammie, hmm. That sounded really cool. Cammie caught Alex's mischievous grin, looked into Sonia's radiant face, and nodded. "Of course, we can. Same time tomorrow."

Cammie and Alex waited for Sonia to disappear inside the house. Then Alex took the history book out of his pocket and positioned it on the ground. They stepped on the book and were back at Skateland instantly.

TRIPLE JUMPS

Cammie and Alex arrived at Sonia's pond at ten o'clock every day. Sonia had explained to them that by that time, both Monsieur and Madame Parmentier were usually on their way to work. It meant that the three of them would have the place to themselves. With the adults gone, Cammie and Alex could coach Sonia for eight straight hours without being interrupted. At the beginning, they thought of finishing their practice at eight in the evening, thus making it a ten-hour-practice day. Yet they quickly realized it wasn't going to work.

When Madame Parmentier wasn't in Paris working as a typist or shopping, she always hung out at the rink, watching the three of them with her small dark eyes. Cammie found the woman's presence annoying. After about ten minutes of watching Sonia practice her triples and crashing on the ice, Madame Parmentier obviously felt it was her responsibility to get involved.

"But Hilde dear, why do you have to listen to these kids? Mind you, you're a much better skater than the two of them taken together. And honestly, I don't fancy this excessive spinning in the air. I don't think the judges will be particularly impressed with a skater who hops on the ice like a rabbit. Personally, I like you merely gliding around the pond, holding your arms like a ballerina. No, wait, why don't you show me your beautiful spin?"

Sonia, however, seemed completely imperturbed by Madame Parmentier's remarks.

"Thank you, Madame Parmentier, but I need those difficult jumps to be the best in the world," she would say, always sweet, always polite.

"You're the best already!" Madame Parmentier murmured to herself as she took small steps in the snow around the perimeter of the pond. Cammie could see how badly the woman wanted to jump onto the ice, grab Sonia, and carry her away. The woman probably thought that it was her responsibility to protect the poor, gifted girl from the two scoundrels with flashy skating habits. Luckily, Madame Parmentier never dared to step on the ice, apparently too scared to slip and fall. Neither she nor her husband could skate.

"Sonia, dinner is ready," Madame Parmentier would finally say. She completely ignored Cammie and Alex. Not once had they been given an invitation to join the family for a meal. Cammie found that lack of hospitality annoying. After all, the three of them worked so hard at the rink. A plate of French onion soup would help them to regain their strength, and a cup of hot tea would definitely keep them warm.

Finally, after two days of coaching on an empty stomach, Cammie loaded her backpack with containers of Caesar salad and peanut-butter-and-jelly sandwiches. She also packed a thermos of hot tea, and at the last moment, Mrs. Page stuffed a bag of chocolate pretzel skate guards into Cammie's backpack.

"You work so hard, honey, that they won't hurt you. Just look at yourself—as thin as a rail."

Cammie hugged her dorm supervisor. "Thank you, Mrs. Page. They're so good. I'm sure Sweet Blades will start buying them from you soon."

Alex had probably been thinking along the same line, for he too showed up with a backpack bursting out at the seams. When the three of them took a lunch break at noon, Alex took out a bag of chicken sandwiches and a two-liter bottle of water.

"Come on, Sonia, let's eat!" Cammie called as she arranged their food items on the wood bench facing the pond.

Sonia picked up her skate guards. "But Madame Parmentier has lunch ready for me."

Cammie shrugged. "You can go home if you want. I thought you didn't want to waste time."

Alex was already munching on a chicken sandwich.

Sonia looked at the makeshift table uncertainly. "Uh, sure. Actually, sharing a meal with my coaches would be an honor."

She sank on the bench next to Cammie and helped herself to some Caesar salad.

Cammie suppressed a grin. Each time Sonia called her *coach*, she had a funny feeling inside, a mixture of bashfulness and delight. And sometimes, when she saw Sonia following her instructions and getting better, she thought whether one day she might really consider becoming a coach.

Cammie stretched her tired legs and squinted at the sky. Today there was a small break in the clouds, and Cammie could see patches of blue here and there, bright and joyful, like Sonia's eyes. Sonia really looked happy all the time now. Her double jumps were solid, and she was already gaining consistency on her double axel and triple salchow. Her triple toe loop was fine too. Cammie smiled as she remembered that it was the first jump Sonia had landed a year ago. The triple loop, however, still remained a problem.

As though overhearing Cammie's thoughts, Sonia spoke up. "Do you think I should learn all of the triple jumps before I compete against Sonja Henie? Because see, she can't even do doubles. I bet I could beat her now. On the other hand, mastering triple jumps will make me practically unbeatable. I'm sure they will even allow me to compete against men. What do you think, Coach Cammie?"

Coach Cammie, yeah, right. I wonder what you'll say when you come back to your senses, Cammie thought.

"Sonia, it's not the time to talk about competing," Alex said harshly. "Your triple loop is pathetic."

Cammie watched Sonia's eyes widen then get moist. The girl looked as though every hope of hers were being crushed.

"But Coach Alex, the world championships are about to start," she said feebly, brushing a tear off her cheek.

That was exactly what Cammie was concerned about. What would happen if Sonia did master her triples in time for the beginning of the world championships and insisted on competing in the ladies' singles? Cammie had no doubt that with her twenty-first-century technique, Sonia would beat Sonja Henie easily. And then what? Not only skating history would be changed, but Sonia would definitely be disqualified from future competitions in Skateland for cheating.

Alex stuffed the rest of his chocolate pretzel skate guard into his mouth and guzzled down the rest of his tea. "Okay, let's get back to work. Sonia, we want you to start your warmup, and then we'll keep working on your triple loop."

"Well, well, well, here we meet again!"

Cammie was on her way to the Skating Museum. There was only one day left before the beginning of the worlds in Paris, and she was trying to think of the best way to help Sonia with her triple flip. She was so busy picturing three perfect revolutions in the air that when a tall scrawny figure suddenly appeared in her field of vision, screaming at her, Cammie lurched forward, tripped on her toe pick, and fell hard on her right wrist.

"Ouch!" It really hurt. Cammie quickly pulled off her glove and examined her hand. It was bright read and sore, but there was no swelling. Cammie bent and unbent her wrist several times. No, it didn't look as though a bone was broken. With a sigh of relief, Cammie scooped up some snow and pressed it against the red spot. She knew if she didn't apply something cold on the injury, her hand would turn purple blue in a couple of hours.

"That was just the beginning, little girl. You think you've outsmarted everybody, huh?"

Cammie straightened out to see Winja's crooked figure advancing menacingly toward her. As usual, the Witch of Injuries's limbs were heavily bandaged. She had dropped one of her crutches on the sidewalk, and she twirled the other one between the fingers of her right hand—the only part of her body that appeared uninjured.

"Your mission is over, Cammie!" Winja sang in her squeaky voice. "No more travelling to the past. We're going to my rink instead, where I have a nice comfortable wheelchair for you. You'll take a long rest, and I'll get a bonus. But first of all ... "

The witch paused, still playing with her crutch. Mesmerized, Cammie watched the long metal object slide between the woman's little and middle fingers, rest between the thumb and the index finger for a second, then twist, spin, and go through the same routine again.

And there's no place for me to hide, a thought flashed in Cammie's mind. The witch had cornered her in a tight spot on the eastern side of the Skating Museum. Because Wilhelmina had closed the museum for renovations—at least, that was her excuse for letting Cammie and Alex wander through the past—Cammie had never seen a living soul around.

And Alex must be already inside, Cammie thought sadly, watching Winja's crutch catch the sun as the witch spun it faster and faster.

Cammie took a step back; the witch followed her eagerly. Cammie moved farther, her back pressed hard against the stone wall of the Skating Museum. That was it; now she was going to get a bad injury. Cammie's wrist throbbed as though reminding its owner that worse pain was coming.

"Help!" Cammie called frantically.

Winja grinned, exposing a set of uneven, yellow teeth. "Nobody's going to help you, kiddo. Now … "

The crutch swung in the air. Cammie closed her eyes, bracing herself for pain.

There was a thud, as though someone had jumped on the ice, followed by a rhythmical scratching of a blade—a sound of someone spinning.

"A-a-ah!"

Cammie opened her eyes. Winja was rubbing her right side, a maniacal glint in her eyes.

Cammie felt her mouth open wide as she stared at the tall, swirling figure next to Winja. The skater exited the spin beautifully, and with tremendous relief, Cammie saw that it was Alex.

"How dare you practice your flying camel spin next to another skater, stupid kid!" Winja bellowed.

"You're not a skater; you're a witch!" Alex said coldly as he took a step closer to Winja.

With surprising agility, the badly injured witch picked up her crutches, rested her arm pits in the cradles, and skated away without giving Cammie and Alex another look.

"Oh, Alex, if it hadn't been for you! Thank you so much!" Cammie had a strong desire to hug her friend.

"No problem. What's this?" Alex pointed to Cammie's red wrist, now wet from the melting snow.

Cammie brought her hand closer to her face and blew on it. It didn't feel like a serious injury—more like a bruise.

"Is it Winja's work?"

Cammie sighed. "It is. Why can't those witches leave us alone?"

"Well, they are upset. Sonia's almost delivered, and that's not good news for them."

"Do you think they know we're coaching her?" Cammie put her glove back on.

Alex shrugged. "Probably not. Though they do see us entering the Skating Museum every day. It's not difficult to figure out that we're up to something. By the way, the worlds start tomorrow."

He gave Cammie a commanding look. "We'd better make sure Sonia doesn't get registered to compete."

"Come on, her triple flip is still underrotated, and we haven't even started working on her triple lutz."

"I told you. For her, it's not a matter of learning a new jump. Her muscles know how to do those triples."

"True, but she couldn't do a triple lutz before."

As they approached the pond still in the middle of their discussion of Sonia's technique, they saw their student working hard already. Today Sonia was wearing a new green skating dress with a matching beret.

"Hi, coaches!" Sonia exclaimed cheerfully as Cammie and Alex put their backpacks on the bench.

"I've been practicing since eight o'clock, and guess what?" Sonia skated around the pond in fast strokes, glided forward, and did a beautiful, perfect triple flip.

"Oh, no!" Cammie said loudly. Sonia was really progressing fast, perhaps even too fast.

"A true prodigy, isn't she?" a dreamy voice said behind Cammie.

Cammie looked around. Madame Parmentier had approached noiselessly and was now watching Sonia's every move with moist eyes.

"Poor dear, so what if she lost her mind? Her skating is … not of this world."

Not of this time, probably, Cammie thought angrily. Her stomach gave an unpleasant twitch as she saw Sonia do an impeccable triple loop. With that kind of progress, Sonia might be able to master her triple lutz today, and then nothing would stop her from facing Sonja Henie at the worlds.

"You know what? I've given this matter a great deal of thought, and I reckon we ought to give the poor girl a chance," Monsieur Parmentier had joined them too and was now eyeing Sonia's huge jumps appreciatively.

"So what does it matter if she calls herself Hilde Holovsky? I'll go to the worlds with her, and I'll personally register her as Sonia Harrison."

"Oh yes, that might work!" Madame Parmentier nodded enthusiastically.

"Sure, the girl will have a chance, and also..." Monsieur Parmentier rubbed his pudgy hands. "Of course, our little guest will share her prize money with us. After all, we've kept her as an honorable guest for so long."

"Right you are, darling." Madame Parmentier beamed and tousled her husband's hair appreciatively.

Cammie gasped. They couldn't be serious. Allowing Sonia to compete would definitely result in her winning the worlds, and that would be wrong. But how could she possibly explain it to the Parmentiers?

Without saying anything to the couple, Cammie rushed to the ice, where Alex was already explaining something to the excited Sonia.

"Alex, the Parmentiers want her to compete at the worlds. They hope to get a share of her prize money."

Cammie looked into Alex's green eyes, now narrowed in suspicion, then into Sonia's, blue and innocent.

"They are going to take Sonia to the worlds and register her under her own name. The skating history will change!" Cammie's heart sank. Would their plan work?

Alex rolled his eyes. "Cammie, there's nothing to worry about. Once Sonia gets her triple lutz, she'll come to her senses, and she won't even think of competing at the 1936 worlds."

"But what if she doesn't get her triple lutz today? She doesn't need it to win. She doesn't even need any of the triples."

"Oh!" Alex frowned, apparently realizing that Cammie had a point.

Cammie looked behind her. The Parmentiers were deep in an animated discussion in rapid French. Cammie saw Madame Parmentier nod several times, looking radiant.

"We need to convince Sonia that she can't compete without her triple lutz," Alex finally said.

"Hilde dear, could you come here for a minute?" Monsieur Parmentier called.

Alex darted forward between the man and Sonia, who was about to step off the ice. "Sonia, the practice isn't over."

"Look, young man, we have important business at hand. Hilde, … er, I mean Sonia, yes, we'll use that name now, needs to get registered to compete."

Sonia's eyes lit up. "Oh yes, Coach Alex, it's true. The competition starts tomorrow. So today is the last day when they accept registrations. So Monsieur Parmentier is right. We need to go to Paris now."

"By the way, do you like the new skating dress I've made her? Her winning dress." Madame Parmentier tugged on Sonia's skirt protectively. "Get the car, Maurice."

"No!" Cammie yelled.

Madame Parmentier stopped mid-sentence, her lips pressed tightly. "I'm afraid you're not the one who makes decisions here, young lady."

Cammie ignored the woman. "Sonia, you need your triple lutz."

Sonia shrugged. "But why, Coach Cammie? Sonja Henie doesn't even have doubles. I'll beat her easily."

"Because, because…" In desperate search for an answer, Cammie looked around at the dark trees and the gray snow. What could she say to make Sonia change her mind?

"Because everybody will say you aren't good enough for a triple lutz. It will make you look like a loser!" Alex blurted out.

Sonia's eyes flashed angrily, making her look like a ferocious tigress. She kicked the ice with her toe and pulled off her beret. Loose locks swirled around her reddened face. "I'm not a loser, all right? I'll get my triple lutz, I will!"

By the time they broke off for lunch, Sonia still hadn't landed her triple lutz. It didn't help that the Parmentiers stayed at the pond the whole time, hovering over the three of them like huge, angry crows. Monsieur Parmentier merely sat on the bench, one leg crossed over the other. The only thing that betrayed his impatience was a slight twirling of his foot. Madame Parmentier, however, showed more obvious signs of frustration. She paced the area around the pond in long strides, the heels of her black shoes digging deep into the snow, her arms folded on her chest. There were angry patches of red on the woman's sallow cheeks, and her black eyes moved from Sonia to Alex then to Cammie.

"She looks like a witch," Cammie whispered to Alex when Madame Parmentier whished by for the umpteenth time, her black gloved hand almost brushing Sonia's back.

Sonia had just executed her triple lutz about six inches away from the edge of the pond.

"Maybe she is a witch," Alex said uncertainly. He took Sonia by the hand and gently led her to the middle of the rink.

"That wasn't a bad attempt though, was it?" Cammie said hopefully. She couldn't wait for Sonia to be delivered, so they would escape from the Parmentiers' daunting presence.

"That lutz was still two-footed," Alex said ruefully.

"Are you sure?"

"Well, she didn't get delivered. It means she still doesn't have her triple lutz."

"Maybe she is delivered." Cammie looked at Sonia, who was rubbing her hands.

"Shall I try again then, Coach Cammie?" Sonia asked.

Cammie sighed desperately. In her right mind, Sonia would never refer to her as a coach.

"Hilde dear … hmm, I mean Sonia, it's time to go to lunch!" Madame Parmentier shouted, cringing under the cold blasts of wind.

"Oh yes." Alex looked at his watch. "Let's eat."

Obediently, Sonia stepped off the ice. Cammie followed her.

"Are you going to feed the world's best skater that junk?" Madame Parmentier shouted as Cammie handed Sonia a tuna fish salad sandwich.

"Americans have never been known for nutritious food, have they?" Monsieur Parmentier said accusingly.

"Hilde … gosh, Sonia, I have made onion soup and *coq au vin*," Madame Parmentier said.

Cammie wrinkled her forehead. "What's *coq au vin*?"

"Stewed chicken with bacon, mushrooms, and pearl onions. It's served with wine sauce," Madame Parmentier said proudly.

"Thank you, but I really don't want to lose any of the ice time. I like tuna salad, and it's enough for me." Sonia took a bite of her sandwich.

At the sight of Cammie and Alex digging into a bag of potato chips, Madame Parmentier blew a loud raspberry. "It's disgusting!"

The couple headed toward the house.

"Good," Alex said. "Let's finish our tea as fast as we can and get back to work."

Cammie took the last sip of her tea and jumped off the bench. "Come on! You'd better try hard now, Sonia."

"I will," Sonia said with determination. "We really need to head to Paris soon."

She skated to the middle of the pond, picking up speed. She got on her backward outside edge, held it...

Go ahead, land it! Cammie prayed. She crossed her fingers, watching Sonia's every move.

"You can do it!" Alex shouted.

Sonia bent her knee, swung her arms. She began to spin in the air...one, two...it seemed as though she would never come down. And then...yes, she landed perfectly, smoothly, and her left leg was extended gracefully behind her.

"You did it, you did it!" Alex rushed to the ice to congratulate Sonia.

"It was amazing!" In a hurry to share her excitement, Cammie jumped onto the rink with her guards on and crashed on the ice.

"Oh for crying out loud!" Cammie sat on the ice in the most stupid position, her legs spread, her arms above her head.

Alex and Sonia were in the middle of the rink laughing at her.

"That was a good one, Cammie!" Alex said shaking his head. "Got too excited, huh?"

"Ugh!" Cammie snarled and stood up slowly, brushing the snow off her parka.

"Are you all right, Cammie?" Sonia's face was so close that Cammie could see every freckle on the bridge of her roommate's nose.

There was something strange in the way Sonia spoke. Oh yes, she had said *Cammie*, not *Coach Cammie*.

"It happened to me several times. Are you sure you aren't hurt?"

"I'm fine." Cammie was still staring at Sonia. Could she really be—

"It's not a good idea to practice in the Icy Park anyway," Sonia said. "What are we doing here? Why aren't we at the Green Rink?"

"Yes!" Cammie stared at Sonia, unable to hide her excitement. Sonia was talking as though they were in Skateland, and it could mean only one thing.

"She is delivered!" Alex shouted. He ripped his wool hat off his head and threw it up in the air.

"Alex?" Sonia gave him a questioning look. "What are you shouting for? What's going on?"

"You landed your triple lutz, that's what!" Alex cheered.

Cammie joined Alex, who was clapping his hands, dancing on the ice.

Sonia smiled shyly. "Well, it's sweet, but why are the two of you so excited that I landed my triple lutz?"

She took a quick look around. The wind had really picked up, and the dark trees shook their heads angrily at them.

"I'm cold, you know," Sonia said. "Let's go back to the dorm, okay?"

Cammie and Alex exchanged uncertain looks. It would take a lot of time to explain to Sonia what had happened to her. On the other hand, how could they make Sonia step on the history book unless she had at least a general idea of what was going on?

"Sonia, you know what? We're not in Skateland," Alex said softly.

Sonia looked confused. "Where are we, then? What's going on?"

"Don't you remember anything?" Cammie asked carefully.

Sonia squinted her eyes. Cammie could tell that she was thinking hard.

"Well, the last thing I remember is waiting at the Main Rink. I was about to skate my number, and then..." Sonia spread her arms. "I don't remember."

"Well, listen—"

Before Alex could finish his sentence, Sonia's eyes became round. "Did the witches do something to me again? Oh no!"

She looked at her feet then stretched her arms forward, apparently trying to make sure she wasn't injured.

"But I feel fine, and I'm not afraid to skate. And yes, I've just landed my triple lutz. So..." Sonia looked at Cammie and Alex hopefully.

Cammie knew that fear was Sonia's main concern after she had been viciously attacked by the Witch of Fear two years ago.

"No, it wasn't the Witch of Fear," Alex said.

"Nor was it Winja," Cammie added.

"But then...what happened to me?" Sonia looked as though she was afraid to hear the answer.

"Look, Sonia, we'll explain everything when we get home, okay?" Cammie said.

"Sure, but where are we now?" Sonia asked, studying the pond and the black trees surrounding it.

"Never mind that. We need to get out of here." Alex took the history book out of his pocket.

"A-a-11 right, let's get going," a French-accented voice said, and Madame Parmentier appeared, closely followed by her husband. The man swirled a car key in his hand.

"You don't want to miss registration, do you, Sonia?" Monsieur Parmentier said.

Sonia stared at him blankly. "I'm sorry, I don't understand. Where do you want me to go, sir?"

"To Paris. To the world championships." Monsieur Parmentier looked slightly surprised, and Cammie knew why. After being so anxious about making it to the competition, Sonia suddenly acted as though she didn't understand what was going on.

"You're about to beat Sonja Henie, remember?" Madame Parmentier said sweetly.

A faint smile appeared on Sonia's face. "What? You've got to be kidding, right?"

Madame Parmentier frowned then glared at Cammie and Alex. "What do you mean *kidding*? Hasn't it been your desire all along? To become a world champion?"

Sonia opened her mouth, closed it again, and shook her head. "Me? World champion? Oh no, what are you talking about? I'm not ready yet."

"Look, we've had enough of this rubbish. You're going with us, period!" Madame Parmentier reached for Sonia's arm but missed, for Cammie had pulled her friend away.

"Alex, get the book ready, quick!" Cammie shouted.

Alex's fingers trembled as he opened the book to the introductory page. He put the thick volume on the ground, and the book began to grow.

"Come here, Sonia, step on the page," Alex said.

"What's this?" Sonia stared at the book with interest.

"We'll explain later. We've got to go!" Cammie nudged Sonia in the direction of the book.

"She's not going anywhere!" Madame Parmentier advanced on Sonia, her husband trailing behind.

Cammie pulled Sonia away from them, but Madame Parmentier's black-gloved fingers had already closed around Sonia's arm.

"Just put your foot on the page, Sonia, quick!" Cammie shouted.

The Parmentiers wouldn't let go of Sonia. Cammie raised her left foot, her blade glittering menacingly at the couple.

"Leave her alone, or I'll cut you!" Cammie yelled.

Apparently stunned, Madame Parmentier dropped Sonia's arm for just a second, but it was enough for Alex to grab Sonia by the shoulder and pull her forward. To avoid falling, Sonia had to take a step forward, right onto the introductory page. Now the three of them stood on the book, the wind ruffling the yellowish pages.

"Skateland!" Alex shouted.

The Parmentiers' shouts intensified, but a split second later, they were muffled by the howling of the wind around Cammie, Alex, and Sonia as the world began to swirl faster and faster.

THE RINK OF THE FUTURE

I can't believe it!" Sonia ran her fingers through her hair, looking shocked.

The three of them sat on the leather couch in the lobby of the Skating Museum. Cammie and Alex had just told Sonia what had happened to her.

"So you have been travelling through the history of figure skating to find me?" Sonia's voice sounded hoarse. She coughed.

Alex smiled at her. "Don't worry; it was fun. All those places we visited ... just wait till we give you all the details. Not now, though. We've got to see Wilhelmina first."

"Did you miss all the practices?" Sonia asked, looking troubled.

"We did practice moves in the field for a week," Cammie said. "We missed the rest of the practices, though. So what? The important thing is we found you. And you know what? I bet after visiting all those countries, I'll ace the skating history test."

Sonia smoothed the creases on her green skating dress and folded the beret in her hands. "It's so weird. I really believed my name was Hilde and I was about to beat Sonja Henie at the worlds ... How long was I missing?"

"Uh, a little more than two weeks," Alex said.

Sonia rubbed her forehead. Her hand froze. "My parents are probably worried sick. Do they know what happened to me?"

Cammie didn't want to make Sonia upset, but she couldn't lie. "Wilhelmina called them, yes."

Sonia jumped off the couch. "I'd better call them."

"Sure. Let's go to Wilhelmina's place. She's expecting us. You can call your parents from there," Alex said.

Sonia was already buttoning the old-fashioned coat Madame Parmentier had made for her. "Let's go."

Alex pulled the heavy front door, letting in a draft of cold air.

"After you," he said gallantly as he stepped away for Sonia to walk out.

"A-a-ah!" Sonia screamed so loudly that Cammie covered her ears instinctively.

"Hey, what?" Before Cammie could say another word, she felt herself being lifted off the floor. In another second, strong hands grabbed her arms and pulled them together behind her back. Cammie made a feeble attempt to kick the attacker with her blade, but she couldn't move.

"Okay, girl, easy now!" a croaky voice said.

Ropes tightened around Cammie's wrists and her ankles. In another moment, she was thrown on the ground, her nose pressed hard against the granular snow.

"Let me go!" Alex yelled behind Cammie. Apparently he too had been attacked.

"Bind the boy before he escapes. Ouch!" a whiny voice bleated.

The voice surely sounded familiar. Cammie had heard it many times.

"Winja!" Cammie screamed. Snow got in her mouth; she gagged. Someone raised her head by the ponytail, and Winja's gaunt face loomed in front of her.

"We meet again, huh? Only this time I call the shots!" A bony finger touched Cammie's cheek.

The witch's touch felt like electric current rushing through Cammie's body. She squirmed; her body stiffened. Oh how she wanted to plant her blade in the witch's belly, but she couldn't do it. The rope was too tight.

"Oh, don't be naughty, little one!" This time, Winja tapped Cammie on the nose.

"Get your dirty fingers off my face!" Cammie spat out.

"Oh, we're being a little too excited, aren't we?" The witch's pale lips formed a pout, and then Cammie's face was pressed against the snow again.

"Don't you dare tie me!" Alex's loud voice came from somewhere behind Cammie.

"I'll be honored to ensnare the world's best skater myself," another familiar voice said.

Cammie gritted her teeth in frustration. That was undoubtedly the Witch of Pride.

"And don't you dare spit, champion! You'll ruin my new co-oat!" the Witch of Pride sang. "You know, I think I'll tighten these ropes a little more. You're pretty strong, boy."

"So what's our next step?" Winja asked.

"Get them inside, you idiots! What're you waiting for? Someone may see us."

The Witch of Fear! Cammie remembered her voice too. She shivered. So they had been attacked by the whole gang of witches. Things didn't look good.

Cammie felt herself lifted off the ground. The street swirled around her then she saw the front door of the Skating Museum; they were going inside. It got darker; now they were in the lobby. *Bang!* Cammie fell on the hard floor. The witches must have thrown her down unceremoniously.

"Ouch!" Cammie grimaced at the dull pain in her right shoulder.

There was another thud, followed by Alex's loud voice. "Just wait till I get my hands on you, witches!"

"Oh no, I'm so scared!" A harsh, almost male voice said sarcastically.

And this is the Witch of Destruction, Cammie thought, desperately trying to get into a more comfortable position. All she could see was the sign where museum hours and ticket prices were displayed.

"You didn't tie the red-haired brat, Fear!" the Witch of Destruction barked.

The Witch of Fear laughed. "We don't have to worry about her. She is still under our curse, don't you see?"

"What makes you so sure?" Winja's squeaky voice asked.

"Huh, look! How are you doing, Sonia?" The Witch of Fear asked.

And to Cammie's utter shock, Sonia answered in a quiet, monotonous voice, "I'm not Sonia. My name is Hilde Holovsky."

Sonia sounded as though she wanted to say something else, but her last words got drowned in the raucous laughter that came from about a dozen throats.

"Yes!"

"Fantastic!"

Cammie made a feeble attempt at turning to her other side. She didn't understand why Sonia acted as though she hadn't got delivered. Maybe they had done something wrong or left out an important detail. Cammie really, really needed to see Sonia's face. She bent her knees and started pushing herself to the left side.

"Now be still, girl!" The voice belonged to the Witch of Destruction, and it sounded right over Cammie. In another moment, Cammie felt a kick on the side, and she rolled over. What she saw made her grimace.

Alex sat leaning against the receptionist's counter, his hands and feet tied. The Witch of Pride stood by his side in her fox coat, looking at him mockingly. The leather couch in the middle of the lobby was occupied by six witches. Cammie recognized Winja and the Witch of Fear, and there were some other evil-looking women she didn't know. Cammie didn't see Sonia; she had to be behind Cammie's back.

"See? The girl is still zonked. Well done, Witch of Confusion!" the Witch of Fear yelled.

"You bet! I always do my best," someone cackled behind Cammie.

There was a sound of something hard scratching against the linoleum floor, and a very old woman emerged leaning on one crutch. The woman had a very peculiar appearance. Her long uncombed hair was partially blond and partially red with gray streaks. One eye was heavily made up, while the other bore no traces of eyeliner or eyeshadow. Cammie also noticed that one of the woman's gloves was green, the other blue, and she had only one skate guard on.

"I did my share of the job too. The girl is as proud as the devil himself," the Witch of Pride said smugly. "And you know what I think? The two of us deserve a reward for a job well done."

"Applause for the Witch of Confusion and the Witch of Pride!" the Witch of Fear shouted.

The rest of the witches scowled and brought their hands together with obvious reluctance.

"And as for the reward..." The Witch of Fear made a meaningful pause. "How about a pair of nice custom-made boots and blades for both of you?"

"Yes!" The Witch of Pride clapped her hands. "Make my blades gold, please."

"Heh-heh-heh!" the Witch of Confusion snickered. "Do I look like I need new skates?"

"And why not?" the Witch of Pride said derisively. "Your blades are all scratched, and they probably won't last through another sharpening, and your boots are falling off your feet."

"True, but... ah, who cares? I only attacked the girl for the fun of it. Besides, I felt I had to do the best job before I retired," the Witch of Confusion croaked.

"Oh, you're retiring! But why?" Winja shrilled.

The Witch of Confusion shrugged, which caused her crutch to slip from under her. The old lady appeared not to have noticed it at all. In fact, she seemed to be able to walk reasonably well without crutches.

"Old age isn't a skater. It can't be fought," the Witch of Confusion said with a throaty chuckle.

"But what are we going to do without you? The two of us make the best team," the Witch of Pride grumbled.

"Well, we'll just have to train someone else," the Witch of Destruction boomed. "Now back to business. What are we going to do with these pitiful skaters?"

"We're not pitiful!" Alex yelled.

The Witch of Pride twisted her face in the expression of fake bewilderment. "Oh, you're not? I beg your pardon. But you will be, and sooner than you think. You know what idea I have, fellow witches? We're going to send them to the future. How about that?"

Silence fell so deep that Cammie could hear the sound of her own breathing. The witches seemed to be weighing the pros and cons of the suggestion.

"To the future? But what good will that do?" Winja screeched.

"Don't you understand?" The Witch of Pride put her hands on her wide hips. "You know how figure skating has advanced in the last hundred years, don't you? Even elite skaters like Ulrich Salchow, even Sonja Henie, wouldn't stand a chance against juvenile-level kids of today. Don't you think in another hundred years our sport will develop even further?"

There was a short pause, and then the witches started clapping their hands.

"Cool!" Winja squealed.

"Those were the words of a true witch!" the Witch of Confusion yelled.

"Awesome!" the Witch of Fear barked.

"So what are we waiting for?" the Witch of Destruction exclaimed, marching toward Sonia. "Hey, witches, do you want me to tie this brat too?"

The Witch of Pride waved her manicured hand at her. "Sonia isn't a threat to us. She's still so confused that she may actually go to the future willingly."

"Ha-ha-ha!" Apparently the witches had found the idea amusing, for they roared with laughter, slapping themselves on the thighs, exposing their sharp teeth.

Cammie shivered. She couldn't believe what she had just heard. The witches were going to send the three of them to the future. But what would they do there? And how about Skateland, Cammie's parents, her friends? And of course, none of them would be considered a good skater a hundred years from now.

"Hilde Holovsky, we invite you to join us on an exciting trip to the world championsip!" the Witch of Confusion said.

Sonia stepped forward, bowed her head, and approached the witch obediently. Cammie shook her head. So Sonia wasn't delivered after all. And they thought she was all right. Cammie gave Alex a helpless look. Her friend appeared equally puzzled.

"Up to the dome then! Get the brats!" the Witch of Fear barked.

Two young witches in black rags grabbed Cammie by her arms and legs and carried her up the spiral staircase. Cammie remembered the witches from her trip to the Black Rink a year ago, but she didn't know their names.

"So we got you this time, didn't we?" One of the witches stuck out a tongue at Cammie.

"No you didn't!" Cammie said gloomily.

The witch's eyes glared, and she slapped Cammie on the cheek. It didn't hurt much, but the witch's fingernails were dirty, and Cammie squirmed with repulsion.

"Move on, all of you!" the Witch of Fear yelled from the lobby.

The rest of the witches walked up too, giggling and cheering. Behind her back, Cammie heard Alex shouting at the Witch of Pride. Sonia, however, was quietly walking next to the Witch of Confusion as though she didn't care. Up higher and higher they climbed, passing halls that displayed different skating periods. Cammie and Alex had never gone that far before, and now Cammie wondered what was awaiting them in the dome.

The staircase led them up to a plain-looking landing with a metal floor. There was a door with a handle but no lock. The Witch of Fear leaped ahead of everybody and pulled the door open. As the black-ragged witches carried Cammie into the hall, she had to close her eyes, almost blinded by the bright light that was pouring down from the glass dome.

When Cammie finally looked around, she saw that the hall was completely empty except for a circular rink that filled up most of its space. The ice was smooth and untouched and had the most unusual color Cammie had ever seen. In fact, there wasn't any distinctive color at all. Though solid, the ice was transparent, and it shimmered with tiny rainbows. As the witches brought Cammie closer, she felt that the ice was vibrating slightly, and she even heard faint music emanating from it.

"It's beautiful!" The words came out of Cammie's mouth before she could even think.

The Witch of Pride grinned. "You like it, huh? Well, I hope you'll enjoy your life as a skating mediocrity too. I think we can untie them at this point."

"Hey, no! They'll run away. Besides, this jerk has been threatening to beat me up," Winja whined as she pointed to Alex.

The Witch of Pride scratched her chin. "Hmm, that's true."

"Just throw them on the ice, idiots! They'll head straight to the future," the Witch of Fear shouted.

"Oh yes, but don't step on the ice yourselves, witches. You never know what secrets a strange rink may hold. Remember the Purple Rink?" the Witch of Pride yelled.

There was a unanimous shout of oh's and ah's. As scared as Cammie was, she grinned at the memory of the witches' pitiful encounter with Melvin Reed's Purple Rink a year ago. The purple ice was so pure that no witch could touch it without getting hurt. In hot pursuit of Cammie and Alex, the witches had slipped, fallen over the prostrate Witch of Pride, rolled onto the ice, and got second degree burns.

One of the young witches had apparently noticed Cammie's smile. "You won't find it particularly funny now!"

In another moment, Cammie felt herself being hurled in the air; she flew right toward the glittering ice. Oh, no! She braced herself for possible pain from the impact, but as she fell down, she had a weird sensation of the ice absorbing her landing. As Cammie lay sprawled out on the sparkling surface, she felt strangely secure. The ice of the future wasn't even bitterly cold, just pleasantly cool.

Bang! Alex crashed onto the ice next to her. Cammie squinted expecting him to gasp from pain. Instead, Alex shrugged and gave her a bewildered look. "Hmm, it didn't even hurt."

Sonia flew across the ice and landed on both feet. Cammie saw her roommate grin as the girl approached Cammie and untied her ropes.

"Ah?" Before Cammie could say something, Sonia set Alex free.

"Sonia! So you aren't crazy?" Alex cried out. He flexed his hands.

"We thought you still believed you were Hilde," Cammie said.

Sonia beamed at her. "I was only faking it, of course. I didn't want the witches to tie me, also. I figured I might be able to loosen your ropes later if I were free."

"Thank you so much!" Cammie hugged Sonia. "That was quick thinking!"

"*I* should be thanking you and Alex!" Sonia helped Cammie to get to her feet.

Alex skated up and embraced the two of them heartily. "That was awesome, Sonia. Hey, if it weren't for you, we'd be history. Hmm, I mean lost in the future."

"I like this ice!" Sonia said dreamily. She did three twizzles on her right foot then switched sides.

"The ice is incredible. You fall on it, and it doesn't hurt at all. Do you girls want to skate?" Alex went into a fast back spin.

A moment later, the three of them skated merrily around the rink.

"Hey! Why are they still here? They should have moved to the future already," Winja's worried voice called.

"I don't know," the Witch of Pride said dully.

"Somebody messed up, and badly!" the Witch of Destruction roared.

There was a sound of something falling on the floor, followed by a deep oh!

"What's that, Confusion? The brats didn't go to the future. Do you know who made a mistake?" The Witch's of Fear voice sound menacing.

"You know what, witches, I think it would be me," the Witch of Confusion said lightly.

"You? What do you mean?" The Witch of Pride grabbed the Witch of Confusion by her multicolored hair.

The Witch of Confusion didn't seem to notice. "I've been sending my spells at the kids all the time to keep them confused. But my coordination isn't that good anymore, so I think you, my dearest witches, got the full blast of my confusion spell by mistake."

"I'll kill you!" The Witch of Pride roared.

"Wait! Not before she undoes the spell!" the Witch of Fear warned. "We'll think of the punishment later."

"Who cares about the punishment? I'm re-ti-i-ring," the Witch of Confusion sang.

"Undo the spell, you stupid witch!" a chorus of scared voices roared.

Next to Cammie, Sonia performed a beautiful triple loop.

"Terrific!" Cammie did a fist pump and cheered. A triple jump, that was cool. It confirmed the fact that Sonia was delivered after all.

Sonia whirled around and did a triple toe loop.

"The brat is doing triples!" the Witch of Fear roared. "The curse isn't there anymore. So that's how you bewitched her, Pride and Confusion!"

"She was cursed. I swear!" The Witch of Pride stomped her foot angrily.

"The girl was surely confused. You all saw her," the Witch of Confusion grumbled.

"Well, whatever happened, no reward to either of you!" The Witch of Fear approached the rink and stared at Sonia with her bloodshot eyes.

Entering her triple flip, Sonia ignored her completely.

"I'm going to file a complaint!" the Witch of Pride shouted.

"Silence, everybody!" The Witch of Destruction raised both hands in the air. "We need to send the brats to the future first. Then we'll deal with the slackers."

"Oh, yeah! Wait a minute!" The Witch of Confusion closed her eyes for a second then did a weird circular motion with both arms and muttered something unintelligible. "Now you aren't confused anymore, witches, so—"

"The book! We forgot about the history book!" The Witch of Pride slapped herself on the forehead.

"That's right. We are all idiots!" The Witch of Fear poked the Witch of Pride on the rib with her long fingernail.

The Witch of Pride wailed, grabbing her side.

"So where's the book?" the Witch of Destruction inquired in an angry voice.

"The brats have it, of course," Winja spoke up from the floor where she sat, rubbing her knees.

"Now give me the book!" The Witch of Fear approached the rink and stared at Cammie, Alex, and Sonia. Her narrowed eyes turned into two crimson slits.

Cammie dashed to the other side of the rink, Sonia following her closely. Alex, however, stayed where he was, his fists clenched.

"Did you hear me, boy? I don't like repeating myself." The Witch of Fear stretched her skeletal arms toward him. The red glow in her eyes changed to burgundy then purple.

Cammie shuddered, her knee buckled, and she fell.

"Are you all right?" Sonia rushed to Cammie's side.

"Stay where you are, Sonia!" The Witch of Fear's voice grew louder and shriller. A moment later, Sonia tripped over her toepick and crushed on the ice next to Cammie.

The Witch of Fear let out a bone-chilling laughter. She turned to the rest of the witches. "See how little it takes?"

"The book! Get the book! What're you waiting for, Fear?" the Witch of Destruction barked.

The Witch of Fear looked a little hesitant.

"Why don't you, Destruction, try stepping on that ice instead of bossing us around?" Winja wailed.

The Witch of Destruction straightened up. "Okay, cowards, watch me!"

She quickly jumped onto the glistening ice. Cammie's heart sank when she saw that the ice of the future wasn't hurting the witch in the slightest. Strong and muscular, the Witch of Destruction reached Alex in two seconds and grabbed his shoulders.

"Get off me!" Alex snarled.

The witch squeezed his shoulder tightly. Alex grimaced.

"Give me the book, boy. That's all I want!" The Witch of Destruction grunted.

Alex jerked backwards, clenched his fists, apparently trying to put up a good fight, but he was no match for the huge, muscular witch. Alex raised his right foot, aiming at the witch's shin, but she dodged the kick easily.

"You nasty—" Alex yelled, but the witch's hand was already in his pocket. And just a second later, the Witch of Destruction raised the history book above her head.

"Good job! Now let's send the brats—"

Before the Witch of Fear could finish her sentence, a loud shriek came out from the throat of the Witch of Destruction.

Astonished, Cammie fell backwards, hitting her bottom hard. She forgot about pain immediately, mesmerized by the sight of the Witch of Destruction lying on her side, kicking her blades hard against the iridiscent surface. The woman shook her right hand violently.

"Get this thing off me, it hurts!"

The history book hung from the witch's palm as though it were attached to it with epoxy glue. Apparently it was causing the woman tremendous pain.

"What's wrong?" the Witch of Pride shouted, her eyes bulging.

The music coming from the ice became stronger. It was no longer pleasant but rather sinister, the cold sound of a celeste, mingling with the monotonos rumbling of drums.

"Witches, I'm scared!" Winja bleated, hugging herself.

"Don't be ridiculous!" The Witch of Fear stepped on the ice tentatively and shifted her feet. Apparently satisfied, she moved toward the Witch of Destruction, who was still writhing on the ice.

"Take it, please, take it!" The Witch of Destruction stretched her hand toward the Witch of Fear.

"Okay, okay." The Witch of Fear bent down, but the moment her fingers closed around the book, she let out a high-pitched shrill. "It's burning my hand!"

What's going on? Cammie turned to Alex. He caught her questioning look and shrugged. The witches had already touched the history book when they sent Sonia to the past, and it hadn't caused them any pain.

"Is anybody going to help us or what?" The Witch of Fear rose on her knees, trying to crawl off the ice. The book still clung to her hand that was already red and swollen.

"Can't you just throw the book away?" The Witch of Pride actually looked amused.

"Wouldn't have thought of it myself," the Witch of Fear snapped.

The Witch of Destruction gritted her teeth and pressed her blade against the book, trying to separate it from her hand. It didn't work. Instead, now the witch's blade was attached to the blue leather volume too, which only allowed the woman to lie crawling on her side.

"Now, you two, go help them!" The Witch of Pride pushed the two black-ragged witches in the direction of the ice.

They scowled but obeyed, and a moment later they lay prostrate on the ice, squealing with pain. Their fingers were glued to the book.

"Cammie!"

Cammie took her eyes off the screaming witches. Alex stood by her side, holding Sonia's hand.

"Let's get out of here. I bet they won't even notice," Alex whispered.

The three of them jumped off the ice. As they had expected, the witches ignored them completely. Cammie, Alex, and Sonia crossed the hall and pushed the heavy door open. They sat down on the cold metal floor to put on their skate guards.

A moment later, Cammie heard a loud thud, followed by screams from more witches.

The floor shook under a dozen feet pounding hard; the door swung open. The horde of witches ran out, closely followed by the skating history book that now rolled among the startled women, landing on their shoulders, hitting them on the heads. Each time the book made contact with a witch's body, the witch yelped.

"Leave me alone, stupid book!" Winja screamed, flailing her bandaged arms.

The book bounced off the witch's shoulder. Instinctively, Cammie reached for the volume and caught it. It felt perfectly normal in her hand. The commotion stopped immediately, the witches froze in their spots.

"Run!" Alex shouted as he sprinted down the steps.

Sonia and Cammie followed, Cammie clutching the book.

"Oh no, you are not getting away, kiddies. Get them!" the Witch of Pride yelled.

Cammie ran as fast as she could, occasionally skipping one or two steps. Alex and Sonia were slightly ahead of her. Behind her, Cammie could hear the horrible sound of blades scratching against the metal steps. None of the witchs had managed to put on their skate guards, and with mean satisfaction, Cammie thought that now the witches' blades would be hopelessly dull.

They were on the first floor already. They crossed the lobby, pulled the front door, and ran outside. Cold wind slapped Cammie in the face, causing her to look away. She heard the museum door open and slam shut.

"Get them!" the Witch of Destruction boomed.

"Cammie, come on!" Alex yelled.

Cammie ran faster, but the witches were closing in on her already. Cold fingers squeezed Cammie's wrist. She kicked hard but missed, and then half a dozen more hands lifted her in the air—

"Freeze! Don't move!"

Immediately, everything became quiet.

"Let her go!" A low male voice spoke from somewhere behind Cammie.

A split second later, Cammie felt the witches' fingers loosen. She fell in the snow. The witches stepped aside, and Captain Greenfield's worried face appeared in Cammie's field of vision.

"Can you get up, Cammie?" Captain Greenfield stretched his hand toward her.

"Uh, I think so." Cammie grabbed his hand and pulled herself up.

The witches still stood around her, silent and immobile.

"Read them their rights, Lieutenant Turner," Captain Greenfield said.

Lieutenant Turner approached, swirling blade brakes in his hand.

"You ladies are under arrest. You have the right—" He bent down to reach for the Witch of Pride's blades.

"No-o-o!" the witch bellowed, jumping away from him. "Run, you idiots!"

With shrieks of horror, the witches scattered in different directions, stumbling on their dull blades.

"Stop in the name of Skateland law!" Leiutenant Turner said. This time he sounded a little uncertain, the blade brakes dangling in his hand.

The Witch of Pride let out a loud whistle, and a moment later, a beautiful silver icemobile appeared from around the corner. The Witch of Pride jumped in the driver's seat and immediately was smothered by half a dozen witches who had leaped in after her.

"Wait! I can't take everybody!" The Witch of Pride spread her arms, pushing the witches away, but they clung on to her tight.

"Home!" the Witch of Pride shouted, and the icemobile moved forward.

"Wait! Wait for me!" Winja howled. With amazing dexterity, she hooked her crutch over the rear bumper of the icemobile and glided behind, her hair flowing wildly in the wind.

The witches who hadn't managed to get a spot in the icemobile skated frantically behind.

"Stop in the name of the law!" Lieutenant Turner shouted again. His voice shook slightly. He gave Captain Greenfield a sheepish look.

Captain Greenfield grinned. "It's okay, lieutenant. We're after the kids, after all, not after the witches."

He turned to Cammie, Alex, and Sonia. "Get into the icemobile, you three!"

THE MYSTERY OF THE SKATING HISTORY BOOK

W here are you taking us?" Cammie asked glumly as the icemobile shot forward. She was ensconced in the back seat between Alex and Sonia. The two Skateland policemen sat in the front.

"To jail?" Alex asked irritably.

Lieutenant Turner gave him a smug look, but Captain Greenfield merely chuckled. "And why would you think that?"

"You can't take them to jail. They've saved my life," Sonia said firmly.

Lieutenant Turner rolled his eyes. "Yeah, right."

"Lieutenant!" Captain Greenfield said sternly. His voice softened as he addressed Sonia. "Of course we're not going to jail. I'm only taking you to Mrs. Van Uffeln's house on her orders."

Ah, that was okay. Cammie sighed with relief and leaned against the back of her seat. Funny how being around witches had made them suspect every adult of trying to hurt them. Actually, it was great that Skateland cops had decided to visit the museum this afternoon. Had they not been at the entrance, the witches might have escaped this time with Cammie as their trophy.

Cammie put her hand into her pocket, took out the history book, and smoothed out the leather cover with her fingers. Now the book was small and innocent looking.

"It doesn't burn me, you know," Cammie said softly. "I still don't understand why the witches wanted to get rid of it."

"It's probably like the purple ice, burning everyone who is rotten inside," Alex said.

"Well, the witches used it before to send Sonia to the past."

"Hmm." Alex frowned.

"Here you go!" Captain Greenfield put his foot on the brake, and the icemobile screeched to a stop in front of Wilhelmina's house.

The five of them walked up the snow-covered steps leading to the porch.

"After me, please. I need to make an official report." Lieutenant Turner squeezed himself between Cammie and Alex brusquely. Ignoring Alex's menacing glare, the young man pressed the doorbell, looking impatient.

The door lock clicked, and Wilhelmina appeared in her usual wheelchair. The old woman wore a white sweater and crisp gray pants. Her glasses dangled on a silver chain.

"Mrs. Van Uffeln, the three students you summoned are delivered safely—" the young man began to say.

Before Lieutenant Turner could finish his sentence, Wilhelmina rose in her wheelchair. "Here you are, all of you! So you found Sonia. Excellent job, Cammie and Alex! How are you doing, Sonia?"

"…to your house. Lieutenant Turner reporting!" Bob Turner said, looking annoyed. Apparently he didn't like the fact that his effort wasn't being appreciated.

"Thank you, officers, you are dismissed. Though I may need your assistance later," Wilhelmina said.

Cammie saw her wink at Captain Greenfield.

Captain Greenfield nodded to Wilhelmina.

"Now get inside, all of you. I want to hear what happened." Wilhelmina motioned for Cammie, Alex, and Sonia to come in and locked the door behind them. "Christel, *Christel!*"

Wilhelmina's daughter materialized in the lobby, a dust sweeper in her hand, her face sour. "More guests, I see. It's dinner time, and you didn't tell me you were expecting company."

"Well, we have company now." Wilhelmina smiled widely. Her eyes twinkled.

"I haven't made enough food for five people. I thought it would be just you and me," Christel said stubbornly. She tapped her foot with the dust sweeper.

"Well, you'll have to buy more food, then," Wilhelmina said nonchalantly. "Besides, I want you to stop at Sweet Blades too."

"We don't need dessert. We still have plenty of those deformed chocolate pretzel skate guards from the nutty cook," Christel snapped.

"As much as I enjoy Mrs. Page's baked goods, they won't be enough for the occasion. Come here, Christel, I've got to tell you something."

With obvious reluctance, Christel approached the wheelchair and lowered her head.

Cammie watched Wilhelmina whisper something into Christel's ear. The younger woman frowned slightly then her eyebrows rose in surprise. Her face brightened.

"Is that right?" Christel eyed Cammie and Alex with amazement bordering on awe.

"It is," Wilhelmina said simply.

"Well, in that case …" Christel swirled the dust sweeper and looked at her slippers. "Just give me a moment to change, and I'll get on the road."

She ran out of the lobby.

"I told her that you rescued Sonia from the witches. Well, children, make yourselves comfortable. Take off your skates, and we'll have a nice chat by the fireplace," Wilhelmina said to the three of them.

Cammie, Alex, and Sonia took their seats in the leather armchairs in the living room. The room was warm and cozy. Sonia curled up in her armchair, her feet tucked under her. She still hadn't uttered a word since they came to Wilhelmina's house, but the warm, slightfully bashful smile was definitely Sonia's.

"How are you feeling, Sonia?" Wilhelmina interrupted Alex right in the middle of his description of the witches' attack.

"I'm fine, thank you," Sonia said cheerfully, and Cammie could tell that she really meant it.

"How are your triple jumps?" Wilhelmina asked.

Sonia's blue eyes lit up. She sat up straighter. "Oh they are very good, actually. I finally landed my triple lutz."

"That's very good, Sonia. It means you can move to the junior level. Very, very impressive. But…" Wilhelmina leaned forward. Her gray eyes found Sonia's, blue and innocent. "Do you realize to whom you owe that brilliant technique of yours?"

The expression of joy on Sonia's face was now replaced with puzzlement. "I don't know what you mean. My coach?"

Wilhelmina nodded. "That's right. Your coaches." She emphasized the plural ending in the word *coaches*.

Sonia looked confused. "Coaches?"

"Yes, coaches. And I don't mean Coach Ferguson, though she has obviously done a lot for you. But now I want you to know that your friends, Cammie and Alex, have demonstrated excellent abilities as coaches."

Sonia's eyes left Wilhelmina's face, moved to Alex then to Cammie. "I don't understand."

"Well, kids, speak up!" Wilhelmina crossed her legs and folded her arms. Her posture suggested that she was all attention.

Interrupting one another, trying not to leave anything out, Cammie and Alex told Wilhelmina how they had helped Sonia to get her triples back.

Sonia sat staring at them with her mouth wide open.

Wilhelmina's deep eyes rested on Sonia's small figure. "What exactly do you remember?"

Sonia raised her head. "I was at the dress rehearsal ready to skate my number and … and that's it. And then I was someone else … a girl named Hilde, and

I was skating on a pond in France, and Cammie and Alex were there."

Sonia's face turned red. "I didn't realize they were there to teach me. I thought they had just come to take me back home."

Wilhelmina nodded. "Of course, they wanted to take you home. But they were your coaches too." She went into a long explanation of how the witches had forced Sonia to believe she was Hilde Holovsky.

Sonia lowered her head again, and Cammie thought her friend was going to cry.

"You're free," Wilhelmina said. "Cammie and Alex have done everything to help you. See, you were confused. You almost made a terrible mistake of competing against a champion of the past. That was the witches' evil plan, and from what Cammie and Alex told me, I see that the people you stayed with in France played a big part in it too. The Parmentiers' greed played along well with the witches' demonic scheme. But Cammie and Alex worked hard to help you with your technique. So once you could land all of your triple jumps, your muscles sent a signal to your brain. And then your mind became clear again. That's how it worked."

"Oh!" Sonia's eyes became huge, and she gazed at Cammie and Alex as though she saw them for the first time. In another moment, she jumped to her feet and put her arms around Cammie. "Thank you! Oh, thank you so much!"

"It's okay." Cammie freed herself from Sonia's embrace. She didn't feel her friend had to thank her. After all, she had only done what was right.

Sonia turned around and for a moment, Cammie thought that she was going to hug Alex too. But then Sonia's cheeks turned pink, and she merely mumbled. "Oh Alex, if it weren't for you ... I don't know where I would be now."

"Come on! You don't have to thank me," Alex protested, but Cammie saw that her friend was delighted. "It was actually fun to travel through history. And we almost went to the future too."

Alex's last words reminded Cammie of what she wanted to ask Wilhelmina. "Mrs. Van Uffeln, what will figure skating be like in the future?"

Something glinted in Wilhelmina's gray eyes. "And why do you want to know that?"

"Well ... " Cammie couldn't think of a good enough reason. "You see, the witches almost sent us there. If only they had gotten their hands on the skating book—"

"They did, but it burnt them," Alex interrupted.

Wilhelmina chuckled. "Did it really?"

"Yes, just like the purple ice," Alex said eagerly. "Mr. Reed told us last year that a bad person couldn't step on the purple ice without getting hurt. It must be the same with the skating book, right?"

"Hmm." Wilhelmina leaned back in her wheelchair, looking thoughtful. "It's a good question, Alex. Problem is, I don't have the answer. You see, when I wrote the book, I didn't even think it would have magic powers. But you're probably right. The skating history book is a description of all the best that ever happened in our sport. So naturally, as I was working on it, I had my mind fixed on the beauty and purity of skating. I believe I somehow managed to transfer my feelings and emotions into the book. And of course, being evil and corrupt, the witches can't stand being around anything that is righteous and good."

"But—" The word came out of Cammie's mouth before she even had a chance to think.

Wilhelmina gave her a curious glance. "What?"

"The witches already used the book once when they sent Sonia to the past. Why didn't they get hurt then?"

"Oh!" Wilhelmina put on her glasses and stared at Cammie through the thick lenses. Her eyes now appeared even bigger.

"To tell you the truth, I haven't thought of it. But you know what? I think Alex and you are the reason."

"I beg your pardon?" Alex blurted out.

Cammie felt equally shocked. What did Alex and she have to do with the mystery of the history book?

"When the witches first took Sonia to the past, they had an ordinary book with them. Well, almost ordinary…" Wilhelmina grinned and took her glasses off again, letting them dangle on the silver chain. "Apparently the book already had some magic powers, and so did the Skating Museum. The combined energy of the book and the museum appeared to be strong enough to propel people to the past.

"But!" Wilhelmina raised her index finger. "Before you, Cammie and Alex, went to the past to rescue your friend, the witches could use the book all right. And after your completed your mission, they could no longer touch the book. Now do you see the connection?"

Cammie frowned in concentration. "Not really."

With the corner of her eye, she saw Alex shake his head.

"The two of you went to the past to help your friend. Your intentions were pure and honest. Your mind was set not on personal gain or revenge but on a very selfless mission of assisting another skater. Now I believe that your righteous motives left an indelible imprint on the book, making it impossible to be used for evil purposes. What did you say happened to the witches when they touched the book?"

"The book burnt them," Alex said.

Wilhelmina nodded. "Here you go."

"It's good the witches failed to send us to the future," Cammie said. "If we got there, we probably wouldn't be able to make it past the preliminary level."

Sonia nodded in agreement.

"That's right," Alex said. "We would look like total amateurs."

Wilhelmina looked amused. "And it bothers you a lot, doesn't it? I don't see why it should. No skater ever performs outside his time. There were great skaters in the past, and there will be wonderful skaters in the future too. By the way, do you guys know why there are no wax figures at the Rink of the Future?"

Cammie looked at Alex, caught his blank stare, and shrugged. Sonia gazed at Wilhelmina with anticipation.

"Wax figures represent something that already happened. See, everything that took place in the past is over; it's finished, done. It's frozen, just like wax figures. Do you remember me telling you that history can't be changed? It's because everything that happens in time is final. The past time freezes over, like ice. Or we can turn it to wax figures and show it to future generations. On the other hand, the present is alive and evolving, and as for the future ... "

Wilhelmina's eyes brushed Cammie's face then moved to Alex's and Sonia's. "The future is mysterious and uncertain. It is beyond our grasp. It's hidden in the realm of possibilities."

The older woman closed her eyes for a moment. Cammie sat, her hands clutching the arms of the chair, afraid to move.

"So the Rink of the Future is empty," Wilhelmina said slowly. "And let me show you something else. Where is the history book?"

"Oh!" Cammie took the book out of her pocket and handed it to Wilhelmina.

Skateland president ran her fingers over the cover gently then opened the book to the last page. "There is no word *end* here, do you see it?"

Cammie craned her neck and looked at the page. Wilhelmina was right; the page was completely blank.

"There is a reason for that," Skateland president said. "The truth is that skating history isn't over. Life is going on, the history is unfolding right in front of us, and, more importantly, you are the ones who will make things happen in figure skating."

Wilhelmina raised her face from the book and looked Cammie, Alex, and Sonia straight in the eyes. "You, my dear friends, are the present and future of figure skating."

There was silence in the room. The only thing Cammie heard was the cracking of the logs in the fireplace and the distant howling of the wind outside.

"All right, so much about theoretical discussions for tonight," Wilhelmina said as she carefully put the skating book on the shelf above the fireplace. "I hear Christel's footsteps in the lobby, and if I'm not mistaken, my daughter is ready to serve us a sumptuous dinner."

"I brought some takeout from Figure Skater's Finest Food. Barbecue chicken with baked potatoes and Caesar salad. And the surprise too," Christel breathed out. Her cheeks were pink from the frosty air, and without her usual sour expression, the woman looked much younger and prettier.

What surprise is she talking about? Cammie thought.

"Thank you, Christel. All right, my dear friends, let's go to the kitchen and have a feast." Wilhelmina motioned for the three of them to follow her and Christel to the kitchen.

Cammie hadn't realized how hungry she was until she put the first piece of delicious barbecue chicken in her mouth. She closed her eyes and squinted with delight.

"Here, put some on your potato." Wilhelmina pushed butter and sour cream containers closer to her. "And you, Sonia, get some bread. Today is a celebration, so you don't have to count your calories. Look at Alex!"

Alex, who had just put another chicken breast on his plate, grinned. "It's been a long, hard day."

"Exactly." Wilhelmina took a big sip of her water. "Although you may want to save some room for the big surprise."

"And what is it, Mrs. Van Uffeln?" Alex asked as he helped himself to another baked potato.

"Well, if I told you, it wouldn't be a surprise anymore, would it?" the older woman said lightly.

Cammie finished her meal and thanked Wilhelmina and Christel. She felt warm and completely relaxed. The continuous pressure of having to do something to help Sonia was now gone. Instead, happiness welled up inside her. She enjoyed being in the company of her friends. And there was also Wilhelmina, the president of Skateland. The lady who had the reputation of a strict and demanding leader was now kind and hospitable, like a loving grandmother.

"Now once we are all fed, it's time for the surprise." Wilhelmina clapped her hands and turned to Christel. "Which is … the Trophy Treat!"

Sonia's mouth dropped open. "Oh!" Immediately her face turned pink, and she lowered her eyes.

Wilhelmina grinned at her. "Yes, I presumed Sonia would be the only one of the three of you to know about the Trophy Treat. Is that right, Sonia?"

Sonia's blue eyes appeared brighter against her flushed face. "Uh, I guess so."

"Well, if that's the case, why don't you tell your friends about the Trophy Treat?"

Sonia nodded and straightened up in her chair. "The Trophy Treat is a dessert, a Skateland special that is served once a year to the residents of Skateland who won medals at our annual competition."

Cammie and Alex exchanged looks.

"The reason the two of you never heard of it is that you have never been invited to Skateland Annual Winners' Party," Wilhelmina said. "You, Alex, only moved to Skateland this season. And you Cammie failed to win a medal last year."

Cammie hung her head, feeling sad as she thought of her unfortunate experience at the last year's annual competition. She had been working very hard on her program, and Coach Ferguson had told her that she was ready. And then Isabelle, whom Cammie had considered a friend, had slipped her a gold magical pin. The pin was supposed to make the person who had won it in a competition skate her best. But because Cammie's pin had been stolen, it had done just the opposite. Instead of having the skate of her life, Cammie had fallen on every jump and messed up every spin. Naturally, she had come in dead last. Therefore, there had been no winners' party for her.

Wilhelmina squeezed her wrist gently. "It doesn't matter, Cammie. I believe there will be future victories in your life. However, what Alex and you have done is far more meaningful than winning a medal in a competition. As you rescued your friend from the clutches of many witches, you showed real guts and determination. And for that, you deserve a reward. Christel, bring in the Trophy Treat!"

"But I haven't done anything," Sonia said in a small voice.

Wilhelmina reached across and patted her hand. "Cammie and Alex have been working so hard to rescue you. And now you are here, and we are going to celebrate. Now—"

"Here comes the Trophy Treat!" Christel put a huge rectangular box on the table. The box was decorated with illustrations of Skateland streets and rinks.

Cammie thought the box was about four feet high. She wondered what could be inside. Judging from the size, the box could contain a coffee maker or a vacuum cleaner. But there probably was a cake inside, because Sonia had referred to the Trophy Treat as dessert.

Christel took off the lid, and Cammie couldn't suppress a gasp of admiration.

"Wow!" Alex exclaimed next to Cammie.

A huge trophy made from dark chocolate sat in the middle of the table. The trophy was wrapped with garlands of gumdrop flowers of every possible color.

"You can choose from quite an array of flavors." Christel pointed to the bright blossoms. "Strawberry, cherry, raspberry, cranberry, blueberry, orange, tangerine, lemon, grapefruit, grape,...hmmm, what else?"

Wilhelmina folded her arms. "Let me see: apple, pear, watermelon, cantaloupe, apricot, peach, plum...I think that's it. Correct me if I forgot something."

"Cool!" Alex studied the trophy ravenously. "I think I might want to try some plum and tangerine blossoms. And a little bit of chocolate too, of course."

Wilhelmina gave him a coy smile. "You think that's all the trophy has, huh?"

Alex looked at her as though he didn't know what she was talking about. Cammie too was confused. Was Wilhelmina playing some kind of a game with them?

"Open the trophy, Christel!" the older woman said.

Christel took off the top layer of the massive chocolate structure, and—

"What's that?"

"I can't believe it!"

Cammie and Alex screamed in amazement at the same time, and Wilhelmina chuckled. The trophy was hollow inside. Watching their awe-struck faces, Christel tilted the trophy slightly, and a whole array of medals of different shapes, sizes, and colors spilled out onto the table.

"Help yourselves!" Wilhelmina said. "This trophy contains medals of all flavors that skaters particularly enjoy."

Cammie and Alex moved closer and studied the contents of the trophy. Some of the medals were made of dark, milk, or white chocolate; others looked like cookies: chocolate chip, oatmeal raisin, butter, and sugar cookies. There were also brownies and Danishes, turnovers and muffins. Some of the medals were of traditional round shape; others were oval, rectangular, or even octagonal.

Cammie took a bite of a big chocolate chip medal and squinted with delight.

Wilhelmina winked at her. "There is more."

"Uh!" Cammie rose in her seat slightly as she watched Christel take another layer off the chocolate trophy. There were more medals, this time with the flavor of cakes, pies, and fruit tarts.

"I don't even know what I want!" Cammie spread her arms. "There are too many of them."

"I wish I could try a medal of every flavor!" Alex said ravenously.

Sonia smiled at him.

"Let's go down to the last layer, and then you will decide," Wilhelmina said brightly.

As Christel removed the next layer, Cammie saw that the best goodies were at the the bottom of the trophy. The third layer medals were made of ice cream of all possible flavors.

"Now it's time to enjoy yourselves. Dig in!" Wilhelmina made a wide gesture, inviting the three of them to fill up their plates.

"By the way, I would recommend a lot of tea with these medals. This way you can eat more," Wilhelmina said as Christel put a plate with bags of Tea Stop and Tea Position, Wilhelmina's favorite, on the table.

They celebrated for a long, long time until Cammie felt she couldn't possibly swallow another bite. And after Christel put away the rest of the Trophy Treat, they spent more time by the fireplace, where Wilhelmina entertained them with stories of her old skating days and how she had met some famous skaters. And then at some point, Cammie felt that she couldn't keep her eyes open anymore. Her arms and legs were tired too; all she wanted to do was sleep.

Wilhelmina must have noticed it, for she clapped her hands, causing Cammie to raise her head. "It's almost midnight! Oh what was I thinking? Time to call it a night, skaters. Let me call the cops now."

Skateland president punched three numbers on her cell phone. "Captain Greenfield? Yes, I want you to take the kids to their dorms, please."

Cammie stifled a yawn. She felt so full and warm.

"Well, the three of you can take a break tomorrow and go back to practices the day after. By the way, now that Sonia is here, we can schedule the show for next Saturday night. How about that? Will you all be ready?"

Cammie looked at Alex and saw him grin. "Sure."

Sonia nodded.

"Yes, and you, Cammie, still need to retake that history test, right? How much time do you need to study for it?"

Cammie felt her lips spread in a huge smile. "I think I'm fine. It shouldn't be too difficult after travelling through the past for more than two weeks."

"I agree."

The doorbell rang, and the three of them followed Wilhelmina to the lobby, where Captain Greenfield already waited for them.

They glided along the dark street in the police icemobile. It was late, and Skateland was sound asleep. Cammie thought that it was really nice of Wilhelmina to let them take a day off. There was no way she could be up at five in the morning.

The icemobile stopped in front of the girls' dorm. Cammie and Sonia jumped out of the sled and bid Alex and Captain Greenfield good night.

"I'm going to sleep for ten hours," Sonia said dreamily as they walked up the porch.

The door opened, and Mrs. Page grabbed them by the hands, looking more excited than Cammie had ever seen her.

"Oh girls, you are finally here. When Mrs. Van Uffeln called and told me Sonia was all right, I was beside myself with joy. You poor dear, you must be exhausted!" Mrs. Page hugged Sonia so hard that Cammie feared she might crush the small girl's ribs.

Sonia laughed. "I'm happy to see you again too, Mrs. Page. And you're right; I'm kind of tired. I'll go to bed, if you don't mind."

Mrs. Page was now hugging Cammie. "Oh, of course! It's late. But before we call it a night, how about a treat? I have my bear cookies and—"

"No!" Cammie and Sonia shouted at the same time.

Mrs. Page's eyes widened, then the woman pursed her lips tight, looking hurt.

"Well, I didn't think my cookies were *that* bad."

"Oh, it's not that!" Interrupting each other, Cammie and Sonia told Mrs. Page how Wilhelmina had rewarded them with the Trophy Treat.

Mrs. Page pressed her hands to her chest and shook her head as though she couldn't quite believe what she had heard. "Trophy Treat! How about that? Well, I can't compete with Skateland's specialty dessert, of course, but guess what? I just got a call from Sweet Blades. You won't believe it. They accepted my chocolate pretzel skate guards!"

Mrs. Page looked so joyful; Cammie could see that the woman had been waiting for hours to share the wonderful news with them.

"It's great, Mrs. Page. I know how hard you worked on those chocolate pretzels. And they are delicious." Sonia kissed the dorm supervisor on the cheek.

Tears appeared in Mrs. Page's eyes, and she brushed them off with the tips of her fingers. "Thank you. You know I couldn't mold the dough in perfect shapes because I don't have artistic talent. But Mr. Reed made some cookie cutters for me, and now my chocolate pretzels look like perfect skate guards. They are so beautiful now! Unfortunately, I can't show them to you. The bakery has bought them all, but—"

"Oh, we'll be happy to look at them some other time," Sonia said sweetly.

Cammie giggled. "Not just see them, I'm sure, but also eat quite a few."

The History of Figure Skating Show

Stars dotted the sky, and the gray ice of Main Square Rink shimmered with tiny particles of light. Melvin Reed had probably sprayed it with some of his magical solutions, because now the ice arena looked almost like the Rink of the Future.

Cammie stood at the end of Straight Line Footwork street in a black velvet dress. From her spot, she could see rows and rows of seats mounting over the rooftops. Hundreds of excited faces stared at the ice. Her parents were somewhere in the stands too, and as Cammie thought about them, joy washed over her.

Soft music began to play, and dozens and dozens of golden, magical snowflakes filled the air. They swirled and bounced off the ice, and as they flew up again, their color changed to silver. The audience applauded, and a moment later, a dozen little girls in silver skating dresses skated to the middle of the rink to perform their Snowflake Dance. Cammie could tell that the girls were trying to do their best, and the dance was really beautiful.

The girls skated away; the enchanted snowflakes vanished from the air too, and then Wilhelmina appeared on the ice of the arena wearing a black silk dress decorated with sequins. Wilhelmina did a series of backward crossovers and then went into her famous combination spin. Cammie tried to count the revolutions but lost count after seventy-six.

Wilhelmina exited the spin and positioned herself in the middle of the arena. A tiny microphone appeared in her hand.

"Welcome to Skateland's annual show. Tonight, we are going to take you all through the history of figure skating."

As Wilhelmina started telling the audience about the first skates made from animal bones and how the first steel skates had appeared, Cammie thought of her history test. She had taken it the day before, and it turned out to be surprisingly easy. During the test, whenever Cammie struggled with a question, she would close her eyes and see Dutch skaters chasing each other on the canals, Renate among them. Then her mind would take her to England, and she would look at the special figures. Thomas could draw them so well, and—

"Figures number now!"

Cammie opened her eyes. It was good that Liz had nudged her on the side; otherwise, she might have missed her entrance. Cammie hurried to her patch alongside other thirty-one skaters. She went into the T-position, drew her breath … at the stroke of the music, Cammie went into her first figure eight, trying her best to stay focused, to make her circles perfectly equal. After completing the second tracing, Cammie skated away.

"Ah!" came the collective gasp then a storm of applause.

I must have messed up my figures again, Cammie thought. Of course, what else could have caused such an excited reaction from the crowd? She closed her eyes, too scared to look back.

"There!" Dana shouted behind her.

Ah, whatever, Cammie thought and opened her eyes. She would have to endure the coaches' rebuke sooner or later, so she might as well find out how badly she had done.

"Wow!" This time, it was Cammie who couldn't contain a shout of joy and admiration. Even as he had promised, Melvin Reed had gone beyond the special effects he had demonstrated during the dress rehearsal. The first and the second figure had turned red and yellow again, but this time, the colors shone in the dark, as though there were a lamp hidden underneath. To Cammie's great delight, the first and second tracings of her figures had blended together, and now an almost perfect orange eight sparkled in the middle of her patch. It was the best Cammie had ever done.

"I did it!" Cammie clapped her hands.

"Well done!"

Cammie turned around and saw Coach Ferguson's smiling face. "It's been a long time, huh? Well, I'm glad your skating has improved. By the way, congratulations! You passed your history test."

"Oh, great!" Although Cammie had been sure she wouldn't fail the test this time, it was still nice to have her coach tell her she had definitely passed.

"And!" Coach Ferguson gave Cammie an enigmatic look. "Mrs. Van Uffeln also told me that you demonstrated excellent coaching skills. It looks like there will be someone to replace me when I retire."

"Oh no!" Cammie laughed. Surely, Coach Ferguson didn't mean that. She was way too young to retire, and besides—

"Quickly, change! The French group number is coming in ten minutes." Coach Ferguson was back to her usual self—all business.

Cammie rushed to one of the temporary locker rooms in a tent on a side street. She quickly changed into a knee-length skirt and a short jacket. She glanced at herself in the mirror. Not bad.

"Cammie, it's time to go!" Coach Ferguson called. The rest of the girls were already outside.

Amazingly, this time the French number was easy too. Cammie actually enjoyed herself doing ballet moves: exaggerated arm motions, long smooth glides, and spread eagles on bent knees followed by two-foot spins.

She looked up. The dark sky seemed to sway around her; the bright stars were like friends watching her every move, winking at her, encouraging her.

Cammie curtsied and skated away. Loud applause from the audience followed.

"Hey, that was good! You almost looked like a French skater." Alex slapped her on the back. He looked handsome in his black pants and a white shirt.

"Almost?" Cammie grinned.

"Look, Jeff is doing his number." Alex pointed to the ice, where Jeff was posing as Jackson Haines. Jeff's ankle had healed just in time for the show. Even though the doctor had recommended going easy on jumps, Jeff could still do a very good imitation of Jackson Haines's half jumps and spins.

"I can't believe it. Jeff looks just like Jackson Haines," Cammie said.

Alex nodded. "Amazing, huh? Who would think that Jeff never saw the real Jackson Haines skate?"

"Look, now he's doing a quadrille dressed as a bear." Cammie pointed to their friend.

Jeff skated very fast doing multiple three turns and rockers. But the best thing was his artistry. Somehow, Jeff had managed to get the audience involved in his routine. With circular hand motions, he beckoned the people to join him on the ice, and when they refused, he sighed, faking disappointment. He nodded as the audience applauded for him, and at some point, Jeff winked at someone in the stands. It had to be a girl, but Cammie wasn't sure.

"He's better than he ever was. Jackson Haines's autograph has really lit a fire in him," Cammie said.

Alex chuckled. "You bet. I need to get ready for my number. You watch me."

He waved at Cammie and moved away from her. Five minutes later, Cammie saw Alex doing jumps in the middle of the arena. She gasped as she saw him fly up in a huge axel. It seemed to her that he had covered the distance of over twenty feet. But Alex didn't do any multi-revolution jumps, and when he left the ice breathing hard, Cammie couldn't help teasing him a little.

"I thought we would see a beautiful Bernard jump," Cammie said nonchalantly.

For a moment, Alex looked as though he were going to snap at her. Then his lips spread in a grin. "Only after you do a scratch spin in the middle of a patch session."

They laughed together.

"No, honestly, I thought you would do a double axel and a couple of triples," Cammie said.

Alex shook his head. "No. Steve Duncan is doing the evolution of jumps, remember?"

They watched Steve Duncan, a handsome African American boy, show how triples had evolved from single jumps. After Steve skated away, beaming and waving at the cheering girls, Jessica McNeil and Peter Deveraux did a pairs demonstration. They showed the audience how it had taken years for pairs skating to progress from simple gliding on ice to challenging athletic moves including lifts and throw jumps. Afterwards, Sandra Newman and Kevin Sawyer performed several dancing numbers, and they received a standing ovation from the audience for their beautiful artistry.

And then it was time for the last part of the show, and Sonia appeared in the spotlight, small and light in a sparkling green dress. With hands clapsed against her chest, Cammie watched her roommate fly across the ice in huge jumps. Sonia seemed to be suspended in midair, performing her triples effortlessly. Cammie thought that since her abduction, Sonia had improved even more. And yet, for some reason, Cammie didn't feel jealous at all. Of course, she understood that Sonia was a much better skater; it would probably take Cammie years to get to that level. And yet there was no envy, just joy.

Why? Cammie asked herself. *Why aren't I feeling jealous at all? Instead, I'm happy for her.*

"That's what a coach feels," a voice said next to Cammie.

Cammie looked around, right into the smiling face of Coach Ferguson.

"Seeing your student do her best is the greatest joy a coach can ever experience," Coach Ferguson said. "I am truly blessed, because with all the students I work with, I have this feeling very, very often."

Cammie nodded, her eyes still firmly fixed on Sonia gliding on her backward outside edge in preparation for her triple lutz.

"It's a new jump for her. She only got it a week ago." Cammie clenched her fists. "Come on, land it!" she whispered.

Sonia bent her left knee, picked hard with her right toe …

Oh, please! Cammie closed her eyes, too scared to look. The audience roared and applauded.

Cammie opened her eyes and saw Sonia gliding backward on a secure outside edge, a happy smile on her face.

"She did it!" Cammie breathed out.

She turned to Coach Ferguson. "Did you see it? She landed her triple lutz!"

Coach Ferguson put her hand on Cammie's shoulder. "And she couldn't have done it without your help."

"Alex worked with her even more," Cammie hurried to explain.

"It doesn't matter. You also contributed to her improvement. That's what's really important."

The applause intensified. Cammie looked at the middle of the ice where Sonia curtsied, beaming with joy.

"I've got to run and tell her what a great job she has done," Cammie said to Coach Ferguson.

The coach gave her a wink. "Go ahead. This is something that can't wait. Do it now!"

listen|imagine|view|experience

AUDIO BOOK DOWNLOAD INCLUDED WITH THIS BOOK!

In your hands you hold a complete digital entertainment package. In addition to the paper version, you receive a free download of the audio version of this book. Simply use the code listed below when visiting our website. Once downloaded to your computer, you can listen to the book through your computer's speakers, burn it to an audio CD or save the file to your portable music device (such as Apple's popular iPod) and listen on the go!

How to get your free audio book digital download:

1. Visit www.tatepublishing.com and click on the e|LIVE logo on the home page.
2. Enter the following coupon code:
   c115-9264-b149-358c-cef6-15e1-0b54-470e
3. Download the audio book from your e|LIVE digital locker and begin enjoying your new digital entertainment package today!